AN ECH[...]

"I just want to forget," Megan said, looking up at Jake with eyes that had seen too much. "But my dreams won't let me. Why won't they let me forget?"

Jake wrapped his arms around her. Pulling her securely into his lap, he tucked her cheek against his chest.

"Megan," he said softly, running his hand in slow circles across her back and repeating her name over and over in a murmuring whisper as he felt the strangeness of holding her, the rightness of comforting her. "I won't let anyone hurt you ever again. I promise."

His words echoed in the hushed silence of the kitchen, echoed in his mind, echoed in his heart as something deep within him remembered saying these words to this woman sometime—sometime.

———

"The author has a way with descriptions that bring her characters' feelings to life."

—*Affaire de Coeur*

Harper
Monogram

THE
COVENANT

Modean Moon

HarperPaperbacks
A Division of HarperCollins*Publishers*

HarperPaperbacks   *A Division of* HarperCollins*Publishers*
10 East 53rd Street, New York, N.Y. 10022

Copyright © 1995 by Modean Moon
All rights reserved. No part of this book may be used or reproduced in any manner whatsoever without written permission of the publisher, except in the case of brief quotations embodied in critical articles and reviews. For information address HarperCollins*Publishers,*
10 East 53rd Street, New York, N.Y. 10022.

First printing: October 1995

Printed in the United States of America

HarperPaperbacks, HarperMonogram, and colophon are trademarks of HarperCollins*Publishers*

❖ 10 9 8 7 6 5 4 3 2 1

THE COVENANT

Prologue

6 June 1872

Sam Hooker went east from the Choctaw Nation into Arkansas an hour after sunrise. Only his knowledge of the scrub oak, rocky hills, and still-trickling creeks marked the boundary. If he had been on an official mission, that knowledge would have forced him to stop. Members of the Choctaw Lighthorse had no authority outside the Nation.

But this was not an official mission. This was a vendetta.

He reined in the big sorrel and sat easily, studying a trail a boy could have followed.

A vendetta against him.

Its roots had remained hidden in mystery for two days, but its existence was as clear as the trail he followed. And its fruits?

Sam pulled a scrap of fine white cotton fabric from his shirt pocket. He had plucked this bit of cloth from a tree branch at the start of his journey. Although he had never seen it before, he recognized the delicate embroidery as part of a woman's petticoat.

Sam stuffed the fabric back into his shirt pocket.

The fruits of this vendetta were something he couldn't yet consider.

He was meant to follow this trail; that much was apparent. And follow it he would, in his own way, at a pace some suspected but few believed. And the devil take those who led him on this chase. A grim smile barely twisted his features. Those he followed would prefer the devil's retribution to that with which he would repay them.

He stopped again at noon to rest his horse and compose his thoughts. The trail was getting fresher. Tonight he would be upon them.

Twice during the day he had become aware of other men behind him. From the vantage point of a rocky bluff, he focused a long field glass and looked back: Army. Six men.

Probably following the same vermin he followed. They hadn't been too concerned about Indian national boundaries either.

Sam calculated the distance between them. He wondered briefly if they would be help or hindrance and then decided he had no choice. There were five men in the party he followed, five men and one woman. He had no doubt he could kill all five men, but could he do so without putting the woman at even greater risk?

And could he stand to wait until he felt he had a chance of bringing her out alive, knowing what would be happening to her while he waited?

He made no fire that night, letting whoever looked back think that the army's fire was his. He gave the soldiers time to fill their bellies and then rode slowly, openly, up to their lone sentry.

"I want to speak to the officer in charge."

"Holy hell! Where did you come from, mister?" The young sentry's voice shook and his hands tightened on his rifle.

"Easy, soldier. I'm not a threat to you. I want to speak to the officer in charge."

"What's the problem, private?"

The officer materialized behind the sentry, gun drawn and aimed at Sam's midsection, as quietly as Sam himself could have.

Sam nodded, both in appreciation of the stealth and in recognition of the man. He'd fought with him in the war against the north. It seemed strange to see him now in Union blue, strange to see only lieutenant's bars on his collar, strange to see a tactician like him herding green troops after offal. But this man was another old wolf like himself; they could deal.

He left the army camp two hours after midnight with the promise of an hour's head start and the knowledge that the five men ahead had robbed the train at Limestone Gap, killing the two soldiers on guard and escaping with an army payroll destined for Texas.

He left the camp with the memory of his private conversation with the lieutenant.

"Just tell me why you need the time. Give me a reason to let you go in ahead."

"Because they may have your gold," Sam told him, "but they've got my woman."

The lieutenant paled and sat silent for seconds. "It might be more merciful to wait and go in with us. To let her die. After three days there won't be much left of her."

"There will be life," Sam told him.

Now, as he reined his horse to the south to begin the circuitous route to the outlaws' camp, he looked up at the stars.

"There *will* be life," he swore.

1

There were times, later, when Megan wondered if she should sell the house. There were times when she wanted to take Pandora and Shadrack, get in her flashy new little car, and leave the house and Lydia, all those she had seen and those she hadn't. What stopped her was the increasing worry that what she really wanted to leave behind was herself, and that she couldn't do—yet.

There were none of those questions the day she first saw the rambling old farmhouse, with its wide shaded porches, only the sure knowledge that this was the home she had been looking for, the one she tried in vain to describe to Dr. Kent.

"Don't you have a home with your father as long as you want?" He never argued, just prodded and probed and pried around the edges of her mind and seemed, somehow, mildly disappointed in her.

"In Washington, D.C.? After what's happened?"

"Or here in Tulsa?" he'd asked softly.

"I have a house here," she had answered, equally softly.

"Not a home. Never a home. Never a place where I felt I belonged."

"You can make it your home, Megan."

"Not that house. Jack McIntyre molded it and made it what he wanted as surely as if he'd lived there. I don't think I'll ever be strong enough to change it." She smiled at him in hesitant explanation. "One Christmas when my father was out of the country, I spent the holidays with my roommate at her grandmother's house. It was the only true home I think I've ever been in. There was laughter and warmth and comfort. I was a stranger and yet I felt welcomed, a part of the family. That's the kind of home I want, and that's the kind I will have. But not in the shadow of my father."

"But why Prescott?" he had asked her in a later session. "Why not here?"

Why Prescott? She closed her eyes and pictured the southeastern Oklahoma town in its postcard setting, houses clustered at the base of a hill and just beginning to sprawl into the valley.

"Because there," she told him, knowing nothing else would satisfy him, "I won't be Jack McIntyre's daughter or Roger Hudson's widow. There I can just be Megan, and maybe I can find out who Megan really is."

How strange, she thought, that Roger and his sister had to die before she found the place in which she thought she could really live.

She was fragile. Dr. Kent said she might always be fragile—witnessing brutal, senseless death tended to have that effect on people. But she was stronger, both physically and emotionally, than when she had returned to the States, stronger even than when she had taken possession of this poor mistreated house that Roger's sister, Helen, had long ago turned into a rental.

She had plenty of privacy; the house sat about four miles outside the tiny little town of Prescott, Oklahoma, a town that she'd belatedly discovered had lost all its businesses except for a post office and general store. Her place butted up to the side of a mountain. There was only one other house on that road, farther up into the woods than hers, and while the man she occasionally saw driving past on his way up that road in a sleek, new black Jeep looked vaguely, impossibly familiar, she never bothered him and, thank God, he never bothered her.

She knew that later she would want to announce she was not just another in a long line of tenants but part of the community; later she would want church socials and gossiping at the general store and trading recipes and herbs with the local women. But for now, all she wanted was to heal. So she avoided Prescott and drove twenty miles to the county seat at Fairview for her supplies and to hire the few needed tradesmen she employed, and mostly she kept to herself as she weeded and replanted overgrown flower beds, scraped and painted abused cabinets, and scrubbed and covered windows. At night, tired, exhausted from the work she had done but not tired enough to sleep, she curled up on the sofa with the two young black cats that had adopted her. Then she took out the journal that Dr. Kent had insisted she keep and tried to make sense of what had happened and how she had become the person it had happened to.

June 3

I painted the smallest bedroom today: emerald green, a color that will look wonderful with white enameled woodwork. The floor is in worse shape than I thought, so I think I will enamel it, too, and stencil it. Then lace curtains. If it doesn't work out, I can always do it over—something Roger would never have understood.

The cats woke me up about three this morning—again—fussing and fretting in the way only black cats do.

But I didn't hear anything or see anything when I walked through the house looking out all the windows. A dog, maybe—or maybe I just need to corral my paranoia. I'm not in South America anymore. I saw my neighbor go through this afternoon. I almost waved at him.

And—God!—I'm avoiding, even in the journal I created so I didn't have to hide my thoughts.

Did I love Roger? Did I ever really love him, or did I think he would somehow magically rescue me? And did he love me? Or was the temptation of being married to Senator McIntyre's daughter just too great for him to resist? Did I base my marriage on a lie, put us both through four years of misery?

—help me oh God somebody please please help me—

Suddenly, after all her weeks of work, all her weeks of healing, the terror was back, as strong as the moment the hand had clamped over her mouth, dragging her back into the trees, into safety, while she watched the others die.

When would it end, Lord, when would it end?

She knew what she ought to do. She ought to turn to one of the other sections of this multifaceted journal and explore that sudden cry for help. Dr. Kent had promised that bringing all the shattered segments of her life together in one book would help her gather into herself all those portions that seemed to be forever lost, had promised that by exploring all the choices she had made, the actions she had taken, even the ones she hadn't as though she had, she could finally make herself whole.

But she couldn't do that. Not tonight. And she couldn't lose herself in sleep. Not tonight. The fear still clawed at her too fiercely. The dreams would come tonight: Roger, Helen, the small staff at the clinic. The green of the soldiers' uniforms. The shots. The screams. The blood.

She sat up quickly, and the black tomcat yowled a complaint. She looked at him, forgetting for a moment what she had meant to do. Then she released her breath, shook her head, and closed the journal.

"Come on, you two," she said, and her voice sounded strangely harsh in the silence of the night. "Let's go paint a floor."

Something was going on at the Hudson place, had been going on for months, even before this newest tenant moved in. Jake Kenyon had attributed it to the activities of the last renter. Now he wasn't so sure. The new woman was an improvement on the lowlifes Helen's place was usually rented to. He supposed if he had to have anyone living at the base of his road, she—whoever she was—was all right. At least she had arranged to have all the dead cars hauled away and was trying to clean up the outside of the place.

Was she the only one living there? After the workmen left, he never saw anyone else, which in itself was odd. She was a young woman; he had noticed that much on the rare occasions he saw her outside, camouflaged in baggy clothes and chopped-off hair.

She might be the only one living there, but she wasn't the only one prowling the place. He'd seen tracks earlier in the year, in the woods. Now the activity seemed to be confined to the hours of darkness, but only when the moon was bright. As it had been last night; as it would be tonight.

He'd turned off the house lights early to let whoever was out and about think he wasn't there or was already asleep. Now he waited in his Jeep at the top of his road in the shadows of a moonlit night so bright he could almost see color. He waited alone except for Deacon, the big black German shepherd that had been shot up as badly as he had and left with him to die—and except for the 9-millimeter automatic revolver he had cleaned and loaded and kept nearby. Once a cop, always a cop, he thought. And once nearly a dead cop, always wary.

Deacon growled once, a low, quiet warning.

"I hear it, boy," Jake told him.

He'd parked at an angle so he could see the Hudson house despite the overgrowth of trees and leaves. Even so, his view was impaired. But the clear night air carried the slightest noise and magnified it, and the sound of vehicles was unmistakable.

Vehicles, plural. More than one. And no headlights.

Some of the last tenant's friends come to pay a visit on the woman living there alone?

"Let's go take a look," he said to the dog, and eased the Jeep into neutral, coasting downhill without starting the engine until he heard shouts and the unmistakable sound of a door being kicked open.

He heard her scream over the roar of the Jeep's engine as he turned into the woman's driveway. It sliced through the night, through the clutter of cars that surrounded the small frame house, raking a chill down his spine that only dimly echoed the terror in the woman's voice.

He felt a moment's hesitation as he recognized the cars: black-and-whites, county cars, all with their light bars dark, and a couple of unmarked ones. But only for a moment. The woman's terror was a palpable thing; there was no way in hell he couldn't go to her rescue.

He ran his car up into her yard and slammed from it at a run, into the house. A dozen men stood around, guns dangling ineffectually from helpless hands. The woman knelt in a corner of the room, dressed only in a thin white shift, her arms clasped over her head, her unearthly wails tearing through him.

Mark Henderson, the sheriff's first deputy, crouched beside her, his hands on her shoulders.

"Get your hands off her." Jake's voice cut through the room.

"Kenyon—"

"Now."

Jake felt a soft brush at his knee and heard Deacon's warning growl. Reluctantly Henderson released her.

"Now move away."

Jake dropped to his knees in front of the woman. She looked at him with terror-glazed eyes, but he knew she didn't see him. "No one's going to hurt you," he said softly. "It's all right. I promise no one will hurt you."

He continued speaking in a lulling monotone, wondering if she even heard, until her screaming stopped. She looked at him, and this time he thought he saw something, at least. He held out his hand, careful not to touch her. "No one will hurt you," he promised. "No one."

Slowly, cautiously, she reached for his hand and grasped it in both of hers. He saw silent sobs shake her body, felt the desperation in her grip, but at last she was quiet.

"What in the hell is going on here?" he asked with deadly calm.

Henderson spoke carefully, avoiding looking at either Jake or the woman. "You're not sheriff anymore."

"Thank God for that. At least I won't have to answer for whatever you've done here tonight. What happened?"

"We were executing a search warrant for methamphetamines—"

"You what?"

"An informant told us a buy was going down here tonight. You know how hard we've been trying to get something on Max Renfro."

"You stupid sons of bitches," Jake muttered. "Look around you. Max Renfro hasn't lived here for more than two months, as you would have known if you'd bothered to ask instead of trying to hotdog it."

"Then why did she scream? What set her off?"

Jake shook his head. He spotted a state cop in the crowd, one who ought to have known better, and spoke to him. "What would your wife or daughter do, Kelso, if a dozen armed men broke into your house in the middle of the night when she was alone?

"Has anyone thought to call an ambulance? Or begun to consider what hell there's going to be to pay when she realizes what's happened here?"

He looked back at the woman, too quiet now, who still held his hand in a death grip. "If she ever again realizes anything," he added softly. "Did any of you rocket scientists think to look for ID?"

"There's this." A cop from Fairview, out of uniform, stepped forward to hand Jake a black notebook but backed off when Deacon growled.

"Give it to me." Jake reached for it and took it in one hand. A quick glance showed him a diary of some sort, and he dropped it on the floor beside the woman.

"We'll need that for evidence," Henderson said.

"Of what, incompetence? You want drugs?" Surreptitiously, he nudged the notebook toward the dog. There wasn't any point in giving away all his secrets.

Deacon sniffed the notebook once and whined softly.

"There aren't any drugs in that notebook," Jake said. "From the looks of the place, there aren't any drugs here at all." He eyed the white walls, the spartan furnishings. "This damn place looks like a convent. A purse, a wallet, a name?" he asked again as he felt the woman's grip on his hand lessening, as he felt her growing weaker. "And would one of you stir far enough to find a blanket or a robe, something to cover her with?"

"Hudson," someone said from the back of the room, holding a wallet out toward the group. "Megan Hudson."

Now Jake knew what had set her off, why she held on to

him as though she feared for her life, but not why she was living here. What in God's name had brought her?

"Congratulations," he said. If it hadn't been for the woman kneeling before him, he would have taken great pleasure from his announcement. "You have just managed to terrorize Senator Jack McIntyre's daughter, Roger Hudson's widow." And Jake's sister-in-law.

In the end, he took her home with him. He couldn't justify doing so, not even to himself. Maybe it was because of the one entry in her diary he had seen: —*help me oh God, somebody please please help me.* And maybe it was because she finally looked at him instead of through him, recognizing him although he knew that was impossible, and whispered, "You came," just before slumping unconscious in his arms.

And he took the notebook, because he knew it was something she wouldn't want careless or curious eyes peering through.

He carried her, still unconscious, practically weightless, into his dark house, into his bedroom, and laid her on the bed. The moment he turned on the bedside lamp, she sprang up, shedding the blanket he'd wrapped her in. He saw darkening bruises on her arms where rough hands had held her and recognized from the look in her eyes that she was seeing something he couldn't see.

She began rubbing her hands down her arms, scrubbing them.

"Bath," she whispered.

"No, Megan. Not yet. Not now."

"Bath," she insisted, her voice broken, her scrubbing actions fiercer. "Dirty. So dirty."

"Megan—"

When she moved a hand to cover her mouth, he recognized the action barely in time to grab the wastebasket and hold it for her as she heaved up the meager contents of her stomach and continued to retch until she lay back, exhausted.

"Oh, hell," he muttered. He didn't dare leave her to go for a cloth. He yanked the case off one of the pillows and handed it to her. She looked at it blankly for a moment and then scrubbed at her mouth.

Maybe she wasn't completely with him, but she was more here than she had been. A few things could explain her actions. Did he want to know? Did he want to open this ugly can of worms? It didn't matter. He had to ask and then, maybe, she could have that bath.

"Megan, were you raped?"

"Not me." She moaned into the pillowcase. "Some of the others. I couldn't stop it."

At that moment he knew what Helen's last hours must have been, knew he'd have to deal with that knowledge. But not now. Tonight this woman needed him.

"Not then. Tonight. Were you raped tonight?"

She looked at him over the edge of the case. Once again he saw recognition in her eyes, but her words told a different story.

"Six men. One of them is dead now. I couldn't stop them."

"Megan." He closed his hands on her arms, not wanting to hurt her, not knowing how to draw her out of a past hell into the hell this night had become for her. "Think. Tonight. Prescott, Oklahoma, June third. Did one of those bastards come in early? Did one of them hurt you tonight?"

She shuddered once, but when she looked at him again he saw reason and sanity in her eyes. "Not tonight," she said, through tortured vocal cords. "They all came at once. I was alone, and they came crashing in. Why did they do that?"

Because they could, he could have answered. Because at best the local law had succumbed to mindless paranoia, at worst to greed. But he didn't tell her that.

"They made a mistake," he told her. "They thought some-one else lived in your house."

"They can do that? In this country?"

"Yeah." He realized he still gripped her arms, so he released her. "Are you with me now? I was worried for a while."

He saw a hesitant smile lift the corner of her mouth. "I was worried too."

He didn't think it possible, but he felt a chuckle break from him, as reluctant as her smile was hesitant.

"You're my neighbor, aren't you?" she asked.

Jake nodded.

"I saw you come through from town this afternoon. I almost waved at you."

"I almost waved at you."

"Thank you." She swallowed once and blinked back tears and, he suspected, memories. "Thank you for coming. My name is Megan Hudson. I'm planning—I was planning to live here." She shook her head and smiled again. "Thank you, Mr.—?"

Maybe not so many memories after all. At least not current ones. "Kenyon," he told her. "Jake Kenyon."

She recognized the name. Her mouth opened in a silent *oh,* and her eyes filled with shock and secrets and shame. "I didn't know. I had no idea you—"

Jake shook his head. "There wasn't any reason for you to know. I didn't know who you were either. Sometime we will have to talk about Helen, but not tonight. You're not strong enough right now, and I'm not sure I am. What I need to do now is get you looked at by a doctor."

"No." Her voice was remarkably firm, remarkably adamant. "I've had enough doctors to last me a lifetime."

"Sorry," he said abruptly, easing himself off the bed and away from her.

What was happening to him? He had caught himself

about to take this woman, a stranger in spite of their convoluted relationship, into his arms and tell her he would never let her be bothered again by anything or anyone.

"Trust me on this," he said instead. "You've been through a shock, may even still be in shock. And you seem to have some gaps in your memory of what happened tonight. Let me get a doctor up here to examine you. Then you can have that bath you asked for and maybe get a good night's sleep."

"The what I asked for?"

He closed his eyes briefly. The image of her scrubbing herself, begging to be clean, floated clearly before him. "See?" he said. "Gaps. Trust me."

"This had better be important."

Jake grimaced as the man's sleepy words over the telephone reminded him of the time.

"Sorry, Patrick," he said, "but I need a doctor up here."

"Jake?" Now the man on the other end of the line sounded wide awake. "Have you gotten yourself shot up again?"

"No." Jake hurried to reassure his friend. "There's no blood, at least none that shows. But you'd better tell Barbara to bring her I-might-have-to-take-this-to-court bag of tricks. And you might want to bring your camera."

"And my tape recorder?"

"I don't know if you'll get an interview. If she says no, that's it. But I'll have plenty to tell you."

"She?"

"Just hurry, will you?"

Jake left Megan to Barbara's tender mercies while he and Patrick drove back down the hill to Megan's house. He found the switches for all the lights and left Patrick to record on film the travesty of trampled flower beds, shattered door and facing, muddy footprints in what had been an almost monastically clean house. Deacon found two half-grown cats huddled and hissing in the closet in the one room of the house that contained any color, a rich green that screamed of life and hope. A corner of the floor had been painted a bright clean white before it had been tracked over. In that corner, too, was the beginnings of a decorative painted pattern, also in green: vines and leaves, budding, reaching, opening.

He rescued the cats, now busily complaining, and carried them into the kitchen, where he found their dishes sitting neatly on a mat near a tightly closed container of food. He fed them, gave them fresh water, and cleaned up and refilled the overturned litter box in the adjacent small room where Megan had installed her washer and dryer.

Then quietly, calmly, he gave Patrick the names and agencies of each man who had taken part in the raid and told him what had been said, and by whom, as they returned to Jake's house.

"No interview tonight," Barbara told them. "She's exhausted and asleep."

"Is she all right?"

"She will be."

"Damn it, Barbara. You know what I'm asking."

"Yes," she said. "I just don't know *why* you're asking, or why it's so important to you. By your own admission you've never spoken to this woman before tonight."

"Barbara—"

"Jake," she said, echoing his frustration, "except for the bruises on her arms, there are no signs of physical abuse. The emotional abuse is a lot harder to spot. She gave me the name of her psychiatrist in Tulsa, and I woke him up too. He's concerned, but not overly so. He told me, and I have to agree with him, that Megan Hudson is a remarkably strong young woman."

"Strong?" Jake asked. "Did you look at your patient, doctor? She's about as strong as—"

"Maybe too strong. Dr. Kent told me that in spite of weeks of therapy she's consistently resisted facing the true horror of what she's been through. And in spite of the gaps and inconsistencies you mentioned, she's still sane, and she's still alive."

The moon had long since set; the sun had not yet made its way over the mountains in the east. Jake kept vigil. Seated in an uncomfortable chair he had dragged in from the kitchen, his feet propped on the opened drawer of the nightstand, he watched the woman sleep. She slept tightly and protectively curled, as though even in sleep she found no rest. He wondered about the familiarity of his actions, because he knew he had never watched over any other woman the way he was watching over Megan Hudson. He knew he had never felt the same unexplainable sense of rage and pain as he felt when he glanced at the shadows beneath her eyes and at the bruises on her arms. And he knew he had never before felt the same sense of desperation and frustration that he felt when he remembered Barbara's words: *She's alive.*

Sugarloaf County, Choctaw Nation Indian Territory, 1872

I must release this fear and hatred before its poison destroys me and the little that has been left to me.

I once thought myself a strong person; now I know that until the events of this summer I had never been tried.

I killed a man.

It seems strange that I can write those words so calmly and yet cannot bear even to think of the events that led up to an act completely alien to the person I once was. But perhaps this is merely another symptom of the madness I feel growing ever stronger within me.

If only I could bear to speak of what happened. But I cannot. And even if I could bring myself to do so, I know it must remain our secret. To reveal it would bring only shame and possibly death.

So I will write. I will spill everything out on these pages, and then I will commit them and, please God, the madness that threatens me to the fire.

On the last day of my youth, I had returned home from my exile at boarding school. Our father was not at home, which was not unusual. Surprisingly, though, he had not remarried as both Peter and I had thought he must do, and do quickly. Only Peter met me when Aunt Peg's driver delivered me. Only Peter laughed with me when I told him that the tollgate keeper at Backbone Ridge had recognized me and claimed he would not charge me a cent to return home but had charged Aunt Peg's driver and maid double the usual toll for a white's passage.

Only Peter was there to argue with me when I insisted on going immediately to Granny Rogers's cabin to see her and—Peter knew this too; he teased me unmercifully—to see Sam.

"He won't be there, you know," Peter told me yet again as we set out on the short journey on foot. But I had dressed in a stylish and sophisticated new walking costume that I had purchased in Little Rock for the express purpose of stunning Sam Hooker into realizing I was at last a woman grown, and I wasn't about to have my plans thwarted by something so simple as Sam not being at home.

We passed the creek, and although Peter looked at it with great longing, he also glanced at the embroidered hem of my skirt and with great restraint refrained from suggesting we go wading.

If I had let him win the argument about our visiting Granny Rogers's house, if I had let him convince me that Sam was not at home, if we had gone wading as we had done so many times before, would any of the subsequent events have happened?

But we passed the creek. And my life—all our lives— changed.

The men came out of the woods just past the first curve after the creek crossing: six of them, on worn sweat-stained horses, crowding around me. The fat one, the one I later learned was called Puckett, already had his rifle in hand and aimed.

"Well, well, well," he said, in a voice I still hear in my nightmares. "What have we found us, boys?"

Peter had lagged behind, a valiant but reluctant escort. Now I prayed his reluctance would save us. "Run!" I cried to him. "Get Sam!"

I saw the fat man raise his rifle, heard the sound of it being fired, and saw my beloved brother fall into the bushes.

"Get Sam?" the fat man asked. A grin split his face, revealing horrid blackened teeth before he spat out a stream of tobacco juice. "Sam Hooker? You wouldn't be his special treat, now, would you, little girl?

"Get Sam," he repeated, choking on a laugh. "Now that is purely what we meant to do. But I think I just changed my mind about the how of it."

He yanked me by the arm, pulling me up and across his legs and the saddle in front of him so that the pommel bit into my middle. I landed with a gasp and immediately began struggling. He only laughed, ripping my new and frivolous little hat away and grabbing a handful of my hair as he pushed my head down.

We stopped later, to water the horses, and although I felt that surely at least one rib had been broken by my punishing ride, I tried to run away. Puckett only laughed when I was hauled back to him. He ordered one of the men to take my boots and then, still smiling, he kicked me, hard, in the ankle. But for the man holding me, I would have collapsed with the pain.

"You won't run again, you Injun-lovin' little bitch," he said. And again he laughed.

They tied my hands together in front of me. This time when we rode away, I rode astride, my feet dangling, my ankle screaming, in front of the fat man. I had thought my earlier ride demeaning, but nothing had prepared me for the indignities of this man's groping hands and the pressures of his body against mine.

"Wouldn't have mattered one way or the other if that Injun kid with you had gotten away," the man called Puckett told me. "Hooker ain't home. Won't be for a couple more days. We found that out just yesterday. Thought we might wait for him and finish settling an old score when he did show up. Now we'll just wait until *he* finds *us*."

And he would. I knew that with every breath I took. Sam would come for me.

Puckett laughed, spewing stale breath and spittle across my cheek. "Yep, he'll come. I wonder if he'll like what he finds any better than the last time I left him a present."

An hour or so later, the five other men pulled up around us. "Damn it, Puckett," a tall gaunt one said. "We're tired of waiting. We're far enough away. It's time."

Puckett looked at the sky. "It's too early to make camp."

"We're not talking about making camp, damn it, we're talking about the woman and you know it."

He jerked me back against him, and I felt the swift stabbing pain of a rib giving way. "Yeah. I reckon this is as good a place as any." He bent over and lifted my skirt, grabbing a handful of my petticoat. "Give me your knife," he said to someone, I couldn't see who, who did as he said, and then he ripped a wide swatch from the embroidered ruffle. "Hang this on a branch, about eye level," he said. "We wouldn't want him to miss seeing this spot when he comes through here in a couple of days, would we? Wouldn't want him to miss knowing what we done."

All the men dismounted, leaving me on the horse. For one impossible moment, I thought I might be able to escape. Then Puckett turned and hauled me down.

One of the others carried me, kicking and struggling, to a grassy spot beneath a huge old hackberry tree. They tied a rope to the one already around my wrists—"Just until we all get a good look at what we've got," Puckett told me—and handed the length of rope to one of the other men.

He tossed the rope up over a branch in the tree, stretching my arms up, pulling me up, until I stood balanced only on the tips of my toes. I felt the rough texture of an old root and the bristle of pine needles through my sensible black stockings, along with the screaming pain in my right ankle.

Puckett stood in front of me now, so close the bulk of him blocked my view of the other men. I felt my blood roaring in my ears, felt my heart trying to pound its way out of my chest. I closed my eyes against the fear, but still the stench of him enveloped me.

He lifted his filthy hand to my face and gripped my jaw, forcing my head up. When he saw that I watched him, he grinned, turned his head, and shot a stream of brown tobacco juice to the ground, just missing the hem of my skirt.

"Sam Hooker will kill you for this," I whispered against his hand.

"We hope he tries, little girl. We purely do hope he tries."

Then his hand left my chin and reached for my buttons, those tiny buttons marching down the front of the new dress I had been so proud of, knowing that the first time I wore it would be when I finally returned home.

Would Sam ever see me in it?

Of course he would.

I had to believe that.

Sam would come for me.

He wouldn't let this happen.

Sam would come in time.

Should I hate him because he didn't come in time?

Should I hate him because the men who took me were there, looking for him, and I was merely incidental to their planned revenge?

Should I hate him because once, long ago, before he returned from Texas, before the war, he killed two of Puckett's brothers while attempting to arrest them?

Should I hate him because, although those men might have taken me, they would probably have done what I prayed for them to do: killed me quickly instead of keeping me alive for Sam to see?

Should I hate him? Or should I look into his eyes and see the guilt that torments him when he looks at me?

And if I cannot hate Sam, who then can I hate?

Please, God, if there really is a god, give me someone or something to hate. Because—perhaps—if I hate, I will have no room in my heart for the fear.

I could no longer feel my hands, still tied as they had been for days, but now the rope was pegged to a stake that kept me from running away. Running? The pain in my ankle where Puckett had kicked me had subsided to a dull roar that only throbbed beneath the swelling. Unless I moved it. Crawling, maybe.

No. Not even that.

My skirt and shirtwaist clung to me in tatters, my only cover against the chill of an early June night in the mountains. And if I really felt anything, it was the chill and the pebbles and shale and pine needles on the uneven ground that abraded my already raw back.

I would die. Soon, I thought. I'd passed hunger a day ago. They gave me water, barely enough for drinking, never enough for washing, but only when they stopped for their meals. Other than at those times when one of them visited me, day or night, it was not to bring me water or food or anything else for my benefit.

I'd heard them talk about selling me to someone in Mexico. That would never happen. I was light-headed most of the time now, too weak to sit in the saddle without being tied. I'd never survive the trip.

They would kill me first. I'd promised myself that.

I no longer fought when one came to me, no longer screamed, no longer cried, no longer lay there silently enduring the obscenities to which they subjected me. No. I had a litany, a well-thought-out monologue, which I repeated with as much fire as I could still dredge up. Maybe soon, one of them would believe me. Maybe soon, one of them would be convinced that somehow I really could carry out my threat. Maybe soon, one of them would put his knife to my throat and end this living hell.

I saw a shape moving in the darkness, approaching with a stealth that only the one supposed to be on sentry duty ever used. The shape dropped down beside me. I didn't bother to look at him.

"I'll kill you," I said, though my voice was no more than a hoarse croak. "If you leave me alive, I will escape. I will find you and I will kill you. Slowly. Painfully. A knife in the gut? A piece at a time? My mother was a witch, you know. She taught me about survival, about secret ways of hurting a man, about—"

"Shh."

I felt fingers on my lips, silencing me—gentle fingers— and heard quiet, gentle words.

"I'll have you out of here in just a minute."

He was a dream, he had to be. I'd gone completely insane and was seeing visions, hearing voices.

But the hands had left me now and were working with the rope over my head.

Then they were under me, lifting me.

"Sam?"

"Hush," he whispered. "It will be all right, I promise. But please be quiet while I get us out of here.

"Sam?" Now? After all that had happened?

In answer, he hugged me tightly against him and crept with me into the woods.

"Sam," I whispered. "You came. I knew you would." At last I surrendered to the weakness claiming me, to the tears I had refused to shed since the first day, and to the blackness I had held at bay for so long—too long. And at last I spoke the words I had felt through every fiber of my being but which I should never have voiced—not to him. "But you're too late."

2

She awoke in that time *before sunrise when the birds had already awakened and started their search for the day's food, calling to each other—pleasant sounds in a world gone mad. She didn't have to turn her head to know he was there, but she did so anyway, to look at him, as she looked at him each morning, with a mixture of love and fear and regret. He sat in a chair near her bed, feet propped on a packing crate, head thrown back against the uncompromising chair. And for once he slept—lightly, she knew—and for once he might be getting some needed rest.*

He would never sleep beside her—that she knew too. But he would remain nearby. He would watch over her. It was more than she had any right to expect. For her, it would have to be enough.

Megan felt the kiss of a light breeze on her face as she awoke, and she lay there, eyes closed, enjoying its caress until the dreams and memories of the night jumbled together behind her closed lids and brought her upright in bed: a strange bed. And outside the opened windows she saw a strange porch and a strange tree-shaded yard.

She heard a noise, a slight scratching, scrabbling sound, and turned her head to see an enormous black dog rising to a sitting position between her and the hall door. She knew she'd seen it before, but had it been in her dreams? In her memories?

"Am I—" Her voice was hoarse, barely audible, and she found her throat raw and reluctant to let her force words through it. Still, she tried again. "Am I supposed to be afraid of you?" she asked.

In answer, the dog rose and walked toward her. She wondered if she should try to run, wondered briefly if she were still trapped in some bizarre nightmare. But when it reached the side of the bed, the dog butted its head under her hand where it lay on the sheet beside her.

"I guess not," she said, answering her own question and giving in to the dog's wordless command to rub its head. "But am I supposed to know you?"

The dog whined once, whirled away from her, and trotted out of the room.

She supposed she ought to get up, follow the dog, and try to find out where she was, but at the moment she wasn't sure she had the strength. Instead, she sank back against the pillows, sorting through what she was pretty sure were memories of the night before: the raid, the soft-spoken woman doctor, the man with the kind hands and the dark anger-filled eyes.

"Good morning. Deacon told me you were awake."

Megan looked up at the sound of the voice. Ah, she thought, this one had been a memory. But had he been? The voice was the same, and the eyes, although she saw no anger in them this morning—but the rest of him? Had the man she saw last night looked like the man standing in the bedroom doorway? The height was the same, the lean almost hungry-looking build, the dark complexion and even darker hair. But hadn't he been older? Looked more—lived in? Wouldn't she have noticed the angry scar that cut upward across his left cheek or the other one that marred the back of his right hand?

"Do you know who I am?" he asked softly. "Or where you are?"

Memories flooded against the walls of her mind, more than she could handle right now and more than she could bear to share with this man.

"You're Jake Kenyon," she said, "my neighbor. And this must be your home?"

He smiled then, reluctantly, almost as though rewarding her for something, and nodded toward a chair. "I didn't think to pick up anything for you when Patrick—Dr. Phillips's husband—and I went back down to your house last night to lock it up. There's a shirt of mine, and a pair of sweatpants with a drawstring waist. The bathroom's the first door on the right. You'll find clean towels and a new toothbrush in there. I'll have breakfast ready by the time you are."

"Mr. Kenyon—"

"Later, Megan. After breakfast."

The bathroom was small and obviously cut out of another room in the manner she had noticed in her own almost-as-old house, because the light fixtures and outlets and even the window were slightly off kilter. But it was clean. The fixtures gleamed. And a pile of thick clean towels and a new toothbrush, as well as a comb and a new bar of soap, waited for her on the top of a small oak washstand.

Megan closed the door behind her and carried her handful of clothes into the room. She placed them on the washstand and sank down onto the edge of the tub. She glanced back at the door and saw the reflection of herself staring at her from a full-length mirror.

I almost waved at you.

She had said it. So had he. Why? Why would anyone who looked like him even consider waving at someone who looked like the woman she saw in the mirror?

Too-thin arms and legs sticking out from a plain white cotton shift. Too-sharp cheekbones and too-large eyes beneath, nondescript light-brown hair that had been cropped off in an attempt to disguise her in her flight through the jungle, and that she'd not yet had the energy or the inclination to restyle. She couldn't see the salty tear tracks on her cheeks, but she could feel them.

When had this happened to her? When had she become indistinguishable from any of the numberless refugees in any of the numberless camps she had visited over the last five years?

Three months ago. She knew the answer to that question. Or did she? Were the events of three months ago what had truly changed her? Or had she started the change long before that—when the disillusionment had begun?

She frowned at her reflection, thrown uncompromisingly back at her from the mirror, and then frowned at the mirror. It seemed a vanity out of keeping with the harsh dark man who had stormed into the middle of a dozen others to pull her back to safety and sanity.

Helen! Oh, God, Helen. Of course there would be a mirror. Jake Kenyon? Jake Kenyon was more than just her neighbor; he was Helen's husband. And he would want answers. Soon.

Maybe not, she told herself as she reached for the faucets and started the flood of water from the shower. Maybe he had accepted the official story. Maybe he wouldn't need to hear any more. Maybe she wouldn't have to tell it again. Maybe she could push it so far back she would never have to think of it again. . . .

Later, scrubbed, polished, and toweled dry, Megan

slipped into the soft faded sweatpants, tied them about her waist, and pulled up the legs until they bagged over her ankles and the pair of gray boot socks she had found neatly folded with the clothes. Then she pulled on the equally soft cotton shirt. Too long and too wide; nevertheless, it fit her like an old friend, and she smiled as she rubbed the impossibly familiar fabric across her suddenly sensitive arms.

She'd shampooed, too, and done the best she could with her hair, and for the first time in months she wished for makeup. But she'd only be hiding behind it, as she had hidden so many times in the past. Maybe it was time she quit hiding. She shook her head and shuddered. Who was she kidding? Hiding—protecting herself from emotional pain— was all she knew how to do, all she'd ever known.

She lifted her chin and threw back her shoulders. She was ready, as ready as she'd ever be, to face Jake Kenyon and his questions.

The dog waited for her in the wide hallway outside the bathroom. "Deacon, is it?" she asked. Again he butted his head under her hand before turning and trotting down the hall. At a door toward the end, he stopped and looked back.

She didn't really need a tour guide, she realized. The house was small, smaller than hers. Only a couple of other doors led off the hallway, and the one Deacon guided her through opened into a large combination living-dining area. A massive stone fireplace dominated one end of the room, with a glass-fronted wood-burning stove butted up against it beneath a rustic carved mantel. Again, she saw only a couple of closed doors indicating other rooms, or maybe closets, before she followed Deacon through an opening to the right. The long narrow room they entered had obviously once been a porch; its history was apparent from its sloping ceiling to its numerous windows. But now it was a kitchen and small breakfast room, functional and—unintentionally, she suspected—cheerful. And empty.

The pine table was set for two, a kettle boiled on the stove, and the oven gave off a suspicious warmth and an unmistakable aroma.

"Mr. Kenyon?" she said cautiously. "Jake?"

"Be right with you." She heard his voice from inside a room of some sort at the end of the kitchen. "Grab that kettle, will you, before it boils over? All right! Here it is."

Megan switched off the burner just as Jake Kenyon emerged. "I knew I had some somewhere," he said, opening what she recognized as a box of tea bags.

"There's coffee and orange juice," he told her, "but Barbara—Dr. Phillips—said your throat's probably going to be irritated for the next few days, so I thought you might like some tea with honey." He nodded toward a small jar on the table. "It's local. It's really pretty good."

"Tea will be fine, thank you," she said, as awkwardly polite as he.

"Sit down. Yes. Why don't you sit down while I put everything on the table? It's ready."

"Everything" turned out to be crisp bacon, which she couldn't eat without discomfort, and fluffy scrambled eggs and melt-in-your-mouth biscuits, which she could. Remarkably, she was hungry. Famished. More so than she had been for months, maybe even for years. With her barely aware of it, Jake kept her cup filled and passed her the butter and honey and the plates of eggs and biscuits. Eventually, though, she realized that he had finished eating, pushed his plate to one side, and now sat with his coffee, just watching her eat and smiling at her in a way that reflected not humor so much as some sort of satisfaction with either her actions or his.

"I'm sorry," Megan said, placing her fork carefully on her plate and clenching her hand on the table beside the plate.

"For what?"

"For—" She grimaced. "This was really very good. You shouldn't have gone to so much trouble."

"It wasn't any trouble. Barbara's mother feels sorry for me, so every couple of months she sends me a few batches of her homemade frozen biscuit dough. All I had to do was stick these in the oven while I fried the bacon and eggs. But why shouldn't I have gone to some trouble for you?"

"Because I've inconvenienced you enough already. I really am sorry."

Megan knew the time had come to confront the night before, because if she didn't do it now, she might never be able to, and this man deserved honesty from her, if nothing else.

"I really lost control last night, didn't I?" she asked. But she knew the answer without waiting for one. "I just want you to know I'm not always so irrational."

"It was an irrational situation."

She found a hesitant smile. "Yes, it was. But I can't imagine anyone else—you, for example—collapsing in a corner and screaming loud enough to bring a neighbor from a quarter of a mile away."

He reached over and took her hand. "Actually, I was already on my way down the road when I heard you. No, I wouldn't have acted in the same way if they had come in on me like they did you, but then I wouldn't have been alive to have breakfast the next morning."

No, she realized, he probably wouldn't have been. That huge dog of his would have warned him that someone was prowling around; he would have been armed by the time the first boot hit the porch, and he would have started firing when the door came crashing in. And he would have been dead. Dead like the others—

"And I don't have the same kind of memories you do, either."

She tugged her hand from his, and he let go. She clasped it with her other hand and looked around, anywhere to avoid the questions in his eyes and the questions his two very obvious scars raised in her. A familiar-looking black notebook lay on the cabinet just beyond his left shoulder. When he saw where her attention had fixed, he turned and lifted the book.

"Yes, it's yours," he told her, handing it to her. "I thought you'd want it safer than leaving it for careless eyes."

"You read it?"

He shook his head. "Only a line or two—just enough to recognize what it was when the deputy handed it to me."

Megan folded the notebook against her. "There aren't that many deep dark secrets in it. Probably not as many as there ought to be. The psychiatrist I saw when I returned suggested I use this as a kind of therapy—you know, talk out what had happened even if there was no one to listen but myself."

"I'll listen."

Megan closed her eyes and leaned back against the chair, sighing. "I was afraid you'd say that. But I knew you had to."

"Yeah. I have to. I have to know how much the official version of the story left out."

"And why I'm alive when no one else is?"

"That too."

Would he believe her? Was it even worth trying to convince him?

Yes, she decided. This man deserved the truth.

"I'm alive because of a series of events that never should have happened," she told him.

"None of it should have happened," he reminded her. "Tell me."

She nodded, swallowed once, and focused on the pattern of leaves and sunlight in the trees outside the window behind Jake. "I'd worked with Project Food for about five years, and we had been supplying the clinic at Villa Castellano almost that long. I'd even made a few trips there, but I don't think Roger even realized that we did so, until the country's aid appropriations bill came in for some real serious objections. My father has always supported that aid, and I guess Roger saw a way to benefit—he said—everyone, even though he'd been pressuring me to quit for over a year. Before I knew it, he had scheduled a junket and had us all in this tiny little village, along with reporters from *Time*, *Newsweek*, even *People*—and Helen.

"Roger said she was filming a documentary, but I suspect there was more campaign rhetoric involved in it—in the whole trip—than impartial journalism. Roger and I had already had what was for us a major disagreement about how this was being presented to the media. You know, the 'this is your tax dollar at work' suggestion rather than plainly stating that all the work there was being done by private contributions.

"We'd gone into a nearby village for the last episode of the media trip before taking the reporters back to the landing strip. One of the women there was in labor. There didn't seem to be enough time to get her into the clinic to the doctor—she had a midwife—but she also had this houseful of scared, crying kids and a husband who came up to me and said, 'Señora, you help my wife?'

"I'd met her on a previous trip. She'd befriended me then, and I had given her oldest daughter a scarf she admired. I couldn't say no, and Roger didn't want me to. I know he was afraid of what I'd say to the reporters if I had any time alone with them. So he left me in the village while everyone else went to the airport to see the reporters leave.

"The woman's husband walked me back to the clinic later, although it seemed hours before he could get away to do so. We were almost to the edge of the clearing when we heard the sound of vehicles arriving. He stopped me. And when he saw they were government—army—vehicles, he pulled me back into the shadows.

"The staff came out. The soldiers came pouring out of their transports, shouting, running into the various buildings, carrying out supplies and equipment, and rounding up anyone they found inside.

"Helen came out of the main office with her minicam in her hand. I think she really thought she could stop them. The officer in charge—I don't know who he was, but Roger did. He recognized him when he came out of the office behind Helen. He said, 'You,' only that, and I think he knew then he was going to die. The officer knew who we were. He looked at Helen and said, 'Señora Kenyon, you should have left with the others.' And then he shot her.

"I'm sorry, Jake," Megan told him, finally looking at him, daring her already shattered voice to fail her further. "But it was quick. It was by far the most merciful of all the deaths that day."

He closed his eyes briefly, but not before she saw a quick flash of pain. "Thank you," he said. "Go on."

"My guide had his hand over my mouth, or I would have screamed. And then it wouldn't have mattered if I had, because there was so much noise no one could have heard me. And when it was over, there was nothing left but death and burned-out buildings, and two weeks of hiding in the jungles, and finally getting to safety, where no one wanted to hear the truth of what had happened. Not even my father."

When she fell silent, Jake pushed up out of his chair and walked to the back door. "I—I have some things to do now but I'll be back in a little while to take you home—if you want to go."

Megan nodded and stood, reaching for the plates on the table.

"Leave those," Jake said. "I'll do them later."

"It's no trouble."

"Leave them, I said."

Megan whirled around, for the first time in longer than she could remember feeling a burst of healthy, heady anger. "You go do whatever manly, macho thing you feel you have to do to get over what I just told you, Jake Kenyon, but I'm the one who had to tell you, I'm the one who has to stay in this house right now, and I'm the one who's doing the damned dishes!"

"Fine. Whatever you say!" Jake yanked open the back door. Deacon scrambled to his feet to follow but Jake made some gesture with his hand. "Stay," he commanded, slamming outside and letting the screen door bang shut behind him.

"Fine," Megan whispered, feeling her anger drain from her. She owed him thanks, gratitude, and only God knew what else; she had just told him how his wife died. And then she had yelled at him. She never yelled at anyone, but she had yelled at Jake Kenyon—yelled at him when what she wanted to do was slide her arms around him and hold him, or be held by him, until the horror of the telling faded away.

What she was going to do instead was clear the table and do the dishes. She glanced at the skillet on the stove and at the clutter on the table. She hated doing dishes.

Somehow, during the simple procedure of putting the kitchen in order, the horror did dull. When she had finished her task and Jake still hadn't returned, Megan made herself another cup of tea and leaned against the counter, holding her journal.

The telling had helped. Maybe the honesty Dr. Kent had insisted she give her journal would help too.

She heard the sound of birdcalls outside the open kitchen door and felt again the gentle breeze, although no longer quite so cool, that had awakened her that morning.

Jake's home was quiet, peaceful, almost timeless, lulling her into a sense of security she couldn't remember ever feeling before. If the raid last night hadn't ruined it for her, she could have this same feeling in her own home; she knew she could. All the elements were the same—except maybe the ages of their houses. His had to be much older than she had first thought, had to have seen so much more life, so much more pain, so much more joy. Had to have been . . .

Megan shook her head as that thought eluded her. All she needed was to become as fanciful as her father said she already was. Work helped keep her from that. And she knew where there was more work to be done in this house. She tossed the notebook on the table and started toward the bedroom, but as she stepped into the living room, she stopped, puzzled.

A fire? she thought. In June? She knew there had been no fire in the fireplace when she came through the room earlier. In fact, there had been a wood stove in place in front of the now-open hearth.

Nor had there been a huge frame balanced on four kitchen chairs in the room.

Megan caught her hand to her mouth. There definitely hadn't been two women in long dresses working over the quilt in that frame.

One of them stood. She was Choctaw, as one would expect in this part of the state, rail thin, and old enough for her black hair to be liberally silvered. She handed a pair of scissors to the other woman, who was young and, surprisingly, white, with soft brown hair and a face that was more than pretty but not yet truly formed because of youth and innocence.

"Liddy," the older woman said, "I've been trying to figure out how to say this, and there's no other way but just to say it. Don't fall in love with Sam."

The younger woman looked up and smiled, seemingly not bothered by the warning. "Granny Rogers, you know I've loved him since I was twelve years old."

"I know you think you have, child. I know you've built him into some kind of hero in your mind because he's a Lighthorseman, and because he turned his back on his daddy's people and returned from Texas, but your daddy's not going to like it. And Sam's having been a Ranger and having worn the gray isn't going to make Daniel Tanner like it. He's going to send you back to those white relatives in Fort Smith. And when he does, you're going to find a young man you can build a life with, someone to share your dreams."

The girl called Liddy clipped the thread from the stitch in front of her, jabbed her needle into a pincushion, and lifted her chin defiantly. "Sam is my dream."

The older woman shook her head and dropped her hand onto the girl's shoulder. "But you're not his. You never can be. Sam has no dreams left, child."

"Megan?"

She heard Jake calling her from what seemed to be a great distance away and turned toward his voice. When she did so, she heard Deacon's low whine and once again heard the birds and realized they had been strangely silent while she—while she what?

She turned again to face the living room, and it was as she had seen it earlier that morning: no fire, no quilt frame, no women.

She sagged against the door facing.

"Megan, are you all right?"

Was she? Or was she finally, and in spite of all her denials, losing her mind?

"Jake, is—" She stopped herself before the words escaped. She couldn't ask a man she had just met, no matter how intense that meeting had been, if his house was haunted. "I'm fine," she said.

He came into the kitchen and looked at her intently. "Are you sure? You looked a little strange there for a minute."

Had she now? She wondered how he would have looked had he seen what she just saw—provided, of course, that she had really seen anything.

"Yes," she told him. "I'm sure. I was just—I must have been—I guess I—"

"I'm sorry," he said. "I shouldn't have insisted you tell me.

And then I shouldn't have left you to deal with it by your-self."

Was that what she had been doing? Oh, God, she thought, please let that be what had just happened.

3

Megan sat huddled in a corner of the green bedroom. Jake had been gone an hour, maybe two, with a promise to return from town with a new lock for her front door and the necessary supplies to repair the damage to the facing.

She ought to get up—she knew that—ought to change out of Jake's clothes, ought to start a load of laundry because she knew she could never, until she had washed them, put against her body clothes that had been pawed over by careless hands, ought to start tucking back into their proper places all the things that had been nudged and shuffled and displaced by the men who had invaded her home the night before. Ought to. But couldn't.

The cats had followed her into the bedroom, watching while she stood there, holding back all the emotions that hammered behind her eyes and at the back of her throat.

It was still early. Unbelievable. But the light flooding into the room through its many windows was the pale, watery green of early morning sunshine filtered through thousands of still tender leaves on the sheltering oaks and hackberries and wild cherries in the neglected and overgrown side yard. That yard was to have been her next project. After this room.

She'd been painting the floor when they burst in on her, had painted perhaps a quarter of it a clean gloss white, and in one corner had even begun the stenciling pattern. She supposed Jake had closed the paint can when he came back here, had saved that much for her. But that was all he had been able to save. There was nothing clean about her floor now, nothing glossy, nothing white except the smeared footprints tracking across the bare wood, a set of them looking as though whoever had made them had stopped and wiped his feet, smearing the green of the stenciling and the white of the floor with the dried mud and what appeared to be barnyard already on his shoes.

They'd all wiped their feet, at least figuratively, on her hopes for this home. Had they destroyed them?

Unable to stay in the desecrated room any longer, Megan scrambled to her feet and searched through her closet until she found a pair of loafers and stuffed her feet into them. The laundry would have to wait. Changing out of Jake's clothes would have to wait. She had to get out of this poor violated house. Later she'd decide whether or not to come back into it.

Jake had long ago gotten involved in a running wager with Patrick Phillips about which traveled faster in Pitchlyn County, good news or bad. Neither of them had been able to come up with a definitive test, so the original money remained unclaimed. But since what had happened at Megan Hudson's place the night before would be judged good or bad primarily by which side of a well-defined political line one stood on, he supposed it didn't matter which moved faster. Because the news would have traveled. Rolley P would play hell trying to keep this mess quiet.

He'd gone back up the hill to his place and exchanged his Jeep for a well-used Dodge pickup before coming into Fairview and had backed the truck up to the loading zone of the feed store/lumber yard/hardware store/garden center. Leaving the key in the ignition, he ambled into the building. Years before, a corner behind the painting supplies had been cleared out to make way for Fairview's version of a spit-and-whittle club, an unofficial coffee shop and unashamed bastion of male-only bonding.

He stood at the counter no more than fifteen seconds before the half dozen men noticed him and fell silent. Yep. Faster than a speeding bullet. Sometimes he wondered, and once after a few too many shared cold beers, he had even asked why Patrick bothered printing the newspaper. Patrick had answered quickly and much too intensely for the mellow mood they had worked so hard to establish: Someone's got to try to find the truth.

"Hey, Kenyon. What brings you to town this morning?"

Jake glanced toward the table. Walt Harrison, owner of the place and brother-in-law of Rolley Pierson, the current sheriff, occupied the chair at the head of the table, the one under the sign that proclaimed POLITICS SPOKEN HERE, and from the smirk on Walt's face Jake could tell that more than politics had been spoken this morning and Walt knew all too well what brought Jake to town.

"Heard you had some trouble out at your place last night," Walt called out.

"Nope, not my place," Jake said. The clerk who came to the counter was new since last week. Jake hoped he had more sense than the last one, but since Walt tended to hire minimum-wage workers and fire them rather than promote them, he doubted it. But he gave him the list he had scribbled on an envelope. "Go ahead and load these in the green pickup out front," he told the man. Then he lifted a couple of boxes of shotgun shells from the counter display. "And bag these with the small stuff but put them on a separate invoice."

Walt stretched just enough to see what Jake had put on the counter. "Going varmint hunting?" he asked.

"Nope."

"Hell, Kenyon, you're just full of information this morning. Grab yourself a cup of coffee and get neighborly while Mack loads up your stuff."

Since Walt Harrison had never been neighborly in his life, Jake interpreted the invitation to mean, Come tell these folk all you know about what happened, so my wife's brother won't get on my ass for spreading the news.

"Sure, Walt, don't mind if I do."

He poured a half cup of sludgy coffee into a foam cup, grabbed a chair, and flipped it around to sit straddling it slightly away from the crowded table. He took a sip and looked at the gathered crowd. He knew most of them as Walt's regular cronies, but he recognized a couple of them as pretty dependable tradesmen and wondered why they were still sitting around in the middle of the morning.

"So," Jake said. "What's been happening in town since the last time I came in?"

"Not much," Walt told him. "Not much. Hear you've got a new neighbor, though."

"Not all that new."

"Hear she's a looker."

"Now where did you hear a thing like that?" Jake asked quietly.

"Hear you took her on up to your place to spend the night last night."

"Damn, things must really be slow in town if you're keeping track of me again." Jake smiled genially as he got up, stretched, and tossed his cup into the fifty-gallon drum that served as a trash barrel. "Did you also hear that I'm closing the private road that runs in front of my place and the

Hudson place down to the county road? Oh, and just in case anyone's thinking about going hunting out there, both places are posted as of today, because it might be dangerous. My *new neighbor*"—he purposely mimicked Walt's intonation of the words—"is a little spooked way out there in the country. I figure she'll feel better with a weapon in the house, but I'm not sure she's going to be too careful about what she shoots at; you know how transplanted city women can be. Come to think of it, I'm not sure I'll be too careful either."

"Come on, Jake." Walt slapped the table with his hand. "Aren't you going to tell us what happened last night?"

"Why should I?" Jake asked pleasantly as he looked over at the clerk, who was wrestling with the door Jake had included in his list. "I told Patrick. You all can read about it in another hour when the paper comes out. I thought it would be more important to tell you what *could* happen—in the future.

"Now if you'll excuse me, I'll help Mack with those supplies. You fellows take care. Enjoyed the visit."

Patrick looked up from helping load bundled newspapers into the back of a minivan. He stretched and waved the driver of the minivan on his way and then walked out to the alley where Jake had pulled his pickup to a stop.

"You work all night?" Jake asked.

Patrick grinned. "Of course not. Do you think my wife would let me abuse this body like that?"

Jake grinned back. He knew damned well that Barbara would let Patrick do just about anything he wanted. "Good. Then you won't mind giving me a hand after you get things squared away here?"

"That depends. Is it thinking or working?"

Jake laughed. "Working. Remember that gate you've been promising for the last year to help me fix?"

Patrick's grin faded. "Are you expecting trouble?"

"Not really. I just thought it might be a good idea to discourage nosy visitors."

"Yeah. How is she today, Jake?"

"I'm not sure. For a while, she seemed all right. Maybe Barbara ought to take another look at her."

"Okay. But it will cost you: dinner tonight at your place. Steaks will be fine if you can't be more creative. I'll call Barbara and have her meet us—where, your place or Megan's? Wherever she finds us. I'll be out as soon as I finish up here."

"You're awfully agreeable, Patrick. I don't always trust you when you give in too easily."

Instead of laughing, Patrick shrugged. "This is a big story. Maybe you'd better prepare Megan, because after these papers hit the streets there's bound to be some interest, at least by the Fort Smith media."

"Damn! That's all she needs."

"I was careful to protect her identity. They might not connect our Ms. Hudson with Senator McIntyre. But even if they do, with your gate up, it's certain they won't be able to get to her without doing some serious trespassing. And you can be sure our good-old-boy sheriff is going to say as little as possible. Has she called her father yet?"

"I don't think so. I don't even know if the phone in her house is in service. Did you notice?"

Patrick shook his head. "Maybe you'd better make sure. The story had to be told, Jake. You know that."

"I called you, remember."

"You called Barbara. I just came along as part of the package."

"I volunteered the story."

"Yeah. But I'm not sure you would if you had it to do over."

"Why would you think that?"

Patrick shook his head, but he was smiling when he stepped back from the truck. "Intuition, I guess," he said. "Steaks. Make mine king-sized if you're going to work my poor body into the ground tonight. Come to think of it, maybe you'd better get the beer too. After all, my labor doesn't come cheap."

By the time Jake had picked up steaks and beer for supper, a few needed groceries, and a couple of take-out burgers for his and Megan's lunch, it was afternoon.

He hadn't been completely honest with Patrick. For a while this morning Megan had indeed seemed all right, spirited even. But that was before he had left her while he went outside to lick his own wounds. Before whatever trip her mind had taken her on while she was alone in his house. Before he had returned her to her own violated home and watched what little animation that remained drain from her.

He probably shouldn't have left her alone. He knew he shouldn't have left her alone. But he couldn't have taken her into town, not without exposing her to more attention than someone much stronger than she was could have handled.

He'd left Deacon with her; he wasn't afraid for her physical safety. But at what point did someone as emotionally fragile as Megan Hudson finally stop fighting and surrender to the horror she had faced?

Damn it! He should have kept her at his place, should have had Patrick deliver the supplies he needed to repair the damage those heavy-footed bastards had caused, should have found some other way to warn off would-be sightseers.

He didn't understand the anxiety that gripped him as he turned off the state highway onto the county road, that grew as his truck rumbled across the cattle guard leading from the county road onto his private lane, that had lodged securely in his throat by the time he turned into the Hudson drive and stopped in front of her house.

It was quiet, too quiet. Not even Deacon came to greet

him. Without turning off the ignition, Jake studied the house and surrounding yard. He glimpsed Megan's car through the partially open doors to the barn where she parked it. He saw no sign of an intruder, no evidence that anyone else had been here since he left Megan alone that morning, which meant that the abnormal silence and her continued absence had nothing to do with outside forces and everything to do with her tenuous grip on emotional stability.

He'd turned off the ignition and opened the truck door when he spotted a fleeting motion at the corner of the south side of the house. He slid from the truck, carefully reaching up beneath the seat as he did so for the 9-millimeter pistol he stored there, as in his Jeep, in a specially mounted hidden holster, and kept his eyes trained on the corner.

They came into sight just as Jake's hand found the automatic—Deacon first, allowing Megan's restraining hand on his collar, then Megan, still dressed in his sweats and shirt but clutching a hoe in her other hand as though she meant to do damage to more than weeds.

"Jake?"

He released his grip on the pistol and stepped away from the truck.

"Where's your Jeep?"

Relieved, he realized she had been acting out of caution and not hiding in a corner somewhere, traumatized beyond ever being able to act again. "I'm sorry." He smiled at her. "I didn't realize you hadn't seen my truck yet. I needed the cargo space for your supplies."

She stepped a little closer as he turned back to the truck and lifted a grocery bag from the cab.

"May I borrow your fridge?" he asked. "Patrick and Barbara are coming out for dinner tonight, and I need to store the groceries—either that or go home first and off-load them, and I'd rather not take the time to do that now."

"Sure," she said cautiously, releasing her grip on Deacon's

collar and walking closer. "Why did you need a truck for a new lock and a—" She reached the side of the pickup and looked into the bed where he had loaded the new door, the framing lumber, the floor paint and polyurethane and another gallon of the green she had been using for stenciling, as well brushes and cleaner. "Oh, my!"

"The county will pay for it, Megan."

He noticed for the first time that she wore garden gloves on her hands, that his shirt and sweats and her face were liberally streaked with dirt, and that she had a couple of dead leaves caught in her cropped hair. But her eyes once again held the spark he had seen at breakfast. He shifted the grocery bag in his arms and reached for the other.

"What have you been doing while I was gone?" he asked with a lightness he sensed she needed.

Megan moved around to his side of the truck and took the second bag. "Getting angry," she said, just as lightly, as she turned and started toward the front door.

Jake grinned as he fell into step behind her. "And who have you been taking that anger out on?"

"Not who," she told him, glancing over her shoulder and grimacing slightly. "What. And I'm not sure I won."

The old house with its high ceilings and long porches and tall, shading trees still held coolness from the night and early morning, and would, like his house, continue to do so until late afternoon. Jake followed Megan through rooms that had not been touched since his visit with Patrick the night before, into the kitchen, which still showed every sign of the quickly aborted but careless search.

Megan scooted her bag onto the scrubbed-pine worktable and turned. "I wasn't ready to tackle this yet," she told him. "I didn't know if I'd ever be ready to tackle it."

Jake found a place for his bag of groceries on the white enameled countertop, spotless before its desecration. "And now?" he asked casually.

Megan gave a soft, almost hesitant laugh. "Remember that mess of weeds and bramble in the side yard?" she asked. "Well, I took my frustration out on it. By the time I got down to what looks like the remains of some stone borders, I knew there was no way on earth I was going to let those overgrown bullies chase me away from here."

Her words were braver than her voice, but Jake plucked a can of cold cola from the bag and saluted her with it before handing it to her. "Good," he said. Should he tell her now what Patrick had said about the news media? He made a quick decision not to. It could be hours before anyone picked up the story. There would be time later, after she was a little more firm in her resolve to stay. Then he realized he couldn't wait.

"Have you called your father yet?"

Megan's smile faltered but she recovered quickly, popping the tab on the cola and drinking deeply before she placed the can on the table.

"Megan?"

"No, I haven't. And no, I won't."

"Do you think that's wise?"

She lifted a determined chin and stared at him. For a moment her eyes filled with pain. But then she fought it down and he saw again the fire, the life, the will to live, and the same stubborn, proud determination she'd shown him when she argued with him. He didn't know why it was so important for him to see those things, to know she felt them, but it was. As important, he realized, as coming back to her this afternoon had been. As important as learning she hadn't spent her time alone huddled in a corner.

Wondering where they had come from and why, Jake pushed those thoughts away. They were as alien to his normal reaction to someone, even a woman as attractive and needy as Megan Hudson, as were the emotions that inspired them. But to keep the life in her eyes he would postpone telling her, for a little while, something he was sure would kill it.

Megan sat at the bench of the long pine worktable in her kitchen listening to the combined thunks and gurgles of her washer and dryer and to the industrious sounds of Jake framing the new doorway and hanging the new heavy wooden door he'd told her she needed and insisted the county commissioners would pay for.

Would they? In order to preclude a lawsuit? Little did they know there was no way she would ever sue, would ever invite attention to herself. Not after the debacle she had gone through when she returned from Villa Castellano. No. Her main reason for moving here was to ensure she could keep a low profile. What a hell of a way to begin.

Jake thought she ought to call her father. She supposed she would if she absolutely had to. But right now she didn't. And right now she was in no mood to try to explain to the senator, yet again, how she had been a victim, only to have him, once again, not believe her.

She heard a mutter from the living room and then Jake humming. Humming, not swearing. He'd told her he enjoyed this kind of work when he'd declined her offer to help him, and for the first time she really believed him.

She'd straightened the kitchen while he worked, then bathed away the dirt and sweat of her marathon gardening effort and changed into clean clothes of her own.

She supposed she ought to get up and tackle the green bedroom, but a light breeze came through the open kitchen windows, fluttering the delicate organza curtains she had hung there. The room was in the northeast corner of the house, with tall, double windows on each wall, making it bright and cheerful in the morning but protected from the afternoon heat. In the few weeks she had been there, Megan had painted and scraped and scrubbed until the tall glass-fronted cabinets and the ancient appliances were a gleaming gloss white, pleasant but sterile. Only the addition of selected accents of color would make it truly a home.

The problem here, as in most of the other rooms, was that she didn't know *what* color. Color reflected the personality and character of the one who chose it, and Megan wasn't sure she knew herself well enough now to make those choices.

The green in the bedroom, yes. For hope. For new growth. But in the rest of the house?

She sighed and stretched, content for the first time in days. She didn't have to choose right away. For now, she could simply enjoy the cool breeze in her clean kitchen, the muffled sounds from her washer and dryer, and the contented noises Jake made as he put her house in order.

She wanted him. She'd wanted him forever. When she thought of him, she saw them in Granny Rogers's cabin, always there, never anywhere else, with their children about them, with her handwork and quilts and dishes marking the cabin as theirs, with him smiling as he lifted a laughing child into one arm while with the other he drew her close to his side.

And she wanted him in other ways, ways she didn't yet understand. Ways that tightened her body, making her ache with a loneliness so great she thought she would die from it. Ways that, were she older, she'd know how to act upon. . . .

"Megan? Can you give me a hand in here?"

Startled, Megan jumped up from the bench, banging her hip against the corner of the table.

It had happened again.

What had happened again?

"Jake?"

She heard a slightly frustrated laugh from the front of the house. "There's someone else here?" he asked, but he didn't wait for an answer—thank God he didn't wait for an answer! "I hate to bother you, but I've dropped the hinge pins."

Rubbing her hip, Megan hurried to the living room. Jake had moved a table near the door to hold supplies and tools but had somehow, without her even hearing, knocked it over. Now he stood balancing the heavy door, looking down at three long pins that lay just inches from his right boot.

She scooped them up and stretched to insert one in the top hinge, but Jake took it from her and pushed it into the opening in the center hinge. "Thanks," he said.

"That's all right," she told him. *She* should be thanking *him,* for interrupting whatever it was he had interrupted, for bringing her back from wherever she had gone. "I'm glad I could help. Is there anything else I can do? Can I get you some iced tea? Or a cold beer?"

Jake frowned, she supposed because he still held the heavy door. "The other pins would be nice," he said.

"Oh. Of course."

"Megan." He shook his head and devoted his attention to setting the pins, but when he had them secured, he released the door and turned to her. "Are you all right?"

"Yes," she told him, "I am. I really am. I guess I'm just a little shaken by all that's happened. Not badly, you understand, but a little."

Jake's mouth lifted in a quizzical smile that was only punctuated by the slash of the scar on his left cheek. "Then why don't we both have a cold beer and sit on the porch for a while?"

She wanted to ask him about that scar and about the one on his hand; she wanted to ask him about the nonexistent women she had seen in his house; she wanted to ask him about her recurring sensations of having known him, or someone very much like him, but not remembering who or when. Instead, she smiled in relief and went for the beer.

She had almost relaxed, sitting beside him in companionable silence on the steps of the paint-peeled porch, feeling the same gentle breeze that had sought out her kitchen, hearing the easy, friendly sounds of the birds in their late-afternoon search for food and the subtle panting noises Deacon made as he lay beside Jake.

Jake. Funny how she knew him and yet didn't. Helen hadn't talked about her husband very much; Roger had spoken about him even less. She knew he had been a Drug Enforcement Agency agent and had overheard Helen complaining to Roger about Jake's leaving the federal government for a go-nowhere job in Pitchlyn County as county sheriff.

Later, Helen had mentioned with chilling indifference that Jake no longer even had that job, since he had been shot, but she refused to discuss it with Megan—not that *that* was anything out of the ordinary—and had given no indication that Jake had come as close to death as he must have to have sustained such scars.

He must still have been recuperating when Helen returned to Washington that last time, just before their fateful junket to Villa Castellano. . . .

The honk of a car horn and approaching engine noises jolted her back to the present and memories of the all-too-recent events of the night before.

"It's all right," Jake said quickly, after one look at her. He held out his hand as if to touch her, to hold her in place on the porch, but drew it back quickly. "I'm expecting someone."

A red pickup almost as disreputable as the one Jake drove pulled into what must have once been a parking and turnaround area near the porch and stopped. Deacon looked up from his relaxed pose on the porch but did not get up as a wiry sandy-haired man about Jake's age jumped from the cab.

"No wonder you need help if all you do is loll around with good-looking women, drinking what is probably supposed to be my beer," he said, laughing as he stepped up to the porch. "Hello, pretty lady." He extended his hand to Megan. "I'm Patrick Phillips. We didn't meet last night because Jake was playing watchdog, but you did meet my wife— Barbara?" he added, in response to her puzzled frown. "Dr. Phillips?"

"Oh, yes," Megan said, at last associating the name with the soft-spoken doctor. She took his hand. "Hello, Mr. Phillips."

"Patrick," he insisted.

He was just as fair as Jake was dark, as open as Jake was taciturn, and Megan felt herself responding to his friendly smile. "Patrick," she said. "And I'm Megan."

"I know. And you have two black kittens and what promises to be a spectacularly beautiful green bedroom."

"Before he learns any more of your secrets," Jake said, while Megan was still trying to decide the best way to ask Patrick how he knew about the cats and the green paint, "you ought to be aware that beneath that good-old-boy routine, Patrick is one fine investigative reporter who just happens to publish the local newspaper."

Megan drew back her hand.

"I'm off duty," Patrick said gently. "At least for the time being." He nodded toward Jake. "I've been drafted by this layabout to help fix a gate he's had down in a ditch since before my first communion." Patrick's smile dimmed. "He didn't tell you, did he. Jake?"

"Oh, hell, don't stop now, Patrick," Jake said with a resigned sigh. "Didn't you bring a copy with you?"

"Yeah. Wait a minute."

Megan watched, more curious than apprehensive, as Patrick jogged to his truck and retrieved something from the seat. Only when she saw he carried a newspaper did she begin to get concerned. But when he unfolded it and placed it in her lap, revealing the headline ILL-CONCEIVED NO-KNOCK RAID GOES AWRY over a picture of her shattered front door with a big muddy footprint beside the remains of the lock, she sank back against the porch post.

"Oh . . . my . . . God," she said on an indrawn breath.

4

Megan turned haunted eyes to Jake as a sense of betrayal almost overwhelmed her. "You did this to me?"

Jake rose gracefully from his seat on the steps, but his actions were less than graceful as he paced a few steps back and forth before stopping beside Patrick and looking down at her. Now two men she barely knew loomed over her. "What was I supposed to do about such a flagrant abuse of power, ignore it? Read the article, Megan."

"I came here for privacy, not to have my name spread all over the local paper, not to invite the media to swoop down on me again, not—"

"Read the article, Megan," Jake insisted quietly.

"I trusted you!"

"*Read it.*"

Megan looked down at the paper in her lap and forced her eyes to focus on it, forced back the fist of terror that seemed to grip her heart, forced herself to make sense of the words she saw on the page:

According to a report filed June 4, the Pitchlyn County Sheriff's Office, acting on an informant's sworn affidavit, led a raid against a purported planned narcotics transaction at what they believed to be the home of a suspected offender with a lengthy arrest record and three convictions for possession of a controlled substance.

Leading a force of twelve men from four state and local agencies, First Deputy Mark Henderson served the warrant at 12:15 A.M. in what is known as a "no-knock" search. Made legal by what was seriously claimed in the last state legislative session to be an infringement of constitutional rights, a no-knock search operates on the presumption that, with warning, a suspect will dispose of narcotics evidence before admitting the officers bearing the warrant.

No narcotics were found. The known suspect was not found. The new resident, who acquired ownership six weeks earlier, as documented by court records and substantiated by tradespeople hired to assist in renovation of the former rental property, was home alone. A neighbor who became suspicious of the late-night activity interrupted the search and affirmed the new owner's lack of involvement with the previous tenant.

Sheriff Rolley Pierson states that the name of the alleged offender is being withheld pending results of an ongoing investigation.

Information received at the *Pitchlyn County Banner* from a reliable source reveals that the victim of this search was not physically harmed but was treated by a doctor for shock following the midnight invasion of twelve armed men.

This surprise raid follows three official complaints during the preceding month against Sheriff Pierson or members of his staff, and a number of protests voiced in official court proceedings by defendants claiming that improper procedures were used in search and seizure or that improper force was used in effecting the arrest.

Megan looked up from the paper, from Jake to Patrick and back to Jake. "You didn't use my name," she said.

"Why would I want to do that to a nice person like you?" Patrick asked.

She looked back at him and grinned. "You didn't use my name!"

Jake took the paper from her, folded it, and handed it to Patrick. "It may come out anyway. Gossip spreads in this county faster than a pasture fire in August. The owner of the lumberyard and his cronies already knew about the raid by the time I got to town this morning. But something had to be done. You see, as long as Pierson's victims were *criminals*, very few people in this county were willing to say anything."

"And we were in luck," Patrick added. "It was a big news day in both Fort Smith and Tulsa, the two most likely outside places to have picked up the story, and by the time they get around to it, if they do, it will be just another in a long line of offenses laid at the door of our dear sheriff. Unless you want to push it, I have a feeling Rolley P is going to play this real low key."

"Which suits me just fine," Jake said. "Until we have enough evidence to take him before a grand jury."

Caught by what seemed to be an alien hardness in Jake's voice, Megan glanced quickly at him, only to find him staring into the distance, his eyes and expression as hard as his voice had been, his features, accented by the slash of the scar, dark and forbidding. For the first time, she knew Jake was a man to be feared. But by her?

o   o   o

She threw herself against him, wrapping her arms around his waist and pressing her cheek to his hard chest. "He's sending me away," she cried, "back to Fort Smith. Please don't let him make me go. Please let me stay here with you!"

She felt the tension tightening his body and felt his hands grip on her arms. She dared to look up and found his eyes glittering darkly with an emotion she had no way of understanding.

For the first time she saw vagrant strands of gray in his black hair and harsh lines that time had etched in his face. It didn't matter. The life that had marked him so had made him the man she loved. "Please let me stay with you!"

His hands tightened even more on her arms as he bent toward her, and she thought for one glorious moment he would kiss her. But he held her still while he separated them by the distance of one step.

"You're so young, child," he said harshly and—because she wanted so much to hear it, hear it she did—wistfully, "and so innocent. I wonder: Could you survive me?"

Whining, Deacon bumped his head under her hand. Patrick was looking at her questioningly, and Jake—Jake stared at her with the same fierce intensity he had focused on that unseen distance just seconds—she hoped it was just seconds—ago.

Megan shuddered and pushed up from her seat on the stairs, finding that the men still towered over her. Familiarity with these—*whatever* they were—did not lessen the fear she felt when she came out of one. What was happening to her?

Seeing questions of another kind building in Jake's eyes, she shook her head, a quick negative answer to anything he wanted to ask.

"Excuse me," she said, but it seemed her voice had as little courage as she did; it had reverted to the hoarse croak of earlier that day. "It's too much," she said. From somewhere she found a tiny bit of strength. "I'm sorry. I suppose I've overdone it. I'm just tired, that's all. I think I'll rest awhile."

"Megan?"

This time it was Patrick who spoke her name, with a wealth of questions in the one word; Patrick who reached as though to touch her; and Jake who stopped him by placing his dark, scarred hand on his friend's arm.

"I think that's a good idea," Jake said. "Patrick and I will be working on the gate near the county road turnoff. I'll leave Deacon with you. If you need us, tell him to get me and bring me back."

"Do you really think this is going to keep anyone out?"

Jake turned from studying the massive pipe gate that still rested in its nest of weeds and briars in the ditch beside the post he had installed months ago.

"Only the mildly curious," he said. "The sightseers, the uninvited hunters who would just as soon find an easier way back to the mountains, and the type of thief who needs a truck to carry away his booty. But at least with this up, I won't have many doubts about the intentions of anyone wandering around on my place or Megan's."

"Interesting," Patrick muttered.

"What is?" Jake asked, as he took a gasoline-powered weed cutter from the back of his truck.

"You never seemed to worry much about the Hudson place before."

"I never had the right before."

"And what suddenly gave you that right?"

Jake paused with his hand on the starter cable. "Hell."

Patrick flashed the grin that had infuriated Jake since the day they started first grade together and nodded toward the ditch. "If you'd just kind of stomp around down there and scare off the snakes, and maybe use that thing like a stick to poke around, I think we can get that big Tinkertoy out of there without contributing to the noise pollution."

Recognizing reprieve, Jake returned Patrick's grin and stepped down into the ditch. "Tinkertoy? I'll have you know that's a product of some expert welding."

"Yeah. Yours and mine—and then didn't you wind up hiring the entire vo-tech welding class to finish it?"

Jake shot his friend a sharp but friendly glare for knowing and remembering too much. Then, working together silently except for muffled groans of effort, the two men wrestled the massive gate from the tangle of briars and tugged and lifted until they had it balanced in place across the pipes of the cattle guard.

Looking across the top rail of the gate at Patrick, who wiped his arm across his sweat-drenched forehead, Jake was reminded of why the gate was still in the ditch after all these months. His body protested even now but at last was beginning to respond as it once had—before he'd either been suckered into an ambush or had stumbled onto something much bigger than his informant had known.

"You okay?" Patrick asked, on a wheezing breath.

"Yeah," Jake said, lying only a little. Eight inches more. That's all they had to lift the damn thing. Then they could release it onto the welded hooks that would serve as hinge pins and be finished with all the heavy work.

Jake flexed his knees and settled his grip on the gate. "On the count of three, city boy. One . . . two . . . three!"

They made it. With a scrape of metal and a satisfying *thunk!* the gate settled into place and the two men collapsed against it.

"I don't suppose . . . you brought . . . any of that cold beer . . . with us," Patrick panted.

Jake chuckled weakly and pushed himself away from the gate.

"So. Where does she go?"

Wishing he had indeed brought some of the beer, or at least a cooler of water, Jake didn't at first realize that Patrick was now wearing his reporter's hat. "What?"

"Megan. When she takes those little mini-vacations. Wasn't that one of those gaps you were telling Barbara about last night? Is this something new since the raid, or a result of whatever the hell really happened at Villa Castellano, or has she always just gone off somewhere in her mind in the middle of a conversation while looking straight at you?"

Jake wiped his sleeve across his forehead and automatically started to unbutton his shirt, but stopped. His upper body was no longer something to expose, not even in a natural reaction against the heat of physical labor, not even when—or perhaps because—the only audience was his oldest friend. "How the hell should I know?"

"Maybe because she's your sister-in-law," Patrick suggested. "You were married to Helen for five years, and Megan was married to Roger for—what—four?"

"Yeah, but I wasn't a part of the life Helen wanted to share with her Washington contacts, and I sure as hell wasn't part of the life good old Rog wanted to share with the Senator's pretty little girl."

"Pretty little girl? That doesn't sound like anything *you'd* say about a female over the age of eighteen, so it has to be a Roger Hudson quote."

"I believe his exact words were, 'She's a pretty little girl. It won't be any hardship being married to her.' Of course, I wasn't supposed to hear them. And from the pictures I'd seen of her—you know, society-page things with her dressed to the nines and acting the role of Lady Bountiful—I assumed she had been around the Washington scene long enough to know what she was getting by marrying Roger Hudson and was agreeable to the bargain."

"You didn't go to the wedding?"

Jake glared at him—he found himself doing a lot more of that this afternoon than usual—and walked to the back of his truck, where he began digging through a box of hardware. "I was on assignment."

"And thank God for small favors." Patrick joined him at the back of the truck and unerringly picked up the gate's locking assembly. "How fortunate that you had something pleasant to do—like deep undercover in some sleazy border town?—rather than endure a Washington society wedding."

"Patrick—"

"I know," Patrick said, sighing. "I'm out of line and I'll back off. But it just makes me so damn mad when you drape your cynicism around you like a shield."

"It's my life," Jake reminded him, not bothering to contradict him, "*my* cynicism, and *my* shield."

"Too true. But you're *my* friend."

Jake gave a quick reluctant laugh and took the hardware from Patrick. "Come on," he said. "Let's get this put together and go find you that cold one you've been begging for."

Patrick nodded, grabbed up the toolbox, and carried it to the gate. "So," he asked. "Do you still think she's a pretty little girl?"

Jake looked at the lock he held, hefted it, and smiled ferally. "One of these days I'm going to stuff *Webster's Unabridged* down your throat."

"It won't shut me up. Barbara tried. Do you still think Megan is a—"

"I don't know what I think about Megan. I do know she's not what I expected. I'm relatively sure she wasn't playing Lady Bountiful in Villa Castellano, that her work there was real and serious. But I'm having a hard time reconciling the woman I've just met with the one who married Roger Hudson. And I'm having a hard time reconciling the way she looks now with the way she looked four years ago."

"Trauma and grief notwithstanding?"

Jake shook his head. "Trauma and grief notwithstanding. The woman I saw in those pictures is gone. Megan is—well, she has a vulnerability that can't be explained by the last four years."

"Or by living through what she survived?"

"I'm not sure it's really touched her yet. She told me what happened at the clinic. The words were there; they were even the right ones. But she told it like someone reporting something she'd read."

"Or can't bear to face."

"Damn it, Patrick. What I'm trying to say is that the Megan I thought I saw in those pictures might have survived, but she wouldn't look like a lost waif, she wouldn't have come to rural Oklahoma to live, and she wouldn't enjoy the hard, physical, dirty labor she's been involved in for the last few weeks."

"That vacation this afternoon wasn't the first one you've seen, was it?"

"No. That was the second one today"—Jake hesitated, remembering her strange reaction when he had come back into his house that morning—"maybe the third. It could be a reaction to the shock she had last night," he added, half hoping he was right, half afraid he was. "Or maybe something completely harmless, like being lost in thought. Barbara didn't seem too concerned."

"Yes, but did my esteemed wife see last night what *we* saw today?"

Deacon whined from the doorway, summoning Megan from her second effort at finishing the floor of the green bedroom. She'd scrubbed and sanded and painted over the ugly footprints, but now tiny white kitten prints tracked across the unpainted portion of the floor. She had captured the kittens, washed their paws so that they wouldn't get sick from licking off the paint, and closed them away in the utility room.

Now she knelt on the floor, determined to apply every ounce of concentration to spreading the gloss white enamel with no sign of a brush stroke, so her mind would be too occupied for any more uncharted side trips. Still, her back and neck were beginning to ache, and when she at last heard the dog she welcomed the distraction of his visit.

She rocked back on her heels, turned to look at him, and recognized a summons in his stance. She felt a moment of fear before she realized that nothing about this highly protective dog even hinted at danger and remembered that both Jake and Patrick were somewhere between her and the road over which any intruder would come.

"What is it, Deacon," she asked companionably, "a squirrel in the front yard?"

Whining again, he whirled and trotted toward the front of the house but paused to look back as though to insist that she follow. She rose to her feet, surprised by how stiff she had gotten in such a short time, stretched toward the ceiling and then toward the floor, and smiled. "I'm coming already."

Her smile faded when she reached the front door and saw a woman standing on the front porch. Did she know her? Or was this another of those weird episodes?

The woman was tiny, fine-boned with a delicate beauty that made Megan instantly aware of her own hospital-escapee appearance. She had smooth golden skin, enormous dark eyes, hair as rich and lustrous as mink caught back at her nape but hanging without a kink or frizz almost to her waist. She wore some sort of tailored khaki skirt and a peach-colored shirt made of the finest, softest cotton Megan had ever seen. And she was undeniably Choctaw.

"Megan?"

Well, Megan thought, at least the woman knew *her*.

"I'm Barbara Phillips. We met last night?"

"Oh, of course." Megan flipped the latch on the screen door and opened the door. "Dr. Phillips."

"Barbara, when I'm off duty," the visitor said, chuckling as she walked into the house and set her bag on a table by the door. "Patrick and Jake promised me you had soft drinks in the refrigerator and a nice breeze on the front porch. You *were* expecting me, weren't you?"

Was she? And then she remembered the food in her refrigerator. *Jake* was, but was she?

"You weren't." Barbara expelled a quick breath and a regretful laugh. "The rats. You might know my dear husband and his best buddy would leave it up to me to explain I'm here for dinner and a house call."

A house call? Megan's first reaction was yet another sense of betrayal, which was ridiculous. Jake had to be responsible for this, and he had been—almost—unfailingly considerate and thoughtful. Her second reaction was one of relief. She remembered this woman as kind and gentle. Maybe she could trust her enough to ask about what had been—or had not been—happening to her.

"Then you're not off duty yet, are you?" Megan asked softly.

Barbara Phillips cocked her head to one side, studying Megan for a moment before she smiled. "And you're not angry."

Megan shook her head. "Of course not. I'm a little unaccustomed to such kindness, but I'm certainly not going to complain about it. Come on back. The kitchen's through here."

"I know," Barbara told her, picking up her bag and following. "Patrick and I spent hours here with Jake when we were growing up."

Megan looked back over her shoulder in surprise. "With Jake? I thought this was Hudson property then."

"It was," Barbara said, plopping her bag onto the pine worktable. "Why don't you sit down," she suggested, "and we'll get this out of the way first?"

"When you were growing up," Megan reminded her as

she pulled out one of the mismatched oak pattern-back chairs and sat down.

Barbara unsnapped the catch on her bag and dug out her stethoscope. "You know about Aunt Sally?"

"No."

"Oh. Aunt Sally Hudson. Roger and Helen's great-aunt."

Megan hadn't even known Roger had a great-aunt, let alone her name.

Listening with the stethoscope at Megan's chest, Barbara frowned slightly, but Megan knew it had to be from her lack of knowledge rather than anything physically wrong. Then Barbara smiled over an obviously well-loved memory.

"Aunt Sally had taught second grade at Prescott almost since before God. Anyway, we all thought she was older than God and had to know at least as much. What most of the kids didn't know was that she had just as much love to give—until Jake's parents died when he was twelve. She took him into her home and took him and all his friends into her heart."

Barbara repositioned the stethoscope. "Take another breath . . . deeper. Okay." She let the stethoscope dangle and raised one of Megan's eyelids, peering at her eye.

"I didn't realize you knew Roger."

Barbara checked the other eye. "Not well. He and Helen lived and went to school in Fairview. We didn't see much of them."

"But—"

"Let's check your reflexes." She tapped Megan's left knee and then her right one. "Okay. Stand up for me, please. Close your eyes, raise your arm out to your side, and then bring your hand around and touch your finger to your nose."

Megan felt a small burst of accomplishment when she felt her finger connect with her nose instead of poking her in the eye, but she couldn't help wondering why Jake and Patrick and Barbara had known so much of Aunt Sally's love if Roger and Helen had wound up with her property.

Barbara walked to the refrigerator and stopped with her hand on the door. "Oops," she said. "Old reflexes of my own. May I?"

"Of course."

Barbara opened the door and removed two cans of cola, which she held up questioningly.

"Yes, please."

Barbara carried both cans to the table, handed one to Megan, and opened the other as she leaned back against the table.

"Is that it, doctor?" Megan asked.

Barbara grinned. "Almost. Are you having any problems? Any confusion?"

Oh. It was time to decide how much to reveal. "A little," Megan admitted.

Barbara nodded. "I talked to Dr. Kent last night. According to him, that's nothing to worry about unless it lingers or gets really bad. He was concerned about what he described as your inability to confront your memories of the attack. He seemed to think this latest insult might have deeper repercussions because of that." She took a deep drink from the cola and waited a heartbeat before continuing. "Any memory loss—that you know of?"

Megan liked this woman. She liked her smiling eyes, her gentle manner, and her quiet grace. Possibly they could be real friends. She shook her head.

"Any hallucinations?"

She didn't yet trust Barbara enough to answer that question honestly, especially after Dr. Kent's comments. The memory of her first weeks back in the States still loomed over her: weeks—first in the hospital, then at her father's house—while everyone she knew, everyone she should have trusted, who should have trusted her, tried to get her to admit she hadn't really experienced what she told them.

"No," she said, turning and walking to the sink, looking

out the double windows above it toward a tree line that stretched across the weedy, overgrown pasture north to the county road, at the glimpse of encroaching hills to the south. She heard the click of the locks as Barbara closed her bag and the scrape of a chair as she sat at the table.

"Dr. Kent also told me he'd recommended you keep a journal."

"That's right."

"Have you recorded the events of the last several hours yet?"

Megan turned around, at last able to face Barbara without wearing a lie on her face. "Not yet."

"I'm not familiar with the procedure he has you using."

"Neither is he," Megan told her. When Barbara raised an eyebrow in silent question, Megan realized how sharply she must have spoken. "It's being developed by a colleague of his, someone he did his residency with. He's using a number of his patients as a kind of test market."

Barbara nodded. "That explains why I haven't heard of it, then. But keeping a journal has been proven to be effective in emotional and spiritual growth. Even if a person does no more than record the events of the day chronologically, there seems to be some benefit in being able to look at events analytically enough to do so. Dr. Kent did stress that he thought this new technique would be good for you. But he said to be sure to call him if you need him."

"Not you?"

Barbara smiled. "You may call me any time you want to, Megan. As a friend, I hope. I can help you find a local doctor too, but I work at the Choctaw Clinic, not in private practice."

"As a friend would be great," Megan said. "I'm sorry, but I've seen too many doctors in the last three months."

"Now you sound just like Jake. No matter how much I complain that he doesn't appreciate my fine education, my dedication, my years of training—"

Barbara was teasing again. Relieved that she didn't have to explain why she was quite literally sick of doctors, Megan opened the refrigerator and took out an ice tray. Jake was sick of them too, was he? Because in spite of Barbara's lightly spoken complaint, Megan knew that Jake held a great deal of respect for her.

The aversion to doctors had to stem from the time he had been wounded. But hadn't that been long enough ago that he had been on the way to recovery by the time Helen joined the junket to Villa Castellano? And if he had been, why wasn't he back at work now with the DEA? Wasn't that the agency Helen used to complain about? Why was Jake still here? And why was she so very glad he was?

"Jake—" Megan started to ask, but a shrill beep interrupted her.

"Damn," Barbara muttered. "I'm not on call tonight, but I guess I'd better remind them. Where's your phone?"

"In the hall," Megan told her. "You can't miss it."

"And your number? Do you mind if I leave it with the clinic?"

Megan shook her head. "No. I don't mind. It's written on the inside front cover of the phone book."

And as Barbara hurried toward the hallway, Megan realized it was just as well that their conversation had been interrupted.

5

Megan sat on the porch steps, leaning against the post of the railing, and listened to the mournful melodic sounds coming from Patrick's harmonica. The night had grown cool, though not cool enough for a sweater, so she now wore a long-sleeved cotton shirt over her Tulsa Oilers T-shirt. But in spite of the shirt she felt chill little shivers and the prickling of goose bumps on her arms, not caused by any weather but by the unexpected yearning Patrick's music called forth from some deep, unexplored well within her.

The light of an almost full moon filtered through the leaves of the ancient hackberry tree. Stars as she could never remember seeing them sparkled like fairy dust across the black sky. And the flickering glow of half a dozen citronella candles brought a soft gentle illumination to the private haven of the porch.

Patrick sat in one of her blue canvas director's chairs, brought out to the porch for this evening, and Barbara sat on the porch floor beside him, resting her arm and her head on his knee with her eyes closed as she listened to him play.

Jake sat on the top porch step, leaning against the rail opposite her. With his head thrown back and his eyes closed he could have been asleep, but he wasn't. Megan knew he was as caught in the music as she was. Still, there was a tension in Jake, a tension that, on reflection, she supposed he must always carry with him.

You're so young, child, and so innocent. I wonder: Could you survive me?

Megan closed her eyes and let the music wash over her. She wasn't young, and she wasn't innocent, and Jake hadn't spoken those words. She didn't know who had said them, or to whom. But if Jake had, how would she have answered him? It was much too soon for either of them to begin any kind of relationship with another person.

Could you survive me?

Who are you?

She drew a ragged breath and opened her eyes. She saw no one new in their intimate group. She hadn't expected to. But who had spoken? *Was* it Jake? Was she hearing words he wouldn't or couldn't speak aloud? She shook her head in a silent, helpless plea: that she had been right in not telling Barbara everything; that Barbara had been right in telling her that some confusion was normal; that she hadn't, this time, heard an unspoken threat in the harshly spoken words.

Jake posed no threat. Not to her, anyway. As dark and as grim and as threatening as she had seen him in the brief time she'd known him, she'd sensed none of that directed at her. On the contrary, except for one brief flare of temper, which she supposed he was allowed, given the circumstances, he had been unfailingly kind to her. Was his just the kindness of one stranger to another?

She didn't think so. Interrupting the raid was probably an act of kindness to a stranger, but not the rest. He hadn't needed to take her home, or call Barbara, or feed her the next morning, or fix her door, or—or this.

Jake and Patrick had not returned to the house until quite a while after Barbara arrived. Obviously they had made a detour to Jake's place; he had showered and changed clothes and, she suspected, shaved. The two men had immediately started unloading things from the back of Jake's truck: a barbecue grill large enough for the four thick steaks she had already seen in her refrigerator; a box with sturdy plastic use-again picnic dishes; small metal pails, each containing a citronella candle to ward off stinging night insects; and various other things that appeared throughout the evening as necessary.

"Thought you might be needing this about now," Jake had told her when he handed her a thermal chest full of ice cubes.

"Yes," she'd admitted. And she had. Her old refrigerator couldn't begin to keep up with the demand for ice that more than one person put on it. "But wouldn't you and your friends be more comfortable at your house?"

He'd smiled then. "Humor me." And she wondered at that moment if she wouldn't have walked into town to get the steaks if he'd asked.

He'd filled and lighted the grill and tossed in foil-wrapped potatoes, and he and Patrick had finished installing the new door lock while the potatoes cooked and the coals burned themselves to what Jake finally declared the "perfect" stage for grilling.

While he took over that chore, she and Barbara had busied themselves in the kitchen, finishing the salad and pouring iced tea for the meal. Patrick had set up a card table on the porch, covered it with a red-and-white checked tablecloth Megan suspected must also have come from the back of Jake's truck, and carried an assortment of chairs from the house.

Dinner had been wonderful, full of laughter, and gentle teasing, and reminiscences that Megan did not feel excluded from even though she had not participated years ago when the memories were made. Not once was Roger mentioned. Or Helen. Or Megan's father. Or Sheriff Pierson.

Now that was over. Everything was neatly tucked away, either in Jake's truck or back in her house, except for the chair in which Patrick sat, making his beautiful, mournful, soul-aching music.

The music faded with a last trembling note that lingered on the air before finally dissolving into the night. Silence surrounded them until the crickets began their melodies again, a whippoorwill resumed its imperious summons, and a bird she didn't recognize began a call that sounded surprisingly like *jakekenyon, jakekenyon, jakekenyon.* Deacon whimpered and got up, scratching his claws against the wooden porch floor as he did so.

Barbara sighed and straightened reluctantly. Silently she patted her husband's knee and rose to her feet. Patrick nodded, tucked the harmonica in his shirt pocket, and stretched up out of the chair. He bent to lift it, but Megan stood and stopped him with a hand on his.

"Leave it," she said softly. "I think I like it better out here. And thank you. For everything."

Then they were gone, with hugs and promises to get together again soon, and Megan was alone with Jake on the candlelit porch.

"I'd better be going too," he said. "Unless you'd feel better if I hung around tonight. Or you could come up to my place."

For a moment she wondered if he were inviting her into the relationship she'd just denied them the right to start. But of course he wasn't. His next words confirmed that.

"I don't think you have anything more to worry about from the sheriff's crew or, with the gate in place, from any casual intruder."

She would be alone, wouldn't she? Funny, but she hadn't

thought of that before this moment. Should she impose on Jake one more night? He'd let her; he'd already volunteered. Would she be afraid?

No, she wouldn't. Not of burglars or police or military. Not of guns or violence or pain or dying. Of *whatevers*, perhaps. She took a step forward.

"Thank you," she said, stretching up. This much was allowable, for her and for him. But he turned and her fleeting kiss grazed his scarred cheek.

She felt a tremor work through him before he stepped back. "For what?"

"For sharing your friends and for giving my home back to me," she told him. "That's what this was all about, wasn't it? Replacing the bad memories with good ones? It worked. I'll be all right tonight, Jake."

"I can leave Deacon with you."

She shook her head. "No. I'll be fine. I promise."

"You'll call if you need anything."

You. In the middle of the night. Holding me.

Good God, where were these thoughts coming from? Had she spoken aloud? No. She couldn't have. Jake wouldn't be looking at her with mild questioning if she had. "I'll call. I promise."

Megan sat on the porch long after Jake left. The light from the candles flickered comfortingly in the gentle breeze. In the director's chair with her legs stretched out and her feet propped on the porch rail, she felt at one with the night, relaxed as she could never remember being relaxed, at peace as she could never remember being at peace.

Coming to Prescott had been the right thing to do.

Coming to this house had been the right thing to do. In spite of her father's objections. In spite of what had happened last night.

In spite of the strange things that had been happening to her.

She hadn't recorded any of them in Dr. Kent's magic book, and maybe it was time she did. All of them? She'd see. The bare-bones facts were so improbable she doubted anyone would believe them anymore than the chimerical *whatevers*.

And who was going to be reading them anyway? This was to be *her* book, her private place, her soul.

Although Dr. Kent hadn't put it quite that way.

She pulled her feet from the rail and stood abruptly, reluctant to leave the cricket symphony for even a moment but knowing, if she didn't do this now, she'd put it off forever.

The house was dark except for the light over the kitchen sink but Megan found her way through it unerringly, first to the utility room to release the kittens from the safe haven to which they had been banished when they insisted on crawling over everyone there, including Deacon, and then to the bedroom she had decided to use until she finished the green one.

She retrieved the notebook from the top drawer of the cherry chest-on-chest that had belonged to her grandmother and carried it back to the porch. There, she gathered three candles on the rail and pulled the director's chair closer, giving her just enough light to see the pages.

The kittens had followed her to the porch, and now one was doing its best to climb the leg of her jeans. She lifted it to her lap and let it curl beside her in the chair, while the other one settled contentedly on her feet.

June 4

I promised in the last entry not to avoid my thoughts or myself or my life when writing in this book. I'm not sure I can do that. I've spent so many years hiding from the truth that sometimes I don't know what it is.

From a move that promised to be quiet, idyllic, perhaps even boring, I seem to have stumbled into something I have no skills to understand.

Who is Jake Kenyon?

And who is the man I see when I look at him?

—no, please no. Oh, God, no, no, NO!

Terror, greater than anything she had experienced, tried to claw its way out of her chest. Megan dropped her pen and shoved the book from her lap.

"Again?" she whimpered. "What is this? Who is this?" Shuddering and suddenly chilled, she scooped the protesting cat from her lap and cuddled him close. "*Why* is this?"

Jake hadn't meant to sleep; he hadn't thought he'd be able to. But after unloading his truck he'd hesitated a little too long by the inviting, oversized couch in his unlighted living room. Giving in to the weakness he had refused to let Patrick see, he dropped onto the couch, intending only to rest awhile, and settled into the familiar hollows of the sofa. His left thigh spasmed once, and his shoulders tensed in their persistent complaint before sinking into the oversized down pillow Barbara's mother had made for him last Christmas. "If a man's going to sleep alone," she'd told him, "he ought to have something soft to hold on to during the night."

Megan would be soft.

He shouldn't be thinking of her this way. It was too soon. But it had been a long time since he'd had anyone, soft or not, to hold on to during the night.

Yes. Megan would be soft. She looked all bones and angles, but he'd discovered that was a lie the moment he'd lifted her to carry her away from Rolley P's intruders. He remembered how she'd grasped his hand last night and how she'd turned in his arms, not even knowing who held her.

Oh, yes, Megan would be soft. He sank deeper into the down pillow, feeling the tension and physical strain of the day ease from him: soft . . . and welcoming . . . at last. . . .

Megan!

He came awake instantly, listening, watching, feeling for the danger that had dragged him from a deep, insensate sleep. He heard nothing, saw nothing, felt nothing except an unremitting dread. Of what?

He twisted his head slightly to look at Deacon. His highly trained guard dog was stretched out on the cool stone hearth with his head between his front paws, snoring. Whatever threatened, it didn't threaten him or this place.

Megan!

He came off the couch in a lunge that had every abused muscle, joint, and scar in his body screaming.

Hell and damnation! And he'd left her there alone, after what had already happened in that house.

Keeping to the end of the room, away from the lighted kitchen and windows where shadows could give away his intention, he whistled softly for Deacon, slipped out the front door, eased open the door of his truck, and retrieved his pistol.

Deacon whined once and Jake stopped, listening.

"I hear it too, boy," he said softly. An engine in the distance. But where? With the way sound carried in these hills, it could be in the mountains behind him, on the abandoned road that bisected the Hudson place, or down on the county road. The only place he could be sure the sound wasn't coming from was Megan's house. No noise floated up from there.

Speed? Or stealth? Starting one of his vehicles would give whoever was lurking around ample warning to leave—or to finish whatever evil had prompted this middle-of-the-night foray.

Stealth, he decided. He wanted to get his hands on whoever was skulking around Megan. And if she had been harmed—

With a cold, clear certainty that betrayed all his years of training and shocked him with its intensity, Jake knew that if Megan had been harmed, Rolley P wouldn't have to go through the motions of pretending to find evidence for prosecution, he'd only have to identify the body of the man who had done it.

But stealth didn't mean slow. The narrow road wound around rocky outcroppings and the contours of the hillside for more than a quarter of a mile between the two houses, but Jake took an almost straight path through the woods, across one creek, and down one slight outcropping that cut the distance in half.

He came out of the woods at the hedgerow near the rear of Megan's house. He paused, listening, but still heard nothing. And even though Deacon appeared unconcerned, Jake's sense of dread hadn't lessened.

Why hadn't she called? She'd promised. Unless she hadn't been able to. Unless she didn't know she was in danger.

Keeping in the shadows, Jake eased from the hedgerow, through the overgrown yard, and around the side of the house.

The candles still flickered on the porch, and Megan—Jake felt an inordinate sense of relief when he saw her sitting, unharmed, in the canvas chair. And an inordinate sense of anger when he realized how exposed she had let herself be.

And then he saw the way she clasped the squirming kitten, the way she stared into the shadows of the night, not really seeing anything.

"Megan," he said softly, stepping from those shadows.

At first he thought she didn't hear him. He stepped closer to the porch, careful not to alarm her.

"Megan, what happened?"

She jerked to her feet and the cat struggled free, clawing its way over her shoulder and knocking over the chair.

Whatever he had expected, it was not that she would run from the porch and fling herself against him. Whatever he had expected, it was not that he would feel this wild rush of desire grip him and hold him, as tightly as he held this slender woman in his arms.

"You came!" she whispered.

What the hell was she talking about? Of course he came. He would always come to her.

And what the hell was he thinking about? He felt her shudder—a tremor caused by terror, not passion—and remembered that not quite three months ago she had seen her husband murdered, had seen Helen shot down, had seen atrocities she couldn't yet speak of and then spent weeks escaping through the jungle.

She had come to Oklahoma to recover, only to fall victim to Sheriff Pierson's incompetence, and tonight she had experienced still another—another what?

Whatever it had been, she'd had just about all the emotional trauma she could handle. She didn't need to confront his own physical and disturbingly emotional needs. Needs? For years he'd thought himself incapable of needing anyone. What was it about this woman that evoked this sense of belonging, of closeness, to someone he had known only by reputation—and had not liked what little he'd known—until twenty-four hours earlier?

Another tremor worked through her, calling him back to the night, to the unexplained sense of urgency that had brought him here, to her terror. Placing his hands on her shoulders, he stepped back from her, distancing himself in every way he could.

"What happened?"

She shook her head in a quick, jerky denial. "Nothing."

"Nothing?" he asked. "*Nothing* has you trembling so you

can barely stand? *Nothing* had you running off that porch as though the devil were after you and I was your only hope of heaven? What happened?"

"I don't know!" she cried. "All right?" She sighed and dropped her head, not looking at him. "I don't know."

I don't know was hardly better than *nothing*, but at least Jake felt some familiarity with it. And did he honestly know what had brought him down the mountain in the middle of the night?

He gentled his touch and his voice as he drew her to him for what he knew must appear to be no more than a quick, comforting hug, then turned her, draping an arm over her shoulder as he walked her back to the porch.

But once on the porch, she balked and refused to enter the house, even when he held the wooden screen door open for her.

"Not just yet," she said, as she slipped from under his arm. She walked back to the steps and stood looking out into the night, aware, or perhaps attuned, to the night sounds, but Jake saw that this awareness was appreciation, not fear, and he eased the screen closed and walked to join her.

"I once thought I would never again enjoy being out in the night," she told him. "But just listen to the music the creatures make, look at the canopy of the night sky, and breathe in that wonderful aroma of fresh breezes and new growth. There's nothing here but us and nature. It's the most freedom I've ever felt."

"You're not afraid to be so far from town?"

Megan made a sound that could have been laughter, could have been derision, and eased herself down to sit on the top step. "Prescott is close enough for groceries and fuel and mail. After what I've been through, though, it's a relief to be away from the crowds and the meanness of even a place as small as Fairview." She shook her head and gestured toward the hillside. "There's nothing out there that's deliberately going to hurt me."

Jake remembered the reason he had come to her, the sounds he had heard in the distance, and her fear. He eased himself down to sit between her and the porch railing. "Are you sure?"

She turned to look up at him in the flickering light and grinned ruefully.

"Of course not." Her smile faded as she drew in a deep breath. "Once I would have been. Once I would have been sure that this countryside is as idyllic as it looks. Once I would have trusted law enforcement to protect me, my country to defend me"—her voice caught—"my father to believe me. Once I would have been sure that I was safe in my own home."

And now she didn't. Whoever Megan Hudson had been when she went to Villa Castellano, either the woman Jake had thought or someone entirely different, she'd come back more changed than she herself even realized.

"I'm sorry," she said. "You don't need me unloading on you."

"No, but maybe you need to unload."

She gave him a whimsical smile. "Thanks. Maybe you do too."

His own loss of innocence had come years ago, and there had been no one to listen, to understand, to share the awful aloneness that had followed. There seemed little else to do. He lifted his arm to her shoulder and hugged her close to his side. "Maybe later," he told her.

She sighed and accepted his offer of comfort for what it was, for all it could be at this time, and they sat in companionable silence for several minutes before he made himself speak. "What upset you earlier?"

She drew another deep breath and straightened, moving slightly away from him and staring out into the night. "I really don't know," she said finally. "A flashback, maybe? A dream?" She shook her head, denying either her words or the memory. "I thought I was awake," she told him, "but it could have been a nightmare. Whatever it was, I'm glad you came back."

Sugarloaf County, Choctaw Nation Indian Territory, 1872

I awoke in a cabin with vague memories of having awakened there before. For the first time I was consciously aware of feeling protected and comforted and safe. Through the open door, I saw the bright light of late afternoon, but in the dimly lighted cave of the room, everything was cool and quiet. I lay in a wide bed with a dusty-smelling but infinitely comfortable feather mattress.

I was clean.

My ribs and ankle were securely wrapped. The damnable insect bites had, for the moment, ceased to torment me. And beneath the long, soft, intact shirt I wore, my body carried the scent of nothing more offensive than strong soap.

I heard noises from outside and fear crowded into the room, into the bed with me.

I turned slightly and felt a heavy, steady weight by my side.

Sam's big revolver, the one I had never seen him without, lay on top of the light cover within easy reach of my hand.

"I'll never hurt you. No one will ever hurt you again." I touched the revolver as the nebulous memory of his— Sam's?—words danced through my mind. *"You don't have to be afraid of anyone ever again. Not even me."*

But I *was* afraid.

Almost too afraid to move when I looked through the open door and saw Sam's bare shoulders and chest as he pulled his shirt over his head and began washing in a shallow basin he'd placed on a stump just off the narrow porch. Almost too afraid to move when I saw a face from all my nightmares step from the edge of the woods. Almost too afraid to move when I saw Sam spin around, reach for the gun that had hung from his hip since long before I met him, and realize that he no longer wore it—that I had it.

Puckett loved to talk. I had learned that about him—and more—in the three days he had held me prisoner. He loved to spew forth his bitterness and his hatred. He loved to tell someone how he was going to wreak his revenge.

This day he laughed the laugh I had grown to recognize as the harbinger of pain, pointed his rifle at Sam, and spat his ever-present tobacco before beginning to speak in a low voice. I could not hear his words, but I didn't need to. I knew first-hand of his hatred for Sam. I also realized, dimly, that if I could not hear his words, perhaps he could not hear me.

My fear almost kept me quiet, praying he would do what he had to do and then leave without finding me. But I couldn't let him. It has to be further evidence of my madness that I honestly don't know whether I went to the doorway to rescue Sam from Puckett's revenge or because, since becoming the creature Puckett made me, I had promised him and myself that I would kill him.

My bound ankle supported me, but with the weight of the gun dragging my arm down and the pain in my ankle hindering my steps, I made my way to the door in an odd, shuffling gait and found when I reached it that I was almost too weak to raise the pistol.

But I did. Oh, yes, I did. To warn him or not? That was my only decision as I looked at the fat, filthy outlaw who had somehow found us.

A glance around showed me Sam's rifle perched against the tree stump a long reach and a mere moment away from his hand.

I wanted Puckett to know—I *needed* Puckett to know that I was able to keep my promise.

I raised the pistol in both hands, fighting to keep it steady, and aimed at the biggest and best target he presented me, a target I had threatened when he thought my words only idle threats: his belly.

I didn't warn him, at least not intentionally. It must have been some movement, some sound I made. He turned toward where I stood in the shadows of the cabin doorway. I knew the moment he saw me. His mouth parted in a feral smile that showed his rotten teeth, and he began to laugh. He was still laughing when I pulled back on the trigger. He was still laughing when my bullet caught him in the belly.

I heard his laugh over the reverberations of the pistol firing. I hear it still, in my sleep, in my quiet moments, and in the times when the madness threatens to overtake me.

Sam reacted as Puckett collapsed, snatching up his own rife, rolling and tumbling out of the line of fire, behind the tree stump, and finally standing to go to Puckett and kick his weapon out of the way before running to my side.

He said nothing at first, simply took the pistol from my clenched hands.

"I killed a man," I said.

He took careful aim at the man on the ground and fired once. "No," he said, "I killed him. And he was vermin, not a man."

Vermin he might be, but I knew too well what could come

of this. "He's white," I reminded him. "You could hang if this becomes known."

"And you? What could happen to you?"

Nothing could happen to me, but Sam Hooker was not yet ready to see that. The worst had happened. And if I walked and talked and even looked as though I still lived, I knew the truth. Much more than my youth had been killed on that bright June day. I was dead, as dead as my dreams. As dead as the outlaw on the grass in front of that tiny little cabin. . . .

Sam sent Puckett's horse on its way with a slap and a yell. "In case someone's following him," he said, "this should attest that he left." Then he pulled aside briars without uprooting them and dug a grave on the outer edge of a small overgrown cemetery plot he found between the cabin and the bank of a slow-moving creek. I thought it a sin to put Puckett's body with those of the decent dead, but I saw the wisdom in Sam's choice—in a matter of days the briars would so completely mask the turned earth that no one would find a new grave—so I kept my silence.

Sam had wanted me to return to the safety of the cabin, in case any of Puckett's men had escaped the soldiers he now told me had gone into the camp after he had carried me away. But I knew there was no safety anywhere. I compromised, though. Holding his pistol in my hands, I sat on a fallen tree just inside the encroaching forest, out of sight of anyone who might stray into the homesite but able to watch Sam as he worked.

Along with the rusted shovel, Sam had found an abandoned tarpaulin in the one outbuilding—truly remarkable finds in this land where the inhabitants used and valued their every meager possession—and had rolled Puckett's body into the canvas and then into the grave. He had just started shoveling the rock-laden soil back into the shallow hole when his head jerked up. He dropped the shovel and grabbed his rifle.

"Stay out of sight," he said, in an urgent but quiet demand.

I needed no further warning; I had no desire to see again or be seen by any of the men who had made my life unbearable. I slid down from the tree and shrank farther back into the forest.

But the man who eventually rode to the edge of the clearing, hesitated, and then sheathed his rifle before dismounting and walking toward Sam was no one I'd ever seen before. He wore the blue wool uniform of the Union, the U.S. army, dusty now and travel stained. He was tall—as tall as Sam, which was rare—and thin, and he wore his years heavily, almost painfully.

Sam lowered his rifle fractionally. "Captain," he said, which I thought strange since I clearly saw lieutenant's bars on the man's uniform coat.

"Hooker." The officer spoke quietly, wearily, and did not correct Sam's mode of address. He nodded toward the grave. "I'll have to see that."

Sam nodded and knelt beside the grave, reached down, and pulled the canvas away from Puckett's face.

No! I wanted to scream. Don't let him see! He'll take you away! But of course I didn't. Coward that I had become, I huddled in the woods.

But when the lieutenant saw who lay in the grave, he surprised me. "Good," he said. "I was following him, not you, you know. He deserved to die. In fact I half expected to find him and the others dead when we staged our raid. I do thank you for the sentry, though. With him taken care of, it wasn't quite the rout it could have been. I take it the woman was still alive when you reached her?"

Sam didn't answer. Instead, he again covered Puckett's face and started to rise.

"Pull him out of there."

Sam swiveled to look at the officer.

"I need to make sure there's nothing under him."

Sam nodded and moved to the end of the hole. He grabbed the body's wrapped feet and tugged and pulled until Puckett lay like a fat cocoon on the briar side of the grave. The officer looked into the hole, then jumped down and stomped around in it for a while, kicking at whatever loose dirt had fallen in, before he climbed back out, nodded at Sam, and the two of them tugged the body back to the edge of the grave and rolled it in.

"Where's the woman?" the officer asked.

"If I told you she was dead?"

"I'd say you didn't get very far in almost three days. Not many things would explain that. An injured woman might; a dead one wouldn't."

"And if I told you there never was a woman?"

"Ah, that would mean you lied, something I've never known you to do. But it would also mean that what you carried out of that camp was the army payroll. Did you, Hooker? Is that what happened to it?".

For a moment Sam stood quietly, shoulders slumped, his weariness so tangible it pained me. "Oh, hell," he said quietly. "The others? What did they say?"

The officer shook his head. "One dead sentry and one dead—leader?"

With a nod, Sam acknowledged the accurate guess.

"And three others beyond questioning. It was quite a carnage," he said companionably. "One of his crew and three of the boys masquerading as men the army sent me to train hightailed it out of there at the first shots faster than any green colts you've ever seen. Who knows where they'll wind up, or when. The rest didn't stand much of a chance against seasoned fighters."

"So it all came down to you and him?" Sam said.

"And now you and me."

"We've never been enemies," Sam told him.

"And we don't have to be now. Just tell me where the payroll is."

Sam shook his head. "I didn't stop to look for it. And I saw no sign of their having done anything with it in the days I followed them. If it wasn't in the camp, I have no idea where it is."

"Maybe the woman does."

"No."

"Hooker, it's the only way."

Sam slammed his fist into his other hand. "Right now, no one knows she's gone. I'm going to get her back before anyone does. Do you have any idea what her life will become if anyone learns what she's been through? She'll be the one who is punished, even though she's clearly the victim. No. I won't let you do this to her. She's been through enough—too much—already."

"*Your* woman, you said."

"In that I did lie," Sam said quietly. "She's not my woman. She's never been mine, and now it's pretty obvious she never will be. But that makes no difference. I still can't let you talk to her."

"Then I suppose I'll have to take you in for killing this piece of trash. Too bad. If he'd had just a drop of your Choctaw blood, you'd be within your jurisdiction."

"His name's Puckett," Sam told him. "Tyndall Puckett. There's a reward for him in Texas, or used to be. Probably there's a price on everyone in his gang. You could claim the money. Get rid of that blue uniform. Get yourself a nice ranch somewhere out west where the war isn't still alive."

"Find myself a woman and settle down?" the lieutenant asked. "I don't think so. Because the only woman I'm interested in finding is the one who can tell me where the payroll is."

"I can't," I said, stepping closer but leaning weakly against a tree out of his sight.

"Stay back," Sam ordered.

"Oh, I will," I told him. "I surely will. But I still have your gun, and I won't let him take you. Puckett's been responsible for taking too much away from you already. I won't let him cost you your life."

"I don't want to cause you more pain," the officer said. "I only want to know what you heard."

I felt a wild laugh try to break through. "What I heard?" He made it sound as though that were something over and done with, as though I didn't still hear everything that had been said. "I heard about a wonderful little place in Mexico where I could continue to exist in the same kind of torture I knew for three days. I heard of other women they had taken and what they had done to them."

Sam didn't know the next part; I'd heard Granny wonder too many times to think he did. Now might not be the time for him to learn, but I couldn't stop myself.

"I heard of how Puckett hated Sam for only doing his job and how he had killed Sam's wife and child because of it. I heard in excruciating detail what they were going to do to him when he came for me, and what they were going to continue to do to me."

The gun was too heavy to hold. I let my hands drop, but I didn't release my grip on it. And now I was tired. Weak, exhausted, drained. And that man in the blue uniform, the uniform of someone who should be protecting me, not harassing me, wanted still more.

"I didn't hear a thing about the army or its payroll. And I have nothing else I can tell you about Puckett or the—or those who traveled with him."

Did he believe me? I thought at the time he did, because he left. Sam carried me back to the cabin; by that time I was too weak to walk, even with his help. And a day later, much too soon, Sam told me, but much too necessary to postpone the trip longer, we set out for home.

6

He was near. She always knew, *always felt this same sense of safety, relief, regret. He gave so much and she so little. How long could he continue to tolerate this hell their life had become?*

The breeze was the same: light and caressing, luring Megan from a sleep that had been deep but not particularly restful. With her eyes still closed, she stretched and felt the slide of her jeans against her leg. Curious, but not yet ready to leave the comfort of sleep, she stretched again and realized that beneath the light sheet that covered her she was fully dressed except for her shoes. The last thing she remembered was sitting snugged up to Jake's side on the porch, watching the night and listening to the music of the night creatures.

Reluctantly she opened her eyes. Her bed. Her house. Her yard beyond the open and uncurtained windows.

She heard a noise and turned her head.

"This is getting to be a habit," she said to the big black dog just rising to his feet.

Deacon whined, trotted to the side of the bed, and butted his head under her hand, just as he had the day before. This time, though, he didn't turn and leave the room. Instead, he stretched out on a small rug near the foot of the bed and looked up at her expectantly.

She took a strange sense of comfort from the dog's presence and from the knowledge that, for the second time, Jake Kenyon had carried her to bed. But it had to stop, before she once again became so dependent on someone else that she could not function on her own. Still, a few more minutes of feeling part of a protected and secure world couldn't hurt too much, could it?

She lifted herself up on her elbows, glancing about the room to make sure Jake wasn't there to hear her holding a one-sided conversation with his dog.

"Does this mean you haven't been told to fetch me?" she asked, stretching her hands up over her head to grip the decorative metal railing of the headboard and yawning hugely. "Or that your master doesn't quite have breakfast ready?"

A big man, his huge belly hanging over his belt. She gagged at the stench coming from his rancid clothes, his unwashed body, his rotten teeth.

Megan sucked in a startled breath and bolted upright in the bed. Good God! Where had that come from?

She glanced at the dog. He was now watchful, but she felt sure it was because of her abrupt actions, not because someone else was in the room.

Of course no one else was in the room. The man had been a memory, not an intruder.

She swung her legs over the side of the bed and sat slumped on the edge of the mattress, fighting the reaction of her nerves to something that had seemed as real as a physical attack. A memory, she told herself again. But a memory of what?

Jake wasn't in the house, but Megan found enough signs of him to know that he had been there until only a short while ago: a pillow and a neatly folded afghan on the sofa, a rinsed cup in the kitchen sink, a pot of still-fresh coffee.

Megan didn't know whether to be relieved or disappointed when she found his note tented beside the coffeemaker, but she poured herself a cup of coffee, checked the water level in the bowl Jake had set down for Deacon, and refilled the kittens' bowls with fresh kibble and water before unlocking the back door and carrying note and coffee out onto the narrow porch.

The back porch had once been screened, but by the time she'd arrived the screens were in such bad shape she'd had them ripped out and carted off, along with the years' accumulation of debris she'd found there. They were scheduled to be replaced, as soon as certain spongy portions of the floor were repaired, and in anticipation of that she had set a round metal table and two chairs on the porch so she could have her morning coffee while watching the sun rise over the mountains to the east.

The sun had long since risen by the time Megan sat in one chair and propped her feet on the other. She didn't have the sunrise to admire, and for a change the hills failed to work their gentling magic on her.

Reflectively she sipped her coffee and considered Jake's note. What it said was straightforward enough. He'd had to take care of some things at his place. He'd left Deacon with her until he returned. What it didn't say was why he'd felt it necessary to spend the night and why he'd felt it necessary to leave his dog.

She'd been a basket case lately. She thought she'd hidden it fairly well; maybe she hadn't. Of course she hadn't. In the short time since they'd met, she'd either been screaming her head off, quaking in terror, staring at something no one else could see, or listening to something no one else could hear.

Should she tell Dr. Kent?

Was it safe to tell Dr. Kent?

Megan's father had denied all she'd said about who was responsible for the carnage in Villa Castellano, but the fact that she had made the accusations had been politically embarrassing for him. Just how embarrassing she wasn't sure. Embarrassing enough so that putting a mentally unbalanced daughter away in some safe place might be expedient?

She hated herself for thinking that of her father. Once she wouldn't have doubted him. But now, as much as it hurt to admit it, she no longer trusted him not to put his political career before any concern for her—which pretty well ruled out telling Dr. Kent about anything as potentially dangerous to her continued freedom as hearing voices and seeing visions.

Barbara. Could she risk their fledgling friendship by confiding in Barbara? Or would remaining silent and refusing to share what was becoming a major factor in her life put an end to the intimacy that true friendship required before it really began?

The notebook. Oh, God, where was it?

She hadn't seen it since she had pushed it off her lap the night before.

She hadn't seen it since Jake had walked out of the night to share her loneliness.

Megan hurried through the house. She found the new front door locked but the screen unlatched and knew how Jake had left, locking her in securely with his guard dog, locking out the world. She was glad he had assumed the role of protector, but why had he? Two days ago they hadn't even known each other.

Jake had been busy on the porch. He'd straightened the

overturned chair, disposed of any lingering debris from their impromptu party, and apparently extinguished all the citronella candles before placing them safely on a small table near the living room windows. But the notebook?

He'd been careful with it before; it made sense to think he'd be careful with it again. Megan backed into the house, latching the screen but leaving the wooden door open to let the morning breezes enter, and looked around the room.

A double window fronted the room, overlooking the porch and shady yard. In front of that window, she had placed all she had been able to find of her mother's things: two comfortable reading chairs, a round table, and a lamp. Preferring to curl up on the couch and let the kittens snuggle next to her, she hadn't used the furniture since she'd been here, other than that first day when she'd noted with satisfaction that it had survived the years in her father's attic much better than she had feared.

Jake had placed the notebook and her pen on that table.

Had he read it? Was that why he had sat with her through the night?

Megan wiped her hand across her face, sighing as she looked at the innocent-looking black book. He hadn't needed any reason revealed in it to think she needed help. And even if he had read it, what would he have seen, a cry? A plea? What on earth was so strange about that?

Nothing—except that she wasn't sure she knew who was doing the crying.

And right now she wasn't sure she wanted to find out.

She carried the notebook into her bedroom and buried it in the drawer with her cotton nightgowns. Later, she promised herself. When she couldn't put it off any longer.

Today was not a day for introspection or housework or gardening, or even trying to coax this poor abused house back to life. Too much had happened for her to carry on as though nothing had.

Quickly she changed out of the shorts and sandals she had put on that morning after her shower, into jeans and a long-sleeved shirt. Sitting on the edge of the bed, she laced her feet into hiking boots. "We're going exploring," she told Deacon, who had dropped into an expectant sitting position by the bedroom door. "Unless, of course, you've been given different orders. Want to go?"

He cocked an ear at her and scrambled to all fours.

"I thought so," she said. "Me too. Let's get out of here."

Megan knew from looking at a map that the Hudson place and the one to the south of her—Jake's, as she had so recently discovered—fit together like chunks of a Tetris puzzle, forming a huge rectangle. Jake owned a lot of the mountains and a little of the valley; she now owned a lot of the valley and a little of the mountains.

She'd once mentioned going hiking in those mountains to Sarah North, the woman who ran the store in Prescott that served as gas station, grocery store, post office, and lunch counter. "Oh, be careful," Mrs. North had warned. "Those mountains go all the way to Texas without anything to mark your way but old logging trails that all look the same. You can get lost in there and never be found—and never find your way out except by accident."

Megan had never flown over that part of the state, but she had no reason to doubt Sarah North's warning. There were towns to the west, even towns farther south in the Ouachita National Forest, but they were widely scattered, and the section line roads, which she had thought divided the entire state of Oklahoma into one-mile squares like an enormous checkerboard, seemed not to exist in this part of Pitchlyn County.

Her house nestled up to the base of the first hill of the range, while Jake's was farther up the twisting road that climbed the hillside. She wouldn't go that far, she decided.

Hiking was like sitting on her porch enjoying the night;

she hadn't been sure she'd ever again feel free enough to do so. She grimaced. She might have recovered some of her bravery, but she wasn't foolish enough to risk cresting the hill and getting trapped in a labyrinth of trees and slopes and contour lines.

But if she stayed on the north slope, if she kept the distinctive peak of Sugarloaf Mountain which guarded the Arkansas border to the north and east in her sight, she couldn't get too lost.

"Besides," she said to her companion as she directed her steps toward the tree line that stretched at an angle in the overgrown field behind the house, "you know the way home, don't you, Deacon?"

He woofed once and wagged his tail, as though acknowledging that they were playing hooky, then took off at a determined pace that challenged her to keep up with him.

It was a beautiful morning, too beautiful to be stuck inside a house with nothing but hard work and disturbing memories.

The tree line bordered what appeared to be an old roadway, overgrown now and impassable to any but the hardiest of vehicles. It led in a meandering northeasterly angle toward the county road in the valley, or in a direction she thought must lead to Jake's house. The valley held little interest for her this morning, and while she had no intention of going as far as Jake's, she turned and began the uphill climb.

A narrow creek cut across the roadbed, complete with lush overhanging trees, water-smoothed stones, and a small, happy gurgle of water. Deacon plowed into the water and splashed upstream. Megan chuckled, and the music of her delight blended with that of the stream as she followed along the bank.

Laughter. Delight. Curiosity. Things she'd been afraid she'd lost forever. Thank God she was alive again!

She followed the creek around a bend and stopped, sure that this spot had been created just for her, for this time.

Sunlight filtered through the leaves of the oak, hackberry, wild cherry, and other trees to play over the surface of tumbled stones, some flat, some in surreal shapes, surrounding a small shallow pool fed by a splash of water from a ledge from which the rocks had fallen.

"Ohh," she whispered on a slow exhalation of pleasure.

Deacon had already scrambled over the naturally formed damn and was swimming slow figure-eights in the center of the pool. Megan could see it wasn't deep enough for her to swim, but the thought of wading in that clear water enticed her into reaching down and dipping her fingers to test the temperature, into casting a practiced eye over the bottom to judge the safety of the gravel in the streambed, into scrambling onto a flat rock and tugging off her boots and socks and rolling up her jeans.

She let out a small shriek when she stepped into the pool and found the water colder than she'd thought it would be, then laughed when Deacon's head shot up and he came paddling toward her. "It's okay," she assured him, laughing. "For the first time in a long time, it really is okay."

She ruffled the long, soft hair on his neck, found a stick near the bank to throw for him to fetch, splashed in the water, and played as she never had been allowed to do as a child until she realized later, reluctantly, that she was tired. It was a pleasant tiredness, one that tempted her to stretch out on one of the sun-dappled rocks and soak up the sunlight, the soft shaded breeze, the beauty of the location, the absence of pressure or doubts or questions, the memory of Jake holding her sheltered by his side the night before. . . .

She woke slowly, aware that the sun had moved across the morning sky by the patterns of light and shadow it now cast; aware that Deacon, his coat now dry, snored gently as he lay beside her on the rock; aware that the gentle breeze had died;

aware that the birds, once almost overwhelmingly noisy, were now silent. Aware of childish laughter coming from the pool.

Surprised, Megan recognized the young woman she had seen in Jake's living room. She—Liddy—wore the same long dress she had worn before, but now it was tucked up between bare legs to allow her to wade in the pool. A boy several years younger splashed farther out in the water, bare-chested, his straight black hair plastered by the water against the golden-brown skin of his forehead and his rounded cheeks. His black eyes danced with humor.

"What would that rich white aunt of yours think if she could see you now, Liddy?" the boy asked.

"Perhaps she would refuse to let me live with her."

"What good would that do? You know our father isn't going to let you stay here."

"Why not?" she asked, with a formality at odds with the picture she presented, wading barefoot in a mountain pool. "He needs someone to manage his house—I'm sorry, Peter. I didn't mean to remind you."

"Don't worry, Lydia. I love my mother, but she's dead and pretending she didn't exist or refusing to talk about her won't bring her back. And her being gone isn't going to get you out of doing what *your* mother wanted."

"I can go to school here."

He snorted his derision and, scooping up two handfuls of water, splashed it at her.

"Oh, Peter!" she shrieked. "Don't get me wet!"

"Don't get you wet? Liddy, you're standing in the pool in waterfall canyon. You don't make sense about anything these days."

As Lydia's eyes misted, Peter stood up in the pool and waded toward her. "I'm sorry, I would not hurt you for the world, but you know our father would never let you marry Sam Hooker, even if Sam felt that way about you. Which he doesn't. You must go to Fort Smith, to your aunt."

"Oh, Peter, I'm going to miss you so much!"

"And I will miss you. But when you are a woman grown, and have finished your schooling, you may come back. Who knows," he said, thrusting out his lower lip in a mock pout, "perhaps then you may teach others of us who do not have rich relatives to send us to the States for our education."

Lydia chuckled and sniffed. "Do you think the Council would let me?"

"Of course. You will have a brother who is a citizen. And a father."

"Will he be? Still, I mean?"

"I think he must marry again very soon," Peter said in an all-too-adult voice. "I think Daniel Tanner cannot risk having the law and therefore his status change. No, I think he will ensure his citizenship by taking another Choctaw wife."

"She will be good to you."

"Of course she will," he said, grinning widely. "I am very lovable."

Lydia laughed even as tears coursed down her cheeks, until a sound from the bank drew her attention. A tall travel-worn man stood there, holding the reins of an equally travel-worn sorrel horse. His dark hair showed strands of silver, and his hair, his clothes, and even the day's dark stubble on his jaw wore the dust from his ride.

"You're back!" Lydia cried, and then, as though realizing how she must look, gamboling in the water like a child with her skirts up almost to her knees, she stopped in her initial glad rush to his side of the pool. "I was so afraid I wouldn't see you before I left."

Megan stared transfixed. I know him, she thought. But who? And from where?

You're so young, child, and so innocent. I wonder: Could you survive me?

An image of a man asleep in a straight-back chair flashed through her memory. She blinked it away. A vision within a vision? Even with all the strange happenings, that was too much.

"I couldn't let that happen," the man said. He gave the girl a tired smile. "I knew you'd never forgive me."

"I'd forgive you anything, Sam Hooker," Lydia said softly.

Peter choked and splashed a handful of water toward his sister, and Lydia flushed. "I mean—"

The man she called Sam smiled again. "I know what you mean. I also know this need you have to say whatever comes to mind. You won't be able to do that where you're going, so I've brought you something to help, a way to share thoughts that no one around you wants to share."

Lydia waded from the pool and across the stone dam to stand in front of Sam before she dropped her skirts. "You brought something?" she whispered. "For me?"

With a brief nod the man turned, drew something from a saddlebag, and handed it to her.

Lydia turned the book over in her hands before opening it. "A diary," she said on a soft sigh. "And you inscribed it."

Too much! Megan swore silently. Too much!

For the first time, she remembered the dog at her side. Weren't animals supposed to be psychic or something? If she was seeing ghosts out there in the creek, shouldn't Deacon be upset? He was awake now but watching her, not anything in the pond. And it was too pat. A diary, for God's sake?

The trio in front of her were oblivious to her or to the dog, oblivious to anything except their own scenario. Seeking something substantial, Megan reached for the dog and grasped a handful of his fur. He woofed once, gently, raised his head, and then, with a surprising lunge, jumped up from the rock and plunged into the shallow water of the pond.

He sees them, Megan thought for just a moment before the dog skirted the edge of the water and clambered up the opposite bank, barely missing Lydia, Sam, and the horse as he disappeared into the woods.

Gradually Megan became aware that the birds were once again singing, small creatures were rustling through the fallen leaves in the woods surrounding her, and the breeze played across her face. Lydia, Sam, and Peter were gone, as surely as Deacon was gone, leaving her more alone than ever.

"Stop it!" she whispered, forcing her hands into fists. No one had been there. She had been dreaming. That's what it had to have been.

Dreaming while wide awake?

As she had been dreaming in Jake's living room?

Yep, it was lockup time, all right.

"Oh, God," she moaned. "What is it? What is going on?"

She heard Deacon's deep bark from somewhere in the woods and reached for her socks and boots. All she needed to make this day perfect would be to lose Jake Kenyon's highly trained dog.

She fought back a giggle when she realized how improbable that was.

But, hey! Wasn't this the day—the *second* day—for the improbable?

She dropped her sock when a tall man emerged from the woods on the opposite side of the small pool in almost the exact location where she had seen—where she had imagined seeing—Sam Hooker. Jake. Thank God, it was Jake. But maybe she shouldn't be too thankful, not with him staring at her as though he could read all the thoughts roiling around in her confused mind. Deacon joined him then, tail wagging, tongue lolling, very full of himself for having found his master and brought him back to join their holiday.

Jake studied her silently for several seconds before bending down to scratch Deacon behind the ear. "Are you spoiling my dog?"

It wasn't the question she had expected, but at least it was one she could live with. "Yes," she told him, dredging up a grin and retrieving her sock. "I thought that was why you left him with me."

Jake skirted the pond and crossed the dam to her side, still studying her but not with his earlier intensity. "I should have known he'd find some way to bring you here," he said. "This is one of his favorite places."

"Yes. Well," she said, finishing with her sock and tugging on her boot, "it might be one of mine too, if it wasn't so far back to the house."

He grinned at her. "Do you even know where the house is?"

"Sure," she told him, pointing. "Downstream about a half mile until the creek intersects the old road, down the old road another half mile or so to a curved pine tree a landscape architect I know in D.C. would give his right arm and half his family to be able to clone, then almost due west along the base of the hill and across an overgrown pasture until I stumble onto either the house or the road that runs in front of it."

"I'm impressed," he told her.

He should be, she thought. She'd come a long way from the woman who once couldn't find her way across town without the aid of an accomplished taxi driver. But that was another life and a long hard lesson ago. Now she had other things she had to find a way around. That knowledge made her defensive and gave a sharp edge to her attempt at humor. "That's nice. *I'm* hungry. But I'm also about a mile and a half of hard walking from lunch."

"Not necessarily."

Suddenly it dawned on her to be suspicious of his appearance. Again, she thought. Immediately following one of her *whatevers*. Ridiculous, she told herself. There could be no connection. But her suspicion thickened her words. "What are you doing all the way out here?"

He laughed and held his hand out to her. "Am I following you is what you mean, isn't it? Now that's an interesting idea. But no, I'm not. I had pretty well finished up what I had to do and was on my way back to your house when Deacon intercepted me."

She took his hand and let him help her up from the rock.

"So I'm farther up the hill toward your house than I thought I was?"

He released her hand the moment she was on firm footing. "Probably not," he said, giving her a maddening smile.

She missed the touch of his hand. Megan denied that thought almost as fast as she recognized it. This was, after all, a highly emotional time. It would be easy to confuse her need for some sort of stability in her life with the strength and security Jake Kenyon seemed to represent.

"Do you often speak in circles?" Megan asked.

Jake chuckled. "Probably about as often as you walk in them," he told her.

"Oh," she said, understanding at last. "Just where, precisely, am I?"

"Follow me," he said. "After one trip, you'll know all the landmarks, but the first time can be kind of tricky. You're about a city block from the road that connects our two houses, and much less than halfway up that road."

She grimaced. "So I was lost after all?"

"What are you talking about?" he asked, gesturing and waiting for her to cross the dam ahead of him. "You're not lost. You know the way home; you're just not exactly where you thought you were."

7

Jake ordered Deacon, wet from one last stolen splash through the pool, to ride in the bed of his truck, but even so—even with Megan sitting all the way across the bench seat, as close to the door as she could get without seeming rude—the cab of his truck seemed filled. But with what?

Who was this woman who had disrupted the order he had painstakingly restored to his life? She certainly wasn't the spoiled child-woman he had thought her to be when Roger Hudson married her. He could no more reconcile the Megan he had so recently met with that young society girl than he could with the woman who had found the strength to walk out of a South American jungle.

Or with the woman he had first seen cringing before an insensitive deputy.

Since he had carried her into his house two nights ago—God had it only been that long?—he had seen her vulnerable and angry, confused and contented, distant and much too welcoming.

And she was Roger Hudson's widow.

Roger Hudson's *recent* widow.

She had lived four years with a man he could barely tolerate. And then had watched him be murdered.

He forced himself to remember how fragile Megan truly was—had to be—emotionally as well as physically.

While he would not have wished that kind of death on anyone, while he could grieve for the loss of her life, his marriage and his love for Helen Hudson had been over long before he had returned to Oklahoma, long before she had left him wounded and alone in a hospital room while she returned to Washington, long before she had taken that fateful junket to Villa Castellano.

But unless Roger had shared that information with her, Megan didn't know it. And Jake was beginning to wonder if Roger Hudson had shared much of anything with his young wife. Certainly not an interest in her work.

Would she go back to Project Food? *Could* she go back after what had happened? Why should it matter to him?

It didn't. It wouldn't.

Just as it didn't matter that when he had walked out of the woods he had found Megan looking as though she had just taken another one of those damned vacations that were beginning to worry the hell out of him.

"That's it?" she asked in a small voice when they rounded the second turn and her house came into view. "I walked all morning and wound up no farther from my house than that?"

"Yep," he said as his truck rumbled over the last hundred potholed and eroded yards of road to the turnoff for her drive.

She glared at him, but he saw a reluctant grin trying to break through the confusion that had filled her eyes since Deacon had brought him to her.

"Yep?" she parroted. "I'll probably have terminal blisters because your dog led me on a merry chase, and all you can say is Yep?"

"Yep." He chuckled and watched a slow flush cover her delicate features when her stomach growled an unmistakable signal. "And buy you lunch, unless you've got something a lot more interesting and a heck of a lot quicker than anything I saw in your refrigerator last night."

"Oh, that's not—"

"Sure it is," he told her. There was no way he was going to go off and leave her alone, not right now anyway. Not until she had recovered, temporarily at least, from whatever haunted her. "I'm hungry, you're hungry, and I have to go into Prescott anyway." He braked to a stop in her turnaround. "Let's check out the house, grab your keys and whatever else you need, and head for the Prescott Palace."

Megan glanced down at her woods wear. "Like this?"

He shook his head in mock dismay. "Haven't you been to Prescott before?"

"Of course I have."

"And you still have to ask about dress code?"

Megan chuckled. "Sorry. Old habits. But where is the Prescott Palace?"

"At the Mall, where else?"

He watched her process that piece of information, knowing the exact moment when she identified the Prescott Mall.

"Where else?" she asked, letting her grin break free to animate her delicate features. "Come on in the house. I need about five minutes. Even the Palace requires that much grooming."

Jake parked in the vacant lot probably once intended for a town square across the road from the long tin-roofed building that housed Sarah North's emporium. Three gas pumps crowded up against the covered wooden porch with its long bench. That bench was now occupied by two septuagenarians in look-alike bib overalls and gimme caps. The men, strangers to Megan, nodded and smiled when Jake opened the screen door for her, and she could practically see the speculation dancing in their eyes.

Sarah North looked up from behind the counter in the alcove to the right of the front door and flashed a big smile. "Jake Kenyon! It's about time you got your body off that hill and down here. Your mail outgrew your box a week ago."

She turned to Megan and her smile softened but seemed no less genuine.

"Are you with this woods rat, or did you just happen to walk in at the same time?"

Megan grinned, succumbing to the gentle teasing which was so alien to the life she had led and yet, she knew instinctively, a necessary part of the new life she hoped to make here. "I confess. I came with him."

"Good. Thought you two would figure out who each other was a lot faster than you did."

Sarah North didn't fit Megan's idea of local gossip, wise woman, or crone; she was too young, at early fifty-something, and too wholesomely normal-looking with her gray-streaked short red curls for any of those roles, but she apparently filled at least one of them. "You knew?" Megan asked. "And you didn't say anything?"

"Why should she?" Jake asked easily as he guided Megan into the alcove that housed the lunchroom. "She had a lot more fun speculating on how we'd find out."

"Did you come in for your usual load of cholesterol and calories or just to give me a hard time?"

"Food, woman," Jake said, nodding at Megan to take a seat on one of the old-fashioned spinning stools.

Sarah produced a clean towel and wiped the already spotless counter. "He wants a double cheeseburger and fries." She looked at Megan appraisingly. "But you? How about some truly excellent chicken salad on homemade whole wheat bread?"

It *was* truly excellent, and Megan was still eating heartily when Sarah poured herself a cup of coffee, leaned a hip against the counter, and spoke companionably to Jake.

"So," she said. "Have you heard about Rolley P's latest foul-up?"

Jake only raised a brow before reaching for another French fry.

"Of course he has, Sarah," the woman said to herself. "Foolish question. What I should have asked is, How much more have you heard about Rolley P's latest foul-up than what Patrick put in the paper? Like, who was the poor victim his crew went in on?"

Megan had already placed her sandwich on her plate. Her stomach roiled; there was no way she could eat more. Instead, she ordered her hand not to shake as she lifted her glass of tea.

"You!" Sarah's voice sounded eminently confident in spite of the shock it carried. "Oh, you poor thing! They came in on you! You must have been terrified." She exhaled a rough sigh. "That idiot. That incompetent. Jake, if something isn't done about him soon, this county—"

"All right, Sarah," he said quietly. "I understand; you don't have to convince me. But please, the last thing Megan needs is sightseers out to look over the county's latest wonder."

"Jake, I'm not—" She turned and patted Megan's hand. "I won't say a word about this," she told her. "I promise you. But Jake has to know, and he has to have told you, that somehow someone *is* going to find out and *is* going to tell."

Megan dredged up a smile. "I know," she said. "Experience has already taught me that lesson. But I appreciate your concern, Mrs. North."

"Sarah."

"Sarah," Megan repeated, accepting what had to be an inevitable informality. She did appreciate the woman's concern. And she appreciated Jake's; she really did. Even if it was beginning to seem just a bit too much.

"Sarah," Jake said firmly, "can you make a couple of keys for me, or is your machine still broken?"

Sarah shot him a glare, but whether to signal to him that she knew better than to let the conversation get maudlin, or in protest against his maligning her store, Megan couldn't tell.

"Of course I can." She grinned at him. "The part came in yesterday."

Jake grinned back. "And speaking of parts," he said, taking a key from his ring and handing it to her, "can I have some delivered here for a while?"

"You know you can. What's the matter? Is that road of yours finally impassable?"

"Something like that. Are you sure it won't be an imposition?"

Sarah North shook her head. "Not as long as you have them bring anything really heavy into the storeroom and not just drop it on the loading dock like—which reminds me. While you're here . . .?"

Jake laughed. "The loading dock, right?"

Sarah nodded. "Right. Two cartons." She busied herself with their dishes until Jake was out of hearing range and then leaned across the counter. "He's a good man."

"I thought he must be," Megan told her. "He's certainly been good to me." And for her.

"No, I mean *really* a good man. The kind they don't make too many of these days."

Was that a warning in Sarah's normally friendly voice; the kind you'd better not take advantage of? How? Certainly not as a woman. Until barely three months ago, Jake had been married to Helen Hudson, a supremely beautiful, supremely confident, supremely talented woman. It seemed almost obscene that he would be interested in someone else so soon, but even if he were, surely it wouldn't be her. Not looking the way she did now. Not as confused as she was now.

"I try never to take advantage of my friends," she said evenly, answering the warning she had heard with one of her own.

"Well, of course not," Sarah stuttered. "I didn't mean, I— well, heck! That's what I get for sticking my nose in where it doesn't belong. Henry's always telling me I'm going to get myself in a mess with my meddling; I just never believed him until now."

What *did* you mean, Sarah North? Megan thought. But she wasn't confident enough to ask. Surely this woman hadn't been matchmaking. That seemed as improbable as thinking Megan could take advantage of Jake.

"All I meant was, you've got to be having nightmares about what happened, here and—before. Jake is a good man to call on if you need help getting through tough times. For that matter, you can call on me."

"Sarah?" Megan asked as she lifted her tea glass. She needed to change the subject, and she needed some answers. "Have you lived in this area very long?"

Apparently Sarah needed a change of subject too. "All my life, why?"

"Did you ever hear of—" Should she do this? Could she not do this? "Did you ever hear of someone named Sam Hooker?"

Surprising her, Sarah leaned against the counter and laughed. "Oh, honey, you've been hearing those old stories about buried treasure. There's no gold on your place or Jake's, trust me. Sam Hooker was a lawman. He wouldn't have robbed a train. And if he'd caught the robbers, he would have turned in the gold, not hidden it to come back to. Besides, even if he had hidden it, as much as those stories have circulated, someone would have dug it up by now."

Megan propped her elbows on the counter and stared at the woman. "Then he was a real person?"

"Maybe," Sarah told her. "And maybe the man we've heard

of is more myth than truth. It's sometimes hard to tell. And of course no one's still alive who would have known him."

"But there was—"

Megan heard Jake's footsteps on the old wood floor and clamped her mouth shut and her rioting thoughts firmly in place. He came into sight, dusting his hands. Without asking, Sarah handed him a towel, and he walked behind the counter to the small kitchen sink and began washing. "Have you had a chance to make those keys yet?" he asked.

"Not yet. We've been talking."

He turned off the water and twisted around to smile at the two women. "Good. That gives me time for another glass of tea."

One of the keys was for her. Jake handed it to her when they reached the massive pipe gate. Megan looked at the key and slid from the truck seat to follow Jake when he went to open it.

"It isn't really heavy," he assured her, "just a little awkward. See?" He opened the padlock and slid the short length of welded chain away, then lifted on a metal bar until the tail slid out of its opening and the gate swung freely on well-balanced hinges. Jake pushed the gate to the opposite side of the road and hooked it to a post.

"Wait here," he told her. "I need to drive the truck through."

Such a lot of trouble, Megan thought. And even though he had built the gate, this was trouble he hadn't thought necessary until she had arrived.

"Is the gate the reason you're having your deliveries made to the store?" she asked, after they had closed and locked the gate, climbed back in the truck, and braked to a stop in her turnaround.

He studied her as though he didn't want to answer. "In part," he admitted.

"Why didn't you put it up before?" she asked.

"When Renfro lived at your place?" Jake shook his head. "Megan, didn't you ever hear that it isn't smart to lock the fox in the henhouse?"

"But what if Patrick and Barbara decide to visit? What if I decide to have more work done on the house?"

"Anybody welcome out here will know to contact us first. As for the other—it might be a good idea if you waited before hiring any more work done."

Megan felt a chill shudder through her. That sounded suspiciously like one of Roger's orders, softly phrased, at least in the early days of their marriage, but an order just the same.

Jake must have seen her mutiny building. "Just for a few days," he added, "until we see how Rolley P is going to treat this: whether he's going to let it die down and hope we won't take him to a grand jury, or whether he's going to roll around in his own stink. Strangers talk. They spread gossip and bring other strangers around. Neither one of us needs that right now."

Didn't Jake really mean that *she* didn't need that right now? she wondered.

Whatever he meant, he was right.

She looked at her house, peaceful in the shade of the huge old trees surrounding it, and suppressed another shudder. It didn't bother her to lock out the world; she'd wanted to do that for a long time. What bothered her was the nagging suspicion that, much like the farmer with the fox, she had locked something in the henhouse with her.

She nodded her agreement, opened the door, and slid out of the truck. Jake got out too and walked to her side. He hesitated for a moment, then lifted his arm to her shoulder and began walking with her toward the house. At the porch he paused again and whistled for Deacon before mounting the steps.

He'd insisted that she lock the door when they left. Now he took her key from her, opened the door, and sent Deacon into the house ahead of them.

"I still have some things to do on my own place," he said, looking down at her. "And I need Deacon for a while. Will you be all right?"

"You don't have to baby-sit me, Jake," she said, but without heat. It had been a long time since anyone had cared enough even to ask about her needs.

"I know that. I also know you've been through some serious trauma and might feel a little better with someone else around to help keep the world at bay for a while."

Yes, he was a good man. And if he tended to hover a little closely, maybe that was all right too, for a while. She gave him a tired smile.

"What I've been through today is a lot of walking and an abundance of good food. I think I'll nap for a while."

"You're sure?"

Megan stifled a yawn and then a little laugh. "Do you think I really need Deacon to watch me sleep again?"

Jake chuckled too, ushered her into the house, and called for his dog. "Lock the door," he said. "And rest. I'll check on you later."

Rest. As welcome as it had sounded, Megan found that rest eluded her. Finally giving up on a nap, she unlocked the back door and carried a glass of tea out onto the porch. She heard the sound of sharp claws on the screen and opened the door to let the kittens out, but after a few minutes of her attention they wandered off in the direction of the side yard, leaving her alone.

Alone. Was that the problem? She hadn't been alone since the raid. Yes, Megan reminded herself. She had been. For brief periods of time. And each time, something strange had happened. She settled into one of the chairs at the wrought iron table, propped her feet on the other, and stared into the distance at the tree line of the abandoned roadway.

You've got to be having nightmares about what happened, here and—before.

Was that what was happening to her? Nightmares, while wide awake?

She'd been handling her recovery so well. Surely, if this kind of thing was going to happen, it would have happened before now. Or had the raid been the impetus her already fragile emotional state had needed to push her over the edge?

The alien sound of a ringing telephone jarred her from her musing. The telephone? No one had called her unlisted number in weeks, and she had grown comfortable with the quiet. For a moment she considered how nice it would be if she could put a gate on her phone line the way Jake had put one on the road, or at least a gadget to tell her who was on the other end of the line, friend or intruder, but that technology would be a long time coming to this small rural phone company.

For a moment she considered just ignoring the summons. But she'd been trained well; sighing, she went to answer it. It could be Jake, and he'd worry if she didn't. Megan shook her head. Worry? He'd probably come charging down the mountain.

"Please hold."

It wasn't Jake, Megan thought, as she heard the woman's impersonal voice and then canned music.

She knew only a couple of people who thought so much of themselves and their time that they didn't even realize how incredibly rude this type of summons was. One of them was her father. The other was Dr. Kent. She didn't want to talk to either of them right now. Could she just hang up?

And answer even more questions later? She held.

"Megan." She relaxed only marginally when she recognized her doctor's voice. "I've been trying to contact you all day. How are you, dear?"

Paranoid, Dr. Kent. Why are you really calling?

The thought came immediately and firmly lodged itself in her consciousness. He'd never initiated a call to her before. But he'd never been awakened in the middle of the night by another doctor about her before, either.

"I'm much better, thank you," she said pleasantly, unwilling to expose her suspicions yet. "I'm sorry you missed me earlier."

"Have you been out?"

Curious, was he? So was she.

"Oh, yes," she told him. "It's absolutely gorgeous here in the early summer. I had a nice hike in the woods today, and then I went to lunch with a neighbor and a woman I met in town." It was truth enough to salve her conscience until she explored her feelings about revealing more.

The brief silence spoke eloquently of his surprise. "You've recovered then from the—from the unpleasantness two nights ago?"

"Emotionally and physically, yes," she said, hoping that was true. "With the help of friends, I've repaired the damage to the house. As a matter of fact, I had those friends to dinner last night. I've talked through my anger, at least enough to realize that what remains is a healthy reaction to an unjust legal loophole that permits a raid of that nature."

She sighed. Showing a little angst wouldn't condemn her.

"And I realize that accidents do happen. I appreciate your talking to Dr. Phillips the other night, but I'm sorry she bothered you. After a good night's sleep, I was able to put the shock of the incident into perspective."

"I see," he said finally. "Have you spoken with your father yet?"

Was that the reason for his call? If so, he'd wasted his time and hers. From previous sessions, he already knew her answer. "And tell him what, Dr. Kent, something else for him to disbelieve? No, thank you."

"Megan. Someday you're going to have to talk with him."

"I know that. And I will. Someday when the memory of his denial, of his essentially calling me a liar, accusing me of trying to ruin his career, and then abandoning me to face alone the feeding frenzy the press made over my audacity in surviving and in daring to say what no one wanted to hear, doesn't hurt so much."

"He didn't, you know."

Didn't what? Megan wondered. "Is he still sponsoring the appropriations bill?"

At one time Dr. Kent's calm voice had seemed comforting; now, even though as soft, as quiet as always, he seemed to be screaming at her. "Are you journaling what's happening to you? Are you at least working in that way toward healing your anger and the trauma you've been through?"

The journal.

Oh, lord, the journal.

And those two condemning entries.

"Actually, no."

"Megan, it could help you immensely if you would at least try."

And no one would ever see it but her. Unless, of course, someone *wanted* to see it. Someone who knew without a doubt that it existed and suspected what it contained.

She knew what she had to tell him. "I tried, Dr. Kent. I made several entries, in fact. But even as a teenager, I never kept a diary. Everything I write seems stiff and forced. And to be honest, I find more healing in digging weeds or scraping paint. I'm sorry. I know you were counting on my input for your associate, but perhaps you can find someone more comfortable with the concept who can give you a more objective evaluation of its benefits."

She heard him sigh. It was the first sign he had ever given her of any emotion, and she had no way to interpret it. "Will you at least keep the notebook," he asked, "and consider the possibility of working in it? I'm not asking for a commitment, but if it's there, handy, you might find you do want to explore some things in it at some later date."

She thought quickly. Her early entries *were* stiff and forced and completely nonincriminating. "All right," she told him, "I'll keep it. But I'll probably never write another word in it."

As she thought it would, that promise seemed to satisfy him. After only a few more questions and comments, all inconsequential, he urged her to call him if she needed him and hung up. To call her father and report to him, Megan thought, and then released the thought as uncharitable. What Dr. Kent did or did not do was out of her control, as was any information she had already given him.

But he wanted her to keep the notebook. A doctor's concern or more? On the uncertain chance that it was more, she would keep the book. Keep it in an open and obvious place. Keep it without making any further entries. Keep it after making sure that the two incriminating cries for help were no longer contained in its pages. . . .

Ten minutes later, she sat on her bed, not sure she'd be able to stand if she tried. Beside her, the black notebook lay open but purged of the last two entries. Those, she held in her hand.

She'd been going to tear up the pages, but some grim fascination had made her read them again.

And answer one of her questions.

The *whatevers* had not started after the raid; they'd started just before it.

Two consecutive entries on two consecutive nights contained semicoherent, almost hysterical pleas. The words were written in the same flowing script, in a handwriting that would have been beautiful if not for the scrawl of panic that marred it. A handwriting that didn't match any of the other words on the pages. A handwriting that wasn't hers.

8

The tracks were faint and in a location almost inaccessible by vehicle. And they'd definitely been made after the late May rains by someone driving in from the south and east, being careful to keep below the first ridge and out of sight of curious or casual eyes.

Jake leaned against a tree and surveyed the ridges and valleys spreading out before him in the vast, undulating terrain. A little of it was primal forest, most of it old second growth, and some the overgrown remains of long-abandoned forty-acre allotments. All of it was wild and untamed.

He still shuddered when he topped the first ridge and started into the hills, still found himself looking back over his shoulder, and he supposed he always would. But daily now, except for the day before, he searched a part of his place or a part of Megan's. He didn't know what he sought, just that he must. He didn't know who was coming onto the property or why, just that someone was.

Travel at night would be more difficult for an intruder, he speculated, even someone familiar with the old logging trails and the locations of the worn-out fences with their rotting posts. Without lights, it would be easy to drop into a washout or over a ledge. With lights, in a location where there ought to be none, whoever it was ran the risk of being spotted. But it appeared that the time after dark was the time of choice. Unfortunately, the nights he had watched and waited, no one had come.

And when they did come, what in the hell were they doing back here?

Whoever it was had been at this particular location not too long after a rain and had stopped in a patch of mud that later dried, keeping the impressions of a wide deep-treaded tire and a large booted foot with a worn-down wide, flat heel.

Two people had gotten out of the vehicle—a four-wheel drive of some sort because nothing else could have gotten to this spot—one on each side of it, and had walked a short distance, each in a different direction, before returning to the vehicle, turning it around, and leaving in the same direction from which they had come.

The trail of the two men on foot was too cold for Deacon to follow. The good side of that bad news was that no one had left anything for Deacon to find, either.

These tracks weren't made last night by the vehicle Jake had heard then; he still hadn't found any sign of that one. But they couldn't have been here more than ten days or for that matter, because of how quickly the ground dried up here, less than eight or nine.

Jake knelt down and plucked a broken and brittle briar vine from the trail. If this were the first time he had found sign of trespassers, he would probably write it off—as hunters, someone out spotlighting a deer. He wouldn't like it, but he wouldn't be overly concerned. But he'd heard no unexplained rifle shots, and, in spite of all his contacts, no gossip.

No, whoever had been here was after something more than out-of-season game. He was pretty sure the search had begun about the time Max Renfro moved out, which he now knew was because Megan's attorney had evicted him so she could take possession.

And while he had seen evidence of trespass in several locations, this particular intrusion, as did most of them, just happened to be on Hudson property. "Now what does that mean?" Jake asked softly.

Deacon whined once, as though trying to answer, and came to Jake's side.

Still looking with narrowed eyes over the sprawling landscape, Jake ran his hand through the dog's ruff. "I know, boy," he said. "I don't believe in coincidences either."

He could try to follow the vehicle's trail, but that would be futile. If he were lucky to find enough signs to get any kind of decent fix on its direction, as soon as it met up with one of the old logging roads he'd lose it again.

And it was getting late. Not late as in dark, true dark wouldn't come for hours yet, but late enough on the southeastern side of the ridge for the shadows to be warning that night approached. Late enough that he figured it was time he made the mile or so hike back to where he had left his pickup. And late enough that his body had begun to complain of not enough sleep and too much physical effort the last two days.

Back at his place, he showered. He debated shaving but decided not to because Megan might think that smacked too much of a male ploy. For the same reason, he dressed in work clothes, clean but nothing that would feed any possible suspicions that this was more than a neighborly visit.

From his refrigerator he took two steaks and a loaf of Barbara's mother's French bread he had gotten from the freezer earlier, a bottle of wine, and the makings for a salad.

He needed feeding, but that wasn't the reason he was taking the food to Megan.

She needed caring for.

And maybe, if he ever again got rested, he'd understand why it was that he was the one who needed to do the caring.

He found her sitting in a canvas chair on her front porch, holding a tall glass of iced tea and with her slender, elegant, bare feet propped on the porch rail.

She looked freshly scrubbed and shampooed, and her light brown hair framed her delicate features like a halo, showing in them an ethereal beauty he'd never glimpsed beneath the stylish hair and careful makeup he remembered. She wore more of her shapeless clothes, but now, even though he didn't know why she wore it, he knew what was beneath that disguise: fragile bones, long slender legs, and a body that was too thin right now but had gentle feminine curves in all the right places.

She watched him from her vantage point on the porch, not moving, while he parked in her turnaround and off-loaded the bag of food. Only when he approached the porch did he see the confusion in her eyes and realize that she was studying him with an intensity that was frightening when he thought of what unknown doubts she was processing.

He propped a booted foot on the first step but did not move closer to her. Instead, he cocked his knee and rested the bag on his leg. "Peace offering," he said, nodding toward the bag.

She nodded her head once, a tiny little gesture that seemed to negate her dark thoughts, and formed her features into a smile—a smile that second by second became genuine, warm, and at last welcoming.

"Why do you need a peace offering?" she asked softly.

Deacon had no qualms about approaching her. He'd already climbed onto the porch, nosed at the two sleeping kittens near Megan's chair, and rested his head on her thigh. Lucky dog, Jake thought, surprising himself. It seemed that Megan wasn't the only one having intense thoughts.

And she wasn't the only one having trouble making her smile appear natural.

He nodded toward Deacon. "For taking your new best friend away from you this afternoon," he said. "Will steaks and homemade bread again make it up to you?"

"That depends," she said, seeming to shrug off some last indecision. She patted Deacon's head, swung her feet down from the railing, and placed her glass on the railing where her feet had been. She stood and walked toward him but stopped just short of touching him.

"On what?"

She grinned a four-alarm all-stops-out grin that melted him clear down to his boots before he had time to dodge, before he'd even realized he needed to, and filled him back up with a wild, angry longing he couldn't understand and a frustrated, futile heat he would have denied just minutes before, wanted to deny now.

He wanted this woman. Wanted her now, wanted her always, had wanted her since before time. And he was never going to have her.

Damn! He pushed away all the strange emotions, as he tried to push away the desire that had just ambushed him. This was the last thing he needed now; it was the last thing *she* needed. The need to care he'd been experiencing was a humane if not understood need, but this was something much more basic. Yeah, it was basic, all right, he acknowledged, as his body continued to make all too clear to his unwilling mind just how basic it was, and how little his rationalizations of the past two days and attempts to convince himself that this didn't, shouldn't, or couldn't exist had affected what could only be embarrassing to both of them and unwelcomed by her.

Damn!

"Depends on what?" she repeated after him. She reached out but hesitated again, looking at him strangely, intently, as though suddenly aware of where his uncontrolled thoughts had taken him. Her radiant smile faltered and then returned, tremulous and as false as those he had seen in her pictures. He watched as she straightened, tensed, and then deliberately relaxed, feature by feature. She lifted her hand and took the bag from him. "On who made the bread, of course," she said lightly, with only a hint that the lightness was as false as her smile.

Jake followed Megan through the quiet, shadowed house to the kitchen, which had been rearranged, scrubbed, and now appeared spotless. He glanced at the neatly displayed dishes behind sparkling glass and white-enameled cabinet doors, and at the clean white counter, bare of clutter, bare of anything except one pale blue antique canning jar holding a spray of wild flowers and pasture grasses. Color. Not much. But Megan had gone to a great deal of trouble to bring it into the house.

She'd gone to a great deal of trouble *in* the house.

Megan slid the bag onto the pine table and lifted the loaf of French bread from it.

"From the looks of the house, you didn't get much rest this afternoon."

Her hand clenched on the top of the paper bag. "Yes. Well, some days are like that," she said with a shaky laugh.

He remained silent, knowing that sometimes that was the best way, the only way, to question.

"I had a telephone call," she admitted finally. "From Dr. Kent."

He walked to the table and began helping her lift groceries from the bag, not drawing back when his hand brushed against hers, sensing, without knowing why, that she needed the contact. "Problems?" he asked.

"Nothing I can't handle," she said softly. "I hope."

"Megan—"

She lifted the loaf of bread. "This is the same kind of bread we had last night, isn't it?"

He nodded, not willing to change the subject but not

wanting to force her into talking about something unpleasant. And the mysterious telephone call had obviously been that.

"Have you realized," she asked, still softly, still obviously trying to find a safer topic, "that we've known each other for two days and this is the fifth time you've fed me?"

No, he hadn't realized. At least he hadn't found it necessary to keep track of the number of meals. Sharing a meal with her had seemed so natural, so necessary, he hadn't even questioned whether he should, except for last night when he had invited guests; he'd just accepted that he would.

He'd never been accused of being overly sensitive, but something in her voice caught at him. He lifted the steaks from the bottom of the bag and placed them on the table. "Am I imposing?"

He turned to look at her, and he could have sworn that for a fleeting moment he saw in her eyes her awareness of him as man that matched the awareness he had felt on the porch, still felt, of her as woman.

She sucked in a sharp breath and turned away from him. "Of course not," she said quickly. With jerky motions she crossed the room and knelt in front of a lower cabinet. "I don't have a charcoal grill," she said, rummaging through the cabinet, "but I have one of those electric-griller things. You know, the kind of thing you get as a gift and think it's going to be so wonderful and then never use—"

"Megan."

Her words quieted, her hands stilled. With what he could read only as reluctance, she swiveled to look up at him, her face pale, her eyes dark.

Embarrassing and unwelcomed. Well, hell. He'd sure called that one right. *She's not for you, old man. Not now. Not ever.* The words swirled through the silence surrounding them. From a book he'd read? A film he'd seen? Something he'd heard that had surfaced from his unconscious to taunt him with unwanted truth? It didn't matter. What mattered was what he could do now to salvage the situation.

"I need a friend," he said softly. "You need a friend. I need a meal; you need a meal." He rested one hip against the table and dragged up a smile. "Deacon needs a bone. That's all this has to be."

She gave one last tug at the box in the cabinet, pulling it out to the floor, then sank down to sit cross-legged beside it. "The problem is," she said, finally looking back at him with eyes that held more pain than any ten people should ever have had to bear, "is that sometimes I feel so *damned* needy. Don't let *me* impose on *you*. Please, Jake."

He crossed the room in three strides, reaching for her. Hesitating only slightly, she placed her hands in his, and he tugged gently, bringing her to her feet and into his arms. He felt what seemed to be an almost instinctive resistance in her, but he had only a moment to wonder about her reaction before she surrendered to the haven he offered her.

And it was a haven. He promised her that silently. He promised himself.

"Do you know," he asked gently, "how few people there are in my life who would worry about imposing on me?"

She shook her head against his chest and pulled away to look up at him questioningly. "About as many as there are in mine?" she asked.

He caught her back to him in a hug that he was careful to keep passionless. "We're quite a pair, Megan McIntyre." He refused to call her Hudson. The woman he held in his arms would never willingly have been the wife of someone like Roger Hudson—not if she'd known what he was.

With one last quick tightening of his arms, he released her. "A hungry pair," he said lightly. "Let's get that gadget unloaded and fired up so we can eat."

                    o   o   o

They sat on the front porch, side by side in the canvas chairs with their feet propped on the rail. The tiny old side table between them held a flickering citronella candle, their stemmed glasses, and the last of the wine.

Megan sighed, sank more deeply into her chair, and let the breeze and the music of the night creatures wash over her. She hadn't thought, when this evening began, that she could be comfortable with Jake ever again.

Her reaction to him tonight had stunned her with its intensity, but it hadn't surprised her. She'd had hints over the past two days that she was marching blithely along toward something much more involved than a familial relationship, much more involved than a neighborly friendship, much more involved, obviously, than Jake wanted to be. Much more involved than she had any right to be—at least until she straightened out the mess her life was in.

What surprised her was that she could feel anything at all after the desolation and disillusionment of her marriage, after the horrors she had survived, after the strange, frightening occurrences of the past two days.

The last thing she had expected was to look at Jake Kenyon stepping from his truck tonight and feel her body tightening and readying itself for his possession, to feel the caress of his eyes, intended or not, bringing her to tingling anticipation of a more physical caress, to know that she had waited all her life to know this man, only this man, in all the ways it was possible to know him. And he wasn't hers.

But he had eased them past that horribly embarrassing moment when she had all but thrown herself in his arms and begged him to carry her off to bed and this time not to leave her to sleep alone.

She heard a muted sound beneath the cricket symphony, a sound she had heard often during the nights she had lived here, that of a car's engine. She cocked her head, listening, wondering if this time she would be able to tell from which direction the sound really came.

She turned to say something to Jake and found him listening too.

"I think the hills must capture the sound," she said, "and throw it back without regard for direction or distance or us poor confused city folk who are used to seeing headlights when we hear cars in the night."

Jake's frown eased only slightly. "Possibly."

She grinned at him. "That sounds like a cop talking." During the evening she had passed from painful physical awareness to an easy companionship that allowed her to tease this man. It was amazing. *He* was amazing. Because he was the one who had made that passage possible.

He made a muffled nonverbal response but returned to his relaxed well-fed slouch in the chair.

"So," Megan said. "Tell me about the bread lady. Is she the same as the biscuit lady, or do you have a whole army of women baking for you?"

Jake took a sip of wine, replaced the glass on the table, and crossed his hands over his chest, sighing contentedly as Deacon had earlier when he'd finished off the steak bone. "Just one."

"Barbara's mother," Megan prompted, remembering their conversation the morning before.

"Mattie," Jake said. "Mattie Hinkle. The second love of my life, in chronological order, not in devotion."

"And the first?"

"Aunt Sally, of course." Jake half turned toward her. "You have no idea how many good memories just being here with you, like this, has given me back."

"I'm glad," she said, wondering at his choice of words. *Given me back*, he'd said, not *brought back*.

"I was so angry when I came to live with her. I'd known her forever—my parents had bought the place where I live now right after they got married—but that was when I had a home of my own to go to, and parents of my own to love."

"Barbara said you were only twelve."

He nodded. "A kid high on amphetamines driving his dad's hay truck. The poisons back then don't sound as disastrous as the stuff our kids are killing themselves with now, but it was just as deadly. He came across the center line right at the crest of Backbone Ridge. Dad tried to escape him, but he rammed my folks' pickup into the side of the mountain. They were dead before the medics got there. The boy came out of it without a scratch."

"Oh, Jake, I am so sorry."

"Yeah," he said. "Me too."

"Was that when your interest in law enforcement started?"

"Maybe. I don't know anymore. I don't guess it really matters."

He lifted the bottle of wine and divided the remainder between their two glasses. "Anyway, I think Aunt Sally and Mattie had their first argument over me. I was hiding in the barn, nursing my pain and my rage and my fear of what was going to happen to me when I heard them. They'd been friends forever, had even gone off to Teachers College together."

"Teachers College?" Megan sounded out the antiquated term.

Jake saluted her with his wineglass. "I told you, forever. And I had never heard either one of them raise her voice to the other. But there they were, out on the screened-in back porch, yelling loud enough to be heard halfway to Prescott about who was going to be the one to get to take me—*get to*, not *have to*—to raise and to love.

"I hadn't been able to cry; I thought I was too big for sissy stuff like that. Well, I wasn't. I bawled like a baby. And when I came out of the barn I learned Aunt Sally had won the argument for the simple reason that Mattie already had Barbara and she had no one.

"She gave me the room you're using now. It was still a sleeping porch then and my favorite in the house, but before winter she had it enclosed and insulated, and she had all those double-sash windows installed so I wouldn't feel so closed in. She helped me keep my folks' place at least minimally maintained. And she did love me. For six years. Until she died my freshman year at college.

"And then Mattie came to me. She told me she loved me like one of her own anyway, so I might as well start acting like I was."

Megan felt the pressure of tears behind her eyes. How could she possibly be envious of someone who had lost two families—now a third—to death? "For someone—" Her voice caught and she hesitated but knew she had to say it. "For someone who's had so much tragedy, you've been . . ."

"Blessed?" Jake asked.

"Yes," she said.

"Yes. I'm sorry I let myself forget that for such a long time."

They were silent for several minutes, just listening to the night noises, now augmented by the lonely singing of a distant pack of coyotes. Megan suspected they were both listening to memories from their childhood. She felt vaguely guilty for the bitterness that rose in her when she remembered growing up in a house that was too big, too well furnished, and too restrained for the solitary child she had been. She hadn't had the tragedy Jake had survived; she'd been too young when her mother died to remember anything about her. Well, except the emptiness and, strangely, the guilt of suddenly not having her. But she hadn't had the love either, and just for a moment she envied him that.

"You'd like Mattie," Jake said quietly, interrupting her thoughts. "And Mattie would like you."

Megan swallowed, trying to dislodge an unwanted lump in her throat. "Would she?"

She saw him send her a quick incredulous glance before he chuckled softly. "Yep," he said. "Problem is—or maybe isn't—she'd put you on the bread list. You'd have to get a freezer just to keep up with the food she'd send over. You'd get fat, maybe fall through that rotten back-porch floor. So I guess I've either got to keep you away from Mattie or Patrick and I have some work to do around here."

He did it so neatly, Megan was laughing before she realized that Jake had committed himself to another major job on her house and many more hours in her company.

"Jake, you don't—"

"Mattie's almost eighty now," he said. "Barbara wasn't born until quite late in her life. Her miracle child, she calls her. But when she was younger, she used to walk all over these hills. That waterfall where I found you this afternoon?"

Megan nodded, because he seemed to want some response but she had no idea what.

"That's not only one of Deacon's favorite places, it's one of Mattie's. But she can't get up there anymore.

"In fact, she can't get much of anyplace anymore since her arthritis has gotten so bad. She can't do the fine quilting or crochet she used to do. She can't do much of anything. Except bake. She swears that kneading dough keeps her hands from freezing up completely.

"And visit. She loves to visit. And she loves to meet new people."

Megan knew there was only one response possible. The number of people Jake had drawn into her life had just increased. "I'd love to meet her."

Jake dropped his feet to the wooden porch floor, stood, stretched, and yawned. "I think I'll go over to Patrick's tomorrow and bring my horses home. Do you want to go with me?"

"Horses?" Megan dropped her own feet to the porch, but the sound didn't cover up the small squeak in her voice.

"Two," Jake said. "Do you ride?"

She suppressed a shudder. "Not on a bet, cowboy. But I think I'd enjoy going with you. That is, you *are* going to bring them back in a trailer, aren't you?"

She heard a soft rumbling laugh from Jake as he lifted the table and carried it to its place against the wall. "Trailer," he confirmed. "Sometime after lunch, I think."

Deacon stretched to his feet and walked to Jake's side. Bending, Jake ruffled the dog's fur, then made some motion with his hands Megan didn't quite see.

"This old reprobate's pretty well ruined," Jake said. "I guess it won't hurt to leave him with you a little while longer. It's obvious whose company he prefers."

He was already one step down before Megan realized he was going. Just like that: walking off and leaving his dog there to guard her yet again.

"Jake?"

He stopped on the first step and turned at her soft question. Rising from her chair, she crossed to where he waited. Even a step below her, he was still taller than she, still an imposing figure, especially silhouetted against the dark night.

"I—" What had she meant to say? The soft flare of the candle cast odd shadows across his face, emphasizing the scar. But the scars were a lie, a disguise that hid Jake Kenyon from the world.

With something like horror, she realized she had lifted her hands to his face, that her fingertips now grazed his cheeks. She drew them slowly away, fighting the flush of embarrassment that heated her from her toes to the ends of her ill-cut hair. "I'm—I—Thank you for tonight. Again."

He caught her hands in his and squeezed them gently. For a moment she thought he bent closer to her. For a moment she thought she saw something flicker to life in the depths of his dark eyes. But he released her hands and stepped down one more stair.

"You're welcome," he said quietly. "Don't sit out here on the porch all night," he added, turning as he reached his truck. "And don't forget to lock up the house."

Shaking her head, Megan didn't know whether to laugh or to throw something at him. "And don't forget to brush my teeth and wash my face before I go to bed, right?"

He looked at her, illuminated by the light of his open truck door, and she saw embarrassment written clearly on his face before chagrin replaced it. "I deserved that, didn't I?" he asked.

"Apology accepted," she said lightly. "Now go home." Before she dragged him back up on the porch and embarrased both of them even more than she had already.

She stood on the porch, listening to the sounds of his truck engine until they mingled with the night sounds, and then sat down on the top step and draped her arm over the waiting dog.

"What am I going to do about Jake, Deacon?" she asked. "About everything? Why did he really leave you with me?"

But other than a companionable whine, Deacon didn't answer. Jake was gone. She was alone at last, with a job she didn't want to do but had put off much too long.

Sighing, she rose and blew out the candle. She picked up the wine bottle and glasses in one hand and opened the screen door.

"Come on, fellow," she said to Deacon. "I have a feeling I'm going to need a guard dog, or at least a friendly face, before this night is over."

Then, after locking the door as Jake had insisted, she hurried through her nighttime routine and went in search of something to use for a diary.

9

Megan sat cross-legged in the center of her bed with the ruffled hem of her long white cotton nightgown tucked securely beneath her.

She'd brought the kittens into the bedroom and placed one of them on each side of her and had dragged the braided rug Deacon liked close to the side of her bed.

"Your job," she told the assembled warm bodies surrounding her, "if you choose to accept it, is to drag me back to the here and now if I get really weirded out. All right, guys?"

She shivered once, despite the fact that the mild June night was far from chilly, and looked at the dark pressing in against the walls of open windows. She'd thought when she first moved in that she'd have to find some way to drape those windows but soon realized that was a city dweller's concern. There was nothing for miles that she needed to shield herself against. And because of the terrain on which it had been built, the height of the house at this corner was such that anyone standing outside, trying to look in, would have to use a ladder.

It wasn't what she needed to be concerned about right now, but worrying about a nonexistent prowler seemed, temporarily at least, safer than worrying about the prowling she was getting ready to do.

She'd found a soft old leather ring binder in a box of schooldays memorabilia she'd retrieved with the other things she'd brought from her father's attic. In it, she had placed the two troubling diary entries and a supply of notebook filler paper she had bought for the journal. It lay now on the bed in front of her, along with her pen and the small computer-generated guidebook to Dr. Kent's friend's journaling technique.

She picked up the instruction book and glanced at it, although she'd already read it several times.

Carefully, she replaced it on the bed and looked at Deacon. "It says I can use my journal to—to skip around; I can use it to explore conversations I've had with people or have completely new conversations with completely new people; I can explore my reactions to things I've done or go back and do those things in a completely different way." She chuckled reluctantly. "Sounds like a schizophrenic's dream to me."

But probably no more of a schizophrenic's dream than the life she had been living for the last two days.

She closed her eyes, considering all the strange events of those days. As many as there had been, they seemed to fall into only three groups: semicoherent pleas for help in a strange handwriting in her journal; visions of the young girl, at Jake's house and at the waterfall; and fragmented memories of words and actions that had never happened and of a man she had now seen identified as Sam Hooker.

Were those groups related?

Of course they were, at least two of them anyway. But the third, the diary entries, seemed far removed from Lydia's innocent love for Sam Hooker. Could they be coming from her own subconscious?

If not, this journaling technique would never work. If not, she'd really fallen through the looking glass, and she didn't remember how Alice had gotten home.

She clasped her hands tightly and looked at the notebook on the bed. Which would be the safest for her to explore?

Lydia. If any of them could be safe.

And when?

She'd had no trouble with her journal until June 3. If, as Dr. Kent insisted, she could go back and forth in this thing, why did she have to risk dating it?

She wouldn't, she decided. She'd just let whatever surfaced, surface.

Because there was no way she was writing June 3 or 4 on any of the pages. Not yet, anyway.

"Okay," Megan whispered shakily. She opened the book, settled it in her lap, and read the journal instructions for this exercise.

Picture the person you want to speak with. Remember everything you can about that person. Close your eyes, summoning all the details you can to the forefront of your mind. Now relax. Feel yourself sinking deeply into a place where you and that person are together, where that person's thoughts are open to you. Relax and go deeper. Let go of your disbelief. What do you wish to say? What do you wish to know? Nothing in this place can harm you. Relax. Breathe deeply and evenly. Relax. Pick up your pen. Now write.

Megan stared at the blank page for a long timeless moment, breathing deeply, searching within herself until she found a peace and calm she seldom felt. *Who are you?* she wrote across the undated page. *What do you want?*

The answer came almost instantly:

August 3, 1870
Lydia Tanner—her book

Megan gripped the pen. She wanted to throw it from her, the way she had thrown the notebook the night before. But she wanted answers, and this trip into her psyche was the only way she knew of even beginning to get them.

Who are you? she wrote again. *What do you want?*

And just as quickly as before, the words came.

I hate it here. Aunt Peg is the worst kind of snob. She finds nothing but fault with my clothes and my manners, even with my calling her Aunt Peg instead of Aunt Margaret. I believe she truly hates my father, but that is at least an honest and understandable emotion for someone who insists he was responsible for my mother's death. What I find completely reprehensible is her attitude toward my brother Peter. For her, he does not exist. How can I survive the next two years?

Thank God, I will soon leave here for normal school. Surely I will not find such bigotry among the good Sisters with whom I shall board.

Oh, Peter. I miss him, his laughter and his mischief, so much. He will be grown before I return. And I miss the freedom of wandering in the beautiful woods near our home. And Granny Rogers. And, of course, and without saying, I miss my beloved Sam.

How well he knew me to give me this book in which to confide my thoughts and my fears.

Can he know me so well, can he be so considerate of my feelings, and not love me, if only a little?

Could he have said what he said to me the week before I left and not love me, if only a little?

In two years when I return, I too will be grown, truly a

woman and not the child Sam thinks me to be now.
Perhaps then he will not fear letting me know the depth of
his feelings.

The flow of words stopped as abruptly as it had begun.
"Well," Megan said. She looked over at Deacon, who sat at
attention on his rug; at the kittens, who had migrated toward
each other and were now curled together in a ball; at the
pages in the notebook in front of her. "Well," she repeated.

Of all the strange experiences of the past two days, this
was perhaps the strangest.

She had been aware of holding the pen. She had been
aware of the words springing to life in her mind before being
transferred to the page by the actions of her hand.

But they were not her words.

They were the words of an innocent girl with her whole
life ahead of her.

She looked back at the pages. They were not in her handwriting.

The handwriting was familiar, all right. She had seen it
before, just that day, scrawled across the pages of another
diary, screaming for help.

On a hunch, Jake drove through the woods, as close to the
ridge as he could get without headlights, parked, and hiked
the remaining distance to the top. Where had that vehicle
been earlier? Nothing had come down the county road,
unless it also had been traveling without lights.

It made no sense, these strangers' incursions onto the
property, unless his DEA-mentality paranoia wasn't paranoia
and Renfro or some of his buddies had a non-taxpaid stash or
crop somewhere in the hills. But he'd found no sign of a crop,
no sign of any activity other than the proof of visits, more

than one, in what almost appeared to be an undirected search.

And what had Rolley P hoped to gain by sending his storm troopers in on Megan? Had it been no more than incompetence? Or was there more connection than coincidence?

He shifted his weight to his right leg as he leaned his back against the trunk of an ancient oak tree and looked out over the panorama spread before him. Dark-shadowed and moon-washed or illuminated by harsh summer sun, it never ceased to amaze him that man had once thought he could civilize these hills.

He still found evidence of their attempts in abandoned homesites marked by nothing but caved-in cellars or a foundation planting of jonquils to memorialize those efforts.

He'd flown over this area at night. The darkness was in its own way as awesome as the lights of a large city and as revealing and, except for small isolated pockets where someone had managed to blast out a road and maintain it, went unbroken by any artificial light for miles to the south, to the east, and even, once past a few small towns on the edge of the national forest, to the west.

So why now was he seeing a single, wavering dot of light high on the next ridge to the east?

He straightened away from the tree, concentrating on that light. A flashlight? Maybe. Maybe something stronger. But unless his perception was way off, it wasn't a spotlight being used to blind a deer. And unless his perception was way off, it wasn't too far from the skeletal ruins of an old cabin.

And once again on Megan's property.

He might be able to drive over there without headlights, without killing himself or losing his truck in a ravine, but he doubted it. And even without lights, the straining noise of his truck engine would announce him.

Attempting to walk it tonight was futile also. Whoever was

there would be long gone before Jake got halfway down this hillside, let alone up the next.

But tomorrow, he promised, with the horse and with Deacon, he would. And tomorrow, maybe, he'd finally figure out what in the hell was going on.

Here on the mountain. And with Megan McIntyre Hudson.

After he slept. After he rested. After he got his head on straight and could begin to think clearly about his reaction to her.

He was in his house, on his long comfortable couch, with his head sunk deep into Mattie's down pillow when he realized that he probably wasn't going to sleep. Not here anyway. And it wasn't because of the pain in his leg.

"Damn," he muttered, rising in a long, controlled stretch before bending to massage the damaged muscles in his left thigh.

He wouldn't sleep because he was here and Megan was alone except for a dog, in a house too close to the road in spite of overgrown roadbeds and locked gates.

He wouldn't sleep because Mattie's pillow was a poor excuse for someone soft, and for the first time in longer than he wanted to remember, he wanted someone soft beside him in the night. He wanted Megan beside him.

"Right, Kenyon," he said to the darkness surrounding him. "And what you need to do is run down the mountain, and then *you* can be the one who bursts in on her in the middle of the night."

But what if their friends on the mountain decided to come a little closer to civilization? What if Rolley P decided to send some of his boys back out on some other trumped-up charge? What if one of Renfro's buddies decided Max might have left something worth finding in the house?

Jake rubbed his hands over his face, sighed, and swung his feet to the floor.

No, he wouldn't sleep: not here, anyway. And since he didn't believe Megan would issue him an invitation to sleep with her, he supposed he wouldn't sleep anywhere.

He took the Jeep, because it was the most easily maneuverable and because it was parked pointed downhill, the way it had been two nights ago, and he could make the trip without alarming Megan or advertising it to any prowler. He turned the key without starting the engine, eased into neutral, released the emergency brake, and guided the silent car down the hill to a point just below the creek where he could watch Megan's house but not be observed by any middle-of-the-night caller.

Her bedroom lights were on.

For the first time in years of surveillance, he felt like a peeping tom.

He eased back against the door, trying to get comfortable and wishing he'd brought his truck so he could stretch out his legs. He'd watched her sleep the last two nights; it seemed as though he had always watched her sleep. Why shouldn't he watch over her tonight?

Why should he?

Megan McIntyre Hudson was a grown woman, one who had lived in and survived Washington, D.C., had worked through and survived a South American civil revolt, had walked out of a jungle and then faced down some real predators when the press took after her. She had done all that without his help; why was he so convinced she couldn't make it through the night alone in a locked house with a trained guard dog for company?

And why was her light still on after three in the morning?

Maybe because she was having trouble making it through the night alone?

"Get real, Kenyon," he hissed, as he felt overworked muscles protest throughout his body. "You're sitting here in the dark like some lovelorn testosterone-driven jock guarding his lady love. You've lost it, probably irrevocably."

Why now? At a time in his life when he had finally turned his back on all the turmoil of the last several years and was beginning to work his way back into the human race, how could someone from his past, someone he hadn't wanted to get to know then, have destroyed his hard-won calm?

And why Megan? Even in her full glory as the senator's daughter and Roger's wife, she'd never been a great beauty. Now, after all that had happened to her, she looked more like a waif someone needed to care for.

Maybe that was it. Helen had accused him of being bitter because he'd lost his white knight streak. Maybe the streak was working its way out of cold storage at long last. It was about time, he thought. If that was the case, he could live with this need that had somehow been created in him to care for her.

He yawned, tired beyond belief but knowing he wouldn't sleep. Yeah. He could live with knowing that at long last his humanity was returning. Strange how often he'd seen someone in law enforcement lose it. Strange how easily it slipped away, almost unnoticed. Strange how hard it was to get it back.

He yawned again, flexed his shoulders, and rubbed his face, pleased with his deductions. Pleased that at last he could understand why he was camped out in the front seat of his Jeep in the early morning hours, watching over a house that didn't need it and a woman who not only didn't need it but probably didn't want it.

Human compassion. He liked the sound of that. A good reason.

Yeah, and if that's true, he told himself, this front seat is a waterbed in an air-conditioned suite in the Manhattan Plaza Hotel. . . .

◦　　◦　　◦

He must have slept: he was too cramped in too many places not to have, and the sky was just beginning to show tinges of gray. Sometime since he'd closed his eyes, a light mist had fallen, clouding his windshield and bringing a welcome but mildly uncomfortable chill to the air. Jake twisted his head and his arms, trying to stretch in the confines of the car, and drew in a deep breath. The sounds of awakening birds and other creatures and the clean fresh early-morning scents were almost worth having spent the night in this torture chamber.

Megan's light was still on.

Damn.

He started the engine—maybe he was carrying this silent surveillance too far—and drove to her house. When she didn't meet him at the front door, he knocked lightly, and it eased open beneath his knuckles. Only Deacon, waiting patiently in the front hall with a complete lack of concern, kept him from going on full alert.

He saw a small glow coming from the kitchen—the fluorescent tube over the range, he knew—and a larger one spilling out into the hall from Megan's bedroom.

"Megan?" he said softly, angry with her, as he had been last night, for needlessly putting herself at risk but not wanting to wake her if she had fallen asleep.

When she didn't answer, he eased down the hallway and looked in on her. She lay stretched diagonally across the bed, hugging a pillow to her and with her bare feet peeping out from beneath a long white cotton nightgown that looked like an overlong Mexican peasant blouse, but with a wide ruffle at the hem and white embroidery on the top ruffle instead of varied bright colors.

She slept, but it was not an easy sleep. Deep shadows beneath her eyes and the tracks of tears, most dry now but still visible against too-pale cheeks, gave testimony to that. Before going to bed she'd folded the bedspread and put it aside, and at some point she had kicked off the sheet. And of course, she'd opened every window so the room was as chilly as the front seat of his Jeep had been.

He shook his head. He was still angry with her, but telling her about it could wait until she woke up. He was here now, so he didn't have to worry about her not locking doors or closing windows. Far from the sophisticated city woman he had spent years thinking she was, Megan McIntyre had a distressing vulnerability about her, a defenselessness all out of sync with what she had lived through. And a hell of a dainty little foot.

Which she would probably plant somewhere on his body if she caught him watching her.

Carefully he pulled the sheet up and spread it over her, the pillow, and the notebook and pen he saw peeping from the other corner of her pillow. Not the black one, he mused, but an old, soft, brown leather one.

She whimpered when the sheet settled over her, smiled in her sleep, and turned more fully toward the pillow.

And now Jake found himself in the surprising position of being as jealous of that pillow as he had been of his dog earlier.

"Bah, humbug," he muttered, then carefully, quietly, turned out the bedside light and left her room.

He was here. She knew the moment he entered the room, even though she supposed she was still asleep. If she were awake, she'd feel the tension that tainted all their waking hours. Sometimes she wanted to scream at him; sometimes she wanted him to scream at her, to accuse her of all those ways she knew she wronged him. But that would do no good, because there could be no resolution for those wrongs.

And sometimes, as now, she wanted to reach for him and draw him into the bed with her, to hold him as she now held her pillow. But that would do no good either, because most of their tension sprang from his wanting to do more than just hold her and from her knowing she could never, ever, give him more.

She had to be asleep. Awake, she would find herself cringing from him, no matter how hard she fought it. But asleep—oh, in the blessed peace of sleep she could take the kindness and care and comfort he gave her. Take them, treasure them, and, yes, fall more deeply into that wonderful peace.

Sugarloaf County, Choctaw Nation Indian Territory, 1872

My brother lived.

So sure that he had died when struck by Puckett's bullet, I had not been able to bring myself to ask about him. And Sam, I learned later, not knowing that I had seen Peter fall, had no reason to suspect I thought him dead.

The wound was minor—if having a chunk of flesh torn from one's shoulder by a deadly piece of lead can ever be called minor—and he was able to be up and about by the time Sam returned with me to Granny Rogers's cabin.

Granny's wonderful dark eyes clouded for a moment when Sam carried me into her cabin, but then she became all bustle and business, settling me in her best bed and shooing the men—for now I must count Peter as a man and no longer a child—from the room.

Her examination and her questions were strangely similar, both gentle and probing. She left me for a long while and returned carrying her best china teacup, full of a faintly tinged warm liquid.

"Drink it all," she said, as she sat beside me on the bed. I did, though it was a vile concoction, and handed back her precious cup. She set it on the table beside the bed and leaned forward, taking me in her arms and hugging me tightly. "You will heal," she told me. "You will have your womanly flow. And no one outside this house will ever know what you have endured."

On the day after my return, my brother Peter rode into the small community of Prescott on the Fort Towson road for supplies and mentioned in passing that Granny Rogers was ill with a fever and that I was caring for her because Sam was away on a Lighthorse mission. On his return, Peter stopped by our house, but he told me it looked as though no one had been there during our absence.

Granny prepared her teas and poultices for me several times a day, and I did begin to heal. And I did have my womanly flow. Only then did I break down and cry. I had not realized how much I feared that I carried the seed of one of those animals.

After Sam had carried me in and placed me in Granny's bed, he did not touch me again. And although I always knew he was nearby, I did not see him except when he came to the cabin for his evening meals.

By the time the good ladies from the Presbyterian church at Prescott decided it would be safe to visit fever-ridden Granny Rogers, I was able to be up from the bed to pass myself off as the nurse, while Granny put herself in her best bed, making sure her newest and best quilt was adequately displayed, and assumed the role of languishing patient.

No one ever knew I had been taken.

No one ever knew Peter had been shot.

No one ever knew I was dead inside.

Not then, anyway.

Our father finally returned to our house, not with a wife but with several workmen who immediately began construction of a rock outhouse behind the main house. "Jones has one," he muttered, so I immediately knew he had been down along the Red River visiting some of the wealthy plantation owners, but not for what reason.

And he was not disposed to tell me, for he was very angry with his children.

"What do you mean, spending all your time up here when we have a perfectly good house for you at the foot of this hill?" he said.

So he took us home, chastising us all the way, never looking to see that both his children bore visible wounds.

He also said, "I didn't raise you and educate you to have you acting like a servant for someone beneath your station."

And: "If you're hanging out in hopes of that halfbreed noticing you, stop it. I won't have you wasting yourself on him. I won't have you ruining your chances with a decent man."

I spoke then. "A decent *white* man, don't you mean? How do you think your son feels, hearing you say things like this?"

He looked as though I had struck him, not because of the truth of my words but because I had dared to speak at all.

And I almost told him then that no decent man of any blood would want me if he knew my secret.

"You are going back to your Aunt Margaret's just as soon as I can arrange it."

I wouldn't, but I didn't speak to him of that.

I didn't speak to him of much of anything.

I didn't *do* much of anything.

I stayed in my room, and on those rare nights when I fell into troubled sleep, I woke to find I was biting on my pillow to keep from screaming.

Peter did his best to cheer me, to try to tempt me from the house and the isolation of my room.

"Aw, come on, Liddy," he said one day in early July. "You know the creek is going to be just right for wading. If we wait much longer, it will have dried up to nothing, and the pool will be as hot as the rocks around it."

I could not return to the creek.

"Come on, Liddy. We haven't been to see Granny Rogers in weeks."

I could not travel that road.

"If you can't get out of the house now, how are you going to teach this coming year?"

I couldn't. I knew that. And knowing that, I also knew there was no reason for me to apply to the Nation for permission to teach or even for permission to remain in my father's house. I didn't need permission to remain a prisoner in the house, in my room. I knew that as the white child of an intermarried white citizen I had no standing with the Nation, but because of my brother's citizenship, and of course my father's, they probably would not consider me illegally present. In the eyes of the Choctaw government, I simply did not exist. How true that evaluation was.

In spite of all of Peter's coaxing and finally begging, I refused to apply for permission to teach, an act of stubbornness that held much more fear than strength. Even I knew that. But because I had not applied, I was surprised when Jeremy Hoskins, newly appointed to the Nation's school board, came riding up to my father's house late that summer. He carried with him a completed application, letters of reference from Sam Hooker and a half dozen other respected citizens, and an appointment for me to teach at the school at Prescott.

I thanked him, overwhelmed by the trust that had been placed in me and totally convinced I could not live up to it. I waited until he left to panic, to run from the house to that portion of the rear garden that had not been destroyed during the construction of the latest, still uncompleted, symbol of my father's status.

Peter did not come to coax me back into the house. He did not appear at all in the corner of the garden where I cowered. But after a while—long enough, I later realized, for Peter to have run to Granny Rogers's house and returned—Sam appeared.

He stood beside the rail fence on which climbed the remains of Peter's mother's wild roses, tall and silent and infinitely sad while he studied me. "You have not fared well since returning to your father's house," he said, as though my returning to that house were the cause of all my problems.

"I can't teach," I said. "I appreciate what you have done for me, but I can't go among people. I can't pretend that nothing has happened. I can't pretend that I am the same person who once lived in this body."

"You're a brave woman, Lydia Tanner. You proved that to me more than once. Nothing can hurt you in Prescott. No one will hurt you in the school, I promise you. You wanted this. You prepared yourself for it. Now you must do it."

10

Megan awoke to the now-familiar sight of Deacon waiting by her bedside and to the not-familiar aroma of frying bacon drifting through her house along with the scent of freshly brewed coffee.

Jake was here. When had he come in? But she knew—didn't she?

She looked at the sheet covering her. Jake had spread that sheet over her—hadn't he?

She gripped the edge of the sheet. "Oh, God," she whispered. Because suddenly her memories were all mixed up with her dreams, with snippets of things that had come through in Lydia's—*her*—journal, in those two moments that became more frightening in light of that diary—the ones where she had seen Lydia—and in those strange, vague reminiscences of words she knew she had never heard. "Oh, God."

She found Jake in the kitchen, leaning back against the sink, holding a cup of coffee in both hands, still wearing the clothes he had on the night before as well as several more hours' growth of beard.

He raked a glance over her, and Megan hesitated in the doorway. She hadn't taken time to dress, but merely covered her gown with its matching white cotton robe and run her fingers through her hair. Now she regretted that decision, but not enough to leave the room.

Strangely, she didn't question how Jake had gotten into the house or even his right to be there. What she did question was why he had come, again, almost as though he had known she needed him.

"You should have checked before you came running in here," he said. "I could have been a burglar."

Had it been Jake who came into her room? "I don't think so," she said softly, caught by the intensity in his eyes as he seemed to wrestle with some equally heavy questions of his own. "Deacon would have warned me."

He looked as though he wanted to argue with her about that but thought better of it. Instead, he turned and grabbed another cup from the cabinet, filled it, and held it out to her.

"Anyone could have gotten in this house last night. What good does a lock do when it isn't used?"

"I did lock it," she said. "Oh. I went out on the porch later. I guess I just thought I locked it again when I came in."

"Megan, this may not be D.C., but it isn't any smarter to sleep with all your doors and windows open here than it is in any large city."

She walked to him and took the coffee. "I know that, Jake," she said.

"Then why in God's name did you leave yourself vulnerable to anyone who wanted to walk into your house?"

This was a side of Jake Kenyon she hadn't seen before, and she wasn't sure she liked it. He was beginning to sound an awful lot like Roger Hudson. No, not Roger, she amended. Roger would have been more concerned about the things in the house than about her; Jake seemed truly concerned for her safety.

"I said I thought I'd locked the door. Why are you so angry, Jake? And why do you look like you've been up all night?"

He peered at her over his coffee, closed his eyes briefly, and stared at a spot somewhere over her left shoulder. "Three nights," he said.

"Three nights," she repeated, as a chill went through her. "Since the raid. Why?"

"Damned if I know," he said harshly. "Any more than why I really came down the hill that night and found you surrounded by Pitchlyn County's version of storm troopers, or the second night and had you launch yourself at me as though I was some sort of lifeline, or last night only to find your lights on, your front door open, and you crying in your sleep. And I don't like the not knowing one damned bit, so if you have any suggestions I'd sure like to hear them."

Megan groped for the table behind her. "Could we sit down? Please."

Jake reached the table first and pulled a chair out for her. "Are you all right?"

Megan shook her head as she sat in the chair, pulled her feet up to the rung, and carefully tucked her nightgown around them. "I don't know." She smiled shakily, wanting to reassure him, wanting to reassure herself but not knowing how.

"Three nights," she repeated. She took a deep breath, knowing she probably shouldn't say anything but knowing she had to. "Has anything else happened?"

"You mean strangers prowling around or word about Rolley P's activities?"

She shook her head. "That too," she said, "but I mean—I mean really strange. Things that have absolutely no logical explanation."

He looked puzzled, and well he should, Megan thought.

"You mean like—"

"Like memories that don't belong to you," she said in a small soft rush.

"Memories. . . ."

She knew he wanted to deny it, just as clearly as she saw the moment when he knew what she meant.

"Tell me," she prompted, "please."

"Is it really important?"

"I don't know. Maybe. Probably. Because three days ago my life changed too, and I'm not sure how much the raid really had to do with it."

He took a drink of his coffee, grimaced, and grasped the cup with both hands. "All right," he said finally. "Most of what's happened, I'm not even sure *has* happened. . . ."

"I know," she said, encouraging him when he hesitated.

He lifted one corner of his mouth in a combination smile, acknowledgment, and question. "I'm glad somebody does."

She felt a totally inappropriate laugh building but refused to fight it. Too many times in her life, humor had been her only solace.

"And I'm glad you think this is funny."

"Jake." She reached across the table and placed her hands over his where he grasped the mug.

"I understand, Megan," he told her, unknowingly echoing her own thoughts. "Sometimes black humor is better than no humor at all. Why were you crying last night?"

She shook her head. "You first."

"Okay. But first, do you know that someone is prowling around the place late at night?"

She drew her hands back and clasped them tightly in her lap. "Here, near the houses?"

"No. South of the first ridge. At least I think their exploration is limited to that side. This has been going on for several weeks now, since sometime after Renfro moved out, which was about the time you moved in.

"I was out trying to get a lead on who was prowling when I

heard the cars come in that first night. Now why I was on this side of the ridge, why I was anywhere near your place, is one of those things I can't explain. Why I took you home with me instead of sending you to the hospital is another. But those are fairly normal responses to an abnormal situation.

"What isn't normal is my reaction to you. It's almost as though we had really known each other all these years we've been related, instead of never meeting. It's almost as though there's a shared history between us, and everything I've done has somehow been as a result of that history."

He set his cup on the table and held out his hands, looking at them as though they might hold the answer. "Crazy, isn't it?"

"Not yet," she said quietly. "Is there more?"

"God, woman! What do you want me to tell you?"

"I want you to tell me what you remembered when I first asked you this question."

"And then you'll tell me why you were crying?"

"I think so."

"All right, damn it. Nothing has been specific, just nebulous thoughts, a dream or two; I think one woke me just as I was finally getting to sleep the second night. But tonight—last night, I guess it is now—when you were getting the grill out of the cabinet, I . . ."

"Yes?"

"You know how you have internal dialogues with yourself?"

"Oh, yes," she admitted. "I'm far too familiar with those."

"Well, I guess I was having one, because just as clearly as I hear my thoughts right now telling me to shut up before I get myself committed, I heard a voice in my mind tell me . . ."

"What, Jake? What did this voice say?"

He smiled at her and sighed. "It said, 'She's not for you, old man. Not now. Not ever.'"

Megan sank back in her chair. She closed her eyes and

hugged herself tightly against the chill Jake's words caused.
It wasn't quite as much as she'd hoped for but it was enough.

"Thank you," she said. "Now I know I'm not alone in this."

"In what?" he demanded.

"Ah, Jake," she said with a sad little smile, "if I knew *what*,
neither one of us would be having any trouble talking about
it, would we?"

"Megan—"

She held up a hand. "Bear with me just a little longer,
please. One or two more questions."

He didn't say yes, but he didn't say no either, so Megan
gathered up what little courage she had left. So far she
hadn't admitted nearly as much as he had, but she was getting ready to, and she wasn't sure how Jake would react.

"When you came in my room earlier—you did, didn't
you?"

He nodded.

"And covered me up?"

Again he nodded.

"Did you have some saddlebags with you?"

He didn't have to answer her verbally; she saw puzzled
denial in his expression.

"And did you sit and watch me sleep?"

"No, damn it. Megan, was someone else here tonight?"

"With Deacon in the house? You know that's not possible.
One more question," she said when she saw him searching
for words. "Have you ever sat and watched me sleep?"

"The first night. At my house."

"In a high-back wooden chair with your feet propped on a
crate?"

"Close enough. A kitchen chair, with my feet on the
nightstand drawer."

"And leaning back against the wall?"

Jake shook his head. "There's no way I could have done
that from where I was sitting."

Megan glanced down at the dog by her side. She had no doubt he could sniff out drugs, track down fleeing criminals, and fend off attackers, but he had been absolutely no protection from anything that had happened to her since Jake had charged into her life. She wondered if he would come to visit when Jake charged right back out again, which he might do when she finished her story.

"I didn't know I was crying in my sleep," she said. "I knew I was crying in my dream. In the dream, you were in my room. I was pretending to sleep when what I really wanted to do was ask you to come to bed with me. But I couldn't." For a moment, the pain of the dream overwhelmed her. For a moment, she thought she might give way to tears again, as she had in the dream. "And I knew I never would, and that you would never share any bed with me."

"Megan—"

"And in the dream, I wasn't me, and you weren't you, but we were who we are. Does that make any sense at all?"

"Megan, it was a dream."

"Was it, Jake?" She looked up at him. "Like it was a dream at Waterfall Canyon when you came walking out of the woods at the very place where the same man I saw in my dream had just been standing?"

"Your vacations."

"What?"

He reached for her hands, holding them together in both of his. "I knew something had happened when I saw you there on the rock. But you wouldn't talk about it."

"Well, I'm talking about it now, and I'm scared. Why is this happening?"

"You mean, after all that has happened to you, why are you taking refuge in your imagination?"

Megan jerked her hands away from his. She walked over to the sink and stood looking out the window at the tree line. For a moment she slumped in defeat. She had so hoped he would understand. She had needed one person—one person with whom she could share something.

She gripped the rim of the sink. "If I'm seeking refuge," she said evenly, "then I'm looking in the wrong place, because I'm certainly not finding it. And if it is my imagination, how did I just happen to people my cast of characters with at least one real person?" She straightened her shoulders, her spine, and her resolve and turned to face Jake. "Even though, according to Sarah North, he's been dead for a long, long time."

How had he moved? One moment he had been seated at the table; now he stood next to her.

She watched as he lifted his hand to her cheek and moved his thumb beneath her eye, damming the course of tears she hadn't even been aware of shedding.

"So," he asked, "the man you wanted to invite to your bed is a mysterious, handsome stranger."

She looked warily at him, to find that he watched her too.

"*I* didn't want to invite anyone, anywhere."

"Whatever."

She sniffed back the last of her tears and tried to glare at him, but she saw a glint of gentle teasing humor in his eyes. "Mysterious, maybe," she said. "But how did you arrive at handsome?"

"That's easy. You confused him with me."

"Jake—"

"Shh," he said, wrapping her in his arms. "It's all right, Megan."

It felt so good to be held, so good to be comforted. With a deep sigh, Megan surrendered to his embrace and took the solace Jake offered. For a moment she simply stood there, wrapped in his strength and protection. Until she felt the first faint stirrings of desire deep within herself; until a faint tremor in his arms told her he too was feeling more than protective and comforting. Until she felt his lips brush across her forehead. Until the memory of Helen and Roger drove all but the remnants of desire from her and filled her instead with shamed embarrassment.

Slowly but determinedly she began extricating herself from his embrace. "I'm sorry," she said. "Oh, lord, I'm so sorry."

She felt Jake's hands on her shoulders, but she couldn't face him.

"Sorry for what?" he asked.

"I told you I was needy. Last night. I warned you. And then I threw myself at you this morning. I can't—I just—I can't do this, Jake."

"Can't do what? Can't accept a little kindness when it's offered? Can't offer a little comfort of your own without having your motives mistrusted?" He tightened his hands on her shoulders and tugged, bringing her back against his chest. "Hush, now," he said when she murmured a protest. "I just want you to help hold me up. You've got to remember, you're locked in a hot embrace with a man who hasn't slept more than six hours in the last three nights. Believe me, if I get anywhere near a bed, sleep is all I'm going to be able to do."

"Ha!" she muttered, trying for humor to help ease them past this moment and knowing she almost made it. "It hasn't been that long since I was single. Isn't your next line supposed to be, 'So why don't you hold me while I sleep?'"

He laughed softly but did not release her. "Megan," he said, "look at me."

Reluctantly she tilted her head back and found him studying her with an intensity that seemed somehow familiar. "Whatever we have between us is worth more than just a physical release. I'd be lying if I said I didn't want you; I've been fighting wanting you almost since the moment we met. But I know the timing is bad for us; I know it's too soon. Trust me, Megan. Trust me not to take more than you're willing to give. Trust me to treasure what you do give. Is that asking too much?"

Asking too much? Megan felt her chest tighten, felt those damned tears lurking dangerously close. Jake had just offered her more than anyone else ever had, and he was concerned that he was asking too much?

"No," she told him. "No, it isn't."

Jake slept in her bed, guarded by Deacon, who had at last abandoned her for what must be his real duty. Megan checked on him later, after he had conceded his need for sleep, after she had promised to wake him in a ridiculously short time, and found him sprawled diagonally across the mattress with one of her feather pillows held securely in his scarred hand and tucked under his cheek. He'd tugged off his boots and loosened his belt, but other than that he remained fully dressed.

He was dark against her white sheets, the result of hours outside, and the two scars seemed even more like obscene desecrations as she watched him in the innocence of sleep.

Who was Jake Kenyon? In spite of knowing instinctively she could trust him, in spite of the shared history he claimed he felt with her, she didn't really know him.

He didn't seem the type to have been married to her sophisticated, worldly sister-in-law. And he didn't seem the type to have spent years submerged in the debased lives he would have found in pursuit of those who trafficked in drugs and human misery, although at rare moments she had glimpsed the fervor that would have sustained him as he dragged himself through the morass of suffering his work must have exposed him to.

She suppressed a shudder. He was out of that, thank God. Or was he? Helen had complained when he resigned from the DEA and accepted the temporary appointment as sheriff; if Megan hadn't tuned out Helen that time, as she so often did, she would have remembered Jake was back in

Pitchlyn County. She might know if his resignation was permanent; she might know if he planned to run for the position of sheriff at the next election; she might know how he meant to spend the rest of his life.

She looked enviously at her pillow. The need to slide into bed beside him, to wrap herself in all he had to offer, almost overwhelmed her. That, in itself, was pretty amazing. She wanted him, much more than she had wanted her handsome, charismatic young husband, even before her wedding night had taught her just how little she really meant to him.

Even more amazing, she trusted Jake to treasure what she was able to give.

Treasure. But not particularly want. Because he *had* been married to her sophisticated, worldly sister-in-law until death had separated them. Because even on her best days, Megan had been unfavorably compared to Helen too often to want to subject herself to that humiliation again. And because what she had to give demanded a lot more than just physical release, too.

So her pride conspired with her knowledge of his exhaustion to hold her poised in the doorway, watching him sleep, rather than crossing the few feet that separated them and joining him.

While Jake slept, Megan considered and discarded all the things she would have once convinced herself she had to do that morning. Too noisy, she told herself. They'd all disturb her sleeping warrior.

The notebook drew her. Its soft brown leather cover caressed her fingers like an old friend, and perhaps it was. She'd spent hours with it last night, after she had recovered from her initial shock. Now its pages tempted her to lose herself within them again, to revisit the life they had shown her, to explore more of that life.

That possibility was as frightening as it was tempting, because the neat copperplate script that now filled so many pages still was not her own.

Temptation won. Jake was here. For some reason she felt safer pursuing this other life just knowing he was in the house with her. After another trip to her room to make sure he still slept undisturbed, Megan took the notebook and a tall glass of iced tea out onto the front porch and settled herself in the blue canvas chair with her feet propped on the porch rail.

She ran her fingers idly over the cover, not opening it yet. Lydia Tanner, whose handwriting proclaimed her the owner of this book, led a life completely alien to Megan, yet almost parallel to her own.

The daughter of an influential man, Lydia had lost her mother at too young an age to remember her. As had Megan. Her father had married again, to a woman whose influence and connections could further his career. As had Megan's. Lydia had been moved to a completely different world as a result of her father's ambitions. As had Megan. She had been sent unwillingly away to school. As had Megan. And although this had not yet been fully revealed, she was being groomed to make an advantageous—for her father—marriage. As had Megan.

Coincidence? Or the vagaries of the human mind?

Megan leaned back in the chair and closed her eyes. Had she created Lydia out of her own needs? Had she peopled this story, this alternate life, with a more loving cast because of the absence of love in her own?

Because Lydia did have love. The gentle Choctaw woman Daniel Tanner married to gain citizenship in the rich and fertile Nation had loved Lydia, and Lydia had loved her. Peter, Lydia's young half-Choctaw brother, had teased her, exasperated her, antagonized her on occasion as he grew toward adolescence, but he had given her great joy.

Granny Rogers, who lived near them, had taken Lydia under her wing, teaching her quilting and preserving and physically doing the things that made a house a home, things

Daniel Tanner thought beneath his daughter and so refused his wife permission to teach.

And Sam. Sam who had been raised by his white father in Texas, who had been a Texas Ranger, who had come to the Nation in search of his mother and stayed to marry Granny Rogers's daughter. Sam, who had fought with his newly discovered Choctaw kinsmen in the Civil War in an effort to help preserve their Nation from the already greedy depredations of northern politicians. Sam, who had come home to find his wife and child murdered by outlaws, his Nation in shambles, his farm overgrown, with nothing remaining for him but an aged mother-in-law and the ruined remains of the sawmill with which he had once made his living. Sam, who could not return to being a ranger, because there were no more rangers, who could not return to being a soldier unless he fought on the side of his former enemy in the western Indian wars, who at last found his expertise needed by the Choctaw national police as a member of the Lighthorsemen.

Sam, who had lost everything, including his dreams, and whom Lydia loved with all her young and innocent heart.

Lydia had her warrior, too.

With a wordless moan, Megan slumped in her chair.

Had she really built this life? If so, when had she started? And was there any way, ever, to know the truth?

She sat there for a moment thinking. She had first seen Lydia at Jake's house, and again at Waterfall Canyon. She had felt Sam's presence here, in this house, as well as that of the unknown woman for whom she'd cried in her sleep. From the journal, she knew that Daniel Tanner lived so close to the Rogers's home place that Lydia frequently visited. Where? The present road ended at Jake's house, and she suspected that if she followed the old trail she'd find that it did, too.

Had Lydia lived here? Megan discarded that thought almost instantly. This house was old, but not over eighty years or so and therefore much too new to have been the

Tanner home. And she suspected from Lydia's words that it was not anywhere grand enough for Daniel Tanner.

That mess of bramble to the south of the house.

Megan sat up with a jerk and dropped her feet to the porch. Could it be? She'd been working at clearing out that mess only the day before yesterday and had found—what?

She left the notebook in the chair but carried her tea with her, down the steps, around the corner of the house, then south to the spot where she had been working. She dropped to one knee and ran a hand over the age-smoothed stone just barely showing above ground in the first row. She'd called them borders, had thought they must once have enclosed a formal garden of some sort; now that she looked more closely, she wasn't sure.

She stood and followed this one until it lost itself in still more bramble, then retraced her steps and followed it in the other direction. It cornered, and so did she, following it again in a straight line until it again cornered, encompassing an area the size of a large room, and then continued on until it, too, lost itself in undergrowth. Could it be the foundations of a house? A substantial house suitable for the prestige and position Daniel Tanner seemed to think he had earned?

How long had she known these stones were here? Long enough to have built them into a scenario?

Wake up, Jake. Oh, please wake up. I need you!

Her unvoiced plea stunned her with its intensity.

"No, I don't," she said shakily. "Not because of this. I need *me*. I need to find out what is happening to *me*."

When she returned to the porch, she picked up the notebook. How innocent it looked, she thought, to be so devastating. But no matter how much she needed to learn, she knew she couldn't go back into Lydia's life. Not now.

She looked in on Jake again and found him still sleeping, a little more restfully, she thought. Rather than risk disturbing him, she put the notebook away in a box filled with books and papers in another room, refilled her glass, and went back out onto the porch.

The house and yard seemed to close in on her. She considered going for a walk but for reasons she didn't explore she knew she couldn't go off and leave Jake defenseless in sleep, not even with Deacon here to guard him.

Instead, she settled back into the canvas chair, propped her feet on the rail, and waited as the late-morning air grew warmer, as the sunlight grew brighter, as the creatures in and about her yard forgot her presence and grew more active.

There was a sense of rightness to her waiting, as though guarding Jake in his sleep was something she was meant to do. Maybe it was. And maybe it was just her turn. He'd certainly guarded her enough in the last three days. Although what either of them was guarding against was a big mystery to her in this peaceful moment.

She heard Deacon's low whine at the screen door, and then he bumped it open and came out on the porch.

"Hi, boy," she said softly. "Did you come to keep me company?"

He came to her side, but instead of relaxing to her touch he stood stiffly at attention, watching the drive.

Megan saw two men on foot turn into her drive at about the same time they must have seen Jake's Jeep parked beside the house. They hesitated, but after a moment's conversation they continued toward her.

Megan tightened her hand on Deacon's ruff, but other than that she didn't move; she couldn't move.

A big man, his huge belly hanging over his belt . . .

She blinked and the image disappeared, leaving her watching one slightly overweight man in the uniform of the Pitchlyn County Sheriff's office and the other, a man she had seen in reality and too recently, the deputy who had led the raid on her house.

11

Slowly Megan lowered her feet to the porch floor and rose from the defenselessness of her no-longer-comfortable canvas chair. Instinct had to be moving her feet and legs, because she knew there was no way she could consciously do so.

With one hand on Deacon's head and the other wrapped securely around the porch post, Megan waited silently at the top of the steps for the two uniformed men to approach.

God, she'd grown to hate uniforms! To resent them. To fear them.

And what were these two doing here, a less than comfortable walk in the midday sun inside a locked gate?

The heavier one was sweating profusely. She saw the stains already spread across the tight khaki beneath his arms, and even though his eyes were shaded by the cream-colored western hat he wore, she'd bet the ranch that his face was dripping too.

Good!

The other one was not happy. He watched her as carefully

as she watched the two of them. At first glance he seemed to be all swagger and good-old-boy determination, but when he reached the bottom of the steps and looked up at her, his eyes told a different story. Back down, they seemed to say. You're supposed to be afraid of us, and by God, you'd better act like you are.

For some reason, seeing that expression in the deputy's eyes stiffened Megan's spine as none of her own prompting could have.

She was safe; she had to believe that. This was, after all, still the United States; the raid had been a mistake, a horrible mistake that wouldn't be repeated. And Jake was asleep just inside the house. One yell from her and he'd be on these men like ducks on a June bug, like flies on a cow patty, like—

Megan clamped down on her wildly spiraling imagination. Jake would defend her if necessary, but was it necessary to wake him from the first rest he'd had since these men, or at least one of them, had stormed into her life?

Pressed tightly against her leg, Deacon growled softly. Megan traced her fingers across the smooth cap of his head but didn't say anything, not to the dog, not to the men. They had gone through a great deal of inconvenience to see her; obviously they had something to say. And just as obviously they didn't know how to go about saying it if she didn't cooperate by speaking first.

"Miz Hudson," the heavy one said, sweeping his hat from his head and wiping his forearm across his face.

Megan looked at him. She had been right. His sweat-stained hair lay plastered against his head, and moisture gleamed and dripped across his reddened but too-pale features.

"Miz Hudson," he said again, and waited.

Waited for what? she wondered. For her to speak? For her to acknowledge him? Well, she supposed she could give him that much. She nodded.

He returned the nod, shifted his hat to his other hand, and glanced warily at the dog by her side.

"Your daddy," he said. "Your daddy the senator seems right upset by that unfortunate episode of three nights ago."

So her father knew. How? Dr. Kent? Probably. Unless he was keeping closer tabs on her than she had thought.

"Your daddy seems to think we have overstepped our authority by exercising our legal responsibilities to the best of our ability."

Her father wasn't the only one who thought that, Megan reflected. Marvelous. At last they agreed on something.

"Miz Hudson you have not yet filed a formal complaint. Not having done so, it appears to me you have acted in a highly improper manner by taking your story to the press and to your father without giving our office a chance to refute your accusations or explain our position.

"Miz Hudson," he said, his voice taking on a decided note of exasperation as she remained silent, "do you understand what I'm saying?"

"Not really, sheriff," she said quietly. "Because it appears to me that you have been talking to a lot more people than I have."

"Mrs. Hudson." The other one—what *was* his name? She ought to know it. She had been watching him with her peripheral vision, the way she suspected someone would watch a threat not yet close enough to be a real danger. Now she turned her head, to acknowledge him and to look more closely at him.

He glanced over at Jake's Jeep and back to her, and his eyes were so cold she had to suppress a shudder. "Is Kenyon around?"

"Is your business with him or with me?"

Apparently deciding that meant Jake wasn't there, the deputy glared first at Deacon and then at her. "We don't need you to pretend innocence or ignorance," he snapped, gathering confidence and courage from the thought that she was

alone. "What the sheriff is saying is that we have a dozen people who can swear to your hysterical overreaction to an honest
mistake on the part of people sworn to protect the law in this
county. A dozen people who have lived here most of their
lives. A dozen people who do not have a history of falsely
accusing those in authority of mistreating that authority.

"Now if you will just call your father, have him halt his
inquiries, and explain to him that you are all right—that
seemed to be his major concern—and if you will see to it
that Phillips at the *Banner* gets an accurate rendition of what
happened, we won't find it necessary to rake up old mud
about your previous unfounded accusations."

Megan clutched convulsively at the fur at Deacon's neck
but spoke with studied calm. "Why, deputy," she said, "that
sounds amazingly like a threat."

"No, ma'am." He smiled and turned those cold eyes of his
on her again. Back down! Back down! they warned her. "It
doesn't sound like a threat; it is one. But since there's no one
but us to hear it, I reckon you won't be able to prove it. Now
are you—"

Reacting to the tension of her hand on his neck or to the
threat in the deputy's voice, Megan didn't know which,
Deacon snarled a warning of his own and bared long teeth
that so far she had seen exposed only in an endearing, lop-
sided grin.

"Call him off," the deputy said quickly.

"Why, deputy," she said, knowing she probably shouldn't
but knowing this was something she had to do, "I reckon
that poor little innocent, ignorant me just doesn't know how
to do that. But I'm pretty sure, if you two leave now, I'll be
able to hold him long enough for you to get on down the
road and climb back over that locked gate."

With horror, Megan watched as the deputy's hand inched
toward the gun at his belt.

"I wouldn't do that if I were you," she advised with a calm

she didn't feel. "If you think you have awkward explanations to make now, they're nothing compared to what they will be if you come onto my locked property a second time without provocation and shoot either me or Jake Kenyon's dog for protecting me."

"Damn it, Mark, let's just get out of here for now," Sheriff Pierson protested.

"Yeah, Mark."

Megan jerked around to face the Jeep. Jake stood partially behind it, at attention. His voice carried every bit as much threat as Deacon's, and with his face shadowed by the dark of his overnight beard, he looked every bit as dangerous. "I think it would be a real good idea for you to leave. And I think it would be a real good idea for you to remember what locked gates mean in this country."

"Kenyon, this is between us and Mrs. Hudson."

"Oh, no," Jake said pleasantly. "That's my dog you're getting ready to draw down on, and it was my gate you climbed. I guess that makes it as much my business as anyone's. Now I think I heard Mrs. Hudson ask you nicely to leave."

"Damn, Kenyon. One of these days you're going to stick your nose in just a little too close."

"Oh, I have already, Mark. And it seems your office hasn't been able to do anything about that either.

"Rolley P," Jake said abruptly, nodding toward the road, "leave my dog alone. Take yours and get out of here."

Sheriff Pierson held his hands up, as if acknowledging defeat, settled his hat on his head, and turned toward the road. After one last defiant glare, the deputy turned and fell into step beside him.

Cautiously, Jake eased something through the open window into the interior of the Jeep and walked to the porch. "Good boy," he said, ruffling Deacon's fur. "You did fine. I'll take over now."

Deacon whined a soft welcome and butted his head

under Jake's hand before moving away from Megan's side. Jake stepped up beside her and slid his arm around her, but the two of them stood facing the drive and watching the direction the two men went until long after they had disappeared onto the lane.

Then Jake turned toward her and hauled her into his arms. Megan went willingly, feeling all the strength leave her legs. She clung to him as reaction set in, as slow tremors racked her. "What horrible, horrible, horrible people," she whispered.

"Yes."

"I'm so glad you were here."

"You did fine," he told her, and his voice was as warm and as convincing as when he had said those same words to Deacon, who she knew had really performed well. "You did just fine. But I'm glad I was here too."

"How did you—"

"Deacon woke me. I wasn't sure what was coming, so I sent him out to you while I did a little reconnaissance."

She exhaled a shaky breath, remembering his furtive movements at the Jeep. "And armed yourself?"

"That too."

"Jake, what could they hope to accomplish by coming out here like this?"

She felt his hand in her hair, felt the other on her back as he pressed her closer to him. She didn't resist. She needed his closeness. "They could scare you into not filing a formal complaint about what happened."

"But I don't intend to do that anyway."

"Megan." His hands tightened on her, then shifted to her shoulders as he stepped back. "You have to. Especially now. You can't let them get away with what they did three nights ago. Or with what they tried today."

"Can't I?" she asked. "Didn't you hear what he said? The national press has already tried and convicted me of being a hysterical or maybe even a vindictive liar about what happened at the clinic. I'm not going through that again. I'm not sure—God, Jake, after what I told you this morning, I'm not sure I could stand up to any real investigation into my mental stability."

He shook her, not gently and yet with a compassion mirrored by his words.

"You're as sane as I am," he said. "Probably more so. And if you're having reactions to the horror you've been through, that only proves your sanity. For God's sake, Megan, you can't let these petty little tyrants dictate to you, or you'll never be able to reclaim your life."

"Do you think that's what I'm trying to do?" she asked. "Reclaim my life?"

"Isn't it?"

Was it? Suddenly his touch was as unbearable as the questions she knew she had to answer, at least for herself. She jerked away from him, walked to the edge of the porch and leaned against the rail, holding on tightly, needing something real and substantial to grasp, even if it was only wood.

"I'm not sure," she said, taking a deep breath. "I'm not sure I ever really had a life to reclaim. I think if I'm doing anything, I'm trying to find a life. And I only hope the one I find is mine."

Eventually, Jake returned to his vehicle and retrieved something he immediately stashed in a brown paper bag, and they took Megan's little red sports car up the hill to Jake's house to pick up his truck to go after the horses. They left his Jeep parked beside Megan's house so that anyone who came in, *if* anyone came in, would see it and think he was still lurking somewhere nearby.

"An import?" he asked, as she struggled to hold the little car between the washed-out ruts of the road. "Isn't Congress in a 'Buy American' mode right now?"

Megan flashed him a grin. "It's new, can't you tell? It was reaction, not reflection, and maybe rebellion against my father's betrayal, that gave me the incentive to go ahead and splurge." She bit down on her lip as the car lurched into a hole. "However," she said, "maybe a good old American army-issue tank would have been better for this part of the country."

She had waited apprehensively in Jake's living room while he showered and shaved and changed clothes, but no women appeared, no voices, no quilting frame: nothing but Deacon, who immediately stretched out on the cool stone of the hearth and began snoring gently.

"Some guard dog you are," Megan muttered. "I wonder, is there training for ghost watching?"

"You say something?" Jake asked, walking into the room.

"No." Megan jumped up from the chair almost as fast as Deacon scrambled to his feet. "Not really. I was just talking to a sleeping dog."

Jake grinned at her. "Are you ready to go get some horses? If you're real nice, I'll let you talk to them too."

Riding downhill in Jake's beat-up, shock-sprung pickup wasn't much smoother a ride than the one uphill had been. In self-defense, Megan dug the seat belt fastener out from the crevice of the seats, buckled herself in, and held on to the dashboard for dear life.

Jake's humor had definitely taken a vacation by the time they reached the gate. He got out to unlock it, and Megan followed.

"At least they didn't shoot the lock off," he said, when his key worked smoothly.

"What? And risk letting you know they were coming?"

"Right." He lifted up on the gate and began swinging it open. "Will you drive through so I can shut this behind the truck?"

Megan nodded and climbed back in the pickup, managing, somehow, to reach all the pedals and work all the levers, even though they were adjusted for Jake's length and strength.

"Have any trouble?" Jake asked as he opened the driver's side door.

Megan shook her head and slid across the bench seat. "Piece of cake," she told him.

"Which reminds me. Is the Prescott Mall all right for lunch?"

"Lunch? You're feeding me again?" she asked as she buckled the safety belt in place.

Jake nosed the truck out onto the county road and accelerated before he grinned at her. "Look at it this way. Sarah needs the business and I need the nourishment, so you're really helping the two of us by suffering through some of Sarah's really awful cooking."

"Right," Megan said. "And if what I saw you eat there yesterday fits your definition of nourishment, I don't suppose you'll be around to make me suffer very long."

Jake laughed, but his attention was on the road, on a deep pothole that seemed to have gotten wider and deeper since yesterday, when a meaning Megan had never truly intended for her words struck her.

Not be around? Jake? But he was indestructible, wasn't he?

Maybe not. Even on this rough road, instead of gripping the steering wheel with his right hand, Jake merely rested it there while giving the majority of control to his left hand. The scar was an ugly thing—too ugly to be old, too well healed to be new enough for the wound to be bothering him still, unless the damage to nerves and muscle might never completely heal.

"Jake?"

He glanced over at her, and his eyes narrowed. "What's wrong?"

"What did you mean when you told that deputy—"

"Henderson?"

"Yes, Mark Henderson. What did you mean when you

told him you'd already stuck your nose in a little too close and his office hadn't been able to do anything about it?"

He swung his attention back to the road, this time to a skinny bridge and a narrow turn.

"You knew I came back home after I left the agency and was appointed as sheriff?" He hesitated a moment. "And that I was shot?"

"Helen wasn't particularly free with the details, but yes, I do know that much."

"I didn't want to have anything to do with law enforcement when I came back home, but the County Commissioners convinced me that they needed the 'expertise' I'd acquired while working with DEA. And I guess I still had a drop or two of crusader left in me. "Surprised the hell out of me," he said, almost in an afterthought.

"The current sheriff, the one whose term I was going to fill, was under indictment for several felony charges. We were in the middle of what was, for Pitchlyn County, a crime wave, with more stuff on the street than some metropolitan areas see, and what looked like the organization of a major pipeline looking for a foothold somewhere in this area.

"I took the job. I didn't want to be one of those officious bastards who sweeps everyone out of a department and fills it with untrained and too often incompetent cronies; besides, I didn't have that many buddies who wanted to trade in their federal jobs for the insecurity of a county one. So I kept most of the staff. I only got rid of the ones who had been implicated in previous investigations. Mark stayed."

"He worked for you?"

Jake shook his head. "Mark never worked for anyone but himself, but that wasn't imediately apparent. He gives a pretty good impersonation of a concerned lawman.

"Anyway, I did manage to develop some leads on the drug pipeline, through a couple of carefully cultivated informants. I found someone who supposedly knew about a major drop site. Mark was my backup. He says I didn't give him the right directions, so he and the other agencies were two ridges away from my meeting, damn near to Arkansas. And my informant neglected to tell me that the drop site had recently been used, or that he was the one who used it.

"We went in on horseback, and like the greenest recruit in the world, I rode into an ambush. I did get one shot off before I was left for dead. Sometime after my informant left, my horse wandered back; even the best trained horses can be forgiven for running when the bullets start flying. I managed to get Deacon—he'd been shot too—and me back on the horse and hang on until we got to my place."

"Jake." Megan had twisted in the seat to face him as he talked. Now she laid a tentative hand on his shoulder. So close. He had come so close to death.

He lifted his hand to cover hers before again placing it on the wheel. "I called Patrick. He and Barbara saw that I got to a neutral hospital. My informant showed up later at the local hospital, dead, but with two gunshot wounds instead of just the one I managed to inflict. Rolley P was acquitted of all charges and resumed his badge, and no one in that office has ever come up with a single clue about who was behind the shooting. But it does look like the pipeline has decided to go around Pitchlyn County."

"Jake."

He gave a rueful laugh. "I'd ask you how you spent your summer vacation, but I've already heard that story and it isn't any better than mine."

"When did this happen?"

He glanced at her, lifted a brow, and lifted the corner of his mouth. "Two weeks before you left on your trip."

"God," she whispered. "You were still in the hospital?"

"Yes," he said. "Most definitely, yes."

"And Helen went on a junket?"

Now Megan did see his hand grip the wheel, and when

she looked at his strong, clean, unmarred profile she saw a nerve twitch near the corner of his mouth.

"We're here," he said tightly.

Megan looked up in surprise. Prescott already? It was just as well. Amazing, she thought. Jake would talk about betrayal, violence, and near death, but the subject of his marriage was off limits. Well, a small, silent voice taunted her, isn't yours? Wouldn't you rather talk about almost anything than tell Jake just how bad your married life had been?

None of the spit-and-whittle crowd loitered on the store's porch today. A cowbell clanked merrily as Jake pushed the door open and held it for Megan to pass.

The alcove to the right of the door was empty. Megan glanced into the interior of the store to see Sarah straightening up from a cramped bend over a frozen food chest. She looked toward the door, smiled, and waved.

"Tea's in the blue pitcher," she called out. "Help yourselves and I'll be right there."

"Amazing," Megan murmured as they walked into the lunchroom alcove and Jake stepped behind the counter. "It's like another world."

"No," he said, scooping ice from a small chest into two glasses. "It's the way the world was before we got so crowded that people in the same neighborhood don't know each other. Here," he said, setting the glasses and the blue pitcher on the counter in front of her. "Why don't you fill these while I see if Sarah needs some help?"

Megan filled the glasses and studied the chalkboard menu on the side wall. Chicken salad wasn't on it, but then it hadn't been on yesterday either.

She smiled when she heard Sarah's laughter mingling with Jake's in the back of the store. A friendlier world. She liked the thought of that. A gentler world. A world where neighbors knew each other and helped each other. Her smile faded. But still a world were people like Rolley

Pierson and Mark Henderson could gain footholds and threaten the peace of that world.

The laughter and then the murmur of voices died away. She heard Jake's heavier steps going toward the back of the store, Sarah's lighter ones coming toward her. Megan found a smile to answer Sarah's welcoming one as she rounded the corner into the alcove.

"Good," Sarah said, nodding toward the glasses. "I see you found it all right."

She stepped behind the corner and washed her hands, then took a large potato from a nearby bin, scrubbed it, and ran it through a hand-operated cutter, letting the strips fall into a fry basket which she plunged into the waiting fryer. Then she took a round ball of ground meat from the refrigerator, pressed it into shape, and dropped it on the small grill.

"Now," she said over her shoulder, as she again washed her hands. "What can I fix for you today?"

"Chicken salad?" Megan asked hopefully.

Sarah shook her head but grinned. "Trust me?" she asked.

"After yesterday? You bet."

Sarah nodded and busied herself taking containers from the refrigerator and assembling something just out of Megan's sight around a corner of the counter.

"Where's Jake?" Megan asked.

"Oh, some of his deliveries came in. He's putting them in the truck. Is he ever going to get that mill in working order?"

"What?"

"The sawmill. I told him when he bought it from Tom Haney's grandkids that it was probably too far gone to salvage, but nothing would do but for him to haul it up the hill to that shed behind his house and start reconstructing it. I swear, he could have bought a new one for what he's put into this one. Of course, you can't really count all the time it's taken. He was barely able to get around for weeks, let alone do any physical labor."

Megan paused with her glass halfway between the counter and her lips. Jake had a sawmill?

Had she known about it before? Had Jake and Sarah talked about what kind of deliveries he wanted to have made here? Had he mentioned to Megan what he was doing during those times he had something he had to do on his own place?

No. Megan was certain. Hadn't she wondered, just this morning, how he meant to spend the rest of his life?

Of course, a home-based sawmill didn't make a career, but it was a start. . . .

"Here you go," Sarah said cheerfully, not at all aware of Megan's mental turmoil as she slid a platter and small plate in front of her and turned to the grill and fryer to finish preparing Jake's meal.

"Is it okay?" Sarah asked over her shoulder.

"Oh." Megan looked at the platter. A medley of sliced fresh fruits and cheeses on a bed of lettuce surrounded a small crystal dish of cottage cheese and a matching dish containing a scoop of lime sherbet. The bread plate held two dark, grainy rolls and a curl of chilled butter. "Oh, my, yes," Megan said. "I never expected something like this. Thank you!"

Sarah flashed her a smile. "And I never expected to be able to serve something like that in the Prescott General Store. Thank *you*, Megan."

Jake entered from the front door just as Sarah finished assembling his cheeseburger and poured the fries from the basket onto the side of his platter.

Without asking, she handed him a towel, and he walked behind the counter and washed his hands. He leaned forward to examine Megan's meal. "Looks good," he said. "Where's the beef?"

Sarah spluttered and winked at Megan. "See what I mean?" she said. "And he's one of my more enlightened patrons."

Jake looked at her, all questioning innocence.

"Go sit," Sarah said, waving him from behind the counter. "Eat, and I'll get your mail."

"It does look good," Jake repeated as he seated himself on the adjacent stool. Reaching over with his fork, he speared a slice of cantaloupe and bit into it. "Tastes good, too. Want a French fry?" Without waiting for her answer, he scooted her bread plate near his platter and transferred a half dozen or so fries to it with his fork. "That'll put some meat on your bones."

Megan groaned. "Oh, come on, Jake. The next thing I know, you'll be calling me 'little lady' and patting me on the head."

"Now that's not exactly where I'd want to pat you. *If* I were to pat you, that is." He smiled at her, but it wasn't humor she saw in his eyes, it was something much needier, and it was gone in an instant.

Sarah didn't return to the lunch counter until Megan had surrendered her plate to Jake and he had just speared the last slice of apple.

"Mail," she said, setting a stack of catalogs and envelopes in front of Jake. "Sorry, but it looks like nothing but bills," she told Megan as she set a small pile in front of her. Megan shrugged and smiled at Sarah. She hadn't really expected anything different, but it was amazing how much having her expectations met hurt.

As before, Sarah poured herself a glass of tea and leaned a hip against the counter. "So, is that all your deliveries, Jake? Or can I expect another couple hundred pounds tomorrow? What did you do anyway? It was only yesterday that you asked. You sly dog, you'd already told them to bring your stuff here."

Jake shook his head. "Nothing so devious, Sarah. I knew what delivery service this company uses. I called them yesterday afternoon and made a driver very happy by rerouting my deliveries here until further notice.

"Good meal," he said, finishing the apple. He lifted his tea glass in her direction, and Sarah filled it wordlessly. She gestured in the direction of Megan's glass, but Megan shook her head.

Jake lifted his glass and saluted them. "What mysterious good-looking guy did you two talk about behind my back today?" he asked, raising a mocking eyebrow.

Sarah looked at him as though he had lost his mind. "Tom Haney? Have you had too much sun today?"

Jake choked and coughed out a startled laugh.

Even knowing what Jake wanted to pursue, Megan couldn't help smiling.

He grinned at her, and if she thought she saw an apology in his eyes—well, she supposed that with all the other things she had been seeing, it was all right.

"I guess old Tom might be considered mysterious, he was kind of a hermit, but I really was interested in the one you talked about yesterday. The one who's been dead for years and years. Help me out here, Megan. What was his name?"

"You don't mean Sam Hooker, do you, Jake?" Sarah asked.

"Yes," Megan said. A weird, wild connection struck her, one so obvious that she was amazed she hadn't made it before: the prowlers. "Sam Hooker and the legend of the railroad gold."

"Oh, Jake, you know about him," Sarah said.

Jake shook his head.

"You mean you didn't go treasure hunting when you were growing up on that mountain? Everybody else did."

"Well, of course I went treasure hunting. Patrick and Barbara and I dug up half the county. But Sam Hooker? I don't think I've ever heard of him. What was he, a train robber, a stagecoach robber, or a bank robber? Some of all of those are supposed to have buried their loot somewhere in the county."

"Hush now, he was none of those, and you'd know it if you just thought. He was a lawman like you. Well, maybe not like you. He was a Lighthorseman, but I don't think he was assigned to Peter Conser. I think he worked specially for the Principal Chief of the Nation. At least that's the way I remember the story. The treasure was an army payroll stolen from the train at Limestone Gap."

"And how did it get all the way over here?" Jake asked. "Toward Fort Smith, Arkansas, is the wrong direction for any self-respecting outlaw to be carrying army gold stolen from damn near the Texas border."

"That's the mystery," Sarah told him. Her eyes widened and her voice deepened, as she lost herself in the rhythm of the story. "Or part of it. The other part of it is, did Sam Hooker recover it and, if so, where did he hide it?"

"And of course it has to be around here somewhere, doesn't it?" Jake asked in a gentle mimic of Sarah's voice.

"Well, wherever else?" she asked. "After all, he lived in these hills."

Megan watched as Jake made the same connection to the prowlers as she just had and then discarded it—but not quite.

"I don't suppose you know where?" he asked.

"I don't." Sarah leaned back, pleased with herself for at last catching his attention, and took a long swallow of her tea. "But Miss Mattie might. Rumor has it he was related either to her grandfather or great-grandfather. You know, Megan, your place is somewhere near where their old homeplace used to be."

12

"*Why did you decide* to bring your horses home now?" Megan asked when they were back in Jake's truck and headed toward the northwest in the general direction of Fairview.

"I thought it was time. Patrick's had them since the shooting. And since I can take care of them now, I ought to be doing it."

"You could have taken just as good care of them last week," Megan reminded him. "Why didn't you get them then? Or next week, when you'll be in even better shape. Why now?" Why now, she wondered, when according to Jake, prowlers were crawling over the property. "Are you going hunting? Are you going to put yourself in danger again?"

Jake took one harried look at her and pulled his truck to the side of the road. He turned in the seat to face her and put a hand on her shoulder. "Megan. I'm going to do my best to see that neither one of us is in any danger. You have to trust me on this."

She glanced at the hand on her shoulder, his right hand, his scarred hand, and swallowed a wave of fear that came from nowhere. She looked up, trying to understand where the fear had come from. "I don't want you hurt again," she said.

He lifted just the corner of his mouth. "Believe me, I don't want that either," he told her.

She tried to match his smile. "Trust is easier to give when it goes in both directions, Jake."

"I trust you, Megan," he told her solemnly, and she saw the truth of his words, and his surprise at that truth in his eyes. "I trust you with my life."

"Just not with the little things, like an explanation of what you think is going on?" she asked, trying for lightness. But that was too much effort. "Jake, do you think our prowler could be some poor misguided treasure hunter after the army gold?"

"I don't know. And since I haven't really had time to explore that possibility, I'd just as soon not speculate. We've got enough to worry about without putting treasure hunters on the menu too." He gave her shoulder a gentle squeeze. "But it might simplify things if that's who is coming on the property."

Jake's truck rumbled over the cattle guard and up a lane bordered on both sides by huge old trees and brown-painted rail fences enclosing pastures so neat they appeared almost manicured.

"Nice," Megan murmured. "Very nice."

"You should have seen the place when Patrick first bought it. It was nothing but bramble and briar and half-grown trees as far as you could see. Except where it was full-grown trees and rock."

The lane opened into a wide rectangular area which it skirted to the right toward a cluster of barns, wooden corrals, and outbuildings. Off to the left, shaded now by two big oak trees, sat a two-story farmhouse, neat and well-tended but not ostentatious.

"He's worked hard."

"*They've* worked hard. Patrick was just out of school with a brand-new degree in journalism, and Barbara had been accepted at med school. She wouldn't marry him till she finished, said it wouldn't be fair to tie him down, to her debts or to her schedule. Somehow he managed to scrape together the down payment on this place and then took off for parts unknown to make his fortune. He wound up with the Reuters News Agency, covering mostly eastern Europe, until Barbara finished her residency, and they both came home together."

She heard affection in Jake's voice, pride in his friends' accomplishments, even a touch of envy as Jake braked to a stop beside the house.

He opened his door and stepped from the truck, then turned, retrieved a small bag from behind the seat, and held his hand out toward her. "I need to go in for a minute. Come with me?"

"Sure." Megan slid across the bench seat and let him help her down. "But aren't they both at work? Or does Barbara's mother live with them?"

"They wish," he said, sliding his fingers into the tight watch pocket of his jeans. "And yes, they're both at work." He pulled out a single key.

"For emergencies," he said in response to her raised brow. "They have keys to my locks too."

"And is this an emergency?"

"Maybe a little one," he told her.

Inside, the house was cool and dim, but Megan suspected that in winter, with the leaves gone from the oak trees, this house, like her own, would be flooded with brightness and warmth. She glanced around her, appreciating the homey touches Barbara had made seem so natural. "If this place were mine," she said, "I don't think I'd ever want to leave it, not even to go to work."

He flashed her a reassuring grin. "Yours will be every bit as comfortable," he told her. "You've already made a good start."

"Sure," she said. "One green bedroom, less than half finished. But thanks for the vote of confidence."

"Any time, Megan," he said. He gestured toward the side-by-side refrigerator. "Would you mind fixing us a couple of glasses of ice water while I take care of something?"

Secrets? Great. Just what she needed, more secrets. But she supposed she could give Jake that much. After all, he had given her much more than simply a little trust.

She didn't want water, though. She suspected that Jake didn't either, that his requesting it had been an attempt to keep her occupied while he was gone.

She didn't need busywork to stay occupied; Barbara's kitchen was a treasure trove of wonderful things to examine: handwoven place mats, ceramic canisters, a framed ancient cross-stitch sampler on delicate linen.

Tucked away on a wall in an arrangement of samplers and paintings and photographs, she found a group picture of a tow-headed boy, another boy who was dark and lean, and a tiny little girl. They had towel capes hung from their necks and improvised swords hanging from oversized belts at their waists and were obviously playing the Three Musketeers.

Megan reached to touch the glass covering the picture. How fierce Jake had looked even then. How old had he been, twelve? She recognized the corner of the house in the background as hers and saw that the porch had been converted to his bedroom. At twelve he'd already had good reason to look fierce.

But he had friends.

And she never had.

Determined not to wallow in self-pity, Megan looked

back at the picture. The overgrowth south of the house hadn't been as heavy then as it was now. Megan easily made out the outline of a portion of the stone borders. And beside the kids, to the east, stood a tumble of stones, almost like the remains of a small turret. From the top of the pile on a branch stuck into the stones flew a homemade flag, its design lost in the flutters and furls but obviously of great importance to the three young adventurers.

She heard a noise from the front of the house, a scraping sound and then a blare of music quickly softened to the mellow sounds of a jazz number.

Music? Jake must have finished whatever it was he'd needed to take care of. Megan pushed open the swinging door and walked through the dining room into a large, comfortable den.

Kneeling on the stone hearth, Jake looked up with a medium-sized flagstone in one hand and a sheepish expression on his face. "I should have known that noise would summon you," he said. "Oh, well." He lifted a cassette tape from the hearth beside him, dropped it into the cavity he'd exposed, and then placed the flagstone on top of it.

"Trust," he said. He smoothed the stone back into place and stood up. "Sometimes Patrick and I need to leave messages for each other. Sometimes we just need a safe place to stash things for a short while."

Megan nodded, understanding, promising with her silence to keep his secret. "And the tape?"

"I dubbed off a copy on his cassette deck, so now there's more than one, and also more than just you, Mark, and Rolley P to hear Mark's threat, so that when you—*if* you decide to file a complaint you'll have even more to complain about."

"Thank you," she said.

"For what, Meg?"

"For understanding that I might not be able to file the

complaint." She felt a grin breaking through. "And for giving us the ammunition to help put that wormy overbearing tyrant in his place if I get the courage."

"I think you've got the courage to do just about anything you want, Megan McIntyre," Jake told her. "And I think you're well on your way to recognizing that you do."

Patrick had kept Jake's trailer when he brought the horses to his place. Megan waited in the house while Jake hooked it to the pickup's trailer hitch and backed it into place, but she walked down to the barn while he loaded his two horses: a gentle dapple-gray mare and a big sorrel gelding with a white patch on his forehead roughly in the shape of the state of Texas. When she saw the larger horse, she merely shook her head. Should she be surprised? Maybe. But there had been so many surprises, they were losing their power to stun her.

"What do you call him," she asked, when he had slammed the trailer gate shut and secured it, "Tex or Red?"

"O ye of little faith," he said, dusting his hands on his jeans. "Are you so sure I have that limited an imagination?"

"What do you call him, Jake?"

"Mm," he mumbled.

"Again, please. And louder."

"Red," he said, raising his voice to be heard over her spluttering laughter. "But that's only because he was already named when I got him. She, however"—he pointed to the mare—"has a truly unusual name. I call her Lady."

They stopped once on the trip back to their houses, at a convenience store and gas station, and while Megan sat in the truck, close enough to the pay phone to hear Jake's words, he called Patrick and invited the Phillipses to his house for dinner that night.

"Couldn't you have waited until we got home," Megan asked, when they were once again on the road, not realizing how she had lumped their two homes together as one until after the words had already been spoken, "or called him from his own house?"

"I wanted to make sure I caught him before he got away from the office. And I didn't want to advertise to anyone who might be listening that I had been inside his house."

"Are you saying—"

"Am I saying the phones are tapped? Maybe. Mine, Patrick's, possibly even yours. I don't know for sure, but I wouldn't say anything that I didn't want known on any of them."

"And I thought *I* was paranoid," she muttered.

Jake chuckled. "Haven't you heard the old story about the man who went to the psychiatrist to complain that he thought he was paranoid. 'Why, no, Mr. Jones,' the shrink says to him, 'it's not paranoia; everyone really does hate you.' Well, I don't think everyone hates me, any more than I think everyone is out to get me. But I do believe in being careful."

"And Rolley P is the type who would illegally tap phones, just on the chance that he might hear something?"

"You've had two encounters with his office now, Megan. What do you think?"

Megan thought about her telephone conversations. Only those with Dr. Kent could possibly be of any interest to Rolley P, or to anyone else for that matter. And of those talks, only the last one—maybe. "Oh, damn."

"What's the matter?" Jake asked. "Have you been selling state secrets over a party line?"

"It's a private line," she told him. "At least I thought it was until now. And they're not state secrets, just mine." She rubbed her hand over her face and shrugged. "Fortunately, I didn't trust the person I was talking with enough to be completely honest with him. So if some poor overworked deputy is listening on my line, he's heard Barbara check in with the clinic and give them my unlisted number, which the sheriff probably already knew anyway; he's heard me telling my psychiatrist how much better I feel; and he's heard me cajoling, begging, and bribing various tradesmen to come out and work on the house."

"And he hasn't heard you telling your father, the Attorney General's office, or a best friend back in D.C. or Tulsa what happened?"

"No."

"Maybe he should. Maybe our sheriff would think twice about threatening you again if you'd already told your story to anyone who would listen."

"Technically, *he* didn't threaten me."

"No, but he was present when his first deputy did, and he didn't do anything to stop it."

"Why, Jake? What possible motive could he have for bothering with me? I have no connections here; I didn't even meet the man until yesterday."

"I think I have a motive," Jake told her. "I just don't understand the reason behind it."

"Great," Megan said, running her fingers through her hair. "Do you want to share that insight with me?"

"Not yet." He turned the truck onto their private lane and braked to a stop. "Do you want to get the lock or would you rather drive the truck through?"

"Saved by the gate," she muttered.

"What?"

"I said, I'll drive through the gate," she said, smiling sweetly.

He grinned, reached over, and tousled her hair. "That's what I thought you said."

Whistling, he opened the door and stepped from the truck, leaving Megan fumbling with her seat belt and mumbling to herself. "Yep. 'Little lady' is right around the corner," she said under her breath.

Because of the horses in the trailer and the increasing afternoon heat, they didn't stop at Megan's house but only slowed enough to look down the drive. The house sat in quiet solitude, its front door closed, as they had left it. Megan smiled at the antics of the two black kittens, just barely visible across the distance, as they cavorted on the porch steps.

How peaceful, she thought. How marvelously peaceful after a lifetime without peace. Yes. She had made the right decision in coming here, in spite of what had happened; in spite of what might still be happening. To have a home that was really a home, to have a life that was truly her own—she glanced at Jake—to have a man who loved and cared for her because of who she was, not because of her father or some imagined status.

Except she didn't have Jake.

Damn.

Helen, Helen, Helen, she repeated silently. Remember her. Remember her. Remember her.

Jake didn't look like a grief-stricken man; he didn't act like one. But talk of his marriage was off limits. And, oh, God, in spite of all that Megan hadn't liked and couldn't respect about her sister-in-law, Helen had been talented and charismatic and gorgeous.

Jake grimaced as the truck bounced into a deep rut in the uphill road. He grimaced again and drew his lips tight against his teeth in what she suspected was a reaction to pain as he fought to control the stubborn vehicle and the added burden of the trailer.

And Helen had left this man, her husband, wounded and still in the hospital, to go off on a manufactured junket to further her career.

Soaking wet, Deacon stood guard in the middle of the road when they rounded the next curve.

"He's ruined," Jake said, expelling a sigh as he braked to a stop. "Completely ruined."

But Megan noticed that he didn't sound too upset.

He leaned his head out the window. "Don't think you're going to ride in the cab with us after you've been in the creek, you old reprobate." He jerked his head toward the bed of the truck. "Hop in the back. And be careful of the trailer hitch."

Deacon trotted obediently to the back of the truck and sat on the roadside, looking at Jake.

"Damn," Jake muttered again. "The tailgate's up, and it's got to stay that way until I unhitch the trailer."

He opened his door and stepped down, blocking the path as Deacon rose to his feet and bounded toward him. "No way, dog," he said. "I want a shower, but not right now, and not inside that truck." He looked at the dog and the truck and considered the possibilities. "Do you want to race?"

Deacon woofed once, and Jake grinned. "That's it boy. Race. Whoever gets there first wins a big bowl of ice cream."

Megan's laugh turned to a soft smile as Jake got back in the truck and revved the engine twice before easing back into gear and up the hill.

"You really do love that dog, don't you?" she asked, not a little envious of the easy companionship they shared.

"Yeah." Jake seemed reflective for a moment as he struggled with steering. "He was with me in the agency, you know."

Megan shook her head. "No, I didn't."

"He was. He was kind of a renegade, like me. He saved my butt on a couple of occasions. He didn't take well to his new partner after I left. I learned they were about to destroy him just in time to pull a few strings and get him pardoned to me."

"I'm glad you did."

"Me too." Jake braked the truck to a stop near a small barn. "I'd only had him with me a couple of months when the ambush took place. He repaid me for rescuing him. He took more than one of the bullets meant for me. He saved my life."

While Jake off-loaded the horses and unhitched the trailer, Megan dished up Deacon's ice cream, giving him an extra spoonful and a pat on the head. "Good boy," she told him. "You've earned the right to be spoiled."

When she returned to the barn, she found Jake had already saddled the sorrel and had a rifle slung across the saddle in a tooled leather holster.

"You're going riding?" she asked.

He nodded. "I wish you'd go with me, but maybe it's just as well. The trail isn't too bad on horseback, but it could be a heck of an interesting first riding lesson."

Megan closed her eyes, remembering too well her first time on a horse. Her father had decided she would make a fine-looking equestrienne, so when she was thirteen he'd bought her jodhpurs and Wellingtons, a pink jacket, an English saddle and a highly bred horse, and had hired an Olympic coach to teach her to ride.

What she'd felt when she first mounted the horse was so much more than fear that to this day she couldn't describe it. She'd immediately freed her feet and dropped ungracefully from the horse's back, to her mortification, the coach's amusement, and her father's unhidden contempt.

He'd told her to get back on, and she had, only to feel fear and nausea engulf her. Again she slid down, ungraceful, uncaring.

The third time, her father had stormed over to where she stood by the horse and had lifted her up, forcefully seating her in the saddle with a demand that she stay there.

Megan still didn't know what had spawned the blackness that had come over her. A stable boy told her later that she had started screaming and crying and fighting and finally had fainted. She did remember coming to and seeing her father leaning over her with what appeared to be genuine concern. "I'm never getting on a horse again," she had told him, while she was still too weak to stand up. "Not ever. So you might as well sell it." Remarkably, he had done so, and only Roger had ever made more than a half-hearted attempt to get her on a horse again.

It wasn't that Megan didn't like horses. She did. Lady approached, as gentle as her name, and stuck her head over the corral rail, and Megan gently stroked the smooth length of her nose. She just couldn't bring herself to get on one, not even for Jake.

"This isn't a pleasure ride, is it?"

"No."

"Is it dangerous?"

"I don't think so, or I wouldn't have asked you to come with me."

She looked at the rifle. "But you don't know for sure."

He didn't answer. Megan suspected he remained silent so he wouldn't have to lie to her. "Jake, where are you going and why?"

"That's a fair question," he admitted, "especially since I need your help. I told you someone has been coming onto the property. Well, last night I saw a moving light, one ridge over."

"And you're going to go investigate?"

Jake twisted Red's reins in his hand. "I have to."

"Why now? Why not wait until Patrick can go with you, or—" She realized she'd been about to suggest they involve the law. "Sorry."

"Do you know what could have happened if that raid the other night had turned up the amphetamines the warrant claimed were there?"

"I'd have been arrested?"

"Yes. And your property would have been confiscated."

"You mean the house?"

"I mean the house and all the land."

Megan's hand stilled on Lady's muzzle. "You can't be serious. That's—"

"That's the law, Megan. And Rolley P is the type to take full advantage of it. He wants me gone bad enough, maybe, to plant something on my place. Even though he knows he could never get a conviction against me, he could make a good case for taking my home. What I don't understand is why these forays have moved over onto your property."

"So you're not just going out there to see what someone found but to make sure no one left anything?"

"Right. And I'd like you to know the general direction I've taken. I'm not anticipating any trouble, but it's smart to have someone know where you are. It won't be for long. Patrick and Barbara are coming for supper. I mean to be back before then."

"But what if—"

"I'll have Deacon with me," he said. "And the rifle. If anything happens, I'll fire three quick shots. You'll be able to hear them here, at the house. That will be your signal to call Patrick and have him rouse the troops—the friendly troops."

"Jake, I don't like this."

"Oh, hell," he said. "Now I've worried you. Let me say it again. I would not have asked you to go with me if I thought there was the slightest danger to either of us. You have to believe that."

She studied his eyes, intent on hers, hiding something but completely honest in his concern for her, and his tortured hand clenched on Red's reins.

Trust. It was so easy to ask for and so hard to give.

It was all he had asked of her.

Megan released her gentle clasp of Lady's muzzle and took the four steps that separated her from Jake. Helen be damned. She wanted to trust this man, she wanted to hold him, and someday, soon, she hoped, when they were both healed of their trauma—she wanted to love him.

There. That wasn't so hard to admit, at least not to herself. It would be a long time before she had the confidence to admit it to Jake.

Unless her actions did it for her, and right now Megan didn't care. She slid her arms around Jake's waist. She felt his start of surprise as she leaned into him, holding him in a tight hug, felt the moment his body welcomed her embrace, felt the moment his welcome became more, much more, than either of them could yet act upon.

"Be careful," she said, reluctantly releasing him and moving back one step.

He tucked his hand under her chin and lifted her face to read her eyes. "You bet," he told her softly. "I've discovered a whole lot of reasons lately why I want to take care."

With Jake ahead of her on horseback, Megan followed in the pickup to the ridge. At his instructions, she parked out of sight—of what? she wondered—beneath a tree. He dismounted and walked to the truck, opening the door. For a moment he just looked at her; then he reached beneath the seat and fumbled with something.

The something turned out to be a large silver-colored automatic pistol in a black leather holster.

Jake didn't say anything for a moment; he just watched her. She saw him blanch and saw the nerve twitch once beside his mouth; then he took the pistol from the holster, slid a shell into the chamber as she had seen on countless cop shows, put the gun back in the holster, and stood there.

"Do I have to do this?" he whispered.

"What, Jake," Megan asked, beginning to be frightened. "What's wrong?"

He shook his head. "I don't know. I think Mattie would say a goose just walked over my grave, and that makes as much sense as anything I can think of. Here." He handed her the weapon. "Do you know how to use one of these?"

"No." Megan didn't reach for it.

"Look," he told her. "Just flip this slide—the safety—in this direction, point it like your finger, and squeeze the trigger."

"Do I need it, Jake?"

He took her hands and folded them over the gun and holster. "Probably not. But it never hurts to be prepared. There've been a couple of bears sighted. And snakes."

"The two-legged or the no-legged variety?"

"Look," he said, gripping her hands before releasing them and stepping away. "Just keep the damned gun handy, will you? Run like hell if you have to, hide if you can, but if it comes down to it, use it. I'll feel better knowing you're protected."

The voice didn't sound like his, his words certainly didn't fit the conversation they had already had about this afternoon, and he looked and acted both reluctant and afraid to give her the gun even though he insisted she take it. And now she was afraid.

"Jake, what is it?"

He stepped away from her, shook his head, and looked at the gun. Carefully she placed it on the seat beside her.

"Please. Tell me."

"I don't know, Megan, unless it's just a damned busy goose."

"I'll be careful, too, while you're gone," she promised, searching his eyes for a reason for his strange behavior and finding nothing but the vestiges of a confusion that overshadowed the confidence she had come to expect from him.

"Yeah," he told her. "I'd like that."

"And don't be gone longer than you have to."

"No," he conceded. "Not today."

Although she wanted to slide from the truck seat and take him in her arms, Megan did not touch him again before he left. She sat in the truck and watched him ride down the brushy mountainside on Red. And Deacon, as though knowing he was once again on duty, followed purposefully.

When they had disappeared from sight, she glanced down at the gun. Jake's rifle hadn't bothered her. Knowing he had armed himself this morning with probably this very weapon hadn't bothered her. She'd never hated guns or feared them until recently, and only then when they were in the hands of men gone mad. But this one?

This one seemed to call out to her to touch it, to pick it up, to hold it close. And at the same time she suspected that if she embraced this gun, she'd know what had brought the fear into Jake's eyes.

13

An hour passed. Megan had long since lost sight of Jake and had long since stopped hearing any sounds that might have been caused by his passage.

The sun had moved on in its march to the west and now beat unmercifully through the windshield of the truck; the breeze, what small breeze there had been, had died in the heat. And the gun still lay, untouched, on the seat beside her.

She should have gone with him. If she hadn't been such a coward, she would have gone with him. Now all she could do was wait here. She couldn't go back to the house, even though Jake had as much as told her to wait there. She couldn't abandon her post, couldn't leave him out here all alone. Couldn't go back to his house and risk running into Lydia and Granny Rogers again.

Lydia. And Sam.

Megan leaned her head back until it rested uncomfortably against the empty gun rack at the rear window.

Sam had been a real person. Had Lydia? How could she find out? Lydia was a white woman; she would not show up on the rolls of the Choctaw Nation. Besides, the Dawes Commission rolls hadn't been compiled until the turn of the century, thirty years or so after the first entry in Lydia Tanner's diary.

"Not Lydia Tanner's diary," Megan said, gripping the steering wheel. "My journal. My imagination." She released her grip on the wheel, only to beat against it with one small frustrated fist. "My fears and neuroses finding a unique way of expressing themselves."

She sighed and sagged forward on the seat. Somehow, some way, she'd heard the legend of Sam Hooker. Sarah spoke as though everyone in this area should know it. That had to be it. She'd heard about Sam Hooker and his red horse and his damnable sawmill somewhere. After all, fiction and legend ran rampant all over the eastern part of the state. Tulsa wasn't that far away. The Creek Nation of northeastern Oklahoma was not that different from the Choctaw with their rumors and myths.

And Lydia? asked a small annoying voice in the back of her mind. Did you hear about her too?

Of course not, Megan told herself. Lydia was just—was just—

She sighed and looked up, searching the hillside below her for some sign of Jake. She needed to see him, needed to know he was near.

Lydia was just her, Megan, cloaked in an identity far enough removed from Jack McIntyre's daughter and Roger Hudson's wife for Megan to be able to look at her dispassionately and without prejudice.

"Ha!" Megan pounded the steering wheel again. Without prejudice, maybe. But there had been nothing dispassionate about any of her experiences with Lydia Tanner.

Suddenly determined, Megan opened the glove compartment and rifled through it until she found a pen and a small notebook. If she was going to wait, and she had already decided she was, she might as well put her time to good use. She opened the notebook to a clean page, leaned back in the seat, and studied it for a moment, fighting an almost overpowering urge to throw the notebook far away.

"Okay, Lydia," she whispered, "let's see what you have to say for yourself."

Nothing. After more than an hour of making his way over to the ridge, after almost as long searching the terrain, Jake had nothing to show for his efforts except confirmation that someone had been here and the knowledge that he had needlessly frightened Megan.

And himself.

God, what had all that come from? She hid her fear well, but he knew she felt it, had to feel it after what she'd witnessed at the clinic and experienced here. He'd only meant to reassure her—no, he had been *compelled* to reassure her that she'd be safe. Had been compelled to give her that damned gun. And he'd never been more reluctant to do anything else in his life than place that weapon in her hands.

"A whole damn flock of geese," he muttered.

That was another thing: he was talking to himself more and more, out loud and in strange, restrained monologues in his mind.

He'd found broken bramble marking the place where the vehicle had turned around, had found signs that, as the last time, two men had gotten out, walked in opposite directions, circled, returned to the vehicle, and driven away in the same direction from which they'd come—the south and east, as before.

He'd set Deacon to searching the paths the two men had taken and then had ridden the trail they made in leaving, to a dilapidated fence that marked what he thought must be Megan's southerly property line. They hadn't bothered to cut the fence—it wasn't that substantial anyway—but just drove over it, knowing, as Jake did, that in a week or a month or a year, whenever anyone got around to checking, it would simply look as though it had fallen over from disrepair.

He'd had Deacon on patrol during that ride. Now, as he retraced his route, he again had Deacon searching. Maybe the intruders were looking for army gold. And maybe he was paranoid, because Deacon's highly trained and sensitive nose had found nothing, absolutely nothing to indicate that any kind of narcotic had been anywhere near the men, their vehicle, or within tossing range.

He looked toward the north, toward the general direction of where he had left Megan. He couldn't see the truck, of course, but he felt her there, waiting.

Nothing. Absolutely nothing.

Megan looked at the notebook in disgust. A few disjointed sentences sprawled across the page, but they were her sentences and in her handwriting.

Did this mean she only accessed that part of her who came out as Lydia while in her own home? Or did it mean that Lydia—God, just listen to me! she thought—did it mean that she, Megan, only felt free enough to explore Lydia in a book to which she was—safely?—confined, not on any old piece of paper and certainly not in a book that belonged to Jake?

She ripped her page from the notebook and leaned across the seat to stash the book and pen back in the glove compartment. The gun was there, ominously in the way.

"Hateful thing," she whispered.

Cautiously she lifted it and tucked it away, out of sight under the seat. Then she replaced the notebook and pen. She stretched her legs across the hump in the floorboard and leaned back in the seat, relishing the caress of a tiny errant breeze. She was tired, so tired. She slept, but she never seemed to get enough rest.

She shouldn't sleep now, she knew. Jake was out there, protecting her property. The least she owed him was to stay awake until he returned. But maybe she could just close her eyes for a moment, not to sleep, but just to rest for a tiny little while. . . .

She hurt. Oh, God, she hurt so bad. The pain was constant. From her ankle, to her ribs, to the bruise on her jaw where one of them had hit her.

She wasn't dead. She had sworn she wouldn't see another day without killing one of them or dying. She was beaten and torn and bruised. But she wasn't dead.

Her hair was wet. She felt it against her shoulder. Had it rained?

No, the cloth that covered her wasn't wet.

A cloth covering her? Yes, she felt it now, and clean dry cloth beneath her. And some sort of mattress, lumpy but infinitely better than the rocky hillside.

What now? Panic overwhelmed her. What new torture had they devised?

She heard footsteps approaching on what must be a dirt floor and felt the dip of the mattress as someone—someone big but not truly visible in the dim light—sat beside her. A hand reached beneath her shoulders, lifting her.

No more! She could take no more. She came up screaming and clawing and fighting with every drop of strength in her abused body.

It wasn't enough. He caught her hands in one of his, holding them away from himself, and, with the other, pushed her down on the bed.

She couldn't stop the ragged moan that broke from her. "Kill me. Please. Just do it now and get it over."

"Never."

She recognized the voice, and when she did, she also realized that the hands that held her restrained her from inflicting hurt but were not, in turn, hurting her.

"Sam?"

He released her hands and picked up a wet cloth from a basin on a packing crate next to the bed. "That's right," he said softly, gently, "and you know I'd never hurt you."

Yes. She knew that. But when he brought the cloth to her face, when he touched her, she cringed and shrank away, not from him but from his touch—from the touch of any man— and she felt her fear in the chill that drove away her pain, saw her fear in her trembling hands pushed quickly between them, heard her fear in her raspy breath, smelled her fear in the dank, quiet dark of the little cabin.

Sam drew away from her in a steady, unhurried motion. He dropped the cloth back into the basin and sat slumped on the side of the bed, defeat and a deep pain of his own etched in every tired line of his body.

After a moment he lifted his face to hers, and she saw an agony there that acknowledged her pain and embraced it as his own.

"I'll never hurt you," he said. "No one will ever hurt you again." He lifted his hand toward her and, God help her, she cringed away from him again—cringed away from Sam. He dropped his hand to his side.

Slowly, as though not sure he should proceed, as though not sure he could proceed, he lifted his revolver from its holster at his hip. "Take this," he said, placing it at her side on the bed.

She shook her head, not understanding.

"You don't have to be afraid of anyone ever again," he told her. "Not even me."

o   o   o

A sharp crack jarred her from the dream. Megan sat up abruptly, bumping her knee on the bottom of the steering wheel before she realized she lay in a fetal curl she had assumed on the seat as she slept. "Oh, God," she moaned, as waves of unreasoning panic slammed through her. *Oh, God, oh, God, oh, God!*

And then she remembered the noise. For a moment the hillside was alive with the sounds of screams and shots. Only memories. She forced that knowledge into her consciousness. Only memories. No more real, now, than her dream.

But the noise: a gunshot? Had that been what woke her from the nightmare? Another sharp crack splintered nearby, and she allowed herself to notice what she hadn't before. The breeze had grown to a full-fledged wind, and the sky had darkened with a summer storm.

"Great," she said shakily, pulling herself upright in the seat and looking into the early darkness. "This is just dandy: special effects and everything. But do you think you could hold off with the rain just a little while maybe?" she asked the wind. "Just until Jake gets back? Would that be too much to ask?"

Maybe not. Megan leaned over and rubbed her knee. The thunder continued to roll in from the west, and lightning speared across an almost black sky in the distance. But no rain fell, not yet, though she could smell it in the wind that rushed through the cab of the truck, almost but not quite taking away the scent of her terror.

The sounds of the thunder and the wind lashing the trees masked Jake's arrival. One moment she was alone with the storm; the next, he appeared on Red out of the darkness. She jumped from the truck, knowing better than to run toward him and risk spooking his horse. But oh, how she wanted to!

She waited beside the truck until he rode up to her. He looked at her intently but didn't dismount. "Why are you still here? Are you all right?" he asked.

She nodded. A little lie. She could explain later. "Are you?"

"Yes. But we need to get back to the house before this breaks."

Of course they did. Lightning would soon be skittering all over this ridge. She should have realized that sooner. She would have, if—if what?

Still, she reached tentatively toward Jake, needing to touch him before they were once again separated. Her fingers rested lightly on his knee and she felt his small start of surprise before she withdrew them and once again climbed in the truck. "Don't wait for me," she said. "Hurry on back to the barn. I'll be right behind you."

He didn't, of course. He waited until she had backed the truck from its hiding place, turned it around, and started down the hill before falling in behind her.

Miraculously, they made it. Megan ran into the house and began closing windows against the rising wind while Jake unsaddled Red. She knew the side fronting the porch would be safe from rain, so she ran into Jake's bedroom and closed those, checked the second room, a dimly lighted and closed-up bedroom, and ran back into the living room on her way to the kitchen.

She skidded to a halt. The damned quilt frame was back. The fire in the fireplace was back. Lydia and Granny Rogers were back.

Lydia clipped the thread from the stitch in front of her, jabbed her needle into a pincushion, and lifted her chin defiantly. "Sam is my dream."

The older woman shook her head and dropped her hand on the girl's shoulder. "But you're not his. You never can be. Sam has no dreams left, child."

Jake came into the room with the clang of the screen door and the rough sound of boots on the hardwood floor. Deacon nosed his head under her hand before skirting around the edge of the living room to lie on the cool stone hearth. And the women were gone.

"Whew," Jake said, slapping his hat against his thigh before hanging it on an carved-oak hat rack. "That wind's got a bite to it for a summer rain. How about some coffee?"

"What?"

"And a little light," Jake added, flipping a wall switch that turned on a couple of table lamps.

It was raining, an all-out cats-and-dogs downpour. The room had grown so dark she could barely see until Jake turned on the lights, and the only thing her mind had registered until just this moment was that the women were gone.

"Ah—yes," she said. "Coffee would be fine."

"Megan?" Jake crossed the distance separating them and stood in front of her. She tilted her head back to look up at the questions in his eyes. "Are you all right?"

She wasn't, and she wasn't sure she ever would be, not after today, but a sense of the ridiculous, too long denied, refused to be silent any longer. "Do you have any idea how much time we spend asking each other that question?"

A slow grin warmed Jake's face. "A lot. Are you?"

Her humor faded. "I don't know, Jake. I just don't know anymore. And you? You were gone so long. Did anything happen?"

He lifted his hand to her face, gently rubbing his thumb across her cheek. Damn! Was she crying again? No. Her cheek was smooth and dry beneath his touch. Smooth and dry and needy. She felt her lips part, felt the subtle changes as her body began preparing to welcome more than just his touch on her cheek, felt the heat of embarrassment flare across her face as she realized that Jake had to see, more clearly than she could bear for him to, how vulnerable she had become to him and to his touch.

Slowly a gentle regret filled his eyes. He slid his hand down to rest on her shoulder and turned her, half leading, half pushing, as he walked with her into the kitchen, flipping on the switch for the overhead light and filling the room with brightness.

"I found where someone had been," he told her, giving her an easy push down onto a chair before turning his hands but not his attention to the old-fashioned percolator.

"I know where they came in and approximately when, how many of them there were, and where they went. But not what they did or why."

"Did they do any digging?"

"As in, for treasure?" He didn't wait for her response as he filled the pot with water and the basket with ground coffee. "There was no sign of digging or of rocks being turned over. No sign of shell casings such as a hunter might leave. No sign of a campfire. Nothing, in fact, other than a strange kind of shuffling, foot-stomping search. That's the only thing that would account for the underbrush being trampled the way it was. But that doesn't make any sense either."

He set the pot on the stove and lighted the burner with a wooden match, took a tin from the cabinet, settled himself at the kitchen table across from Megan, and pried off the lid.

"Mattie?" Megan asked when he offered her the tin, revealing several huge chocolate-chip cookies.

"You bet." He grinned and took a bite.

But she wasn't in the mood to be diverted, not from this. "What's going on, Jake? What do these people want?"

"Damned if I know," he told her. "If it were a mile or two over, I'd almost think—"

A formidable flash of lightning lit up the outside sky while dimming the lights in the kitchen, and the accompanying blast of thunder covered Jake's words.

"Think what?"

He frowned, shook his head, and reached behind him to adjust the flame under the coffeepot. "Nothing," he said. "It's so off-the-wall that even your stolen treasure theory makes more sense. . . . "Did you leave any windows open in your house?" he asked abruptly.

"Jake," she said, with a reluctant chuckle, "don't you remember, 'What good does a lock do when it isn't used?'"

"Oh."

The wonderful aroma of perking coffee filled the room with warmth and comfort, dispelling the gloom of the rain sheeting down the darkened windows.

She could sit here with him forever, not thinking about the prowlers on the property, not thinking about Sam and Lydia or the tragic unknown woman who haunted her dreams, not thinking about Rolley P and his threat, not thinking about her father's betrayal, not thinking about the clinic and Roger and Helen and—

She caught back a moan and twisted to one side, disguising it as a cough.

The coffee boiled over. Jake jumped up from the table to tend to it, and Megan slumped in relief. Saved again. Saved from what? From exploring too closely something that had the power to destroy her? No. She was exploring all those things. Hadn't she spent hours with Dr. Kent and that blasted notebook he'd insisted upon? Yeah, right, she remembered. A notebook that except for the two damning entries she'd removed sounded about as personal and soul searching as a résumé.

"Here," Jake said, handing her a mug of steaming coffee. "There's no need to look so discouraged. We'll find out what they want."

She smiled at him, grateful for the coffee but more grateful that he had misunderstood her turmoil. "What time are Barbara and Patrick supposed to be here?"

"Oh, damn!" Jake stopped halfway down into his chair, jerked upright, and marched into a small room off the kitchen. She heard a door open, heard him fumbling with packages, heard the door slam. Jake emerged from the room with two packages wrapped in white butcher paper. "Maybe they'll thaw before midnight," he said as he set them on the counter. "I really had meant to feed them something more original than steak, but I guess this will have to do."

He opened the refrigerator, peered inside, and slammed it shut with a disgusted sigh. "And I left most of the salad makings at your place last night."

She bit back a grin. She suspected Jake would eat steak every night if the decision were left to him. "And it's pouring axes and hammer handles outside and your road is getting more impassable by the moment."

"Yeah," he said in disgust.

"So why don't we wait for the rain to slack off a little, take those steaks and that big truck of yours, slide down the hill, and cook at my house again?"

"You're sure you don't mind?"

"No, I don't mind," she told him, rising from the table and carrying his coffee to him where he stood at the sink. "I like Barbara and Patrick, and I've discovered that in spite of what I once thought, I enjoy entertaining. At least, I'm beginning to."

Megan had heard somewhere that a storm cell never stayed in one place longer than forty-five minutes, and she'd always accepted it as truth. However, either this cell was especially slow or a faster one moved in behind it without any clearing between, because it was well over an hour later before the rain let up enough for them to make a dash for the truck.

Laughing, Megan slid onto the seat, slammed the door behind her, and pushed the hood of her borrowed yellow slicker from her hair.

She looked up in surprise as Deacon jumped into the seat from the driver's side, laughed again, and scooted over to make room for him as Jake climbed in and scowled at his dog at the same time as he ruffled Deacon's fur.

Except for a light sprinkling, the rain had stopped by the time they reached the curve near the creek. Megan rolled down her window, drew in a deep lungful of fresh rain-washed air, and listened to the rush of water so near the road.

"It's really wonderful out here, isn't it?" she asked.

"Yes," Jake said. "In spite of what's been happening, it really is."

They met Barbara's car at the turnoff to Megan's drive, and Jake stopped, switched on his turn signal to confirm that Barbara should enter the drive, and waited until she did before following her in.

Patrick's truck was already there, parked in the turnaround, but Patrick himself was nowhere to be seen until he came hurrying around the south edge of the house.

"There you are," Patrick said, walking up to the side of Jake's truck. "When I saw your Jeep here and couldn't find sign one of either of you, I began to get worried."

"Hey, love of my life," Barbara called, "do you want to give me a hand with this?"

"Sure," Jake called back. "Just let me get rid of this blond intruder first."

Patrick lifted his fists in a mock boxer's stance before grinning at Jake and turning to help Barbara lift boxes and bags from the seat of her car.

"What's this?" Jake asked.

"Dinner," Barbara told him, shoving two flat boxes at him. "I doubted the rain would let up soon enough for you to get your grill going in time to feed us at a reasonable hour, so we're having something truly different tonight."

"Pizzas?" Jake asked.

Laughing, Megan led the way up onto the porch. She unlocked the door and stepped back, allowing her guests to enter first. She held the door for Deacon, but he flopped down on the porch with a tired wag of his tail. Smiling, she went on into the house, flipping light switches, leading her new friends toward the kitchen, and enjoying every moment of their friendly bickering.

Jake and Patrick set their packages on the table. "Salad?" Jake asked.

Barbara indicated a bag. "Right here."

"Drinks?"

Again Barbara pointed. "Jug wine and cold beer."

The house was remarkably cool for having been closed up all day—pleasantly so. Megan opened the windows over the sink for a little more fresh air and turned to survey the room which in the past few days had finally become part of a home instead of just four walls. It didn't have the ambiance of Barbara's kitchen yet, but it was fast getting there.

"Why don't I set the table in here?" she asked.

Jake flashed her a grin. "Good idea." He threw an arm over Patrick's shoulder and led him toward the back door. "Patrick, my friend, while the women tend to domestic things, I've got a little job I need to discuss with you."

Patrick groaned. "I should have known it. You never get me out here unless you have work for me. Now what is it?"

"Just a porch," Jake told him. "Just a little ten-by-thirty screened-in porch. No trouble at all for two accomplished carpenters such as ourselves."

Barbara joined Megan's laughter as she helped her set out plates and flatware and glasses.

"I can't let them do it," Megan said.

"Why not?"

"Because it's too big a job for—for friendship."

Barbara laid a restraining hand on Megan's arm as she started to turn toward the refrigerator. "They love that kind of work. Jake and Patrick did most of the renovations on our house, and all of them on Jake's place. Friendship isn't always doing for someone else, Megan. Sometimes it's letting someone else do for you."

"Are you saying I'd be doing *them* a favor by letting them rebuild my back porch?"

Barbara nodded. "And me. Jake will get to play with his saws and power tools again, turning out custom moldings and trim for the project, and Patrick will be so contented working on something, anything, that he'll put off his plans to redo part of a house that I've finally gotten just the way I want."

They had finished the last piece of two large pizzas when the rain started in again, in earnest, with thunder booming close enough to rattle the glass in the glass-fronted cabinets. The lights dimmed once but remained on.

"Uh-oh," Barbara said. "I bet you didn't think to buy an oil lamp when you moved out here."

"You're right, I didn't." She felt a soft brush at her ankle and looked down to see Shadrack, the larger of the two black kittens, winding around her feet. She reached down and picked him up. "There you are, you sly cat," she said. "Where's your buddy?"

"I thought we left them outside today," Jake said. "In fact, I was a little worried about them."

"We did." Megan rubbed her face against the cat's smooth fur, found it dry without a trace of damp, and listened to his rumbling purr. "But these two are the great sneak artists of the world. Obviously this one, at least, got in past us, either when we were coming in the front door or while you and Patrick had the back door open."

Jake frowned. "Megan, I didn't see them either time."

"You didn't see a black cat on a rainy night? Why am I not surprised?"

Patrick chuckled. "Relax, Jake. Time out. You're off duty, remember?" A loud crack of thunder sounded as lightning struck somewhere near. "Wanna tell ghost stories?"

Barbara groaned. "Next comes a bag of marshmallows, a stick, and a fire to roast them over."

The warmth of friendship. Megan had never known it

until these people came into her life. She smiled over at Jake. She had him to thank for it.

"No ghost stories," Megan said, reaching for the plates and stacking them neatly in front of her. "But how about some real ones. For example, do any of you know the history of those foundation stones on the south side of the house?"

Barbara snagged a last piece of crust from Patrick's plate and munched on it reflectively. "Only that they've been there forever. Mom said—wow, it's been a long time since I thought about them, but they fascinated us when we were kids—Mom said they were the ruins of her grandfather's house. Grandfather Tanner lived there when he was a kid."

"Tanner?" Megan asked. "As in Daniel Tanner?"

Barbara shook her head. "Peter, I think. His dad was some big-shot white entrepreneur who'd come into the Nation to make his fortune, and made several, but nothing was ever good enough for him except the money. You know the kind of man I'm talking about, don't you?"

Too well. Megan was very much afraid she knew more than just the type of man. She nodded.

"Well," Barbara continued, "there used to be a pile of stones out there too, until—when? I guess we were almost grown before we found a nest of copperheads in it and Aunt Sally had it hauled off. Mom said it was the remains of a carbide house."

"A what?"

Barbara grinned. "They didn't teach that in Oklahoma history when I was going to school either, but a lot of the wealthy plantation owners down on the Red River had them. They used them to pump carbide into the house to power their version of gas lights. And Peter's daddy, according to the rumors, not being one to be one-upped, especially not by any Choctaw, had one built for his new house, and I guess it worked fine until it blew up." Barbara's expression sobered. "Killed his daddy, and that's a heck of a punishment for pride. But Great-grandpa Peter got out okay."

Peter Tanner, with a white father, living close enough to the creek to go there regularly, living close enough to what was now Jake's house for Lydia to visit regularly.

"How—how old was your great-grandfather?"

Barbara shrugged. "Fourteen, fifteen. I'm not sure, but not grown because Mom says he went to live with a widow he'd known for years."

"Then he had no—no other family?"

"Gee, Megan, I'm not sure. You know how family history has a tendency to slip away. Mom might know. Why?"

Megan glanced at the friends seated so companionably at her table. She was about to take the biggest risk of her life, and she wasn't at all sure she should.

But damn it, there were so many connections, so many coincidences, she had to tell someone. These people—yes, she knew without a doubt, these people could be trusted. She looked at Jake. "I told you a little of my strange experiences this morning." She glanced at the others at the table. "Jake calls them my 'vacations,'" she said, and knew by their quick darting looks at each other that Patrick and Barbara had been aware of them too. "Oh," she said. "You knew."

"Not what was happening," Barbara said kindly, "just that something was."

Megan attempted a smile that failed miserably. Again she looked at Jake, wanting to plead with him not to lose all regard for her, wanting to shut up and not say another word, wanting at the moment for none of the otherworldly things to have happened. "I told you about only part of them," she repeated. "There's more. And there's something I think I need to show all of you. If you'll wait here, I'll get it."

She felt herself trembling as she rose from the table and felt the chill of fear as she walked through her house—fear of rejection, fear of losing the first true friends she had ever had, fear of losing her sanity, fear of losing . . . Jake.

The chill intensified as she reached the hallway, but

Megan remained lost in her thoughts. Peter Tanner was real too. Sam Hooker, Peter Tanner, the wealthy white father. Who else?

She'd reached the spare bedroom when it finally dawned on her that her chill wasn't completely internal. A draft whistled down the hallway. A draft? In a closed-up house? She hesitated. The breeze seemed to be coming from her room. Slowly she turned and made her way to the end of the hall.

Her room was dark, as it should be. She'd left no lights on. But she had closed the windows. She remembered that clearly. Jake's admonitions about safety and security had been far too fresh when they left the house for her not to have heeded them. So why, then, did she feel the rush of rain-damp air coming from her room?

Slowly she reached into the room and passed her hand over the light switch. The overhead fixture flared to life, freezing Megan in mid step, holding her motionless in the doorway, unable to do more than moan as she looked at the desecration of the place that had been her private haven.

14

With a worried frown, Jake watched Megan as she left the kitchen.

"What is it, my friend?" Patrick asked.

"I'm not sure," Jake said. "We talked this morning about some pretty disturbing things for both of us, and some weird dreams she's been having, but I don't—hell!" he said abruptly. "I might as well admit it, if she's going to. This place has been rapidly approaching the reality of a *Twilight Zone* episode lately, more for Megan than for me, but I haven't been completely immune. I have no idea what she's going to show us, but you can bet the farm it's something she wishes didn't exist."

Megan was gone for a long time before Jake heard her soft footsteps in the dining room as she returned: soft, hesitant, almost shuffling.

She came into the kitchen empty-handed and sat in her chair with her hands clasped together in her lap. Her face had lost the healthy glow it had begun to take on. Now it was pale, almost ashen. Her eyes seemed enormous, and her badly cut hair only added to the impression of refugee, waif, victim.

"Why did your aunt finish the walls in your bedroom with plaster instead of drywall?" she asked in a small soft voice.

"What? Megan, what are you talking about? How do you even know what's beneath all that paint and paper?"

"Because it's all over my bed," she said in that same detached, emotionless voice. She held out her hands, revealing a coating of white dust. "I'll have to change my sheets."

The words took seconds to penetrate, and then he was out of his chair and on his knees beside her, reaching for her hands.

"What?"

Barbara knelt beside him and took Megan's hands. "Go check it out," she said. "I'll take care of her."

Jake heard Patrick behind him as he rounded the corner into the hallway. The light from Megan's bedroom flooded out into the darkness, revealing two small white footprints on the otherwise gleaming-clean wood floor. Jake skidded to a stop in the doorway and looked at what Megan had just discovered.

"Son of a bitch!" he said, and pounded his fist against the door facing.

Rain lashed in through all the windows, now broken, and mixed with plaster dust on the floor. The damage had been done from the inside. Every drawer had been ripped open and its contents spilled out. Clothes had been dragged by the armload from the closet and thrown to the floor, where they had been walked on and kicked around. And someone had fired a shotgun in the room, at the wall behind Megan's bed, shattering the old plaster, revealing hunks of lath and wire, and the plaster had showered in chunks and in dust over her bed, covering her pillows and duvet and the black notebook with its gaping empty rings in a cloud of white.

He heard Patrick's low whistle. "When?" Patrick asked.

"God knows. We left right after Rolley P and Mark did."

"What?"

"Yeah, Patrick." Jake shrugged. "That was why I wanted you to come out tonight, to discuss what had to be a very inconvenient visit for them—they climbed over the gate and walked up from the road—and to share a tape I was fortunate enough to make of Mark conveying Rolley P's threat to Megan."

"That bastard. Do you think—"

"I don't know. We went to lunch, got the horses, and went straight back to my place after I called you. This could have happened any time after noon."

"Go see about Megan," Patrick said gently. "I'll call the report in."

"She's not going to want us to. Don't ask me why, because all I can tell you is it has something to do with her not being believed. It makes no sense to me because she's obviously the victim, as she was in the raid, but—"

"But we have to," Patrick said, "or we just help make Rolley P the tyrant he truly wants to be. She's not alone in this, Jake. Not now. And she won't be ever again, will she?"

Jake turned away from the wrecked room and looked at Patrick, seeing a knowledge in his friend's eyes that he wasn't sure he was ready for. "Aren't you rushing things a little?"

"Am I?" Patrick asked solemnly.

"Roger and Helen have only been dead for three months."

"Yeah, but how long has Helen really been gone, years? I'd lay odds that Megan's marriage wasn't any better than yours."

"You're psychic now?"

"No, just observant. Someone who's been happy all her life isn't so innocently delighted by little displays of affection and the everyday things Barbara and I and even you, my cynical friend, accept as normal. What's the notebook?" he asked abruptly. "And why would someone be interested in it?"

"Unless I'm mistaken, that's what she was going to show

us. It is—" Jake paused and sighed. Megan had enough reason to be shaken without this added blow. "It was the journal she's been keeping since she got out of the hospital. It must have contained a lot of her thoughts about the strange things she's been experiencing."

"But who would care?"

Jake shook his head. "Mark's threat was to expose her as a hysterical woman who overreacts and falsely accuses those in authority, to rake up old mud about previous unfounded accusations."

"Nice fellow, our first deputy. Isn't it amazing how he manages to find his way everywhere he needs to go, and some places he doesn't, but couldn't keep a planned rendezvous with his boss on a clear moonlit night?"

"Yeah." Jake stepped out of the room. "Make the call, Patrick."

Jake found Megan huddled in her chair with her arms wrapped tightly about herself. Barbara knelt beside her, touching her shoulder, speaking quietly, but she looked up when he entered the kitchen.

"Someone trashed her bedroom," he said. "Pretty thoroughly."

"Damn." Barbara gave Megan's shoulder another comforting pat before relinquishing her position to Jake.

He dragged a chair over and sat so close his knees nudged her thigh. "Megan," he said, reaching for her hands.

In response, she hugged herself more tightly and rocked a little, back and forth, back and forth.

"Megan," he said again, more forcefully this time, and held his hands out to her.

She looked at him blankly for a moment and then at his hands. Slowly, cautiously, she released her grip on herself and with tentative care reached for the lifeline he offered. He felt her fingers, slightly rough from her weeks of work, slide across his, then clasp his hands fiercely.

"It's all right," he told her, folding his hands around hers, holding her as tightly as she held him. "I'm here."

"I just want to forget," she said, looking up at him with eyes that had seen too much. "But they won't let me. Why won't they let me forget?"

He gave a tug, freeing his hands. Then, wrapping his arms around her, he pulled her securely into his lap and tucked her cheek against his chest. "Shh," he said. "It's all right."

Over Megan's head he glimpsed Barbara shake her head in a quick negative gesture. "She needs to talk," she said softly. "Cry, maybe scream. She hasn't, you know."

Jake freed one hand from Megan long enough to gesture for Barbara to leave them alone. With a sad, concerned smile for him, she did.

Scream? He'd heard Megan screaming, and it was a sound he never again wanted to hear. Cry? Maybe she hadn't, except in her dreams. Maybe the pain went too deep for the solace of tears. And maybe she knew that if she once started, she might not be able to stop. God knew there were things in his life he'd wished he could put in a box and never have to look at again.

The rain still fell outside, gently now, and its soft pattering rhythm provided an almost hypnotic backdrop for their quiet moment. He ran his hand in slow circles across Megan's back and repeated her name over and over in a murmuring whisper as he felt the strangeness of holding her, the rightness of comforting her. "I won't let anyone hurt you ever again. I promise."

His words echoed in the hushed silence of the kitchen, echoed in his mind, echoed in his heart as something deep within him remembered saying these words to this woman, sometime . . . sometime. . . .

He felt her gathering strength to push away from him, and he didn't want her to leave, couldn't bear for her to leave.

"I'm sorry," she said, her voice muffled, her face still pressed against his chest.

"For what?" He separated them enough to place his hand on her cheek, to turn her face toward his.

"I want to be in your arms," she told him. He saw a terrible honesty in her eyes and wondered how much these words had cost her. "I have since—since we met. But not like this. Not like some damned victim."

He captured her face in both hands and looked deep into her eyes. It was too soon, his conscious mind yelled at him, much too soon, but he wanted her—wanted her with an intensity all out of proportion to the time they'd known each other, all out of proportion even to the trauma they'd shared. Her, Megan. With her cropped hair and baggy clothes and haunted eyes. Not the senator's pretty little girl, not the Barbie doll Roger Hudson had tried to make her.

He felt Megan draw in a hushed breath, felt the thud of her pulse in her temples beneath his fingers, felt the wanting that reflected his own. Saw her lips part slightly in anticipation and invitation.

"Megan," he said on a sigh. Unable to help himself, unable to obey the warnings screaming through his mind, he speared his hands through her hair and bent to her.

Her lips were soft, welcoming. Home.

With a groan, he gathered her close and lost himself in the rightness of the moment. Strangely untutored, strangely innocent, she gave freely of herself, and striving to get closer to him she urged him with every touch to give just as freely to her.

"Will wonders never cease?"

Patrick's voice boomed through the room, and Megan jerked away, fighting an embarrassment she shouldn't feel but that he knew she did. Jake refused to let her go. With a gentle but implacable strength he held her close. He glared at the doorway and found Patrick grimacing.

"I'm sorry, Jake." Patrick sighed. "If it's any excuse, my surprise is for our sheriff's office. It seems they have a deputy as close as Prescott. I'm going down to the gate to let him in."

"Deputy?" Megan whispered. "No. Oh, no."

With a concerned glance at Megan, Patrick left.

"What's wrong?" Jake asked, taking Megan by the arms and halting her attempt to scurry away from him. He could understand her not wanting to file a formal complaint against Pierson for the search, but this was different and disturbing. "Why don't you want anyone to know what's happened?"

"Because," she cried. "Because . . ." She stopped struggling and looked up at him. "I don't know." Confusion and doubt twisted her features. "I don't know. Oh, Jake," she moaned as she drew into herself, "am I losing my mind? Is that what's finally happening to me?"

"No. Good God, no!" he said, giving her a little shake for emphasis. "Barbara!" he yelled.

"What . . ." He barely heard Megan's startled whisper, but he did hear Barbara's steps on the wood floor as she hurried toward them.

"You need a pep talk about emotional trauma and its after effects," he said, rising from the chair with her still in his arms but lowering her to her feet at arms'-length distance. No more closeness. Not now. She was too vulnerable. *He* was too vulnerable. "And since I'm not sure you'd believe me, I'm calling in an expert."

Jake whistled Deacon into the house before the deputy arrived and took him through each room: nothing. Only a strange whimper from his dog when they searched Megan's bedroom. Only a frightened cat hiding in the pantry.

The deputy was new, young, fresh-faced, and untrained.

He'd also been one of the dozen who had burst into the house with the search warrant. "You'd be safer if you kept that gate at the road locked," he said, as he wiped the mud from his shining black boots on the entry mat.

"It was locked," Jake told him.

"And the house?"

Damn the kid, and damn his superior attitude. "The house was locked too."

"Did you find a means of entry?"

Jake shook his head. "We waited for you. Thought you might want to be in on the search."

A fresh splatter of rain hit the porch roof. The deputy grimaced, then looked around the pleasant, undisturbed living room. "It doesn't look like anything's missing."

Jake remained silent after that almost sneering comment.

"Locked gate. Locked house, so you say. And it doesn't look like anything's been disturbed. Are you sure there was a break-in? Or has Ms. Hudson's imagination been working overtime with her alone all the way out here in the country?"

This kid wouldn't have lasted a minute if he were still sheriff, Jake thought, because he never would have been hired. "Who are you, anyway?" he asked. "Rolley P's nephew?"

The kid puffed up. "I don't see what difference that makes. Do you have a report to file or not?"

Jake glanced over at Patrick, who had stopped just inside the doorway behind the deputy. He was wearing a raincoat, one with big flap-covered pockets in a half dozen places. Jake noticed the almost invisible microphone protruding from one of those pockets. He exchanged a knowing glance with his friend.

"Why don't you come with me," he said to the deputy, "and we'll see just how much Ms. Hudson's imagination has to do with this call."

"Holy shit!" The deputy stopped just inside the room and gaped at the destruction. He took another step into the room, and plaster crunched under his feet. "What do you mean, you didn't find an entry?" he said, gesturing toward the windows. "There's your entry."

Definitely untrained. "That would seem to be the case," Jake said calmly, "except for the fact that these windows are about ten feet off the ground outside. And except for the fact that the glass pattern indicates the windows were broken from the inside."

The boy walked to the bed and picked up the open notebook. Jake bit back an oath.

"That book has the kind of surface you could have gotten prints from."

"Oh." The notebook fell back to the bed with a soft thud. "Well, I wasn't told to look for fingerprints. We don't all have kits."

"Since when?"

"Look, I was just told to get a report and get back on duty."

"Deputy"—Jake's voice sounded like a harsh growl in the room—"taking this report is part of *being* on duty."

"Yeah." The kid cleared his throat. "Well—"

"But let me help you," Jake said. "You'll want the names of the witnesses," he prompted, nodding toward the deputy's unopened folder. "Jake Kenyon," he said. "Former sheriff, neighbor." He nodded toward Patrick. "Patrick Phillips, publisher of the *Banner*, friend."

The deputy swallowed once but grabbed his pen and jerked open his notebook, writing furiously.

"Barbara Phillips," Jake continued. "Doctor at the Choctaw clinic in Fairview, friend. And Megan Hudson, property owner and as of about six weeks ago registered voter in Pitchlyn County. Got all that?"

"Yes, sir. When—"

"Sometime between noon—if you'll check to see when Sheriff Pierson and Deputy Henderson went back on duty and add about five minutes, you'll get the correct time—"

"They were here?"

"—and around seven o'clock. That's when we returned to the house, but no one thought to come to this part of it until just before we called you. Got all that?"

"Yes, sir." The young man swallowed again and looked toward the open notebook. "What—"

"Personal papers were taken," Megan said, stepping into the room.

Gone was the trembling, frightened waif of only minutes before. She hadn't changed clothes, hadn't put on any makeup, but suddenly and completely she was the senator's daughter. Not the pretty little girl Roger had talked about but a confident woman who knew the value of power and how to use it. Knowing how much this display cost her, Jake had never been more proud of anyone in his life than he was of her at that moment.

"Nothing of monetary value to anyone," she said. She stepped closer to the deputy and extended her hand. "I'm Megan Hudson, Deputy—"

"Harrison," he croaked. "Charley Harrison."

Harrison. Jake cataloged the name. The son of Walt Harrison, lumberyard operator and Rolley P's brother-in-law or another of his relatives. Did it really matter?

"Deputy Harrison," Megan continued. "We left the door locked, the windows locked, and my cats outside. When we returned, the doors were still locked but we later discovered that my cats were inside. And, of course, we found this."

"Yes, ma'am."

"This is an outrage," Barbara said, squeezing in past Patrick in the doorway and crowding the deputy farther into the room. "If your office wasn't so busy harassing innocent people, if they'd train you to do your job and let you do it, decent people wouldn't have to put up with these kinds of intrusions."

"Yes, ma'am. Uh—ma'am?"

"What?" Barbara asked, changing tactics in the space of a breath and smiling sweetly at the young man.

"Maybe I'd—maybe I'd better look around outside?"

"Good idea," Jake said. "Look out for broken glass beneath these windows."

"Don't worry, my friend," Patrick said, all good-old-boy innocence. "I'll keep him company and hold the flashlight."

Jake stepped to Megan's side and draped a protective arm over her shoulder. He felt tension thrumming through her, although not one sign of it penetrated the calm mask she wore. "That's kind of you, Patrick," he said. "Real kind. I'm sure the deputy appreciates it, don't you, son?"

The young man glanced toward the window, where the wind whipped the rain into the room. He looked down at his shiny black boots and his crisp tan slacks and visibly paled before he straightened his shoulders and met Jake's knowing smile. "Yes, sir," he said.

To have something to do, Megan cleared away the remains of their dinner and washed the few dishes. Barbara helped her. But after one frustrated attempt to make her sit and wait quietly—what did he think she was going to do anyway, break?—Jake began a systematic search of locks and windows which, too soon, took him from the room and out of her sight.

She had finished the dishes and made a pot of coffee by the time Patrick returned, carrying his camera case with him. "Young Charley's mama's going to have to do laundry for him tonight," he said as he set the case on the pine table and opened it. "How old do you think he was? Twenty, maybe?"

Jake had followed Patrick into the kitchen and now leaned against the door facing. "Not old enough to know what to do with the responsibility of the job or the gun he was wearing.

He's probably not a bad kid, but he's way out of his league. Is that the way you read him, Patrick?"

Patrick nodded.

"So," Jake continued, "in spite of the incredible coincidence of having a deputy in this part of the county when we needed one, our boy Charley probably hadn't already been out here tonight to leave this little surprise for Megan?"

"Probably not."

Megan had lifted the carafe from the coffeemaker when Jake's words registered. She set the glass pot on the counter and turned to face him. "Sheriff Pierson didn't—you don't think—?"

His smile carried a trace of sadness and acknowledgment of her continuing disillusionment. "You said it yourself," he told her. "They're horrible people. Someone went to a great deal of trouble today to frighten you. Why, Megan? Pierson's the only one who has anything to gain if you fold up and fly away."

"And the prowlers, Jake?" she asked. "The ones who have been coming onto the property since long before the sheriff had any reason to want me gone? Do they have something to gain?"

"Damn, I hate it when a woman's logical."

"Shame on you, Jake Kenyon." Barbara reached around Megan, lifted the coffeepot, and began filling cups and passing them around. "If you don't mend your wicked ways, I'm going to sick every major feminist group in the country on you." She took a sip from her cup and leaned back against the cabinet. "I think Rolley P's a bag of scum too. And, like you, I hate coincidences. But what if he's not responsible for this?"

Patrick looked over at his wife and blew her a kiss. "Damn, I hate it when a woman's logical."

In spite of the tension, Megan chuckled. "Do we have the Bobbsey twins?" she asked Barbara.

Barbara flashed her an exasperated grin. "Polly and Molly. Frick and Frack. Falter and Fall." Serious again, she studied Jake across the distance of the room. "What do we do now?"

We. After years of being alone, Megan felt that word caress her: We. Not: What does Megan do? Not: Gee it's been fun but you're on your own now, kiddo. Not: I'm not about to get involved with something that doesn't directly benefit me.

"Did you find anything outside?" Jake asked Patrick.

"Lots of mud. And you? Anything inside?

Jake shook his head. "No sign of forced entry. How about keys?" he asked Megan. "Did Renfro leave all his?"

"I changed the locks." she told him.

"Wise move." Jake nodded. "And I changed the front-door lock yesterday."

"With a lock you bought—" Patrick said.

"—from Harrison's Lumberyard." Jake finished.

"That's circumstantial evidence," Barbara said, seeing the familiar trail their thoughts were leading them to.

"I'll bring new glass for the windows out in the morning," Patrick said. "And a dead-bolt lock set I just happen to have stashed away in our leftover remodeling supplies." He set his cup on the table and picked up his camera. "Now I think I'd better take pictures and get on home, or it's going to be morning before any of us gets to sleep."

"It's obvious you can't stay here tonight," Barbara said to Megan. "You're welcome to come home with us for as long as you want to stay."

"No!"

Megan turned to look at Jake. From the expression on his face, the force of his objection had surprised him more than it had her.

"No," he said again, a little more softly. "I think it would be a good idea if Megan stayed with me."

Barbara turned toward the counter, hiding a small grin that only Megan saw as she rinsed her coffee cup. "Of course you do, Jake," she said easily. "But what does Megan think?"

"I mean—"

"I know what you mean, Jake," Megan told him. "Thank you, Barbara, but Jake is right. I need to stay close to home." And to Jake. Jake, who was becoming more and more synonymous with the meaning of home.

So Jake stood with her on the front porch of her house as they watched the taillights of Barbara's and Patrick's vehicles disappear down the lane. Somehow his arm had gravitated to her shoulder again. She could get used to this. Pathetically, gratefully, used to it.

"You'll need a few things," he said. "Enough for a day or two at least."

"Yes." Fortunately she had some clean clothes in the utility room, folded and not yet put away, so she wouldn't have to force herself to return to her destroyed bedroom.

"We can take the cats if you like," he continued. "I haven't had one in the house since I was a kid, but yours are okay. I—I wouldn't want them hurt."

You're a softie, Jake Kenyon, she thought, as she turned in his loose embrace to face him. A big, dark, dangerous-looking softie. She wanted to reach up and brush her lips across his, but that wouldn't be wise, not wise at all. Not after the brief, stunning kiss they had shared in the kitchen earlier. Not after finally acknowledging to herself how much she had come to want this man. Instead, she lifted her fingertips to his cheek and rested them there lightly. "Thank you."

"Megan." His hand now rested at the nape of her neck. His other one lifted and settled naturally on the curve of her hip. "I'm sorry about what happened here. About the damage to your bedroom, the theft of your diary. This has to seem like the most intrusive of—"

"Oh, my God!" she whispered, tensing beneath his touch. "Oh . . . my . . . God."

"What is it?"

She moved her fingers to his lips, silencing him, attempting to reassure him. "How could I have forgotten? Please," she whispered. "Oh, please."

Turning away from Jake, she hurried into the house, hearing the screen door slam behind her, hearing his footsteps following relentlessly. The door to the green bedroom had somehow gotten shut during the evening. Jake's hand covered hers as she reached for the knob. He pushed open the door, reached around her, and turned on the light before releasing her to enter the room.

The closet door was closed too. Megan opened it and dropped to her knees in front of the box of books. She lifted the top and reached beneath the first stack of papers.

"Yes!" she said, drawing forth the brown leather notebook. She eased open the cover for a hesitant look inside. Neat copperplate handwriting covered several intact pages. She hugged it to her chest. "Oh, yes!"

"Isn't that the notebook I saw in your bed this morning?"

Megan nodded. "You were asleep. I didn't want to disturb you, so I put it in here instead of returning it to the drawer in my bedroom. This is what I was coming for when I found the vandalism."

"What is it?"

She rose to her feet, still holding the book close. She had been prepared to show it to him earlier, but the moment had passed. "It's a product of my paranoia," she said reluctantly.

Jake lifted his arm as though to touch her. Megan shrugged and stepped away. "You know, when I saw that notebook lying open on the bed, I didn't suspect Sheriff Pierson or the prowlers on the property. I thought of only one person. I didn't think it could hurt any more than it already did. I was wrong. . . ."

"Who, Megan?" Jake prompted.

"My story really hurt my father politically. Dr. Kent is his friend. When he kept insisting I vent my feelings in that notebook of his, I wondered if he had ulterior motives. I wondered if proving I was more than a little unbalanced wouldn't offset some of the harm telling the truth about Villa Castellano had done. So when the really strange stuff started showing up—"

She sighed and looked up at him. He waited, patient and silent.

"Really strange stuff." She sighed again. "I took it out of the black one and put it in here. So whoever took that journal took about seventy-five pages of instructions and a lot fewer than that of disjointed ramblings and my unsuccessful attempts to be brutally honest with myself."

"And left the book open and empty so you'd know it was gone."

"Who else would do that, Jake? Who else had a motive? Who else even knew about the journal?"

"Only about a dozen other people, including our first deputy," he said. "The night of the raid, one of the officers wanted to take it in for evidence. I took it away from him. It doesn't have to be your father, Megan."

She hoped so. Oh, God, she hoped so!

"It's late," he said gently. "Let's get out of here, go home, and get some rest. Maybe tomorrow we'll be able to look at this clearly."

Home. He said it so easily. Not *my* home. Just home. As though she really belonged there with him. Did she? Could she?

"Yes," she said. "Let's do that."

15

Jake had shown Megan into his small guest bed-room, a room he hadn't even considered the night he first brought her to his home. She had looked at him in weary confusion when he opened the door, threw up the window to let in some fresh air, and turned back the spread to check for clean sheets, but she hadn't protested.

The cats had followed her into the room and curled up on the bed. He'd wanted to join them. He still wanted to.

And she wouldn't send him away.

That was the hell of it: knowing he could open the door to her room and she would welcome him into her bed; not knowing whether she would be welcoming him for who he was or only as another means to escape facing the horror. And not knowing why her reasons mattered so much.

She kept the light on for so long he thought she must be sleeping with it, but at last the sliver shining through the narrow opening under the door blacked out. The living room was already dark, lighted only by the spill from the kitchen doorway. He moved over to the sofa, facing the mantel, and leaned back into Mattie's pillow as he propped his aching left leg on the coffee table.

Damn, he was tired, as tired as though he hadn't stolen a few hours of sleep that morning. So tired that all the pieces of the puzzle swirling around them took on the same size and shape and color.

And now there was another piece: Megan's father.

Without getting up to find a clock or turning on a light, Jake could only calculate the time. He added an hour for the difference in time zones. One o'clock or thereabouts in D.C. Not an unreasonable hour. Especially since the sheriff had told Megan to call her father and her doctor had also insisted she call him.

Jake didn't know the senator or Megan's stepmother other than through a few superficial encounters he'd had because of Roger and Helen. Where had Megan been during those times? When he reflected now, he realized that he should have run into her on any of a number of occasions, but that she had been strangely absent whenever he let Helen draw him into that world. Off with Project Food? Possibly. Or just left out?

As Senator McIntyre's chief of staff and his son-in-law, Roger had lived in McIntyre's pocket and in his house. Helen had visited her brother often, sometimes without Jake, because he knew too well what really drew her to D.C. It wasn't family loyalty; it was power and prestige, even if only secondhand. And wealth, which somehow had managed to rub off on both Roger and Helen.

He eased his leg from the coffee table and stretched up from the couch, feeling bones and joints and muscles all protesting one more step. He didn't need a light to dial the highly guarded, unlisted number or to look it up in his personal directory. He'd long ago memorized it, although three months ago, when Helen had left him lying in a hospital bed, he'd sworn he'd never use it again.

Wilkins, the senator's houseman, answered, repeating only the number as an acknowledgment, and sounding as alert as if it were one in the afternoon instead of the middle of the night.

"This is Jake Kenyon. I want to speak to Senator McIntyre."

"Ah, yes, Mr. Kenyon, I recognize your voice. Unfortunately, the senator is not available."

Jake wanted to growl, but Wilkins was the only person in the senator's household who had not treated him as though he were an intruder, a pariah.

"It's about his daughter," he said. "It's important."

"Miss Megan?" Wilkins asked with mild surprise. "Of course. I had forgotten that you're in the same rural area. I trust she's recovering from her ordeal?"

"Recovering?" Jake bit back an oath. "I suppose. As well as she can, considering that three nights ago twelve armed law enforcement people burst in on her at midnight with a misdirected search warrant, today our local sheriff attempted to blackmail her into not filing a formal complaint about the raid, and tonight someone else broke in, blasted a hole in her bedroom wall with a shotgun, trashed the rest of the room, and stole the journal that the senator's friend, Dr. Kent, had insisted she keep to chronicle her recovery."

"Was she injured?"

Jake couldn't ignore the genuine concern in Wilkins's voice. "No. Not physically," he said, a little softer, a little less aggressively. "Now will you connect me with the senator?"

"I'm sorry, Mr. Kenyon. He isn't here."

"Damn! Doesn't she have anyone she can depend on?"

"You, sir? You seem to have assumed a role of responsibility." As though realizing he had overstepped the bounds of his employment, his voice immediately regained its habitual formality. "I will relay your message to the senator when I hear from him, but I'm not sure when that will be. I believe

I can tell you—for Miss Megan's information, of course—that it is because of her that he is not here. Her allegations about Villa Castellano proved so disturbing that he has personally gone on a fact-finding mission."

"I can't see Jack McIntyre slogging through the jungle," Jake said. "Where can I reach him?"

"I'm sorry, sir. I really can't give you that information. Perhaps Mr. Davies, his new chief of staff, could. If you will leave me your telephone number, and tell me where we can reach Miss Megan, I will advise him of your telephone call first thing in the morning."

"No," Jake said. "Megan is going to be unavailable for a few days, and I'm going to be hard to reach. I'll contact him later."

So the senator had gone on a fact-finding mission, had he? Jake pondered that as he made his way into his dark bedroom. But where? Villa Castellano or somewhere in Pitchlyn County?

He didn't even try to stop his groan as he stretched out, fully clothed except for his boots but in his own bed for a change. What he ought to do was fill the tub with hot water and use that semi-antique whirlpool attachment he kept for the times his body claimed he had overworked it, but right now he couldn't face digging out the gadget and connecting all the wires and grounds. Right now he couldn't face looking at himself in the glare of the bathroom's overhead light.

The scars on his face and hand were bad enough. In the tub, he'd be looking at the mangled mess that was his left leg, at the puckers, marks, and slashes that were permanent reminders of the two bullets that had found his chest and the surgeons' efforts to patch up the damage they had done there.

It was enough to terrify small children and send women shrinking away in revulsion.

Send Megan shrinking away?

He wadded the two pillows beneath his head and lay looking out at the rain-soaked landscape, now lighted by a still-bright but waning moon. He wouldn't go to her. Wouldn't stretch out beside her. Wouldn't gather her in his arms and follow the desires of his body and hers.

For God's sake. He had only known her three days, and it felt as though she had been a part of his life forever. Three days, and he wanted her with an intensity that shocked him with its power. Three days, he reminded himself, during which she had been reeling from one attack after the other.

He ought to go out tonight, ought to try once again to find out who was coming onto the property and why. But he couldn't. Not with Megan in the house. Not after what had happened today.

He wouldn't sleep, he promised himself as he felt his muscles finally beginning to relax. He'd just rest a while and examine Megan's suspicion.

Would the senator send someone to steal her diary? It didn't make much sense, but then little of the high-powered political scene made much sense to Jake. If he had, how did that fit into the pattern of other things that had been happening?

The problem was, nothing fit. Correction, he told himself as he felt his eyelids growing heavy. Nothing *seemed* to fit. Somehow it did, it had to. And if he could only figure out how, he'd have all the answers he'd need.

Megan lay back in the strange bed, wide-eyed, dry-eyed, long after Jake had closed the door behind him and left her alone.

Alone. God, she had been alone so long.

If he had wanted to stay with her, what would she have done? Would she have shamed herself and stunned him with how much she needed him? Or would she have been the good little girl she had always been and denied herself by sending him away?

Always denying herself. Why?

Always deferring to others. Why?

Always accepting second best, or less, as her due. Why?

When she was very small, she had wanted love. Had wanted affection. Had wanted to know she belonged to someone in a special way, not just as property.

Her father hadn't been capable of that kind of love; her stepmother hadn't even wanted to try. By the time Megan finished school, she might have been envious of her friends who seemed to have that missing element, but she had long since stopped hoping for it herself. Not even with Roger had she really expected it. At last she could admit that he had been her father's choice and had seemed as good as any. With him, she had hoped for affection of a sort, respect, a sharing of mutual interests. With him, she had not had even that much.

Why had she been willing to settle?

She'd never thought to question before. But the attitudes of a lifetime were almost impossible to break. She couldn't face those questions any more than she could face the events of the past months. Of the past day.

Lydia. Megan grabbed that thought like the lifeline she had so often needed and so seldom had. Young innocent Lydia, with no more pressing problems than an unrequited love. She might only be a product of Megan's imagination, but in spending time with her, Megan wouldn't have to think about all that pressed in around her, wouldn't have to think about her father's betrayal and her trashed bedroom and stolen journal and the woman who cried in her sleep and Jake, awake even yet, prowling restlessly through the house. Wouldn't think about how much she wanted to open the bedroom door and call him to her. Wouldn't think about how mortified she'd be when he turned her down.

Lydia.

Oh, yes. Safety lay in thinking of Lydia, not in those other things. Quietly Megan slipped out of bed, retrieved the brown leather binder, and carried it back to the bed.

Lydia, she thought again, summoning images of the young girl at work at the quilt frame, wading in the creek with her brother, complaining to her diary of her aunt's bigotry, learning fine stitchery with the sisters at school, and dreaming her girlish dreams of Sam Hooker.

Sugarloaf County, Choctaw Nation Indian Territory, 1872

Megan looked down at the page and frowned. Lydia hadn't dated this entry. But then, Megan had stopped dating her entries too. And Lydia—it was Lydia's handwriting, but something was wrong, terribly wrong. Hesitantly, she again bent over the page.

> I must release this fear and hatred before its poison destroys me and the little that has been left to me.
> I once thought myself a strong person; now I know that until the events of this summer I had never been tried.

Megan bit back a moan. "Oh God," she whispered. "Oh my God." She recognized the emotions of this entry as clearly as she recognized the handwriting. The woman who cried in her sleep. The woman who wanted to invite the unknown man to her bed but knew she never would. The woman who was so different from young Lydia that Megan had believed she had to be herself.

What had happened? What could possibly have changed Lydia Tanner from the laughing schoolgirl who was looking forward with every fiber in her young body to returning home, to seeing Sam again, to convincing him that she was the one to show him the way back to life and to love?

Megan had wanted escape, but she could no more close

the journal now than she could have closed the door on Lydia had she materialized in front of her.

With her heart pounding so hard she heard it echoing around her, felt it in the tremor of her hands, Megan again lifted the pen. For a moment it poised above the page, ominously still. For a moment she thought she might be spared a knowledge she wasn't sure she wanted. But then, taking on a life of its own, the pen began to move.

> I killed a man.
>
> It seems strange that I can write those words so calmly and yet cannot bear even to think of the events that led up to an act completely alien to the person I once was. But perhaps this is merely another symptom of the madness I feel growing ever stronger within me.
>
> If only I could bear to speak of what happened. But I cannot. And even if I could bring myself to do so, I know it must remain our secret. To reveal it would bring only shame and possibly death.
>
> So I will write. I will spill everything out on these pages, and then I will commit them and, please God, the madness that threatens me, to the fire. . . .

Jake woke sometime later as a fresh wave of the storm made a pass over the mountains. He noted the rumble of the thunder still rolling away into the distance as the cause of the noise that had awakened him and saw the trees outside his window, twisting and dancing in the rising wind. He smiled, thinking that anyone out on the mountain tonight was going to be miserable. Then, after listening a moment for the absence of any other noise in the house, he settled back into the pillows.

But something wasn't right. Megan?

He eased out of bed and down the hall. Her door was open, her room dark. Silently he turned the corner into the living room and stopped. The small light from over the kitchen sink cast just enough glow for him to see her sitting on the hearth in front of the open fireplace, legs bent beneath her and tucked demurely under the hem of her tentlike all-encompassing white nightgown, as she had sat other nights brushing her long silken hair. He wanted to go to her, but he'd known the pain of rejection too many times to easily subject himself to it again. . . .

Whoa! Where in the hell had *that* come from? Jake clamped a hand on the door facing to steady himself as a chill went through him. The room seemed to shift and spin and then right itself.

And there was Megan, sitting cross-legged, tailor fashion, on the hearth in front of his wood-burning stove, wearing another of those white India-cotton nightgowns that reminded him of a peasant's wedding dress, that covered her from breast to toe but left her arms and shoulders and her vulnerable throat bare. Her hair was short, as short as it had been hours ago when he'd forced himself to walk away from her bedroom door.

Next to her, as close as he could get without climbing in her lap, sat Deacon. The dog's attentions weren't unwanted. Megan had turned to him, thrown her arms around his neck, buried her face in his ruff, and now held on to him as though her life depended upon it.

Maybe it did, if what Jake had just experienced was anything like the strange episodes she had been trying to explain to him.

He walked across the room, his steps muffled by his socks on the smooth hardwood floor, until he stood in front of her. What he wanted to do was sweep her up in his arms and carry her back to his bed, but he knew that even if she had been willing, his leg wasn't. Instead, he knelt on his right knee. "I give better hugs," he said quietly.

Slowly she turned her head from its hiding place in Deacon's ruff to look at him. She wasn't startled; instead, she seemed almost resigned to the inevitability of his having come for her. In the dim light from the kitchen he saw tear tracks on her cheeks and pain in her eyes.

"Bad dreams?" he asked.

She nodded and closed her eyes briefly. "Something like that."

He held his hands out to her, not touching her but offering, waiting. "Come here."

"Oh, please," she whispered as she unwound her arms from Deacon's neck and took his hands. "Yes."

He pulled her into his arms, and she came willingly, trustingly, holding him much as she had grasped Deacon, as tremors racked her fragile body.

There was nothing sexual in her embrace, far from it. Megan seemed so much a lost child that Jake despised himself for the desire that gripped him. Too soon her tremors stopped, brought to a halt, he suspected, by a supreme act of control. Then she pulled slightly away from him and he saw the tears streaming down her cheeks.

"Don't tell me not to cry," she said, in a determined but tear-clogged voice.

Jake remembered Barbara's admonitions, remembered Megan's too-controlled reactions to events that should have sent her into hysterics. "No," he said, "I won't."

He rose to his feet and tugged on her hands until she stood also. Still tempted to try a grandstand play like sweeping her into his arms and carrying her from the room, Jake felt doubly frustrated, knowing that physically he could not, not tonight, and that he shouldn't, even if he had been able.

Instead, he led her to the overstuffed chair at the end of the sofa, settled into it, and pulled her onto his lap. He pushed her head down into the hollow of his throat and wrapped his arms around her.

He felt her small start before she settled against him. Now he had surprised her. Hell! He'd surprised himself. He'd never thought of himself as being a particularly sensitive person; too often Helen had accused him of being just the opposite.

She cried furtively, with tiny little tremors and whimpers, like someone ashamed or afraid of being found crying. He said nothing, merely held her as he listened to the thunder rumbling in the distance, stroked her arm, her hair, made comforting circles on her back, and felt totally incompetent in this business of giving aid and comfort.

Finally she hiccuped once, twice, and began swiping at her cheeks with her fingers.

So much for all this sensitivity crap, he thought with disgust. He didn't have a handkerchief, and the only disposable paper products in the house were toilet tissue and towels. He leaned over slightly, snagged Mattie's pillow off the end of the couch, and wrestled it out of its case, remembering as he did so another time when he had done something similar for—it had been Megan, hadn't it?—yes, for this woman.

He tried to hand her the case, but she only looked at it, shook her head reluctantly, and continued to wipe her fingers across her cheeks.

"Here," he said as he gently pushed her fingers away and began drying her cheeks with the pillowcase. For some reason, that only started the flood again. But this time, instead of sobs and hiccups the tears came silently, as she looked up at Jake with something like wonder in her eyes, and this time, instead of leaning into his embrace, she finally snatched the pillowcase and buried her face in it.

"Why were you sitting in here hugging my dog?" Jake asked.

She lowered the case and twisted her hands in it. For a long, silent moment he thought she wouldn't answer. "Because it was lonely in the dark," she said softly.

"You could have come to me."

She tilted her head slightly to look at him in the dim light of the room, studying his eyes, his expression, the set of his mouth, weighing what she found there and accepting it. Accepting him. "Now I know that."

The softly spoken words carried a wealth of trust, a wealth of longing. They touched him in a way Jake had never thought possible and at the same time wrapped a crushingly heavy burden around his heart.

"I thought you were asleep," he said. "If not, I would never have gone to bed and left you alone in the night."

"I know. That's why I finally turned off the light. You need your rest, Jake. I've deprived you of it too often."

"And your needs, Megan? What of them?"

"I need to face my past. Isn't that what everyone has been telling me?"

"Alone? In the dark? With nothing but a dog to hold on to?"

"And now you," she said.

The dim light from the kitchen still held them in shadow, and the thunder still rumbled in the distance, but Jake felt as though everything in his life had changed. "Yes," he said, pushing her head back into the hollow of his throat and wrapping her tightly in his arms. "And now me."

For minutes, as Jake listened to the soft sounds of her breathing, to the diminishing rush of the wind through the trees outside, and to the occasional splatter of rain tossed against the window screens, she lay quietly against him. Then he felt her shoulders tense slightly, as though she were gathering strength.

"My mother died when I was four," she said. "I didn't understand why she was gone. Someone, I don't know who, spanked me for crying and told me to act like a big girl. No one would talk to me about her. And later, probably much later but I can't be sure of that either, I overheard my father and the woman who became my stepmother discussing how much I should be told, or whether I should be told at all, because I really needed to forget my mother and talking about her kept me from doing so."

"Bastard," Jake muttered.

"No. Misguided, maybe, but I can't believe he was malicious. At least I didn't then. The night you rescued me," she said, not raising her head, making no effort to leave the safety of his arms. "When I was screaming?"

Jake nodded and rubbed his hand along her arm, trying to dispel the chill he felt.

"I remember some of it," she told him. "And one of the things I remember is thinking that the screams were too much for what was happening. Another was that I wasn't the one screaming, that whatever was happening wasn't really happening, or was happening to someone else.

"There was a girl at the clinic, a young native girl no more than fourteen. She screamed for a long time. I heard her for days as we walked through the jungle before I was at last able to turn off the sound.

"Tonight, when I found the destruction in my bedroom, I heard her again. I thought maybe she was the one. . . ."

Jake closed his eyes against the horrors Megan must have faced. If he wanted to do that, how much more must she? "And now?"

"I worked on my journal for a while tonight. Not for the right reasons—you know, putting all the pieces together—but because I thought I had found another way to escape. It didn't work."

"Megan," he murmured, rubbing his cheek against her soft, sweet-scented hair. "Oh, Megan."

"I think the screams are mine, Jake. And not just for Villa Castellano and Sheriff Pierson's raid but for something else, something buried so deep I don't really know it. And even though I don't want to, even though the thought of discovering something so horrible scares me senseless, I have to find out what it is."

He carried her to bed. To his bed. After all, he had done it before. And if his body protested, that was too damned bad. The need tonight—hers and his—was too great.

He stretched out beside her and gathered her to him in another of those passionless hugs he had been restricting himself to all evening, which she accepted, welcomed even, as she had all evening, and all went well, until suddenly it wasn't enough for him. He cradled her face in his hand and bent over her, telling himself it was just for a kiss, one kiss, one moment of sharing such as they had experienced in her kitchen, that was all, nothing more—and she cringed away from him.

He held himself still for a moment, cursing himself for wanting what he had known he couldn't have, cursing himself for rushing her at a time when she had to be damn near shell-shocked, and then eased down beside her.

"Jake." He heard the stunned disbelief in her voice, but for what, his actions or hers? "I'm sorry. I'm so sorry."

"Shh," he said. Cautiously, gently, he pulled her toward him in another of those damned passionless hugs. "It's all right," he promised, not knowing what *it* was but pretty sure that nothing was all right.

Except, he thought drowsily as he drew her slight weight next to him, as he felt her comforting warmth penetrating the chill that had too long been his life, as he drifted impossibly quickly toward sleep, she was in his arms and in his bed and in his life, this time to stay.

Sugarloaf County, Choctaw Nation Indian Territory, 1872

Of course I taught. On the first day of school I dressed in one of the dresses I had chosen a lifetime before but which now hung loosely on me, gathered the new books I had so carefully selected in that same lifetime, packed them into a satchel large enough to hold Sam's pistol, and allowed my brother to drive me to the small frame building halfway between our house and the community of Prescott.

This should have been a great honor for me. Although not one of the exceptional boarding schools the Choctaw Nation sponsored, this was a school for Choctaw children. The few white children and the even fewer freedmen's children had their own schools, which were less conveniently located than those for the children of the citizens.

Peter should not have been attending this school. He was of the age and of the privileged class to be sent back to the States for a more formal education, but he had refused to go. And although he had not given his reasons, I knew they in part concerned our father's latest moneymaking scheme. Daniel Tanner had decided raising cattle would be more profitable than attempting to raise cotton and had hired a number of workers to take care of the actual physical needs of his cattle and fields. And the workmen still came sporadically to work on the stone outbuilding.

"Lights, Lydia," our father had said when I asked about the building. "As in civilization. As in the gaslights your Aunt Margaret covets and does not yet have. Miners have been using carbide for years. With it contained outside the residence, it's perfectly safe. The plantation owners on the Red River use it."

That, of course, was the crowning argument. No question of safety from fire or explosion could counter it. No expense was too great, no extravagance too wild, when he felt he had been bested. The lighting fixtures he ordered had been arriving all summer, packed in crates of straw to protect the fragile cut glass and delicate crystals and painted isinglass. And if the white workmen seemed surly toward Peter or offensive toward me, our imaginations were working overtime because we feared progress.

So Peter didn't leave. Nor, for long weeks at a time, did Sam. Often I looked down the drive and saw him riding along the road past our house. Often, when I sat on the second-floor veranda outside my room, I felt him near. But he did not approach me. And I remembered him telling the army lieutenant that I was not, had never been, and never would be his woman. I'd known since the day I returned to this beautiful, harsh land that I would never be anyone's woman. Why then did the knowledge that I would never be Sam's bring me so much pain?

Why did his pain bring me so much more pain?

Because Sam *was* in pain. I saw it in the days I spent with Granny Rogers; I saw it in his eyes when he encouraged me to teach. I felt it in the distance he now kept between us, a distance that even when I was in the throes of my childish and probably embarrassing love for him he had not forced himself to keep.

I had eighteen students, ranging in age from tiny little Therese LeFlore to Will Henry. Most of my students were of mixed blood, because Sugarloaf County had been settled primarily by mixed bloods at the time of the removal from Mississippi, and its proximity to Fort Smith had made incursions and later intermarriage by whites or mixed-blood Cherokees from Arkansas possible.

Will's father, like ours, was one of those whites from Arkansas who capitalized on the advantages of Indian citizenship. Unlike ours, he hadn't been quite as successful in his business ventures as he had expected to be.

Will was a bully. With a quarter, or some said less, Choctaw blood, he looked down on those with more. With pretensions to wealth, he looked down on those with less. Peter stood toe to toe, even a little above him, in standing in the community, but several inches shorter in physical stature. Still, he stood up to him, defending those smaller or weaker than himself—and me.

Will decided he was much too important for me to discipline, much too fascinating for me to ignore, and, even though I was older, I was, after all, Daniel Tanner's daughter and would make a suitable wife for him. If, of course, I was or could be made malleable. And if, of course, I could be brought to succumb to his less than subtle advances.

Advances that once I would have met with a sharp slap of the ruler.

Advances that once I would have laughed about.

Advances that, because of his size, brought back too many memories for me to do anything but shrink into a silent shell, leaving Peter, valiant Peter, to defend me.

One day Peter was kept busy with our father's ventures and did not return in time to accompany me home from school. Will intercepted me at the turnoff to the tree-shaded road that led to our house and eventually to Granny Rogers's, a road that held too many memories of another interception, another oversized bully.

He attempted to grab my satchel from me, announcing that he would carry it. And then he attempted to grab me.

I panicked.

I swung the satchel at him, striking him in the chest and causing him to stagger, then tore out across the country-side—straight into the arms of one of my father's imported white workmen.

"Damn, little girl," he said. "What's got you so afraid? Looks like you need a man to take care of you."

Did he mean me harm? I will never know. But at that moment he was all my nightmares, all my fears.

I backed away from him, tugging Sam's gun from the satchel and pointing it at the workman, until I stood pressed against a tree with nowhere to run.

"She has one."

Sam's voice sounded through my panic.

"And if he ever catches you bothering her again," he said easily, "you'll be a dead man."

The man blanched. "Hell, Hooker. She came running right at me. I didn't hurt her."

"I know. That's why you're still alive. But maybe you'd better give serious thought to finding another job. Somewhere far away from here. Starting now."

I didn't watch as the man left. I was too mortified by my loss of control and still too caught up in my fear.

I felt Sam's hands on mine as he pried my fingers from the gun; then, cautiously, he took me in his arms, wrapping me in safety. "I'm sorry," I said. Over and over I repeated it. "I'm so sorry."

"No, I'm the one who should be sorry. I trusted your father and Peter to look out for you. I was wrong."

I became aware then of his arms around me, of his warmth, and of his closeness. Of his size. Of the strength which I knew in my heart, but not in my poor tortured mind, that he would never use against me. With a whimper I pushed him away. And he went.

"Lydia," he said, not touching me now but so close I still felt as though he did. "Lydia, look at me."

I could not step back; the tree held me captive. I tilted my head and looked up into his troubled eyes. "This isn't working, is it?"

I didn't know what he meant. My expression must have told him that.

"I thought that once you returned home you would begin to heal, that you would be able to put at least some of what happened behind you. But you haven't."

"How can I?" I asked him. "Please tell me how to forget."

He closed his eyes momentarily. "I don't know," he said. "But you can't go on this way, losing weight, looking like death, taking flight instead of fighting back."

I dipped my head, unable to look at him any longer. "Fighting did no good."

"Lydia."

I felt his hands on my shoulders, and even knowing who touched me, I tensed. I tensed but I forced myself not to flinch away.

"Oh, Lydia. What have I done to you? What have I done?"

"You?" I straightened my spine and faced him. "You've done nothing except rescue me. Still again."

"And still again after you have been hurt."

"Hurt? No. No, Sam. No one hurt me this time."

"No? Then why are you trembling? Why can you not look at me? You were frightened, and I was not there to prevent it. I want the right to be there always, Lydia. I want the right—"

Thick with emotion, his words broke off.

"What are you saying?"

He looked at me, lifted my face to his with a calloused palm, and curved his mouth in a bitter, twisted smile. "What I should have said to you before you left for school. I want to marry you."

I felt my heart catch before it raced upward to my throat. Once I would have given my life to hear him speak those words. Now I knew how truly impossible they were.

"I can't," I said in a choked whisper. "You of all people must know I can never truly be any man's wife."

"Yes," he said, and I heard the weight of the rest of my empty years in his voice. "Yes, I know."

16

Deacon barked.

The sound was so alien that for several seconds it didn't penetrate Megan's consciousness. Then she jerked awake.

She was in Jake Kenyon's bed. In his arms. And he was smiling at her, a lazy, good-morning, everything's-right-with-the-world, *rested* smile. As though it was the most natural thing in the world, she lifted her hand to caress his jaw and let her fingers trail over the dark stubble of his morning beard and the lower edges of the upward-cutting scar.

Deacon barked again from somewhere inside the house, and Megan heard the sound of a distant engine groaning its way up the hill.

"Someone's coming," she warned, although Jake didn't look the least upset.

"Probably Patrick," he told her. "He does have lousy timing, doesn't he? Good morning."

Jake also didn't seem upset that she had practically crawled on top of him during the night. Megan felt a flush beginning with her toes and climbing all the way to the roots of her horrible hair.

Now both her hands rested on his chest, but when she tried to pull away he captured them, holding her still. "Not yet," he said. "Not when this seems so right."

And it did. Megan stopped her efforts to move and absorbed that knowledge. Everything about them had seemed right since he had come to her last night—everything but that one moment when memories of Lydia had intruded, and that hadn't been Jake's fault.

"How can you tell?"

"That this seems right?" he asked, still smiling contentedly, still holding her hands against his chest.

"No. That it's Patrick who's coming."

He released one of her hands and traced a gentle pattern along her cheek. "Because you haven't managed to completely ruin my dog yet," he said. "That's not his warning bark; that's a demand: 'Let me out so I can go play.' And the only other person he ever played with, before you, is Patrick Phillips. Besides, I'm expecting him."

As she turned her cheek to his touch, warming to it, welcoming it, she felt Jake's breath catch. She tilted her head and saw his eyes darken, saw his smile fade.

"Megan," he said, all seriousness as his hand captured her face and held her still. "In about five seconds, I'm going to kiss you. So if the thought frightens you or repulses you, you'd better tell me now."

Now her breath caught, and the flush that warmed her was not from embarrassment but from something much more elemental. She felt her heart pounding in her chest, felt the answering rhythm of his heart beneath her hands. Felt his hesitancy as he waited for her answer.

"Never, Jake," she whispered.

She saw the doubt in his eyes and knew what she had done to cause it. In a moment that been all tenderness and giving, she had cringed away from him. She didn't know yet why she had done it, other than because of those fleeting images of Lydia that had crowded in on her, but she knew this man had done nothing to deserve that reaction.

"Never you," she insisted. Still he hesitated. Once again she lifted her hand to his cheek. "Never you," she repeated.

The touch of Jake's lips on hers was like coming home. Megan closed her eyes, sighed a welcome, and slid her hand around to the nape of his neck, urging him closer as she moved, impossibly, closer to him.

She had thought her response to their kiss last night was a fluke, a reaction to all the shocks of the day, that nothing could be so right. She had been wrong. She belonged with this man as she had never belonged with anyone else. She wanted this man as she had never wanted anyone else. She loved—

She heard the roar of an engine and the blare of a horn. Jake shuddered once, moved his lips to her throat in a sensual assault that had her heart spinning, and lifted his head. His hand trembled when he cupped her cheek.

"Damn," he said in a breathless whisper. "I'm going to have to have a talk with our friend Patrick, maybe even send him back to eastern Europe."

She saw frustration in his eyes, but he dragged up a smile for her.

"It's too soon for us, Megan, I know that. But I also know there is something between us and we are going to have to explore it." He pulled away and stood up, tucking his shirt into his jeans. "If you want to make a run for the guest room and your clothes, I'll keep Patrick outside for a while. Or if you want to stay in bed a while longer, I'll try to keep him quiet so you can rest."

She knew the frustration he felt; she felt it too. What she wanted to do was stay there in his bed and in his arms and begin the exploration he spoke of. What she wanted to do was forget about the reason Patrick Phillips had come, forget about why it was too soon for the two of them, forget about all the problems that faced them. But she wasn't going to do that. Not ever again. That was the promise she had made to herself in the dark of the night while she sat on a cold stone hearth hugging Jake's dog. That was the promise she was going to keep, if she could—regardless of how painful it became to do so.

"Thirty seconds," she said.

Jake raised an eyebrow in silent question.

"I need thirty seconds to get down the hall," she explained, "and five minutes to throw on some clothes. Then I'll help you with breakfast."

He smiled, leaned over, and brushed a lingering kiss on her cheek. "Good girl," he said.

At the door, Deacon went scrambling outside when Jake unlatched and opened the screen, skidding to a halt and waiting for Patrick to scratch that special place beneath his chin that only Patrick could find. Jake followed more slowly and leaned against the fender of Patrick's pickup. Finally Patrick reached into the open cab of his truck, retrieved a foot-long twisted rawhide chew bone, and sent it sailing across the yard with Deacon in hot pursuit. Then he turned to look at Jake.

"Don't you know the Miami Vice look went out of style a long time ago?"

Jake ran his hand over the stubble on his chin and grinned. "Maybe if you hadn't gotten out here at the crack of dawn, I'd have had time to shave. Don't you have to work?"

Patrick chuckled. "It's Saturday, my friend; I don't have another edition to get out for two days. And dawn's been cracked for several hours."

"So you thought you'd just run on out here, check on us, and finish spoiling my dog."

"Yep." Patrick gave him a quick, remorseless grin before turning solemn. "Bad night?"

Jake nodded. "Bad enough."

"How is she?"

Soft. Tempting. More than he'd ever thought he'd find. All that he'd ever want.

"Okay," Jake said. "As well as can be expected."

"Good." Patrick slammed the truck door. "I left the window glass at her place. I didn't think it would be too smart to risk hauling it all the way up your road and then back down. And I brought the dead-bolt lock set, so we can get that on today too. After you pour some coffee down me. I haven't had nearly enough caffeine this morning.

"Good morning, Megan. You're looking lovely today."

Jake turned toward the porch. Megan had dressed in what had to be record-breaking time and stood there in jeans and a cotton sweater with her face scrubbed clean and her hair whipped into a semblance of style. Her reddened eyes bore silent witness to her grief of the night before, but to him she looked brave and valiant and, yes, lovely.

She grimaced and shrugged. "I look like death warmed over and you know it, Patrick Phillips," she said, but without heat.

Patrick stopped on the step below her, leering and twisting an imaginary mustache. "But on you, pretty lady, even that looks good."

"Ha!" She threw a glance at Jake. "He's your friend; can't you do something about him?"

"Yeah." Jake growled the word, only half in humor, crossed the yard, and mounted the porch. There he threw his arm over Megan's shoulder, ignoring her start of surprise other than to give her a slight hug. "Patrick, old man," he said, "you're poaching."

Silently Patrick looked at the two of them. Then a wide grin lighted his face. "Good," he said. "Now can I please have some coffee?"

Megan surrendered the old-fashioned stove-top percolator to Jake but immediately lighted the oven and began gathering bacon and eggs and frozen biscuit dough while he built the pot and put it on the burner to perk. The actions were familiar enough so that he was able to turn his attention to Patrick's reason for being there and to the events of the night before.

"Did you have any trouble getting enough window glass?" he asked.

Patrick shook his head. "No, but the new fellow at the lumberyard—what's his name, Mack?"

"Yeah," Jake said.

"What's his story? He asked so many questions I may have to hire him as a reporter."

"If Walt Harrison runs true to form," Jake told him, "he'll be needing a job soon. Maybe you can cut a deal."

"Yeah, sure. Anyway, I finally told him a part of the truth, that I was closing in a sleeping porch. Don't know why I didn't just come out and spill the whole story. I'm perverse, I guess. Wanted to see how long this story takes to circulate and what version finally prevails. Young Charley's bound to talk to his family. And you know the Harrisons—all of them, not just Walt—can't keep a secret. If God told them their salvation depended upon keeping one, they'd sell the story of His appearance to the *National Enquirer* and then sell the secret.

"Oh, by the way," Patrick said, as Jake grabbed the coffeepot just as it began to boil over. "Speaking of secrets, I've got one the two of you should know about."

Jake lowered the flame on the burner and set the pot back. He looked up to see Megan watching Patrick with something like dread in her eyes. "Spill it," he said.

Patrick seemed to notice Megan's expression too. "Right. It's bad enough," he said to her, "but not, I think, as bad as you're expecting. Why don't the two of you stop and sit down for a minute?"

Jake raised an eyebrow, but he held a chair for Megan and dropped a hand onto her shoulder.

"I found an anonymous letter under my door when I went by the office last night," Patrick told them. "All it said was that I should contact the police department in Knoxville,

Tennessee, about Max Renfro. Now I don't have any connections with the Knoxville P.D., but it just so happens I shared a couple of assignments with the man who now heads the journalism department at the University of Tennessee. *He's* the one who ought to complain about crack-of-dawn—"

"Patrick," Jake warned.

"Yeah." Patrick fumbled in his shirt pocket and pulled out a sheet of paper. "He faxed me this police report. It seems our buddy Max was run down by a hit-and-run driver last Sunday night."

"How bad was he hurt?"

"How bad is dead?"

Megan gasped, and Jake tightened his hand on her shoulder. "Sunday night?" he asked. "Two nights *before* the search warrant? Our local people didn't know by then?"

Patrick unfolded the paper and read from it.

A routine check for warrants showed an outstanding warrant for possession with intent to deliver from Pitchlyn County, Oklahoma. The sheriff's office at Fairview was notified of Renfro's death at 9:07 P.M. but the deputy on duty was unable to give any information as to the warrant. This officer was advised that Pitchlyn County would contact us Monday A.M.

"And did they?"

Patrick folded the paper. "Don't know. What do you think?"

"I think it would be interesting to find out. And interesting to know how Knoxville found the information so quickly on a state charge on a two-bit hood like Renfro. Could your buddy look into that for us?"

"He could," Patrick said. "As a matter of fact, he already is. But I was thinking we might get more results if we called in some of *your* buddies."

Jake shook his head. "I don't think they're going to be

interested in a botched search warrant, a dead small-time dealer, and a corrupt sheriff."

"Not even with one of their own, still recuperating from being shot up, sitting right in the middle of this mess?"

He felt Megan's shoulder jerk beneath his hand as she turned to look up at him and saw the quick flash of fear in her eyes. For him? Damn!

"But I'm not one of their own, Patrick," he said, looking at Megan while he spoke. "Not anymore except in the strictest interpretation. And I'm not going back when my leave of absence is up. I'd made my mind up before I left; I don't know why I let them talk me out of quitting outright."

"Coffee."

Tensed for an argument, Jake only stared at Patrick for a moment. "What?"

Patrick smiled. "The coffee is ready. I know what it means to come home, my friend. And I know how unsure I was that I was making the right decision. So unsure that I left myself an escape hatch too. So let's drink our coffee, eat our breakfast, and fix our windows. There's no need to fight old fights over again. We're both where we want to be, even if our little version of Eden does appear to have a few serpents in it."

"You're sure you won't come with us?"

Megan tried to ignore the concern in Jake's eyes; it too closely echoed her own.

"I'm sure. You don't need me getting in your way. And I need to do this."

"You're sure you'll be all right?"

Because she wasn't sure, she smiled. "That sounds amazingly like our favorite question."

"Don't," he said. "This is too important for jokes. You're too important."

She looked through the open door to where Patrick

waited beside his truck. "You two will be between me and the road. You've left me a guard dog and a pistol big enough to use as a club if I can't bear to pull the trigger. Nothing can possibly hurt me."

"Except what you find in that damned journal."

"Please don't," she said. "Not when I've finally decided I must do this. Dr. Kent was right, Jake. I have to put all the pieces of myself back together. If what I've found so far seems alien to me, I have to think it's an allegory, even some dreamlike symbolism. It can't hurt me—unless I don't follow it through to the hidden meaning."

"Megan."

She shook her head and stepped back from him. "Go. Please. And remember: you two are there to fix the windows and the lock only. Don't even think about starting the cleanup."

After Jake and Patrick left, Megan wandered around Jake's house with the brown leather notebook clutched to her, trying to find a place that felt right to delve into her mysteries. Finally convinced there was no right place, she dumped her few toiletries out of the tote she'd packed them in and replaced them with the notebook, an apple, a small plastic jug of water, and, reluctantly, Jake's pistol.

Slinging the tote over her shoulder she scooped up the two black cats, which had returned to curl up on the bed.

"Come on, you two. I've neglected you shamelessly the last few days, but I know a place you're going to love."

But as she reached the front door, the telephone rang—as alien a sound in this comfortable old house as it was in her own—surprising her so that she tightened her grip on the kittens she held cuddled in her arms, sending them into a startled frenzy to escape her hold.

"Oh, all *right*!," she said, releasing them to let them drop down onto the back of Jake's sofa.

Should she answer it or ignore it? No one knew she was there except Jake. What if he was calling to check on her? Or

Barbara, looking for Patrick? No, she couldn't ignore it. Once again she was stuck answering a mechanical summons.

She circled the couch and picked up the receiver of the plain black desk phone. "Hello?"

Static-filled silence greeted her and held her quiet and still for a long count of five, before a harsh whisper grated over the line. "You bitch. Go back where you belong before more than a bedroom wall gets blown to pieces."

Megan gripped the phone long after the dial tone hummed in her ear, not truly believing what she had heard. When the electronic squawk signaling a phone off the hook sounded, she jumped, looked at the receiver, and carefully replaced it.

Just as carefully she curled into the chair where Jake had held her only hours before, comforting her, making her feel as though she could face just about anything.

If she worked at it really hard, she could convince herself that all the violence in her life so far, even the damage to her home, had been random, not really directed at her.

But this? Who would threaten her? Why?

All she wanted was to live a quiet, peaceful life. Was that too much to ask?

With a whine, Deacon thrust his nose into her lap and up under her fisted hands.

Jake stopped in the doorway to Megan's bedroom. The travesty inside didn't look any better in the light of day; it looked worse. Rain had lashed in through the shattered windows during the night, mixing with the plaster dust and soaking the strewn clothing.

He heard Patrick stop behind him and sigh. "Does she really think we can ignore this and not try to put it back in some semblance of order?"

"Probably," Jake told him. "It seems she's been surrounded by the kind of people who could do just that most of her life."

He stepped a little farther into the room and bent to retrieve a once-white garment from a pile on the floor. The nightgown he had found Megan wearing—had it just been the morning before? He touched it with a gentleness at war with the rage running through him at the careless hands that had thrown it down. What would have happened if whoever had destroyed this room had found her alone as he had?

It didn't bear thinking of.

"I'm worried about her," he said instead.

"Probably with good reason," Patrick told him. "This is enough to shake anyone up, even without all that's gone before."

"Yeah. Where's Barbara?"

"She was going to wind up at Mattie's after she took care of some errands. Do you think she needs to come on out now? I know she was planning to later, but I can call her if you want."

"It's that damned journal," Jake admitted. "As if all this isn't enough, something strange has been happening to Megan with that infernal thing." And to him, without benefit of the book, he admitted to himself as a vision of Megan, yet not Megan, sitting in front of the fire combing her long hair ran through his memory. He found he was clutching the soft, damp fabric of the nightgown. "Yeah. I think you'd better call her."

He scooped up a pile of the tumbled clothing.

"This stuff will mildew by tomorrow if we just leave it here. I think I'll hang the things that are still on hangers over the shower curtain rod to dry and start a load of the washable stuff through the washer and dryer while you're tracking Barbara down."

A few minutes later Patrick carried another load of wet clothing into the small utility room and dumped it in the basket Jake indicated. "Mattie said she hasn't gotten there yet, but she'll have her call the minute she does."

Jake grunted a nonverbal response as he closed the lid on the washing machine and gathered up broom, dustpan, mop, and bucket. "It's a good thing we know how to batch, isn't it?" he asked, thrusting the broom and mop at Patrick.

"Jake."

Damn. It had been a long time since he had heard Patrick use that voice. It was the one he'd used when he'd come to Jake's dorm room at college to tell him Aunt Sally was dead. It was the one he'd used when Jake had awakened in the hospital and Patrick had to tell him that not only was he facing more surgery but the whole plan to trap the drug traffickers had been shot to hell almost as bad as he had. No arrests, no contraband. Nada. Zip. Nil. It was the same voice he had used in that same hospital to tell him Helen had been killed in a village in South America. And he didn't want to hear it now.

"After we get this little clean-up chore finished, which do you want, inside or out for the windows?" he said.

"Jake. It seems to me that Megan isn't the only one having trouble confronting reality. This has gone way beyond dirty politics. Call the agency. Or let me. It's time to get someone else involved."

"And wind up owing them my soul after all?" Jake asked. "I barely escaped with it the first time I got out."

"Not true, my friend. You had some serious chips and cracks when you came home, but the essential you was still intact. *Is* still intact."

"How much longer would it have been? What if I hadn't come home in time?"

"But you did."

"If I call them in on this, I'll owe them, Patrick. And they want me back."

Patrick took the broom and mop. He sighed and gave a lopsided grin. "I'll take inside," he said. "There's no way I'm risking this body ten feet off the ground with sheets of glass in my hands. But while you're out there climbing around on the ladder, you might give some serious thought to what your not calling in your crew could mean to Megan."

Megan had no idea how long she had been sitting in Jake's chair, holding his dog, when she heard a car horn honking as it approached the house. A horn. And she hadn't heard noises of the engine coming up the hill.

She looked up, distracted. Some time had passed, maybe a great deal of time. For a moment she was frightened, by the approaching car, by the missing time. Then Deacon whined, gave her wrist a wet sloppy swipe of his tongue, and thumped his tail against the floor.

"A friend, hm?" she asked him. Even to her, her voice sounded rusty and unused. She released her hold on the dog, smoothed her hair, and scrubbed at her eyes with unsteady hands, acknowledging as she did that she couldn't look any worse than she had already appeared that morning to Patrick.

Megan heard the car pull to a stop in the drive and forced herself to get up out of the chair and walk to the door.

Yes. A friend.

She recognized Barbara just before her new friend bent toward the open passenger door to help someone out.

Granny Rogers?

Megan stared open-mouthed at the tiny woman emerging from the car. Her hair was totally silvered, and she was much older, but she bore an amazing resemblance to the woman Megan had seen twice now at the quilt frame in this house. She bore an amazing resemblance—to Barbara.

Megan sighed and sank against the door facing. Barbara's mother. Jake's beloved Mattie. She felt as though a huge piece of a puzzle she had been slaving over had just dropped into place. Her conscious mind might not have remembered Barbara the morning after the raid, but obviously her subconscious had and had embellished that memory, aging it and placing it in a scenario that one day she might understand as well as she understood now from where she had drawn the image of the older woman.

Now Barbara was bent over the open rear door into the backseat. She straightened and turned, holding a large split-reed basket that from the way she held it appeared to have some weight.

"Hi!" she called. "The fellows will be here in a bit, but they said to come on up."

Megan stepped onto the porch and smiled at Barbara, but her attention was really on Barbara's mother. She found Mattie's dark eyes focused on her with what appeared to be a sad, knowing smile.

Well, that's just great, she thought. Someone else to feel sorry for me. She gave herself a mental shake. None of these people felt *sorry* for her. What they felt was compassion and friendship, and while these had been missing from her life for so long, she did recognize them as something infinitely precious.

She stepped off the porch and met her visitors in the yard. "Here, let me help you with that basket."

Barbara shook her head. "Thanks anyway. Let me introduce the two of you. Mother, this is Megan. Megan, my mother, Mattie Hinkle."

Mattie's once-slender hand was gnarled and paper dry in Megan's, but her grasp was firm.

"I'm so happy to meet you," Megan told her. "Jake thinks very highly of you."

"And my daughter thinks highly of you, child. I hope you don't mind that I came without an invitation."

"Mind? I've been looking forward to meeting you, and to telling you how much I've enjoyed your bread. Besides, this is Jake's house, and I'm sure you don't need an invitation to visit him."

Mattie smiled at her as she patted her hand. Then she rested her hand on Megan's arm and turned to look at the house. "Yes," she said softly. "Yes!"

Megan looked up in question and caught Barbara's eye. Barbara shrugged and shook her head. "Patrick had talked to Mom before I got there, but the gist of his end of the conversation seemed to be 'Bring food; Jake's working me into the ground.' Anyway, Mom had this ready by the time I arrived."

Megan laughed and turned to help Mattie up onto the porch. "I think Patrick must have two hollow legs. How does he eat so much and still manage to stay slender?"

Inside the house, Megan waited while Mattie settled into a smaller version of Jake's big chair, at the opposite end of the sofa. But when she excused herself to join Barbara, who had carried the basket into the kitchen, Mattie stopped her with a gentle shake of her head and an equally gentle hand on her arm.

"Sit with me, please,"

Wanting to stay but feeling she ought to be helping, Megan looked toward the kitchen door.

"Barbara's all right, child. She knows her way around that kitchen."

"Yes, of course. But can I—" Realizing she was comfortable acting as hostess in Jake's house, Megan bit off her words. If anyone was qualified to act as hostess, surely it was Mattie Hinkle, second love of Jake's life. With a rueful grin, Megan settled on the end of the sofa near Mattie.

"Mom, what's this doing in the picnic basket?" Barbara asked as she rounded the corner from the kitchen carrying a large book.

Mattie reached for it, and Megan saw it was an ornate old photograph album. "I brought some of my special herb-blend tea. Please put the kettle on, dear, while Megan and I visit."

Barbara frowned, but Megan saw at once that it was from confusion. Again she shrugged. "Sure, Mom."

When Barbara left the room, Mattie smoothed her hands over the cover of the album in her lap. "My daughter tells me you are interested in my grandfather's family."

Pictures, perhaps of Lydia? But no. She had already accepted that her dreams, the journal, all the events with Lydia were only her, Megan's, way of dealing with the turmoil in her own life. Still, she clasped her hands together to keep from reaching for the book.

Her throat tightened. Her voice almost deserted her. "You have pictures?" she asked.

"Not many. Most were lost with the house. These, by what appears now to be an almost unbelievable coincidence, were here, in this house, when Grandfather Tanner's house burned."

After she spoke, Mattie remained quiet with her hands folded and still on the album, holding it closed while she studied Megan intently, once again with that sad, knowing smile.

Eventually, though, she seemed to rouse herself from her own version of the mini-vacations Jake and Patrick accused Megan of. She lifted the heavy book and offered it to Megan.

Almost hesitantly, Megan took it. For a moment she just held it, running her hands over the worn padded-velvet cover and tracing her fingers along the edge of the lavishly embossed clasp. Then, with a questioning look at Mattie, who waited, still smiling that smile, she unfastened the clasp and opened the cover.

It was the kind of album designed to showcase valuable and at that time costly photographs. The pages were mats, holding the portraits in place, one, occasionally two, to a page. The first photograph, studio posed, was of a stern prosperous-looking man with light-colored hair and a high, tight collar; the next, of a gentle, almost ethereally beautiful young woman. Both were white; both were unfamiliar to Megan. She began to breathe a little easier.

The next was of a Choctaw woman, a little older than the first woman but dressed in the same expensive fashion.

Smiling at the unaccustomed fashion and poses, Megan turned the page.

Her fingers froze on the book.

Two poses, both portrait quality, showed him slightly younger than she had first seen him at the creek and again a few years older.

"Peter," she said on a quiet breath.

She heard Mattie moving in the chair and sensed she was reaching out to her. Hesitantly she turned the page. Lydia looked up from the old portrait in all her youthful innocence.

Megan sank back against the sofa cushions, eyes closed, gripping the book.

"You know who she is."

Megan looked at her. Mattie's words carried not one hint of question. That was all right. She had plenty of questions of her own. Soon. Just as soon as her heart stopped trying to pound its way out of her chest.

Mattie reached over and drew an unmounted photograph from the back of the book. She placed it across the page in front of Megan and waited.

Lydia as she had become, too old for her years, stood side by side with, but not touching, a tall, lean, infinitely weary Sam Hooker on the front porch of what was probably this house. Beside them, almost as a guard of honor, stood a too-mature adolescent Peter Tanner and the woman Megan knew only as Granny Rogers.

She looked up at Barbara's mother and knew she was dangerously close to hysteria. "Why?" she whispered, knowing no one, least of all this aged woman, could know the answer. "Why?"

17

Mattie tugged the book from Megan's nerveless fingers and placed it on the sofa beside her. With great care, she rose from the chair and crossed the room to the kitchen doorway.

"Megan and I are going outside now," she said. "We will return shortly."

It was probably the way she said it that kept Barbara from questioning her words. Megan knew it kept *her* from questioning.

Mattie returned to stand in front of her. "We will walk," she said. "And perhaps we will find answers. Or at least the right questions."

Megan sat, stunned.

"We will walk," Mattie repeated, and Megan realized through the haze that surrounded her that the woman would probably wait indefinitely for her to rise.

"Yes," she said, suddenly needing to move. "Yes."

Outside, Mattie turned toward the cluster of small buildings at the rear of the clearing. For someone whose hands bore such painful signs of arthritis, she walked remarkably unhampered by the disease. Though unhurried, her step seemed almost determined, as if she had made up her mind about something and now must see it through.

She stopped outside a large barnlike building with what appeared to be double-hung sliding doors as well as a smaller wooden door with a many-paned window. A whimsical wooden bench painted in Shaker green sat beneath a lattice and vine-covered arbor beside the people-sized door. Mattie sank onto the bench and patted the seat beside her.

Megan joined her on the bench. Her mind was full of the questions Mattie had suggested they might find, but she waited, silent, for the woman to speak.

Still, she did not expect the words Mattie spoke.

"Where have you seen them?"

"What?"

Mattie reached over and patted Megan's shoulder. "I suspected you had not told my daughter. That's one of the reasons I brought you out here. But it is time to speak of these things, child. Where have you seen Lydia?"

Oh, my God. She knew! But how?

Megan started to rise, but Mattie's hand restrained her. "Where, child?"

"It isn't my imagination?"

Mattie shook her head. "Where?"

Megan looked away, toward the wooded area stretching down to the creek. "In the house," she said finally. "With a woman she called Granny Rogers."

Mattie's voice filled with awe. "In Jacob's house. Imagine that. Did Jacob see them?"

Megan shook her head. "No. At least I don't think so." Surely if he had, he would have said something when she bared her tormented thoughts to him, wouldn't he? "No."

"And where else?" Mattie asked.

Megan caught her hand to her mouth to hold back an

incriminating sob. "Are you so very sure there was some-where else?"

Mattie nodded, smiled, and gave Megan's shoulder a gen-tle squeeze. "You recognized my grandfather."

Yes, she had. "At the creek," Megan admitted. She might as well; she was damned already. "At the place Jake calls—Peter called—Waterfall Canyon. He called his sister 'Liddy.' Both of them were so very young."

"Lydia was being sent away to school. Sam Hooker brought her a diary to take with her."

Megan twisted around to stare at Mattie. "How did you—"

"Oh, child. I was six, maybe seven, the first time I saw them," Mattie said. "I ran to my grandfather Peter, sure that I had seen ghosts. He questioned me and then asked how I could have seen ghosts when he still lived."

"But how—?"

Mattie released her shoulder and stood, flexing her hands to ease them, straightening her shoulders to ease them too. "In our religion, the old one, everything is vested with spirit. Everything is part of the whole. In our language, 'to go' is the same as 'to have gone.' There is no differentiation as to time.

"I went often to the creek and its natural dam. Even when I did not see grandfather or Lydia or Sam, I felt a peace there, a continuity too often lacking in my world, a harmony with all that had been, all that was, and all that would be."

"Even knowing what later happened?"

Mattie looked down at her. "Do you know what hap-pened?"

Did she? Megan wasn't sure she knew much of anything after Mattie's startling revelation. But maybe she did. And maybe it was time to tell someone.

"I'm having her dreams," she said softly. "I'm having thoughts and memories that must belong to her. I'm—I'm writing her diary."

Mattie studied her silently before turning and looking toward the wooded hillside.

"Good," she said finally, surprising Megan even more. "Good." Her voice was little more than a whisper. "Now, perhaps, the mystery will be solved."

"What mystery?"

Both women turned at the question. Mattie recovered first.

"Jacob." She extended her hand toward him long before he reached her side. "I should have known you'd be out here searching for this lovely young woman. Have you and that scoundrel son-in-law of mine finished your carpentering?"

"Yep." Jake glanced questioningly at Megan before focusing again on Mattie. "What mystery?"

"History, Jacob."

Megan quickly masked her shock at Mattie's statement. But the woman was so straightforward and seemed so innocent she began to doubt that she, too, had heard the word "mystery." Was Mattie hiding the contents of their conversation? Or was she merely attempting to define the mystery?

"I was telling Megan some of my family history," Mattie said, as she turned toward him for a kiss. "Have you shown this delightful child your workshop yet?"

Jake gave her the expected buss on the cheek. "Not yet."

"Well, yes. I suppose you have been busy. But why don't you open it up now? I want to see what progress you've made, and I'm sure Megan would be interested."

"You are, are you?" Smiling, but in such a way that he let Megan and Mattie both know he was only humoring them and not believing for a moment that Mattie wasn't trying to hide something from him, Jake walked to the corner of the building and ran his hand behind a trellis on which grew an ancient clematis, drooping with the weight of hundreds of huge purple blossoms.

He returned with a jailer's ring containing several keys

and unlocked the door. Holding it open, he gave a mock bow and stepped back for them to enter. Mattie marched in determinedly. Megan followed a little more slowly. She felt the weight of Jake's hand on her shoulder.

"Mystery?" he whispered.

"I heard what you said, Jacob," Mattie said lightly. "Do you doubt my words?"

Jake grinned and flipped on a bank of switches, flooding the room with light from various overhead fluorescent fixtures. Megan looked around in amazement. Whatever she had expected from Jake's workshop, it wasn't this professional-looking room that looked to be a woodworker's dream.

Numerous hand tools hung neatly from pegboards on the wall, while workbenches and freestanding power tools occupied the concrete floor space. Against one wall, a set of shelves held sheets of plywood and banks of lumber, and against another stood various projects in different stages of completion.

Mattie walked to the wall with the projects and ran a loving hand over a mock-up of a doorway, complete with Victorian detailed facings in what appeared to be cherry.

"How soon?" she asked.

"Only a couple of days, once I get back in the shop."

Mattie nodded. "I can wait. For this, it will be worth it."

"Mattie's the one who really convinced me I might be able to make something out of my hobby," Jake said to Megan as he too touched the wood, with something approaching reverence. "Do you have any idea how many people are restoring old houses today, how many people are looking for millwork to match that of craftsmen of a hundred years ago?"

Mattie sighed and looked around the shop. "That sawmill contraption you bought from Tom Haney? Where is it?"

Jake nodded toward the second set of doors, those at the back of the workroom. "Under the shed out there."

Mattie nodded. "That's a good place for it. It's not far from where the other one was. I don't suppose there's much left now, what with the ravages of rain and time and the overgrowth, but when I was a child I could still find traces of what had been huge piles of sawdust in what was a cleared area near—well, somewhere near here."

Megan shot a glance at Jake's face. She had an idea of what was coming, but did he?

"Sam Hooker was a lawman." Mattie walked to another delightful bench, a not-yet-painted twin of the one outside, and sat down. "Like you, Jacob."

Jacob lifted one questioning eyebrow before he nodded at her. "Oh, yes. The mysterious Sam Hooker that Sarah North has been telling Megan about."

Mattie glanced pointedly at Megan.

"I asked if she knew anything about him."

"Yes." Mattie nodded. "You would." She looked back at Jake. "His mother was Choctaw, but she died in Mississippi without ever coming west. His father was a white man who took his son to Texas and raised him as white as he could. Samuel became a Texas Ranger, fighting Indians as well as outlaws, until he discovered that he had to know about the half his father had kept hidden from him. He came to the territory in search of his mother's family. He married. He fathered a child. And since there was little need for his skills as an Indian fighter, or trust for this stranger as an enforcer of the law, he made his living with a sawmill, cutting lumber for the new towns going up, for the new homes being built. When war was forced upon us, he took up arms for the Confederacy to defend his new country for his wife and for his child.

"When he returned, he found his wife and child both dead and his wife's mother struggling to keep this place going. Little remained but the cabin, which has become the house where you now live, and the smashed and broken remains of his mill."

Mattie sighed and settled more comfortably on the bench.

"I heard this from my grandfather when I was but a child, so some of the details are a little sketchy. Having proved his loyalties in the war, Samuel was rewarded by being taken into the Lighthorse, which must have been a mixed blessing for him. Whites were allowed into the territory to work only with permission of the Choctaw government, but in order to enforce the laws against a white person, a member of our police had to seek out a U.S. marshal. I doubt that Samuel had been accustomed to seeking help or asking permission from anyone before that time."

"And the army payroll?" Jake asked. "When did that interesting bit of history evolve?"

"Jacob," Mattie chided. "Rumor is not history. Do you honestly believe, as poor as most of our family has always been, that if there were any basis to that rumor there would be anything left of those hills back there other than a big hole in the ground where my relatives had dug looking for what would be a fortune even today?"

Jake laughed. "That's a good point, Mattie. But according to Sarah, the rumor has persisted. How do you explain that?"

"Why should I?" she asked. "Fools who wish to follow rumors will be fools, no matter how much the truth is protested.

"Eventually, Samuel married my grandfather's sister," Mattie said, turning from the rumors of lost gold to her story—a story Megan knew was being told for her benefit. "Therein lies the true mystery. My grandfather would not speak of what occurred, other than to tell me that something very bad had happened to her.

"Like you, Megan?" Mattie asked. Not waiting for an answer, she shrugged. "Who can say? Except, perhaps, you. How bad, I can only imagine from looking at the two pictures we have of her.

"You would think that after the life of turmoil Samuel had already lived, he would find peace in a late marriage. Apparently not. Apparently Lydia, his new wife, had suffered beyond recovery from her own turmoil. From what my grandfather told me, she was terrified of everything, living in constant fear."

"But I don't—"

Mattie raised her hand to silence her. "No, Megan," she said gently. "You survive by denying that fear. Lydia survived by keeping to the cabin Samuel had built near here, not going into town, even to church, unless accompanied by him, or by her brother, eventually even proclaiming that someone was lurking around the clearing, attempting to approach her on those rare occasions when Samuel would leave her alone.

"Agoraphobia? Perhaps. Depression? Surely. Paranoia? Who can say without having known her and what was really happening? All of them treatable today. All of them devastating then."

Megan swallowed a lump in her throat. Her denial had been automatic; Mattie's response too uncomfortably clearsighted; and her story, almost too painful to bear. "What happened?"

Mattie shook her head and rose from the bench. "I think that must keep for a later time," she said.

"Come on, Mattie." Jake said, hurrying to her side as she stumbled slightly. "You can't just leave it like that. You and Sarah have Megan half in love with Sam Hooker."

"As she should be, Jacob. He was certainly someone worthy of love." Mattie patted Jake's cheek. "As are you."

Mattie turned and rested her hand on Megan's shoulder. "And you also, child. Even though I think you have spent a great deal of your life denying that too."

Megan was operating on overload. That was the only reason she could think of to explain why she didn't run screaming into the woods. Instead, she accompanied Jake and Mattie back to the house. Instead, she sat at the table with the others and ate the picnic lunch Mattie had packed. Instead, she helped with the dishes, not even challenging Barbara because of the professional secrets she must have shared with her mother.

And after the dishes were put away, she accompanied Barbara into the living room to join the others. She sank onto the hearth, draped her arm over Deacon's back as he crowded next to her, looked unerringly at Jake who was watching her, not quite but almost in his hovering mode, and said, "I think I must tell you about the telephone call I received this morning."

"Will she be all right?" Patrick asked still again as Jake walked with his friends to their vehicles.

Jake glanced at Barbara, who only shrugged as she helped her mother into the car.

"Jacob?"

"Yes, Mattie," he said, bending to lean toward the open car window.

"Parallels, Jacob. There are many parallels. Don't forget that, don't discount them, and don't assume that you have seen all of them yet."

He patted Mattie's hand and nodded at Barbara, signaling for her to leave.

"What was that all about?" Patrick asked.

Jake grimaced. "Sam Hooker, stolen army gold, and her great-aunt Lydia."

"I repeat," Patrick said. "What was that all about?"

Jake scrubbed his hands across his face. "I don't know," he said. "I'm not sure I know much of anything anymore. Except this." He pulled his wallet from his pocket and extracted a slip of paper which he handed to Patrick. "You were right about getting outside help; the threatening call only proves it. Here's the name and number of my agency contact. I'd appreciate it if you'd make the call from a discreet telephone."

Patrick took the paper silently and tucked it into his shirt pocket.

"And you, Jake. Will you be all right?"

Jake nodded and slapped his friend on the shoulder. "Yeah. Now you'd better get on down the hill. Help Barbara with the gate. Spend some time with your wife."

"And you?"

Jake laughed without humor. "I'm going to see about circling the wagons. And I guess I'm going to have to ask Megan what she knows about Sam Hooker, stolen army gold, and Mattie's great-aunt Lydia."

Jake waited in the yard until Patrick's truck dropped out of sight on its way down the wooded hillside. Then he turned and faced his house. Parallels. If Mattie said there were parallels, there must be parallels, superficial ones anyway. *Don't discount them, and don't assume that you have seen all of them yet.*

Megan waited for him in the living room. At least she had relinquished her hold on his dog, Jake thought, as he stopped beside the couch and looked across the room at her standing in front of the mantel. But she still looked damned defenseless. And, he realized with a start of surprise, guilty. What in the hell did she have to look guilty about?

"Do you know what Mattie was talking about in the workshop?"

Megan nodded. "Come in the kitchen, Jake. I want to show you something."

Jake noted how serious the topic must be for her when he saw that she had started to make coffee in his stove-top percolator. He adjusted the gas flame beneath the pot before he saw the two books on the table at his usual place. One was the ornate photograph album he had seen that day but not examined. The other was the brown leather notebook Megan had brought with her.

"Please," Megan said, pulling out a chair and sinking onto it, leaving him the chair in front of the books.

He nodded and sat down. Megan placed her hand on the old album. "Mattie brought this to show to me. I think you ought to see it too. Obviously, so does she, or she would have taken it with her."

"Megan—"

She shook her head. "I told you some strange things were happening. You admitted as much yourself. I just didn't know how strange."

Carefully she opened the book to a picture of an intense young man dressed in the clothing of over a century before.

"This is Mattie's grandfather, Peter Tanner," she said. "Have you ever seen him?"

She turned the page, and the face of an innocent young girl looked up at him. "Or her?"

Jake frowned as something familiar about the young woman teased at his memory. "No," he said. "Of course not. These people have been dead for decades."

"I have."

He thought he must have misunderstood her, but before he could question her, Megan drew another photograph from the album, an unmounted one, and handed it to him.

"Peter Tanner," she said, pointing to the young man whose portrait Jake had just seen, "the woman they called Granny Rogers, Sam Hooker, and Lydia Tanner, probably Hooker by then, in what is most likely their wedding picture."

"My God," Jake said in a whisper, unable to stop the words as he relived the moment he had seen this woman— or Megan?—sitting in front of the fire brushing her hair. "It's her."

The coffeepot boiled over then, and Jake jumped up to

rescue it, to rescue himself from admitting more than he already had.

Megan got cups and set them on the table and waited quietly while Jake filled them.

"That was my reaction too," she said when he sat down again. "At first."

"What kind of reaction?"

"Denial."

"Megan, what's going on?"

She smiled wanly and pushed the other book toward him. "Read this. And then, if you still want to, we'll talk."

Reluctantly, Jake reached for the notebook. Reluctantly, he opened it. The first page was familiar to him; he'd seen at least part of it the night he first brought Megan to his house. Now, feeling like the worst kind of voyeur, he read the entry.

June 3. Just days ago. Jake read of her anxiety about the noises in the night. He read of her curiosity about him, the unknown neighbor at whom she had almost waved. He read of her doubts and questions about her marriage, her hopes for her new home, her innocent plans for the green bedroom. And then he read the words that had lost none of their impact since the first time he saw them:—*help me oh God somebody please please help me*—

He glanced up and found her watching him with dread and hope clouding her eyes. "Go on," she urged softly. "There's more. Much more."

June 4. The next night. The night he had been compelled to run to her side and she had launched herself off the porch and into his arms the moment she saw him.

She wrote of avoidance and attempting to face the truth. She wrote of her lack of understanding of what had happened in her new home. She wrote of him; she wrote of seeing someone else when she looked at him. And then, in the same handwriting as before, different from the rest of the entry:—*No, please no. Oh, God, no, no, NO!*

Jake felt the terror in her words, felt the panic that must have propelled her off the porch and into his arms. But at what? A flashback of Villa Castellano? Or of something, if at all possible, even worse? Whatever it was, it hadn't been a nightmare, not one experienced during sleep. Her written thoughts, though troubled, had been far too lucid up to that point to have been written in sleep.

He looked up, toward Megan—for what? For an assurance he wasn't sure she could give? For a comfort she needed as much as he did? She wasn't there. Sometime while he read her hidden thoughts, she had slipped away from the table, leaving him to plunder her deepest secrets in privacy.

Though not thick, the book did contain more pages. Was he supposed to read them? Could he bear to read them? The answer to both questions had to be yes.

He realized that his body had assumed the tension he welcomed just before going into danger. And perhaps that was where he was headed. Steeling himself for what he might find, Jake turned the page.

August 3, 1870. He read words written in the same handwriting as the incoherent cries for help but contained, now, without the panic to mar its ornate penmanship.

"What the hell?" he muttered.

Lydia Tanner—her book.

Standing at uneasy attention facing the mantel over the wood stove, Megan eventually heard noises from the kitchen. She rubbed her hands over her chilled arms and thought for the first time in almost an hour of her coffee, cold now, forgotten almost as soon as she had left the kitchen.

She heard the scrape of a chair and the weight of a booted foot on the wooden floor, but Jake did not call her name, and he did not come into the living room to find her.

"He's probably trying to figure out how to call the men with the butterfly nets to come after me," she muttered.

But no, he wouldn't do that. He'd have to send them after his beloved Mattie too.

He came so quietly she didn't hear him, didn't know he was in the room with her, until she felt his hands drop onto her shoulders and draw her back against his chest.

"She loved him very much, didn't she?" he asked softly.

It wasn't what she had expected. She let herself relax into his warmth. "Yes."

"Do you suppose she did know what happened to the gold?"

Megan shook her head. "At least one person thought so. But wouldn't she have admitted something like that in her diary? Especially if she was trying to heal herself?"

"I don't know." Jake rested his chin on her head and wrapped his arms securely around her. "Do you suppose she finally let herself hate him afterward, that in spite of her efforts not to, she let herself blame him for what had happened?"

"I don't know," Megan told him. "I don't know much more than you do. Except that she cried in her sleep. For him. For what they wouldn't have together."

"And Sam?" he asked. "Do you supposed he blamed himself? Do you suppose that guilt for what happened to her ate at him for the rest of his life?"

"I don't know, Jake. I wish I did, but I don't."

"Damn!" he whispered, rocking her slightly in his embrace. She felt him draw in a deep breath, felt him brace himself as though to say something, but all she heard was another regretful whisper. "Oh, damn."

18

"*Do you hear us, Jake?*" Megan asked. "We're talking about them as though they are real persons."

"Aren't they? Didn't Mattie know their story? Even Sarah knows part of it."

No. This was definitely not the reaction she had expected from him. She felt a small bubble of hysteria rising in her. Jake's warmth and protection surrounding her were her only weapons in fighting it down.

"So what are they, ghosts?" he asked softly. "Have you, and I too, managed to tap into some unhappy spirits lingering near the old homeplace?"

She wasn't the only one having problems with the chaos a few pictures and a notebook had brought to their world. She heard it in Jake's attempt at humor; she felt it in a tremor of his arms.

"Not ghosts," she said. "Mattie's grandfather was still alive the first time she saw them."

He held her pressed so close to him she felt him swallow and draw in another breath. "What then?"

"*To go* and *to have gone* are the same in Choctaw," Megan said, repeating Mattie's words. "Do you suppose that what appears to be happening is only the lingering remains of some really strong memories? Or is it possible that somewhere, somehow, what we have seen is still—is *just* happening?"

He didn't tighten his arms around her; he didn't loosen them. Still, she felt Jake's resistance to that suggestion. "And somewhere in the future," he asked carefully, "a hundred years or so from now, someone walking in the woods or the housing development or whatever happens to this piece of real estate by then will see us as we are now and be scared out of their minds by a couple of ghosts?"

"Or not," she said. "Maybe by then what's happening will be so well understood that no one would be frightened. Or maybe someone would really have to be tuned to us to see us. And maybe only the images of the pivotal points, the times when changes could have been made in someone's life linger."

"And this isn't one of those pivotal points?" he asked.

"Is it?" she whispered.

Slowly he turned her in his arms and cradled her face in his hands. "I think, Megan McIntyre, that everything that has happened since I met you has been a pivotal point."

What she wanted to do was take the one step that would erase the distance that now separated them. What she wanted to do was lift her hands to the back of his head and tug him down as she raised to meet him. What she wanted to do was stay lost in the longing and desire she saw in his eyes.

"I think—" Jake's voice, thickened by the emotions she saw in his eyes, faded. "I think," he said, straightening infinitesimally away from her, "that we had better get out of this house before we give some twenty-first-century voyeur a more personal glimpse into our lives than we're ready to share."

Megan didn't move, even though she knew she should; she couldn't move. Not away from Jake, not now. Because this *was* a pivotal point. When had she fallen in love with

Jake Kenyon? The first night he rescued her, the second, or any of the many other times?

And was it love or a reaction to the emotional overload she had been feeling since he stormed into her living room and took her hand and refused to let her succumb to terror?

Jake didn't move either. "Megan, I need a little help with this nobility business," he said hoarsely.

Yes. That was the right word. Jake might be attempting to tease them out of a tense moment, but there was—had been since the beginning—a certain nobility in his actions. Like Sam with Lydia.

You and Sarah have Megan half in love with Sam Hooker.

The memory of Jake's earlier words returned to taunt her. Was she half in love with Sam? Was that coloring what she was feeling for Jake? Was that why she was feeling for him something so strong she had nothing with which to compare it?

"Megan?"

Instantly desire fled, leaving her feeling as alone as she had always been, even though she still felt Jake's hands on her face.

"Megan?"

"Yes," she said, twisting away from him and the confusion she now saw in his eyes. "Perhaps we should get out of the house. . . ."

They walked.

Jake spoiled the idyllic picture of two people out for a leisurely stroll with their dog by strapping on a black leather holster containing a twin of the pistol he had given her.

"For bear?" Megan asked dryly.

"Varmints," he answered, equally dry.

And he was right to take it, Megan knew. This was another truth of their life they couldn't ignore any more than they could ignore the truth they tried to leave in the cabin.

They walked past the barn and corral without stopping. Perhaps remembering a terrified Lydia and her journey by horseback, perhaps wondering if Megan had somehow tapped into that years ago and miles away, as Megan wondered, Jake didn't again suggest they ride.

They crested the ridge where Megan had parked, waiting for Jake the day before, and plunged into the wooded hillside. For a while they seemed to be following some sort of animal trail, but within minutes Megan had lost sight of it and knew that without Jake to guide her back to the ridge she would be hopelessly lost.

They came to a small clearing and paused, and Megan looked out over the ridges and hollows spread out before her.

"I can almost see how Mark Henderson made his mistake," she said.

Jake leaned against a nearby tree and offered her the plastic canteen of water. "What mistake?"

She shook her head at the offer of water. "It's inexcusable, I know, because it was his job to know where he was. And the repercussions were almost fatal. But out here, one ridge really does look pretty much like another. What's one ridge in country like this? I'm not sure I wouldn't find myself one or two or even more ridges away from where I was supposed to be. Especially at night."

Jake grimaced and hooked the canteen onto his belt.

"Where were you?" she asked.

Sighing, he walked to her side and reached around her, pointing to a shadowed peak. "About halfway down on the west side of Witcher Mountain."

"So close," she murmured.

"No. Not really."

"And Henderson? Where was he when you needed the cavalry?"

Jake turned slightly, turning her with him, and pointed to a peak more east than south. "There."

More than one or two ridges separated the two peaks.

More than a simple mistake had kept help from Jake's side. Megan felt it; she knew Jake must too.

She resisted the desire to lean back against him. Instead, she turned. "I'm sorry, Jake. I know how betrayal feels."

"Yeah," he said. "I know you do."

"But why?" she asked. "Surely he had to know he'd be accused of something, if no more than incompetence."

Jake shook his head. "By the time I was able to start making accusations, Rolley P had been acquitted. He'd gathered his supporters and gotten himself reinstated almost as soon as the word got out that I was going to be out of commission for a good long while. Having just gone through the expense of one grand jury investigation, the county wasn't willing to begin another. Ultimately, Rolley P was the one who investigated Mark's action and found him blameless. He's also the one who hasn't been able to learn anything about the death of my informant or any more about who had been making the drop."

"Drop? You interrupted an actual transaction?"

"Yeah. Or who the gunmen were or where they went after using me for target practice."

"Have you been back to the location to see if you can find anything?"

He shook his head. "No. There are some logging roads that would get me pretty close. Now that I'm able to ride, or have my bones shaken the way they would be in a four-wheel drive, I've thought about going. But it's been months. The chances of finding anything, even the exact location, are pretty much nonexistent."

Without the need for words, Megan fell in beside Jake and they started walking again. And while it might seem like aimless wandering to her, she suspected Jake had a destination or a reason for the generally uphill direction they took.

"I was going to divorce Helen," he said, shattering the quiet mood and startling Megan so that she stumbled.

He grabbed her arm, steadied her, and then released her.

"We had talked about it for months, had even come to a tentative settlement agreement. When I woke up in the hospital and found her there, I asked her to go ahead and get the paperwork started. She refused, and for a while, at least until I floated back into consciousness the next day, I thought it was because some remnant of our marriage still remained. Foolish me."

"Jake, you don't have to—"

"Yes, I do. If there's ever going to be anything between the two of us, I have to say it and you have to hear it. The reason she wouldn't go ahead with the divorce at that time had nothing to do with commitment or vows or even the residue of a dead emotion. It wouldn't have been the politically correct thing to do: for her and, by association, for her brother.

"I'm sorry, Megan," he said. "But I didn't care much for Roger Hudson. I blamed him and his manipulations for a lot of the problems in my marriage. It wasn't until the end that I realized that Helen was just as manipulative, just as ambitious, and just as selfish as I had always thought him to be."

Oh, God, she thought. Truth time.

"He was," she said softly.

"What?"

"Roger," she said. "He was manipulative, ambitious, and selfish."

He dropped his hand to her shoulder, touching her again, giving her the needed warmth of contact with him, perhaps needing it himself.

"Somehow I hoped you hadn't realized that," he said.

"It was pretty hard not to after he told me on our wedding day exactly why he had married me."

"God," Jake muttered. "And you stayed in the marriage?"

She had been over this many times in her mind and still couldn't justify why she had allowed herself to be used by Roger for so long, why she had thought herself unworthy of anything more than his neglect and casual abuse, so she took refuge in lashing out. "So did you. Why? Vows, commitment, honor? All of the above or none of it? I had the added benefit of a politically powerful father who convinced me his reelection depended on having a squeaky clean family life, or at least the appearance of one."

He silenced her by the simple but effective means of hauling her into his arms and pressing her face to his chest. "I'm sorry," he said. "I'm so sorry."

Yes. He was. Megan felt compassion in the way he cradled her to him. Compassion and a return of the darker, more intense emotions that had driven them from the house.

And she was sorry too.

What she wouldn't give to have met this man unencumbered by all the mistakes and disappointments of her past, all the emotional trauma and confusion she had endured and was still enduring. All the self-doubt that seemed to be ingrained. All the history she had of not admitting her emotions, her needs, her desires.

What she wouldn't give to be able to respond freely to what she thought she felt for Jake. To what she thought she felt coming from him.

Instead, she pulled away from him, attempting to break their fragile contact, but succeeding only in stepping back, still captured by his hands on her arms. "So am I," she said. "Very sorry. But we all make choices, Jake. And we all have to live with the choices we have made."

"Maybe," he said, looking down into her eyes. "But maybe, just maybe, some of us get another chance."

Maybe they did. Megan smiled tentatively at him. This time, when she stepped away, he let her go.

Little remained among the trees and underbrush to mark what had once been a homesite: a few tumbled rocks from an ancient chimney, a few almost petrified posts from a long-ago rotted fence, a surprising cluster of iris and jonquils and old-fashioned day lilies near what must once have been a front stoop.

"Oh." Megan heard her own reluctant moan when Jake stopped beside the unexpected plants with their dead and drying flower stalks.

"Their cabin, do you suppose?" Jake asked. "It's old. A lot older than any of the other ruins I've found on either of our places."

"I don't know," Megan said as she fought a strange reluctance to approach what surely was no more than a pleasant woodland scene. "From what Mattie said, I thought they must have lived closer to your house."

"Actually, it is," Jake told her. "I've pulled a Deacon on you." He pointed toward an area of the woods behind what would have been the back of the cabin. "There's what once appeared to be the remains of a path leading up to a spot behind my barn. A rock slide has partially blocked it. That's why I brought you around the long way. It's maybe half the distance from my house that yours is."

"Far enough away for privacy; close enough for Granny Rogers to help with Lydia when her fears became too much for her to handle alone or for Sam to cope with," Megan murmured.

"Yeah." He frowned at the spot where the cabin had once stood, squared his shoulders almost as if he were preparing to do battle, and reached for her hand.

Surprised at his actions, Megan slid her hand into his and felt his fingers close securely around her fingers. He tugged on her hand and led her into what would have been the largest, if not the only, room in the cabin.

"No," she moaned as the chill slid over her. "Oh, no. No, please."

She jerked her hand, trying to free herself from Jake's grip, but he refused to let her go.

"Get out of here." Megan had no idea where the words were coming from, only that they must be said. "Please, Jake. You have to leave. Now!"

He didn't bother to lead her out or let her go. He picked her up and carried her from the cabin site and the miasma that filled it to a fallen tree and sat rocking her until her tremors faded, until embarrassment and confusion rose up to battle but not defeat the fear, the threat she felt still coming from the peaceful-looking scene in front of her.

"I don't know what that was," she said at last. "I'd hide it if I could; I'd deny it if I could. Apparently I can't do either."

"Fear?" he asked gently.

Megan shook her head. "More than fear. It was—"

"*More* than fear?"

"Hey, give me a break," she said, attempting humor, anything to dispel the black cloud that still seemed to hover over her and within her. "I know fear."

"Yes," he said, but he didn't smile. "You do."

"And this was—do you believe in instincts, Jake?"

"Yes." He drew a deep breath and settled her closer to him as he rested his cheek against hers. "And I've learned to trust them. They've saved my life more than once."

"That was what this felt like. Like a huge powerful warning, pushing me—pushing you—out of there, before something too horrible to believe happened. Maybe it wasn't their place after all," she offered.

"Twenty-five years ago," Jake said reflectively, softly, "there were still signs of the remains of a barn or shed nearby. I kept digging up pieces of metal and taking them home for my father to identify, which he did. They were the rusted and broken parts of a sawmill and the steam engine that powered it. That wasn't too unusual, I learned later. These hills had been dotted with them before the easy accessibility of commercial lumber. But it was what first got me interested in working with wood, as well as exploring these hills.

"My dad gave up on keeping me at home, so he came down and filled in the old well to make me a marginally safe place to explore. I never liked the place where the cabin had been; not because of any threat but because it seemed, even when I was what?—six, seven?—an incredibly sad place. It still does."

"You didn't feel it?" Megan asked. "You got me out of there so fast, I thought you must have."

"Megan, I saw what something was doing to you, that's all."

"That's all?" For a moment the terror of a moment before was forgotten as she reveled in his admission. "That's pretty remarkable, Jake Kenyon."

He shook his head. "Anyone would have—"

"No. No one has seen what I needed or done what I needed, with or without my asking, ever before. Just you."

"Megan. Oh, Megan."

She felt the tremor back in his arms, felt the tension tightening his body.

"I know it's too soon," he said. "I know the timing is wrong. I know you're stressed out and I'm taking unfair advantage of you. But I want to love you. I want to make love to you until neither one of us can remember anything but each other. I want to make love to you until Sam and Lydia and Roger and Helen and Rolley P and that son of a bitch on the telephone this morning don't exist for either of us."

"Yes," Megan admitted, to him and to herself. "Yes. I want that too. But not here. Of all the places we could be, not here. Please, Jake."

"And not now," he said.

She heard resignation in his voice as he stood and released her to stand beside him. Resignation as though she had rejected *him,* not just the location. Resignation as though he had heard that rejection so many times he had grown to expect it. The same resignation Lydia felt when she admitted that Sam would never share her lonely bed.

Jake remained silent for a moment, as though waiting for her to confirm that rejection. She wouldn't. But Megan realized she couldn't deny it either.

"Let's get you back to the house," he said finally. "You must be tired."

She wanted to tell him it was her head that had been battered, not her body, but she realized that *his* body had been battered, and worse, and if anyone had a right to be tired after their day's—several days'—activities, Jake did.

"Yes," she said, casting one last glance around the ruins of someone's dream. "Let's go."

Back at the house, Jake insisted she nap. She didn't want to, but she suspected it was the only way he'd feel free to rest himself. She took Lydia's journal into the guest bedroom with her, but she didn't open it. When she tried, she found she'd grieved for Lydia all she could bear for a while. Later she would have to return to her; there were too many questions unanswered. But now, in her own life, there were also too many questions unanswered, and she had to try to make sense of one of them: of how—without Lydia, without Sam, without the drama of the last four days—she really felt about Jake.

At last the soft rustling and noises from the guest bedroom stopped. Jake stepped to the partially open door and looked in. In spite of her protests, Megan had fallen asleep. She lay on her side with one hand curled on the pillow near her cheek. While he watched, she twisted in her sleep, drawing the other pillow to her side and wrapping an arm around it.

He could be there with her. With only a few words—or lack of them—he could have brought her back to his house and in minutes have persuaded her that, yes, she really did want him. That, yes, making love was the right and natural thing for them to do and not merely another way for her to defend against her fears, her pain, and, he now knew, her insecurities.

Even if he hadn't done that, he could still be with her. If he went to her now, if he slid into the bed, she would welcome him. He knew that. Why couldn't he accept that she really wanted him?

And why didn't he just get the hell out of the house before he did what *he* really wanted and wound up hating himself?

Megan awoke in an empty house. No one answered her tentative greeting when she left her room: not Jake, not Deacon.

Her eyes felt grainy, her head throbbed, and she felt groggy and disoriented from a sleep that had been both too deep and too brief.

She found coffee, lukewarm but drinkable, in Jake's temperamental pot on the stove, but no note telling her where he had gone. A glance out the back door confirmed that both his vehicles were there. He must have brought the Jeep home when he and Patrick returned.

The horses? She couldn't see the corral from the kitchen, but she realized that leaving her alone without a word, especially after the threatening call she had received, was completely out of character for Jake Kenyon.

Had something happened to him?

And then through the open window she heard the whine of one of his power tools and relaxed against the counter, nursing her coffee and her headache and the residue of the emotions she had tapped into at the cabin site.

Whose emotions? In spite of all the new knowledge Mattie had brought her, Megan still couldn't let go of the nagging suspicion they were *her* emotions. She'd just shared with Jake something she'd sworn never to reveal to a living soul; she'd just felt things with him she'd thought herself incapable of feeling. And *wham!* up pops a psychic wave of fear and threat and, yes, guilt, overwhelming her, holding her powerless in its grip, as she had been powerless so many times in her life.

The last thing Megan wanted to do was ever again set foot within the perimeter of that cabin, maybe Lydia's, maybe someone else's.

She closed her eyes, and all the emotions that had swarmed over her at the cabin came flooding back, pressing in on her, pushing to get out of her.

God! She couldn't go back there.

And that was why she had to go back.

Quickly, before she lost her nerve, she set her coffee cup on the countertop, found her hiking boots where she had dropped them earlier, stuffed her feet into them, and stepped out the back door. Jake had brought her home by the most direct route, up the hill, past the rock slide, and into his clearing from behind the barn, so she knew the way back.

She ought to tell Jake where she was going; he'd be furious when he found out she'd gone wandering without him. *If* he found out. She planned to be gone only a matter of minutes. If she told him where she was going, he'd either try to talk her out of it or insist on going with her.

She glanced toward Jake's workshop when she reached the corral. The power equipment had fallen silent. Was he finishing his task? Or had he begun more of the fine handwork she had finally recognized as his: in the bench under the arbor, in the fireplace mantel of his house, in the trim and cabinets in his kitchen, and in numerous projects in the workshop?

He deserved this time alone with his work, she told herself as she rounded the barn; he'd had little enough of it since she'd been thrust into his life. She knew her thoughts were an attempt at justifying her actions—knew and couldn't help it. She had to make this trip; she had to make it alone; and, God help her, she had to make it now.

She realized just how long her nap must have been when she stepped into the woods and saw the long shadows the trees cast and how dimly the sunlight penetrated the deeper woods. It would be all right, she told herself. Just a few minutes' walk down the hill, a few minutes back up the hill—and a few minutes at the cabin. She'd be back long before dark, long before any danger of getting turned around in the trees.

She was into it before she knew it: a peaceful glen softened by the shadows of what had in the moment she first entered the woods seemed late afternoon and now appeared to be early evening.

She found nothing ominous here, nothing frightening. But then, she was still outside the cabin, not in it.

Megan walked around the perimeter as outlined by the iris and jonquils to the flat stone that must have served as a stoop. She stopped there, reluctant to go farther, knowing that for her own peace of mind she must.

The birds still sang and made little scrabbling noises as they hunted in the dry fallen leaves beneath the encircling trees. A breeze soughed through the glen, rustling the leaves above and the faded flower stalks of the vestiges of the flower garden.

A vision would be nice about now, she thought, with a flash of wry humor: a nice clear vision to explain what she had felt earlier and why. Or maybe not. The feeling had been too intense to have been generated by anything that could be depicted in a "nice clear" vision.

Steeling herself, Megan stepped across the stoop and into grass-covered memories. Nothing assaulted her; she felt only the yearning of what she had once thought an inexplicable sorrow. Oh, yes. Jake's impression of an incredibly sad place was right on target with what she felt here now, with what she had felt too often in the last few days.

But why, then—she curtailed her musing, suddenly sure she would find no answers here—maybe not even, as Mattie had suggested earlier, the right questions—just a repeat of the ones she had already considered.

Her emotions, or Lydia's?

Her fear, or Lydia's?

But what part did Jake have in what had happened earlier? She had felt strongly that he had been as threatened as she.

By what?

Jake? *Or Sam?*

Choking back a sob at that unwanted intrusion, Megan whirled and stepped back over the stoop. No answers, not a one.

In the past few minutes, the shadows had grown threateningly long. Megan glanced up at the scraps of sky visible between the trees. "Oh, lord," she murmured. "Jake's got to know I'm gone by now." He'd be worried, she knew; probably he'd be searching for her.

Worried, not angry. Well, maybe angry too, but justifiably.

And searching, not condemning.

Those two contrasts caught Megan by surprise, slowing her steps and opening a familiar but never truly explored line of thought. Well, well, she thought. She'd gotten answers after all. Not answers for which she had been consciously searching but answers she needed as much as she now needed the rapidly fading light.

Jake wasn't Roger Hudson. She'd known that on one level, but on another she supposed she'd thought all men must be like him—or that she would react to all men as she had reacted to Roger. But if she'd learned anything in these past three months it was that she was strong, a hell of a lot stronger than anyone, including herself, had ever given her credit for being.

Strong enough for Jake.

Strong enough to stand up to him. And to stand beside him.

Strong enough to tell him how much she wanted him.

Strong enough to choose the living, breathing, caring man over the romantic—yet ultimately harmless to her—long-dead Sam Hooker.

"Yes!" she whispered exuberantly. She grinned. She was strong enough to face his fury that she had gone out on her own, because she now knew him well enough to understand that his worry might well take that form of expression.

She was concentrating so hard on the rough trail in the fading light, thinking so deeply of Jake and his concern, and anticipating what she would say to him later about her return trip to the cabin and the epiphany she had experienced that she had no idea anyone else was within miles of Jake's sanctuary—until she reached the crest of the ridge and saw the rooflines of that sanctuary through the trees.

Until a rough hand clamped itself over her mouth.

Megan fought a soul-blackening moment of déjà vu as she felt herself being dragged backward into the trees. She struggled for breath; she struggled to scream; she dragged her feet and grabbed for branches to cling to and then fought and kicked.

And still whoever held her pulled her backward. Pulled her from safety. Pulled her into the nightmare.

"You know, don't you?"

She heard the harsh whispered words, but they made no sense.

"He told you. I said all along he did. And now you're going to tell *him*. Or have you already? I watched you today, pointing and talking.

"Well, he won't get it. It's mine. And you, bitch, are going to show me where it is. Now!"

19

Whoever he was, he punctuated his words with a guttural hiss and a brutal jerk of his arm across her ribs.

But his hand slipped. Not even pausing to think, Megan sank her teeth into the flesh between his thumb and forefinger and jammed her booted foot down hard along his shin at the same moment that she slammed her elbow into what she hoped was his solar plexus.

She heard him grunt with the unexpected pain, but best of all she felt him release her as he gave in to it for one brief moment. It was enough. She unclamped her teeth and twisted away from him, running even as she turned. She didn't pause to scream but gathered breath as she dodged trees and rocks and briars until she felt she had enough in her lungs to spare and then she let it go in a long, keening shriek that should have had dogs howling in seven counties.

She heard Jake's answering yell but couldn't manage to make words. Just his name, "Jake, Jake, Jake," with every puff of breath she could spare.

Jake caught her at the edge of the woods, swinging her

around and holding on to her with both arms. "What happened?"

"Man," she gasped, leaning into his strength while still trying to point behind her. "Man. There."

She saw Deacon as no more than a black blur as he raced into the woods.

"You're all right?" Jake asked, running a hand over her arms, her shoulders, her back, cradling his hand against her face.

She nodded, still gasping from her run. "Just scared. I don't know where he came from. He was just there, with his hand over my mouth, pulling me off the path."

"You went out alone."

She heard the chastisement in his voice, but she also heard his fear and concern. "Later," she said, finally regaining some use of her breath. "Yell at me later. I deserve it."

"And you didn't take your gun."

"Jake." She shook her head against his chest, and then she looked at him, really looked at him. He held that nasty-looking automatic of his in one hand even as he caressed her face with the other. And she'd never know how he managed to hold her so protectively while still standing resolute and ready to do battle with anyone or anything that had chased her screaming from the woods. "Oh, Jake," she whispered, raising her hand to his cheek to give him the comfort and reassurance she sensed he needed but wouldn't ask for.

They heard Deacon's warning bark and a series of growls and a couple of human howls mingled with thrashing noises somewhere between them and the ridge. Jake turned, raising the pistol in his hand. He'd just released the safety when Deacon yelped in pain.

"Oh, God," Megan murmured, turning toward the sound.

"Stay here," Jake commanded. "No, on second thought, I'm not letting you out of my sight again. But for God's sake be careful!"

She nodded and followed him back into the woods. After only a few yards, the sound of a nearby gunshot sent them both diving behind trees.

"Deacon?" she asked, not wanting to, and not wanting the answer she knew she would hear.

Jake, grim-faced and silent, obviously didn't want the answer any more than she did. He hesitated only until he heard the thrashing sounds of someone running through the underbrush. Then, with a sharp gesture Megan felt sure was meant to tell her to stay put, he worked his way forward.

He glanced at Deacon lying motionless beside a large rock. Megan saw the regret in his eyes, regret he had no time to show as he started after the man running recklessly down the hillside.

Megan dropped to her knees beside the dog. "Oh, Deacon," she moaned as she ran her hand over the smooth cap of his head and over his shoulders for one last time— and heard him whimper.

"Jake!"

Her cry stopped him in his pursuit.

"He's alive," she shouted, feeling laughter and tears mingling too close to the surface to be held in for long. "He's alive!"

They sat in the dimly lighted inner office of the downtown Fairview small-animal clinic: Megan, Barbara, and Jake— when he wasn't pacing down the hall to look through the viewing window into the vet's surgery. They'd moved into Dr. Stanton's private office after the fourth person had been attracted to the lights in the waiting room and stopped to see what was happening there on an early Saturday evening. Now Megan wondered if the intrusions of the friendly and just plain curious wouldn't help Jake more than the silence and the waiting.

Of course, Jake being Jake, he had insisted that Barbara examine Megan for any new injuries.

"I have a bruise," Megan said, refusing to impose on Barbara anymore than she already had. "Not even a bad one. We checked that out in the ladies' room right after we got here. I'm all right, Jake," she assured him, knowing that she wasn't, knowing that her carelessness had caused this tragedy. "Unless I get rabies from the bite."

Barbara chuckled. "No, hon. You've got that backwards. For you to catch rabies, that sleaze would have to have bitten you."

When they had discovered Deacon still lived, Jake had sent Megan racing back to the house to call the vet and alert him that they were bringing Deacon in. Megan, having no idea which of the half dozen DVMs listed in the small telephone directory was the right one, had called Barbara.

It was Barbara who had called the correct veterinarian, Barbara who had met them at the clinic along with the vet, and Barbara who was maintaining what conversation there was in the tension-filled room. She walked over to the floor-to-ceiling bookshelves behind a walnut desk and ran her fingers over leather-bound books, a small color television and VCR combination, and a bronze statue of a greyhound dog at rest but wearing her racing silks.

"Looks like there's almost as much money in the private practice of pets and poodles as there is in that of people," she said. "Maybe I went to the wrong med school." She smiled.

Megan saw no envy, no jealousy, and no regret in her expression.

"Jake, sit down," Barbara said firmly as he rose still another time and paced toward the hallway. "You're not going to help matters by wandering back there every five minutes and disturbing Tink's concentration."

"What kind of surgeon has a name like Tink?" Jake muttered.

"A damned good one," Barbara reminded him. "One who's already pulled that bag of bones and bark out of a lot worse mess than the one he's in now."

"Yeah." Jake eased himself down onto a leather wingback in front of the desk. "Yeah."

He shifted once, as the tension returned to his body, and straightened until he sat on the very edge of the chair. "Where's Patrick? I thought he was on his way."

Barbara sighed. "I told you I left a message with his pager. When he gets his story and checks in, he'll be here. You know that."

"And where the hell's the deputy who was supposed to come over? It's not as though the five or six blocks he'd have to travel is any major obstacle."

"Now *that* I can't help you with," Barbara told him.

And neither could Megan. But there had to be something she could do. She'd never seen Jake like this and she never wanted to see him this way again: agitated, yes; worried for Deacon, yes; angry, yes. All of the above. But underlying it all was remorse and a completely inexplicable guilt—that he had no reason to feel.

She rose from her chair and went to stand in front of him. "He's going to be all right," she said, placing her hands on his shoulders. "Deacon's going to recover. He just has to. And I'm sorry. So sorry."

Jake looked up at her. He shook his head and wrapped his arms around her, pulling her closer until she stood between his legs. She felt him shudder as he buried his face against her stomach.

"I almost got you killed," he said. "With all my training and all my experience, I almost got you killed."

She slid her hands from his shoulders to the back of his head, holding him tightly against her. "You didn't send me out in the woods alone, Jake. I'm responsible for that piece of stupidity, not you. You're not responsible for sending that creep after me. And you're not responsible for the incompetence of the sheriff's department."

The muted sound of voices intruded. Megan looked up. They were alone in the room, and she sent a silent thank-you to Barbara for having given them this privacy. But Barbara's was one of the voices she heard, along with a vaguely familiar masculine one. She looked toward the doorway and grimaced.

"Don't look now," she said, bending down to whisper in Jake's ear, "but your favorite elected official has sent Dudley Do-Right to investigate the crime."

She couldn't tell whether the muffled noise Jake made was a cough, a laugh, or a groan, but he hugged her tightly against him one more time before releasing her to stand and turn toward the door.

"Harrison," he said, dropping his hand to Megan's shoulder as he acknowledged the deputy who stood in the doorway with Barbara.

The young deputy from the night before held his clipboard clasped under his arm and gripped his western hat in both hands. "Mr. Kenyon," he said in greeting. He dipped his head toward Megan. "Ma'am." He glanced back toward the hallway. "I'm real sorry about your dog."

"Yeah," Jake said. "Me too. And I'm real sorry that someone attacked Ms. Hudson practically in my backyard. What do you suppose your office plans to do about that?"

Charley Harrison swallowed once and turned the hat in his hands. "I know you don't like me, Mr. Kenyon, and I can understand that, I think. But I want you to know I'm trying to do my job."

Megan felt Jake's hand tighten and then relax on her shoulder, his only sign of emotion until he relaxed his pose slightly. "Maybe you are, kid," he said. "I guess I can give you that."

Charley nodded again, and he, too, relaxed slightly. "I'm going to take this report, sir." He paused and visibly drew himself erect. "I'm going to take it back to the office and file it properly. But I won't have any control over it after that."

"Fair enough, Charley," Jake told him.

"And sir?"

"Yes?"

"Maybe you'd better watch the ten o'clock Fort Smith news tonight."

"What do you mean you don't know?"

Deacon was still in surgery, and Patrick had arrived only moments before.

"I mean, Jake, that if there's going to be something on the ten o'clock news, it's something I don't know about."

"This isn't the story you were out on?"

Patrick leaned against the desk and dropped his head to his hands for a moment, then sighed as he looked across the room at Jake. "The story I was out on was the fiftieth anniversary of Mattie's niece and her husband, coupled with his family's annual reunion bash."

"Patrick Phillips was covering a family reunion?" Jake asked incredulously. "Give me a break."

"I'm sorry that Fairview isn't Beirut, Jake," Patrick said. "Or Sarajevo. Or at least it hadn't been until you came home. Now it's beginning to feel uncomfortably familiar."

"Boys." Barbara stepped between them, holding a hand out to each. "Just because you know all of each other's buttons doesn't mean you have to push them. I thought you grew out of that in first grade."

"Besides," Megan said, unfamiliar with the kind of arguing that didn't lead to all-out war, uncomfortable with the familiarity that let two long-time friends know each other's buttons, and thoroughly uneasy with confrontation. She held her arm up, pointing to her watch. "If we want to know the news, don't you think we ought to turn it on?"

It was a press conference on the Pitchlyn County Courthouse steps. Called by Rolley P. Attended by him and the district attorney, his one friendly county commissioner, his one friendly judge, and all the print, radio, and video media he could summon from Fort Smith and Tulsa.

"Son of a bitch," Patrick said.

"You didn't know."

"Hell, no, I didn't know. I'd have been there with bells and whistles on and pictures in my pocket."

Jake nodded and grimaced at his friend. "I know."

The carillon of the Methodist Church was still ringing in the background as the conference got under way. "Rock of Ages" surrendered to the sounding of the time, which the bells did three times a day: 8 A.M., noon, and 5 P.M. Jake held up a finger for each tone: five.

Rolley P could be seen to have a fine line of sweat beading his upper lip and more dotting his forehead when he removed his cream-colored western hat and stepped up to the speaker's podium and microphone that had been carried out onto the steps. Most of the reporters surrounding him were holding what appeared to be packets of information: reports; photographs, although they weren't visible to the small audience of four gathered around the television; and probably a typed copy of the statement Rolley P read into the microphone.

"While we regret the unfortunate incident that happened at the home of Ms. Megan McIntyre Hudson last Tuesday night, we of Pitchlyn County even more strongly regret the malicious rumors that have since been circulating."

"Who do you suppose wrote *that*?" Patrick asked.

"Shh," Barbara hissed.

"As to the report given our office last night about the reported break-in and vandalism at Ms. Hudson's house, we can only state that no evidence of forced entry was found by our investigating officer. Most of the damage appears to have been done by a shotgun fired within one room.

"According to reliable information—"

Patrick choked.

"Shh." This came from Jake.

Almost immediately a photo of Jake filled the screen, one taken since his attack, showing his scarred face and making him look more like one of the criminals he had hunted for so long than one of the good guys.

"—Jake Kenyon, who filled a short term as sheriff and who is rumored to have circulated the first unofficial complaints concerning the erroneous information given our officers in support of the search warrant, purchased shotgun shells the day before, at the same time that he was purchasing other items, ostensibly for Ms. Hudson."

"Shit!" Jake's hand came down on the desk with enough force to rattle the green-globed banker's lamp.

"Did you?" Megan asked quickly.

"Later," Jake said, frowning.

The sheriff continued. "Ms. Hudson—"

"Oh, God," Megan moaned. Now a picture of her filled the screen, one of the Barbie doll pictures, as she had dubbed them, showing her in all her innocuous fluffy Washington glory.

"—as you will recall," Rolley P droned on, still reading, "is the widow of our own Roger Hudson and the daughter of Oklahoma's United States Senator Jack McIntyre. She is no stranger to notoriety and unfounded accusations, having accused the military of Villa Castellano for the brutal attack on the clinic where her husband and his sister, Helen Kenyon, wife of Jake Kenyon, were murdered, although the best efforts of the United States Senate investigating committee were unable to corroborate those accusations. Ms. Hudson is known to have spent some time as recently as this year in a private sanitarium in Virginia."

"Oh hell, oh hell, oh hell." Megan heard the moaned words a moment before she realized they were coming from her.

"That's enough," Jake said storming across the room to the television. Megan stopped his hand as he reached for the television's control.

"No. I think we need to see it all."

He looked at Megan sadly for a moment but waited until the conference and commentary played to its end before turning off the set and returning to the desk. He rifled through its drawers until he pulled out a multicounty telephone book.

"Who are you calling?" Patrick asked.

"Your buddy, Zack Thomas."

Jake grimaced as he dialed numbers, as he waited, as he repeated his telephone credit card number for the operator and waited again.

"Slow news day?" He asked abruptly. . . . "Got it in one," he said. "You bet it's me. Did you watch your ten o'clock? . . ."

No more than two seconds passed. "Did you ever think to get confirmation on something like that? Or did you just decide it was a good day to trash an innocent civilian? . . .

"Megan Hudson, that's who the hell I'm talking about. The woman who had a dozen men break in on her in the middle of the night. The woman who had her bedroom walls filled with shotgun pellets and a dozen windows broken out during a rainstorm. The woman who's received a threatening phone call and who, today, was assaulted in my backyard." He paused a moment.

"Yeah. That's what I'm talking about, responsible journalism. . . . No. I didn't hear the call." Jake scowl deepened.

"No. I didn't see the assault. I did see her running away from her assailant. I did hear the man running away through the brush, and oh, yeah. Remember Deacon the Wonder Dog, the one who saved my life a few months ago, darling of the media, hero of your six and ten o'clock news for over a week? . . .

"Yeah, him. What about him? Well, he saw the assailant. Real up close and personal. We're at the vet's now. It seems a bullet plowed through his chest from the gun of this uncorroborated imaginary assailant. Unless, of course, you think I shot him, as well as that innocent bedroom wall."

Jake slammed the phone down. "Bastard."

"Feel better?" Patrick asked.

Jake glared at him.

"Imagine," Patrick said companionably to Megan. "Our friend here was once described to me as having nerves of steel and a control over his emotions and reactions that was nothing short of miraculous. In fact, I think the agency was trying to figure out some way to clone that control, or at least teach it to new recruits."

Jake looked at Megan. What was this? A grimace, scowl, glare, or moderately rueful grin? They'd all blended together tonight until she wasn't sure just what each one was.

"At least with Rolley P on the courthouse steps at five o'clock, we can be relatively sure he wasn't the one who tried to snatch you."

"I knew that already," she said.

"How?" Patrick demanded. "You said you couldn't see him and that he sounded as though he was disguising his voice."

Megan shuddered at the memory but refused to give in to it, not yet anyway. Maybe later. "It's simple," she said, trying for a grin, rueful or otherwise, of her own. "The middle I sank my elbow into wasn't soft."

"Jake?"

Tink Stanton stood in the door to his office. He'd already washed up and shed his lab coat. Megan drew herself erect and reached for Jake's hand.

"That's one lucky dog you've got there."

Jake's hand gripped hers. "Lucky would be for none of this to have happened," he said, and she heard the hoarseness he tried to hide with his rough words.

"Yes," Stanton agreed, "but it did. Have you considered he might be part cat? He certainly seems to have the proverbial nine lives."

"I wouldn't know, doc." Now Jake grinned and extended his free hand toward the doctor, but he didn't release his grasp on hers. "You'd be the expert on that, having looked at the inside of him more than you look at most of your textbooks."

Megan shook her head and glanced at Barbara. "Let me guess," she said. "Friends since the first grade?"

Barbara laughed outright, a sound that was full of relief. "No, Tink is a newcomer. We didn't meet him until third grade. Good job, Tink," she said. "I knew if anyone could pull him through it would be you."

Tink's smile faded. "He's not completely out of the woods yet, Jake. I'll want to keep him a few days to monitor his progress."

Jake nodded his understanding. "How about his injuries?"

"The bullet did a lot of muscle damage, which I know you're much too familiar with to think it can't be serious, but it missed the major organs. And it missed his hip. Whoever did this was either in a big hurry or a really lousy shot, thank God.

"He's still under the anesthetic, and he will be most of the night. I come in at seven on Sunday mornings to check my weekend guests. Why don't you meet me back here then, and I'll be able to give you a better idea of when you can take him home."

They caravaned in their three separate vehicles to Barbara and Patrick's home. No one, it seemed, had eaten since the feast Mattie had provided for them hours before, not even Patrick, who had still been too full of Mattie's home cooking to sample the potluck specialties at the family reunion.

They all trooped wearily into Barbara's charming kitchen and dropped into chairs around the table looking at one another silently for several minutes. Jake propped his foot on a nearby chair and began massaging his thigh. When he saw Megan's worried glance, he started to put his foot down, apparently reconsidered, and continued his slow massage. Patrick's stomach groaned a protest, breaking the silence, and he patted it gently.

"That's what I was waiting for," Patrick said, "a sign to show me what I wanted more, sleep or food."

They all groaned, pushed up from the table, and began the task of gathering food, beverages, and utensils for a late-night meal. Megan set the table, and her trips back and forth from the cabinet took her past the group of pictures she had so admired, the one with the photo of the Three Musketeers and the pile of stones they had once stood beside.

She paused and looked at the photo again, at the tough little team that still worked so well together and at the flag sticking out of the pile of stones.

"When did it explode?" she asked.

"What, Megan?" Barbara asked from her hunched-over position in front of the refrigerator.

"The carbide house of Daniel Tanner. When did it blow up?"

"Don't know," she said. "Yes!" She snatched a jar of pickles from the back of the bottom shelf and turned, slamming the door of the refrigerator with a twitch of her hip. "Why?"

Megan looked back at the photo one more time. It had seemed important when she asked. Why indeed? "Don't know," she mimicked, shaking her head. But her attempt at humor fell flat. "I just—don't know."

None of them had much energy after the week they had already endured. Jake and Patrick talked for a few minutes about the slight to Patrick at the press conference, about the repercussions of Rolley P's well-placed innuendos, about the who and why of the attack on Megan, and even, in cryptic comments with curious undertones, about a conversation Patrick had held with someone that day.

Coffee was out of the question. They were wired enough already. Barbara searched for and found a bottle of wine in the back of the cabinet and poured a nightcap for each of them.

"Tell us again what happened, Megan," Patrick urged. "Though I know you damn well don't want to go over it again."

"I don't know what he was talking about," Megan said. "Because it didn't make any more sense then than now. Unless . . ."

"Unless what?" Jake asked.

"Sam Hooker," she said. "And there's no way on earth anybody but you and I and Mattie would know about that."

"Hooker?" Barbara asked. "Who's he?"

Could Barbara not know? Megan wondered. Was it possible that Mattie had never discussed with her own daughter the strange and confusing matters she had so easily shared with a stranger?

"Railroad gold? The old army payroll story?" Patrick straightened up from his elbows-on-the-table position, revealing that he, at least, was familiar with part of the story. "Why on earth would anyone drag that old rumor out?"

"See?" Megan said. "No sense at all."

"Can you remember the exact words, Megan?" Jake asked. "Not just the context, the exact words."

Megan closed her eyes to isolate herself from this warm gathering and almost instantly felt the chill of fear shudder through her, felt the hand clamped on her mouth. Determined not to give into it, she rubbed her hands over her arms and listened with all her senses for that harsh whispered voice.

"'*You know, don't you?*'" she repeated slowly. "'*He told you. I said all along he did. And now you're going to tell him.'"* She went on. "Something about had I already told and how he'd watched us today, and how *he* wouldn't get it, and then: *'It's mine. And you, bitch, are going to show me where it is. Now.'*"

Only the sounds of their breathing broke the silence in the room until Barbara reached for her wineglass. "God," she said.

"Who's 'he'?" Jake asked.

"More important"—Patrick picked up his wineglass and saluted Megan—"how could Sam Hooker tell you anything?"

"Don't," Megan said softly. "Please don't."

Patrick's wicked-looking grin slid from his face. "I'm sorry. Did I stuff my size twelves into my mouth again?"

Jake stood up and held out a hand for Megan. "Yes, but it's probably something we all need to talk about, since Mattie has made herself a part of it. But not tonight. We're all exhausted."

"Yes, we are," Barbara said. "And it's way too late for you to think about going home. Besides, you don't want to go up the hill and chase bad guys tonight. Stay here."

Jake looked at Megan for consent. She nodded. Barbara was right. She didn't want to go back either to his house or to hers tonight.

But now Barbara looked hesitant. Jake understood first. He grinned at his friend. "Give Megan the guest room," he said, answering her unspoken question. "I'll bunk down on the couch in the den."

Megan rose to go with Barbara, but she waved her back into her chair. "It will only take a minute to check out the room. Finish your wine. You too, Jake. Patrick will bring you some sheets and pillows, won't you, Patrick?"

"What? Oh, sure." With a quick nod, he followed Barbara, leaving Megan and Jake alone in the kitchen.

Jake had once again propped his foot on a chair to stretch

out his leg. Now he dropped it to the floor and stood,
stretching muscles that must be screaming in protest. But he
voiced no complaint. He reached out to Megan and waited
until she placed her hands in his, then tugged gently until
she stood before him.

"It's been a hell of a day, Megan McIntyre. Are you going
to be all right?"

Was she? She thought briefly of those few moments that
afternoon when she had thought herself to be strong. When
she had thought she might have a chance for a life with this
man. When she had thought she could handle anything fate
threw at her. But that was before the threat to herself had
become even more personal than the anonymous telephone
call. Before she realized that some time between waking up
in Jake's arms that morning and standing now with her
hands in his, she had lost the ability to defy her fear.

"What does he want, Jake?" she asked. "Why would he try
to scare me into leaving and then not wait as much as a day
for me to do it?"

Jake shook his head. "Mattie said something today about
parallels. I thought at the time she was trying to make some
point about Sam and Lydia. Now I have the feeling there's
something I'm missing. Something we're all missing."

"You mean this is supposed to make sense?"

He smiled as he tugged on her hands again and pulled her
into his arms. "Some of it."

"And there's no such thing as coincidence?"

"Rarely. Random acts of violence do happen. But not
repeatedly to the same person, and not within a period of
days. And certainly not in the backwoods of Pitchlyn
County, Oklahoma."

"Oops." Barbara stopped in the doorway and shrugged.
"Oh, well, since I'm already in the room." She placed the
things she carried on the table. "Here's a new toothbrush,
Megan. All my clothes are made in Munchkinville, so here's a

Sooners' practice jersey for you to sleep in. Don't think about asking where Patrick got that. Your room is the last door on the right, and the bathroom is just this side of it. I'm out of here, but Patrick is making noises about wanting to talk to you, Jake. Shall I tell him to put a sock in it until tomorrow?"

Jake chuckled. "No. Megan's on her way to bed now, before she falls asleep on her feet. But I think I have a couple more minutes before I do the same. Thanks, Barb."

"Yeah, well, what are friends for," she muttered good-naturedly as she backed out of the room, "if not to interrupt every intimate moment."

Jake laughed softly but waited until he heard Barbara speaking to Patrick some distance down the hallway before he spoke. "Is that what this was," he asked, "an intimate moment?"

Megan looked up at him, not even trying to keep the longing from her eyes. That's what this could have been, she realized, except for all the outside forces bludgeoning her every time she thought she might at last fight her way free of them.

No, she wasn't strong enough yet to tell Jake she wanted him. Until she was, she wasn't strong enough *for* him.

"Good night, Megan," he said regretfully, as he dropped his arms from around her.

He wasn't going to kiss her or tell her not to go. He wasn't going to hug her again. He was just going to stand there and let her walk out of this room without him.

"I'll come back here after I check on Deacon in the morning. Then we can decide what we need to do about your security and living arrangements."

Megan drew herself erect. "I'm going to the vet's with you."

"It isn't necessary."

"It's necessary for me, Jake. I'm responsible for what happened to him. If I hadn't gone wandering off in the woods by myself, he wouldn't be near death right now."

"And if I hadn't been fighting my rampaging hormones so

that I had to leave the house to keep from crawling into bed with you, you wouldn't have been left alone to go wandering off into the woods."

Megan tilted her head to study Jake's expression. He looked almost as shocked by what he had said as she must. "Really," she said, feeling a totally inappropriate little smile stealing over her face.

"Of course I'm responsible."

"No, no, no," she said. "The other. Did you really want to crawl into bed with me?"

"Oh, Megan." He stepped away and looked at her as he dragged his hands through his hair. "Yes."

Calm and in control, was he? Maybe once. Not now. Because that one word spoke volumes and worked wonders for her self-esteem. Not only had he wanted to then, he wanted to now. And only—*only?*—his sense of honor kept him from acting on that desire.

She raised up on tiptoes and brushed her lips gently across his. "Good night, Jake." Turning, she picked up her nightshirt. "And don't even think about leaving this house tomorrow morning without me." Soon, she thought. Very soon she'd have to find a way to reconcile his honor with his desire—and hers.

Sugarloaf County, Choctaw Nation Indian Territory, 1872

I do not know how Sam convinced my father to let us be married. Nor do I care. In public he smiles at Sam and at the blooded citizens of this Nation. In private, he told me how I have dishonored him by wedding beneath my station.

If only he knew how Sam has saved us all from dishonor.

Or from public knowledge of it.

But of course I will not tell him. These are matters of which no one speaks, not even those who know the truth.

And now, after months of silence from him, after months of having suffered his displeasure and his absence, he wishes my attendance at his party: the party to show off the new carbide lighting in the house that will never be grand enough or large enough or modern enough or tasteless enough to satisfy his craving for position and power and esteem.

It matters not to him that I am convinced that his lighting is dangerous. It matters not that I am convinced his workmen were at best careless in the construction, at worst incompetent. It matters not that I cannot face strangers or those who once knew me.

Aunt Peg will not come.

I agree she will be eaten by envy, but she will not allow Daniel Tanner to see that. Nor will she grace his graceless home with her disapproving presence.

Could I hide what I have become from her?

Could I hide the sickness within me that now will not even allow me to accept small kindnesses from the man who is my husband if those kindnesses involve touch of any kind?

Could I hide from her the fear that will not allow me to leave the safety of this cabin, which will never truly be a home, or the fact that I have altered all my dresses so that I now have pockets in which to carry Sam's revolver with me at all times?

Peter has been commanded to appear. And Sam has been extended an invitation that has more of the appearance of a royal command.

Is *he* one of the invited guests?

I know no one believes me when I say he lurks nearby. I know that after the first few times when Sam searched futilely for some visible sign of the intruder, even he began to doubt my word.

Who is he? He is tall; I know that from the time he grabbed me. The army lieutenant? The one outlaw who escaped from the ambush? There was a tall thin one, one with a streak of cruelty that still has the power to wake me from my sleep. But surely he would know where the payroll is? And surely the lieutenant, if that is who it is, would have no reason to hide his presence from everyone but me?

Why won't he leave me alone?

I don't know anything!

I don't want to know anything!

Please, God, I just want to die.

20

Jake didn't know what woke him, some slight noise or just a general feeling that something was not right with Megan in the predawn quiet of the house. Damn! How did he know things like that? Or was the problem more basic than an emotional link he had no skill in understanding?

Had someone discovered that Megan was here and come calling to complete yesterday's visit?

Quietly he slipped into his jeans and stuck his pistol beneath the band at the small of his back.

He found Megan sitting at the kitchen table with only the small light from the range hood illuminating her face. She'd propped her feet up on the chair seat with her knees tucked under her chin. Patrick's purloined jersey covered her like a gray tent.

When he stepped into the room, she looked up at him with a haunted look in her eyes that told him she thought this meeting was inevitable and saluted him with the can of cola she clutched with both hands.

"Coke?" he asked quietly. "At this time of the morning?"

"I needed the caffeine," she said. "But I didn't want to wake anyone with the noise of making coffee."

"What's wrong?"

She shrugged. "Nightmare."

"Want to talk about it?"

She shuddered and took a long drink from the can.

"Megan. What was it about?"

"I don't know," she told him. "Lydia, Sam. You, me. Some faceless man who grabs women and demands answers from them that neither one of us has—had."

He pulled a chair to her side and sat as he had in her kitchen, with his knees nearly touching her. He pried the can from her hands and set it on the table and then cradled both her hands in his.

"You've been through some pretty heavy-duty trauma lately. Do you think it might help to talk to Dr. Kent?"

She shot him a look of wounded betrayal. "That time I spent in the sanitarium?"

He nodded, encouraging her by his silence to continue.

"It was really a private hospital. I was there because of my physical condition. And because everyone thought I should be collapsed in a heap after what I'd witnessed."

"Do you think I don't know that?"

It was as though she hadn't heard him. "He made me sound like some kind of nut case in that press conference. And he doesn't even know the half of it."

"Megan."

"I was doing so well. I hadn't collapsed. I hadn't surrendered to it. And then all *this* started happening. So I tucked some more of it away. I'd managed, once again, to get that girl to stop screaming. You helped me with that. I'd even decided maybe I was strong enough for . . . well, never mind for what. Now it's gotten personal, and I'm not sure how long it will be before I *am* collapsed in a heap." She gave a tiny shuddering sob. "I'm not sure what will happen if I ever let the fear win."

"Megan, you're one of the strongest people I know."

Absolute disbelief filled her eyes.

"Trust me," he said. "Barbara tried to tell me that the first night she met you. I couldn't see it then. I couldn't see past your beauty and your vulnerability and your physical fragility."

"Yeah, sure," she said, tugging one hand free and grasping a handful of her chopped-off hair to hold out for his inspection.

"Hush." He reclaimed her hand and held it still. "Your hair will grow back. In time you'll gain weight. You've already started to get color in your cheeks and life in your eyes. And you hold your own in any wisecracking sessions with me and Patrick and Barbara like you've been with us since the first grade too. You're beautiful and vulnerable and fragile and honest—"

"And you believe every word I tell you." Her voice held the same disbelief as her eyes.

"Yes," he said. "I do."

She tried to pull away again but he tightened his hand. "I have a little trouble with some of it. Not because I don't believe you, but because I don't completely believe the concept. But if you told me Sam Hooker was standing in the corner of this kitchen, I'd say hello. If you said we had to get out of Sarah North's emporium because it was going to blow up, I'd carry you and Sarah out of there so fast you'd be dizzy for a week. And if you told me we had to dig up my living room floor because the army gold was buried under it, we'd go shopping for replacement flooring."

"She doesn't know."

"What?"

"Lydia. She doesn't know where it is. Don't ask me how I know that, I just do." She added, in a quiet yet intense whisper, "And I don't know where it is either!"

∘　　∘　　∘

Tink Stanton let both of them visit Deacon. When Jake stepped back, doing his best to disguise his relief but failing completely, Megan leaned forward. Deacon's eyes followed her as she lifted her hand and ran it along his head and shoulders. His tail thumped once, and he rewarded her with a valiant attempt to lift his head and lick her hand.

"That's okay, boy," she crooned to him. "I'm sorry, Deacon. I won't ever do this to you again. You are a fine brave dog. Oh, yes, you are such a good boy. I'm going to see that you get a sirloin steak at least once a week for the rest of your life."

Now she knew how Jake must have felt when he stepped back from the stainless steel kennel: embarrassed. Damn! She blinked once while Tink closed the kennel door and again when she turned to leave the room. Jake grinned and handed her a paper towel from a nearby dispenser. Should she remind him that he had almost needed one too? She sniffed again, wiped her eyes, and returned the towel to Jake.

They had to go back to his house. The horses needed to be fed, and the cats were wandering God only knew where. Megan wasn't sure they had even taken the time to lock any of the buildings after Jake had carried his bleeding dog to the clearing and loaded him into back of the Jeep.

"We can check into a hotel," Jake suggested as they neared the turnoff from the highway to the county road.

"What good would that do?" Megan asked. "We'd just be in unfamiliar surroundings."

"Right. I—oh, hell, I guess I have to tell you this. I tried to call your father. He wasn't there," he added hurriedly when she turned to glare at him. "Wilkins, the houseman?" She nodded. "Wilkins said he was on a fact-finding mission."

"Great," she said, not trying to hide her bitterness, not able to hide the hurt. "I hope he finds some."

"About Villa Castellano."

"Oh."

"And I asked Patrick to call DEA for me. After the threatening phone call. And again today, to fill them in on what happened next. I don't know what help we can expect from them. I don't know how far they'll go, because this is, after all, out of their jurisdiction. But you must know there isn't going to be any help at all from Rolley P and his crew."

She swallowed once, trying to clear her throat of fear and anger and frustration all twisted together in a mass that threatened to choke her. "I know."

"If we're going to stay at the house, we'll need food."

She nodded understanding and he turned, not toward their houses but toward Prescott.

Sarah and Henry North lived in a small house behind the store. Jake parked by their front porch. "Wait here for a moment," he said. "Then I want you to go into the store with us."

I don't want to leave you out here as a target. He might as well have gone ahead and said the words; she heard them anyway.

Sarah answered his knock almost immediately and after a few seconds of conversation reached up alongside the door facing on the inside of the house and grabbed a ring of keys. She waved at Megan as she crossed the yard toward the back of the store, and Jake nodded, so Megan opened the Jeep door and followed them into the storeroom.

"There was a big bunch of folks out here Friday evening after you left," Sarah said, "and yesterday. Where on earth did they get that horrible picture of you, Megan? They kept shoving it in my face and asking if I knew you and where you lived and were you, well—"

"Was I crazy?"

Sarah stared at Megan in awkward silence until she must have seen that Megan held no anger toward her. "Something like that," she admitted. "They were a rude lot, the whole bunch of them. So I gave them what they deserved. I looked at that picture and told them I had never seen anyone who looked like that around here and I didn't expect to."

She grinned a diabolical little grin that told Megan a lot about Sarah North's wicked sense of humor.

"I did tell them I'd heard a rumor about a strange woman living up on Witcher Mountain. Of course, it was getting on toward dark by then, and we all know how hard it is to find the right road in from that one state highway that runs over toward it. I warned them it wouldn't be easy getting there. There was a good chance she had a high fence with some of those security cameras on it, but then again that might just be rumor.

"There was one man, though, Jake," Sarah said without a trace of her earlier humor, "who gave me the willies. A quiet fellow, more polite than the rest of them, and I guess that's what made me notice him first."

"Tell me about him."

"You want to share your reason?"

"Someone attacked me in the woods yesterday afternoon, Sarah," Megan told her. "I didn't see him well enough to identify him, but he shot Deacon."

"Oh, no!"

"He's going to be all right," Jake told her. He glanced at Megan and lifted an eyebrow. "So is Megan."

"Well, I can see that!" Sarah shook her head. "Honestly!"

"The man, Sarah?" Megan asked, turning Jake's command into a request. "Please."

"Oh, yes. Five ten or so. Wiry-looking. Dark hair, receding hairline. Dark eyes. Dressed well—you know, L. L. Bean instead of the usual jeans or overalls. And a regional accent I couldn't place but definitely wasn't from Arkansas or the Cuisinart School of Television Diction."

Jake's eyes glittered with an expression Megan couldn't remember seeing before and with—was it possible?—recognition. "Do you remember when he was here?"

Sarah nodded. "Yesterday morning, midmorning. Yeah, just as the milk delivery got here, because I was doing my best to check expiration dates on the stuff going into the walk-in and this guy was pumping me for information: ten, ten-fifteen or so."

"Thanks, Sarah," Jake said, hugging the woman. "Can I use your phone?"

"Sure. You know you can."

He looked at Megan. "The freezer's still pretty well stocked. Pick out some fresh stuff, will you, while I call Patrick."

She didn't understand; they never called each other at home about anything important. "But what about—"

He shook his head, earning her silence. "If they hear, they hear. We can't afford to play their games anymore."

With her mind only partially on her chore, Megan made a selection of fresh fruits and vegetables, milk, juice, eggs, and, out of habit, bread, while Jake disappeared to use the phone in the back of the store and Sarah busied herself at the front. Jake joined her just as she pushed the cart to the checkout stand, and Sarah hurried around from the lunch counter with a white paper bag in her hand.

"A couple of sandwiches," Sarah said.

"Great," Jake told her. "I would have asked if this hadn't been your day off."

Sarah grinned at him. "You would have asked if you hadn't been afraid I'd hit you over the head with this antique cash register. But you're right. This is my day off, and I'm sure glad we're closed."

"How did you ever manage with that crowd yesterday?" Megan asked.

"Oh, good grief. I almost forgot. I had a helper. He came out yesterday afternoon to apply for a job and got caught up in the whole mess. He said you knew him, Jake."

"An off-the-street job applicant in Prescott?" he asked

with an incredulous laugh. "And you don't know him? Who is he?"

"His name is Mack—Mack—oh, lord, I wrote it down but I've forgotten. He said he'd been working at Walt Harrison's lumberyard but was out of a job as of noon yesterday. If what he did for me is any indication of the kind of worker he is, I sure could use him around here."

Jake's easy laughter faded. "He didn't last long at the lumberyard, even considering Walt's bad temper and hiring practices. Maybe you'd better check his references carefully."

"Why? Do you know something bad about him?"

Jake shook his head. "I don't know anything about him. And all of a sudden that's beginning to worry me."

When they topped the last hill on their way home, a clear view of the valley lay before them. From a distance, they spotted a cluster of cars grouped near the gate Jake and Patrick had installed. It seemed that, thank God, they had indeed locked it on their mad dash out the day before.

Megan heard Jake swear and felt the sudden jolt as he stepped on the brakes.

"Now what?" she asked.

He gave her a lethal smile. "A little off-roading, I think. Are you up to it?"

She nodded. "Are you?" And then she realized what off-roading meant in this part of the country. "Oh, Jake. Your new car. You'll scratch it all up."

"Probably." He turned into a rutted lane. "This place runs parallel to ours for a considerable distance," he told her, "until my place wraps back around it. I was thinking about buying it, even ran a few cattle on it for a while."

The old house and barn were nothing but ruins, which Jake skirted, avoiding them in favor of a trail that angled back toward the mountains. He fought to keep the Jeep on the track until they bounced off the shale-lined path and into a stand of ancient pecan trees and he jammed on the brakes.

"Damn!"

A twelve-foot portion of the fence lay in a tangle of wires and orange metal posts. Jake slammed out of the Jeep and Megan followed.

"The reporters?" she asked as she stood by him while he knelt and examined the downed gap gate of the fence.

He shook his head, walked to the end of the grove on the other side of the fence, and examined the grass there.

"I don't think so," he said. "Could be, but this appears to have been used for a while. The person who trashed your bedroom? The man who tried to grab you yesterday? Both of them—or one of them—could have come through here and circled around to either of our houses, just like I'm planning to do. Damn! I didn't even think of looking on this side of the ridge. But who the hell would know about this access?"

"Jake." Megan put her hand on his arm. "Let's just go home now. Please. I have a feeling we're going to have a lot of time to worry about the whos and whats and whys."

"Right," he told her. "If you drive the Jeep through, I'll put the gap back up."

She saw no path; she had no idea how Jake followed one or even where they were until they entered the tree-lined overgrowth of the old roadbed, somewhere south of the curved pine tree but still north of the creek.

"I know you probably want to check on your place," Jake told her, "but we run the risk of being spotted if we go by."

She shook her head. "I'd rather not confront the physical evidence of someone's hatred just yet. The memories are bad enough."

What remained of the road from the creek to just shy of Jake's clearing was every bit as awful as Megan had imagined it would be, with the way cluttered by young saplings, tumbled boulders, and volunteer cedars and pine trees and every briar native to the area. Megan winced as she heard still another branch scrape along the side of the Jeep. Mentally she added a new paint job to the list of things she already owed Jake Kenyon.

He pulled to a stop in the trees just outside the clearing and left the engine idling as he looked around suspiciously.

"Do you think anyone's up here?"

"I don't know. Probably if any of the reporters made it this far they decided we weren't here and went back to the comfort of their air-conditioned cars to wait for us to show up. As for your buddy, I hope he's long gone. But let me case the joint before you put a boot on the ground."

"Case the joint?" Megan asked. "As in a bad gangster movie?"

Jake grinned and touched his hand to her cheek. "Would you prefer 'run a perimeter check'?"

Megan caught her hand in his. "I'd prefer you to be damned careful and hurry back."

"Got it," he told her. "But just in case something goes wrong, head this Jeep down the road. Don't stop for the gate, just make yourself a new one anywhere you want."

And leave him here alone? No way!

But Jake didn't need an argument right then. "Hurry back," she told him.

He didn't hurry, and it seemed like forever before he returned. "If anyone's been here, they're gone," he told her.

"Good," she said. "Now can we please go in the house and lock the doors . . ." *and make love until all the intrigue and danger swirling around us is just a bad memory.*

"And have lunch?" Jake finished for her. "Whatever Sarah put in that bag smells like 'more.'"

*   *   *

The kittens were in the house. Megan fed them kibble and milk, and after she and Jake finished their lunch, she rose to let them out.

As she passed where he sat at the table, he stopped her with a hand on her arm. "Leave them in," he told her, with more concern than the simple act merited.

She looked at him questioningly.

"That way you'll know where they are. You won't want to go out looking for them while I'm gone."

"Where are you going?"

"First to where Deacon was shot, to see if I can find any evidence as to the identity of that scumbag who attacked you, and then to see if I can pick up any clue as to where he went, *if* he went, and with whom, if anybody, he went."

"No."

"No?" His hand, still resting on her arm, tightened. "What do you mean, no?"

"I mean I don't want you going back out there alone."

He twisted in his chair until he faced her and then pulled her closer until she stood between his knees. Then he tugged her closer, wrapped his arms around her, and rested his head on her breast. Not even thinking about repercussions or unspoken admissions, Megan lifted her hands to his head and held him close.

"I'm the professional here," he said. "I'm supposed to have some idea of how to keep you safe. Instead, I just keep fumbling around in the dark, putting you at risk."

"No," she whispered. "You've saved my sanity, and I know you've saved my life. And at what cost to you? Your privacy's been invaded, your life's been turned upside down, your reputation's been slandered, and your dog's been shot. Now you're getting ready to put yourself in harm's way again because of me, and I don't want you to do it."

He hugged her tightly and released her, standing up so abruptly he scooted his chair backward. "Too bad, baby," he said, reaching for a lightness that didn't exist in the situation, "but a man's gotta do what a—"

She put her fingers on his lips and silenced him. "I know," she said. "But damn it, Jake Kenyon, don't you dare let yourself get hurt."

He made her find the automatic he'd given her earlier, checked it to make sure it was still loaded, and jacked a shell into the chamber.

"Keep it near you," he told her. "You probably won't need it, but if you do, use it. And if you need me, fire a shot. I'll be close enough to hear, and to get back in a hurry."

Then he had gone, leaving her alone in the house with nothing but memories.

Hers. And others that couldn't possibly be hers but were just as real.

Without the comfort and security she had come to feel in Deacon's presence, she felt horribly vulnerable as she waited for Jake to return.

Vulnerable. Waiting. Vulnerable. Waiting.

Disjointed images of her nightmare hammered at the edges of her consciousness. She—Lydia?—someone was waiting. . . .

Damn it, for what? Or for whom?

She hadn't been in the notebook since Mattie had made her revelations. Since Mattie had confirmed that Lydia Tanner Hooker had really lived. Since Mattie had mentioned a mystery.

Damn it, what mystery?

Megan had enough on her plate without the added burden of a nineteenth-century mystery.

But since it just might be involved with a very real twentieth-century one, shouldn't someone try to solve it? And who could?

Megan took the notebook into Jake's bedroom. It seemed safer there, and she had a strange premonition she would soon need "safe."

He had an old-fashioned walnut vanity, the kind with a kneehole and a padded bench, nice but not museum quality. She suspected it was a family heirloom because it was nothing that Jake would choose for himself and nothing that Helen would have kept if not forced to do so.

She seated herself on the bench and opened the notebook on the vanity in front of her. One kitten crawled into her lap, the other curled on the bench beside her.

Megan gripped her pen. This felt different from the other times. They had been scary because the unknown *is* scary. She knew what she was facing now, knew that at least two other people believed in it, knew that Lydia had been a real person and had a diary. This foreboding was brought about not by all those things but by the intuition that she was going to learn something she really didn't want to know.

That she *had* to know.

Sugarloaf County, Choctaw Nation Indian Territory, 1872

Megan looked at those words with dread. Still 1872. But when? Well, there was only one way to find out. She felt a moment's hesitation, as though her subconscious was every bit as reluctant to subject herself to what she might learn as her conscious mind was, and then the pen began to move.

Sam has accompanied Peter to my father's party. He said he must, in an attempt to bridge the chasm that has opened between me and the man who gave me life. Life! The only chance at life I ever had was with Sam Hooker, and now even that has been taken from me.

Sam did not insist I accompany him, but he would not succumb to my entreaties that he remain with me. And I would not succumb to his that I remain with Granny for the evening.

He wore his suit, the one he had made specifically for the times he must attend to the business of the principal chief, and he looked for a brief moment as dashing as when I first fell in love with him.

I had thought in my innocence I could heal his pain. I have only brought him more.

And now he has left me alone, knowing of my fear but unwilling to believe that it is real, that someone stalks me in his absence, that someone wants from me what I cannot give because I do not know.

The leaves have fallen early this year, parched and dull without their rioting colors. How appropriate that the world itself has taken on mourning clothes for the death of my dreams, of my soul. There is as yet no chill in the air to herald winter's coming, only the bare ugly branches and the brittle detritus of the forest's life—

Megan stared at the slash her pen had made across the page, an angry punctuation for the almost palpable terror that seemed suddenly to fill the room. She listened, because she felt sure she must have heard something, must have been jarred from Lydia's world. But the cats still slept contentedly, the light breeze still played with the leaves of the trees visible through the windows, the old house settled contented and still around her.

So the terror must be coming from Lydia. Again.

Did she really want to learn why? No, but she knew that she must.

God help us all. It has exploded. Daniel Tanner's vanity has killed them.

I heard the roar from inside the cabin. At first I thought it to be a vicious and too-close blast of thunder, until I remembered that the sky had been cloudless when last I looked outside, to see if the scrabbling noises in the leaves were caused by the raccoon that so often frequents our cabin looking for an easy food supply.

Against my will I was drawn to the ridge. Through the leafless trees I could see flames shooting upward from what had been my father's house. I could hear the screams of horses tethered too near the flames.

Granny had run from her cabin. She saw me at the ridge and urged me to go with her to be of what assistance we could to the injured. Sam is there. Peter is there.

God help me, I could not go.

Sam is dead because of me. I know that within my heart.

I cannot cry.

I should have listened to Granny years ago when she told me not to love him. I should have stayed with Aunt Peg rather than return. I can ignore that knowledge no longer. Without me, he would have been spared these months of agony. Without me, he would not now be trapped within—*Oh, God!*

Lydia? You might as well tell me. You can't hide in there forever.

Are the words I hear only caused by the whispering of the wind? Are they dragged forth from my fear and my memories? Or is someone truly outside?

I have barred the door. I sit now with Sam's revolver on the table before me.

Lydia? Open the door, Lydia. You know there's no one to save you now.

Sam, I am so sorry. I never meant to cause you pain. Please, oh, please God forgive me. And please, please God—someone—help me. . . .

$\overline{2}\overline{1}$

Jake returned to the location where Deacon had been shot. A few yards farther on, he found the spot where Megan had escaped from her assailant. A few feet away from that, farther along the trail of broken grass and twigs, he found a sprinkling of blood. Good. Deacon had made the bastard earn his escape.

He followed the trail to the old cabin site before losing it in a thicket of briar.

His mouth twisted in a grim smile. The man would have more blood on him than that caused by Deacon's teeth after fleeing through this tangle of blackberry and greenbriar vines. With any luck he'd have picked up a giant dose of ticks and chiggers too.

Jake looked at the thicket. He could probably work his way around it and pick up the trail again. And do what, follow it to where the man had left some vehicle parked? Follow it until he found where another fence had been run down? Then what?

Then nothing. He was at a dead end. Another in a long trail of dead ends.

He thought bitterly of what he had tried to tell Megan. He was the professional; he was supposed to protect civilians from the bad guys. Once he had been more than capable in his job, but not in this morass of intrusions and intrigue and spirits. In this, in what was probably the most important case of his life, he felt no more competent than the greenest rookie.

He was too damn close to it. He'd never understood how being close to a case could do more than heighten an investigator's senses. Now he did. Megan was too important to him. Fear for her clouded his perception.

Parallels, Mattie had said. All right, he'd give her that. But parallels of what? Parallels of a story more than a century old that was too unbelievable to be real, too real to disbelieve? Especially in light of what he had finally forced Mattie to admit that morning. Parallels of the ridicule Megan received when once again it became known she had been a victim? Or even the parallels of Sarah's having—maybe—seen someone from Jake's past, someone who had no business being in Prescott, Oklahoma.

He looked at the sky and at the trail. Had he come so far that he would be unable to hear Megan if she called him?

Face it, he told himself. He didn't want to follow a blind trail to another lost end. He wanted to go back to Megan and lock the doors . . . *and make love until all the intrigue and danger swirling around us is just a bad memory.*

Jake shook his head to clear it. Had that been his thought or another intrusion? It didn't matter; it echoed what he wanted to do. But he couldn't let himself be lost in loving her. Not while the danger to her still haunted this hillside.

He found the door locked when he returned and the house quiet when he let himself in with his key. Apprehensive and alert, he didn't call out. Instead, he worked his way silently through the rooms.

He let out a tightly held breath when he found Megan sitting at the vanity in his bedroom writing in her journal.

He dropped his hands to his sides and turned away from
, unable to watch while he repeated his story. "I called
attie this morning from the store to check on her, to reas-
re her if she had watched the newscast, and to tell her
hat had happened to you yesterday. She told me. She said
e had to warn me."

"About what?"

Jake turned around. He looked at the journal where it lay
nnocuously on the walnut vanity that had belonged to his
mother's family, and at Megan, completely contemporary in
her cropped hair, faded jeans, hiking boots, and pink long-
sleeved T-shirt.

"Maybe you'd better sit down," he said.

She shook her head and remained standing. "Tell me."

It shouldn't have been difficult to do. They were, after all,
talking about someone they knew to be dead. But Megan
wasn't going to like this. He didn't like it. And he knew why
Mattie hadn't wanted to tell either one of them.

"Sam didn't die in the explosion," he said bluntly, knowing there was no kind way to tell her. "Lydia killed him."

The breath whooshed out of her and her knees collapsed.
Jake reached for her as she sank onto the vanity bench.

"No," she said, holding her hands out in front of her to
ward off his words. "No."

"He went home from the explosion, and she shot him as
he walked in the door."

"No!"

"He was found by her brother the next morning. Lydia
was gone."

"Gone? But that means . . . don't you see? Whoever was
lurking around must have killed him and taken her. Oh,
God. Not again."

"Megan. Sam was shot with his own pistol. And Lydia was
seen nearby in the woods several times after that but never
closely enough for anyone to capture her."

A "form of therapy" was how she had once described that
book. A product of her paranoia. A way of putting all the
pieces together. Another way to escape. What was it today?

He sat on the edge of the bed and leaned back against the
headboard, quiet so he wouldn't disturb her—if anything
could disturb her. He watched her reflection in the vanity
mirror. She had her lower lip caught between her teeth, but
other than that she looked as though she were in some sort
of trance.

The longer he watched, the more concerned he became.
He sat up on the edge of the bed.

"Megan?" he said softly.

She made no response; she gave no indication she had
even heard him.

"Megan?" he said a little more loudly.

Still the pen moved determinedly over the page in front
of her: the page in the book that except for the first two
pages contained nothing of Megan and everything of the tortured woman they knew as Lydia Tanner.

"Damn," Jake muttered as he crossed the room. He was
aware of intruding on Megan's privacy as he looked over her
shoulder, but she wasn't aware of it. She didn't seem to be
aware of anything, not even the pen she moved across the
page.

"Lydia." The word hissed through his teeth as he saw the
fine copperplate penmanship fairly leaping off the page—
fine copperplate penmanship made all but illegible by the
panic that propelled it.

"Megan!" He didn't stop to think, didn't stop to consider
the danger of jerking her back to awareness. Jake only knew
with gut-level certainty that Megan was in as much danger
as Lydia if she stayed trapped in the journal with her. He
roared her name and clapped his hand down on her shoulder, spinning her around to face him.

She looked up at him numbly for a moment, as though

not really seeing him. Then slowly, much too slowly for his peace of mind, awareness of who she was and where she was returned to her eyes, followed quickly by the memory of what she had just seen or felt or whatever the hell happened to her in Lydia's diary. Her eyes filled with horror; her already pale complexion paled even more; her mouth opened, as she gasped and dragged in air.

Then she crumpled, reaching blindly for him, grasping him with both arms around his waist as she buried her face against him and shook with sobs that racked her slender body.

Feeling completely ineffectual, Jake stood within her embrace and held her, smoothing her hair back from her face, rubbing her shoulders, her neck, her back, forcing himself to let her cry as he remembered Barbara's admonitions, when what he wanted to do was stop her tears somehow, stop the pain that shuddered through her.

"I couldn't get out," Megan said finally against his chest. "I couldn't get out. And she was so scared!"

"Shh," he said, at last daring to speak, at last daring to try to calm her. "It's all right. You're here now."

"Is it all right, Jake? Everything in my life is screwed up. My whole world is crazy, except you. You're the one stable thing I have to hold on to, and I'm dragging you into the mess with me."

"That's enough," he said. "Whatever is happening is not your fault, understand?"

"Then whose is it?"

He sighed and pressed her face to his chest. "God only knows," he said. The open journal lay on the vanity in front of him. He stared at it over Megan's bent head with something like revulsion. With all that was going on around them, they didn't need the added burden of whatever the hell it was coming through that book and however the hell it managed to do it.

He reached over and slammed the noteboo supposed to be healthy? Some reputable doct you this trip to the Twilight Zone and told yo forays into someone else's terror would heal you

"No." He felt Megan shudder as she drew awa She seemed to pull herself upright on the bencl her shoulders, defying the tears that glimmered ir "No," she repeated. "This has gone way beyond Kent gave me. I think his associate who's develo technique would be appalled at what has happened efforts. It's supposed to put *me* back together, not so who lived in the nineteenth century."

"Then let's put it away," he said, not bothering to h concern for her. "Let's stick it in a closet and leave it and leave Sam and Lydia and all their problems with i have enough trouble of our own."

"I have to go back."

"What?"

"I have to go back. I can't leave her there like that. I to get her through what's happening. She thinks San dead; Sam and Peter went to her father's house. It was night the carbide house blew up. And now someone is ou side her house, trying to get in. Don't you see? I can't abar don her now. Not till Granny gets back. Not till she know for sure."

"Megan." Jake pulled her from the bench and into his arms. "Listen to yourself. There's nothing you can do."

"I can be there. She's telling me this for a reason."

"Megan." He caught her shoulders in his hands and shook her. "Stop it. You can't do anything. It's all been done, long ago."

"But she's so alone!"

"And it's going to get worse."

She looked up at him, and comprehension filled her eyes. "You know what happens, don't you? How do you know?"

A "form of therapy" was how she had once described that book. A product of her paranoia. A way of putting all the pieces together. Another way to escape. What was it today?

He sat on the edge of the bed and leaned back against the headboard, quiet so he wouldn't disturb her—if anything could disturb her. He watched her reflection in the vanity mirror. She had her lower lip caught between her teeth, but other than that she looked as though she were in some sort of trance.

The longer he watched, the more concerned he became. He sat up on the edge of the bed.

"Megan?" he said softly.

She made no response; she gave no indication she had even heard him.

"Megan?" he said a little more loudly.

Still the pen moved determinedly over the page in front of her: the page in the book that except for the first two pages contained nothing of Megan and everything of the tortured woman they knew as Lydia Tanner.

"Damn," Jake muttered as he crossed the room. He was aware of intruding on Megan's privacy as he looked over her shoulder, but she wasn't aware of it. She didn't seem to be aware of anything, not even the pen she moved across the page.

"Lydia." The word hissed through his teeth as he saw the fine copperplate penmanship fairly leaping off the page— fine copperplate penmanship made all but illegible by the panic that propelled it.

"Megan!" He didn't stop to think, didn't stop to consider the danger of jerking her back to awareness. Jake only knew with gut-level certainty that Megan was in as much danger as Lydia if she stayed trapped in the journal with her. He roared her name and clapped his hand down on her shoulder, spinning her around to face him.

She looked up at him numbly for a moment, as though

not really seeing him. Then slowly, much too slowly for his peace of mind, awareness of who she was and where she was returned to her eyes, followed quickly by the memory of what she had just seen or felt or whatever the hell happened to her in Lydia's diary. Her eyes filled with horror; her already pale complexion paled even more; her mouth opened, as she gasped and dragged in air.

Then she crumpled, reaching blindly for him, grasping him with both arms around his waist as she buried her face against him and shook with sobs that racked her slender body.

Feeling completely ineffectual, Jake stood within her embrace and held her, smoothing her hair back from her face, rubbing her shoulders, her neck, her back, forcing himself to let her cry as he remembered Barbara's admonitions, when what he wanted to do was stop her tears somehow, stop the pain that shuddered through her.

"I couldn't get out," Megan said finally against his chest. "I couldn't get out. And she was so scared!"

"Shh," he said, at last daring to speak, at last daring to try to calm her. "It's all right. You're here now."

"Is it all right, Jake? Everything in my life is screwed up. My whole world is crazy, except you. You're the one stable thing I have to hold on to, and I'm dragging you into the mess with me."

"That's enough," he said. "Whatever is happening is not your fault, understand?"

"Then whose is it?"

He sighed and pressed her face to his chest. "God only knows," he said. The open journal lay on the vanity in front of him. He stared at it over Megan's bent head with something like revulsion. With all that was going on around them, they didn't need the added burden of whatever the hell it was coming through that book and however the hell it managed to do it.

He reached over and slammed the notebook shut. "This is supposed to be healthy? Some reputable doctor really gave you this trip to the Twilight Zone and told you these little forays into someone else's terror would heal your own?"

"No." He felt Megan shudder as she drew away from him. She seemed to pull herself upright on the bench, squaring her shoulders, defying the tears that glimmered in her eyes. "No," she repeated. "This has gone way beyond what Dr. Kent gave me. I think his associate who's developing the technique would be appalled at what has happened with my efforts. It's supposed to put *me* back together, not someone who lived in the nineteenth century."

"Then let's put it away," he said, not bothering to hide his concern for her. "Let's stick it in a closet and leave it there, and leave Sam and Lydia and all their problems with it. We have enough trouble of our own."

"I have to go back."

"What?"

"I have to go back. I can't leave her there like that. I have to get her through what's happening. She thinks Sam is dead; Sam and Peter went to her father's house. It was the night the carbide house blew up. And now someone is outside her house, trying to get in. Don't you see? I can't abandon her now. Not till Granny gets back. Not till she knows for sure."

"Megan." Jake pulled her from the bench and into his arms. "Listen to yourself. There's nothing you can do."

"I can be there. She's telling me this for a reason."

"Megan." He caught her shoulders in his hands and shook her. "Stop it. You can't do anything. It's all been done, long ago."

"But she's so alone!"

"And it's going to get worse."

She looked up at him, and comprehension filled her eyes. "You know what happens, don't you? How do you know?"

He dropped his hands to his sides and turned away from her, unable to watch while he repeated his story. "I called Mattie this morning from the store to check on her, to reassure her if she had watched the newscast, and to tell her what had happened to you yesterday. She told me. She said she had to warn me."

"About what?"

Jake turned around. He looked at the journal where it lay innocuously on the walnut vanity that had belonged to his mother's family, and at Megan, completely contemporary in her cropped hair, faded jeans, hiking boots, and pink long-sleeved T-shirt.

"Maybe you'd better sit down," he said.

She shook her head and remained standing. "Tell me."

It shouldn't have been difficult to do. They were, after all, talking about someone they knew to be dead. But Megan wasn't going to like this. He didn't like it. And he knew why Mattie hadn't wanted to tell either one of them.

"Sam didn't die in the explosion," he said bluntly, knowing there was no kind way to tell her. "Lydia killed him."

The breath whooshed out of her and her knees collapsed. Jake reached for her as she sank onto the vanity bench.

"No," she said, holding her hands out in front of her to ward off his words. "No."

"He went home from the explosion, and she shot him as he walked in the door."

"No!"

"He was found by her brother the next morning. Lydia was gone."

"Gone? But that means . . . don't you see? Whoever was lurking around must have killed him and taken her. Oh, God. Not again."

"Megan. Sam was shot with his own pistol. And Lydia was seen nearby in the woods several times after that but never closely enough for anyone to capture her."

"Capture?"

"She went mad," he said sadly, knowing how she must take this news. "Completely mad. And eventually she just disappeared."

"No," Megan said, whispering the denial he knew she must make. "No, no, no, no, no. She was terrified the night of the explosion, absolutely terrified. But she was sane, Jake. As sane as—"

He jerked her off the bench and shook her until she looked at him. "You are!" he said. "Don't doubt it for a moment. Oh, Megan," he said. "Oh, hell!"

Her lips parted in shocked surprise under the onslaught of his mouth. Too long. He had wanted her too long to be gentle, to be teasing. To coax. He wanted her, not the doll of her Washington days, not the wounded and troubled Lydia: Megan. With her cropped hair and wall-to-wall problems and surprising self-doubt and indomitable strength that right now was undergoing a battering of a different kind from the bombardment he was making on her senses.

Megan. Shy and smart-mouthed. Full of doubt but with a will of iron. Too fragile to have endured all she had been through; but she had.

Megan. With a beauty that haunted him. With soft curves beneath her disguising clothes. With a touch that tormented him. With a breathless, throaty, unendurably sexy voice moaning his name.

Jake made one last effort to reel in his senses. He tore his mouth from hers, lifted his head, and looked down at her. Into eyes that showed a desire as great as the one he felt. At a mouth trembling from his kiss. At a longing he had thought never to see on a woman's face. She lifted her hand to his scarred cheek.

"Oh, yes," she said. "*This* is what I was going to tell you yesterday. This is what I wanted to happen when I returned from the cabin. And this is what I was afraid I would never be able to tell you, after . . ."

After what? But the time for asking was gone. Megan lifted her other hand to his cheek, lifted her body to fit against his, lifted her mouth to his in supplication and demand.

They found their way to the bed, backstepping, stumbling, never releasing each other, and fell onto it in a tangle of arms and legs and moans and even an unexpected soft laugh. The bed where he had lain alone for too many months. The bed where he had taken Megan that first night and wanted to crawl in beside her in spite of her vacations and the trauma she had been through. The bed he had shared with her in frustrated, unrevealed passion two long nights ago.

Jake was shy of his body. He had not been with a woman since the shooting. He had not thought he would ever be with one again in the harsh light of day. But when finally they dispensed with the last of their clothes, when finally he was revealed to her in all his scarred, battered, tarnished glory, when finally he heard her small gasp of dismay, he saw no revulsion or pity in her eyes. He saw compassion. And a fierce warrior's glare.

"I could kill him," she said. "I could kill whoever did this to you with my bare hands."

And he believed that this soft, gentle woman would do just that. Because he knew that if anyone truly harmed her, he would do the same.

And he accepted that had his scars been on her body, he would not have loved her less. Loved her. Yes. That was a knowledge that had been hovering just outside his consciousness until this moment. And it felt right. It felt more than right; it felt inevitable.

And it felt returned. Although Megan had not said the words, she would. He knew that as well as he knew the desire she felt for him was surprisingly new to her.

She had bent her head to the long scar on his chest where the marks of the sutures still showed in a neat rows along each side of the jagged line, had trailed her fingers to his thigh, to the tortured muscle there, leaving warmth and healing each place she touched.

Leaving warmth and healing in a heart that had been too long alone.

Laughing in triumph, Jake lifted her head and gathered her close. Maybe it hadn't been too long for him to be gentle, after all.

Megan lay caught close to Jake's side in the aftermath of their passion. Their arms and legs were still tangled together, although he had moved slightly to one side to shift his weight from her. She felt a light breeze through the open window skim across the fine sheen of perspiration covering her body and shivered slightly.

Jake groaned, fumbled for the sheet, and threw it over them.

Amazing, Megan thought. Here she was, stark naked with a man she had known for only five days, and the only need she felt for a covering was to protect her from the chill.

Amazing. She had had sex—had *made love*—with this same man and for the first time in her life had not been left feeling used or still wanting. She felt a frisson of anger try to work its way into her contentment—anger that it had taken her this long to know how love between a man and a woman should be. Anger that for some reason she had accepted that what she had known was all she was entitled to. She pushed the anger back. She knew she would have to confront it later, as she would have to confront many things. But right now all she wanted to was to lie here in Jake's arms and share this marvelous moment with him.

She slept. As exhausted as they both were, the only thing surprising to Megan about that was that she awoke as soon as she did, just as the dusk of early evening was sliding into the dark of night.

She turned, still caught in Jake's arms, and found him raised on one elbow, looking down at her with his eyes still shadowed by exhaustion, and she knew without asking that he had stayed awake, on guard, protecting her.

"You're a wonder," he said, lifting a hand to trace his fingers along her cheek and jaw, to draw them with teasing slowness across her lips. "Another blessing in a life of undeserved miracles."

"I won't leave you," she promised. She felt a slow flush rising. He hadn't asked her not to. He hadn't asked anything of her. She pushed that away to be considered later, with the anger. He might not have asked in words, but Jake Kenyon had told her that he wanted her. That he needed her. "You'll have to tie me up and ship me off to get me out of your life now, Jake."

A slow smile warmed his scarred face. "Thank God."

Yes. He wanted her. *Forever?* He hadn't said, he might not yet know, but to Megan it felt like forever. Had, she realized now, felt like forever from the moment she saw his hand reaching for hers in a roomful of uniformed men.

It had been too long for her: a lifetime of emptiness, loneliness, and unexplained longing. She lifted her hand to Jake's neck and urged him down to her.

"I thought this was never going to happen," he murmured against her throat. "That I would never know your sweetness or your passion."

He would never sleep beside her, that she knew.

Part of Megan wanted to hold on to that thought, to explore it, even to share it with Jake. Another part of her recognized that it came from another time in her life, a time she could not allow to intrude in the now of her and Jake and this moment.

"Shh," she whispered, rising to meet him. "Love me, Jake. It's been so long. Too long." Her words, like her earlier thought, cried for exploration, cried for understanding, but she could not give them that. Not now. "Please, just love me."

Where is he? He promised never to leave me to face danger alone again, and now he's gone. Gone to confront Daniel Tanner in a vain attempt to reconcile us when I need him here! Here with me. That's not a raccoon outside, that is a human being.

He's dead. Oh, God, he's dead. Dead because of Daniel Tanner's vanity and my fear.

Dead. And whoever is outside the cabin knows that, knows that without Sam I am defenseless. I don't know. I swear to God I don't know where the gold is. Sam? Sam, I need you. Oh, God, Sam, I am so sorry.

When Megan awoke again, the room was dark, lighted only by a spear of light from the hallway. She smelled the aroma of coffee before she heard his footstep and before she felt the bed shift as Jake sat beside her.

She scooted up against the headboard and into the curve of his arm, taking the sheet with her to cover herself, unsure of the etiquette involved in morning after—evening after—encounters. Stop it! she told herself as her insecurities started to spin out of control. This was Jake. And they had just spent magical hours together.

He'd pulled on a pair of jeans but remained shirtless, leaving his scarred chest and back exposed and vulnerable. That, more than anything he could have said, convinced Megan that their emotional closeness had not dissolved with their physical parting. She smiled and took the coffee cup he held out for her.

"We have to talk," he said.

Yes, they did. About many things. Too many things?

"Do you have a dartboard?" she asked. "We could pin topics on various parts and toss to see where we start."

Jake shook his head, and in the shadows Megan saw his jaw tense.

"The first topic has to be your safety, Megan."

"And yours."

She might as well not have spoken.

"Physical and emotional," he said. "I want you to promise me you won't work in the notebook again. At least for a while."

"Why?"

"Because you couldn't get out of it today. You admitted it, but you didn't have to. I called your name several times before I finally shook you."

"But nothing would have happened. Eventually I would have finished the entry."

"What if someone had been breaking in the house or sneaking up on you? Would you have been aware of that any more than you were aware of me? It isn't safe right now." He gave a short bitter laugh. "Later we'll discuss whether it ever will be safe."

"All right," she said.

"Just like that?" he asked.

"I don't like it, but I'm not an unreasonable person. You have a valid point."

He lifted the cup from her hand and set it on the night table, then turned her in his arms, holding her loosely against his chest while he rested his chin on her head. "I have to keep you safe. You know that, don't you?"

You were frightened, and I was not there to prevent it. I want the right be there.

Again the memory of other words and another time tried to intrude. Again she pushed it away. "Yes."

"And that I would never willingly hurt you?"

I'll never hurt you. No one will ever hurt you again.

"Yes."

He let out a tension-laden breath and turned her to lie against his shoulder. "Good."

"Why does that sound as though you're going to say something I won't like?" she asked.

"Probably because you won't. We need to get you out of here, to someplace safe, and the safest place I can think of is your father's house in Washington."

"You're right," she said, knowing where some of his tension had gone; it had come to her. "I don't like that plan at all. Especially if you're going to stay here and play hotshot."

"Megan—"

"What if the plan all along has just been to scare me away?" she asked.

"From what?"

It made no sense, but nothing else did, so Megan threw it out for his consideration. "What if someone has stumbled over the old story of the army gold and believes it. What if that same someone wants me off the property to have the freedom to search for it."

"Whoever would do that would have to be—"

"Around the bend," she finished for him. "Completely unpredictable to anyone trying to find him. Completely unpredictable if confronted. So if I leave, you leave. We let whoever it is dig up the property until this whole area looks like moon craters, and then we come back together."

"That's a completely unreasonable solution," he said.

"I know. The alternative is that we both stay here and catch this nut. Together."

Jake's arm tightened on her shoulder. He didn't like this idea, but she'd known he wouldn't. "This person has gone beyond eccentric treasure hunter, Megan," he said. "He proved yesterday, if not before, that he is dangerous. And what if he's not after the army payroll, then what?"

"Then let's look at it. Maybe the two of us, talking about it, can drag up some minuscule little item that might make sense of the whole."

"Maybe." He hugged her tight before reaching for the

coffee, taking a sip, and handing it to her. "Okay," he said. "We have the nighttime intrusions onto the property: mine too but mostly yours."

"Right," she said. "The phone call, the vandalism to my bedroom, and the attack yesterday."

"Max Renfro," he added, "dead in a suspicious hit-and-run *before* Rolley P executed the search warrant." Jake paused, and Megan knew he had decided to reveal another piece in their shattered puzzle. "And a stranger at Sarah North's store this weekend who might be tied to Renfro."

She digested the news quietly for a moment before adding a piece he would deny but that she knew belonged. "And Sam and Lydia."

"Megan, if we're going to add those two, we might as well throw the attacks on the clinic and on me into the pot and— oh, my God!"

"What? What, Jake?"

He took the cup from her and turned until he was looking into her eyes. His face wore a look of such self-derision it hurt to see it.

"What is it?" she asked in a whisper.

"You told me. You told me the first morning we had breakfast, and I paid absolutely no attention to your words."

"I told you *what*?"

"You told me Helen and Roger knew the army officer in charge of the attack on the clinic, and he knew them. How? Why would a middle-ranking officer in a tiny little country know Roger and Helen? Why would Roger take one look at him, say '*You*,' and know he was going to die? Your words, Megan. Remember?"

Not knowing where he was taking this, not knowing how to react to the intensity now thrumming through him, Megan could only nod. Those had been her words; that had been what happened.

"Carry this a little further, Megan. Why would Roger and

Helen, who above all loved their creature comforts, ever have gone to Villa Castellano? Did it make any more sense to you than it did to me?

"And why, considering how much your place is worth even at raw land and mineral prices, did they turn a valuable piece of property into nothing more than a cheap rental for a two-bit drug dealer?"

"Okay," she said warily. "Why?"

"Access, Megan. Access to the privacy of the mountains behind us and the road in front of us. Perfect for that damned pipeline that was starting up before—"

"Wait!" Megan grasped Jake's arm and tried to shake him. "Wait! Are you saying Roger and Helen, my husband and your wife, were involved in some sort of international drug ring? Oh, Jake. Listen to how improbable that is. They didn't need the money. Why on earth would they do that?"

"What did the man say to you yesterday, Megan? 'He told you where it is. I knew he would. And now you're going to tell him.' Who did he mean? Not Sam Hooker or Tyndall Puckett. He'd been watching you and me, so not me. Who, Megan? Who else but your husband? God, I never liked him, and I hate to put this on him. But if not this, what?"

"What are they after, Jake? What would Roger have told me about?"

He looked at her. In his eyes she saw sadness, regret, and, above all, a surety that she couldn't doubt and he could no longer deny. "About the location of the drop that went bad the night I was shot."

And now she knew why he wanted to deny it. It was unconscionable, unthinkable. "That too? But wasn't that on Witcher Mountain?"

He nodded. "Two miles away. At least that's where I interrupted it. But I don't know where the contacts went after I was shot, and, as you said yesterday, what's a ridge or two in country like this?"

He closed his eyes, masking his thoughts from her. "Parallels," he said. "Mattie told me to look for them. But, God, this is unbelievable, even for a paranoid like me. There's got to be another answer."

Megan looked away from his bowed head toward the darkness outside the window, looked and tensed. "Then you'd better find one in a hurry," she told him, "because there are lights on the ridge."

22

Jake leaped up from the bed and pushed shut the hallway door, closing the bedroom in darkness, before he crossed to the window. Enough moonlight filtered into the room to outline him and reveal the tension that held him watchful.

"Who—"

Jake slashed a hand through the air, motioning her to silence. Megan waited, every sense attuned to what were clearly headlights near the spot where she had waited in Jake's truck. And with the silence she heard it, the noise of an engine, not the one on the ridge but another one, groaning up a steep hill. But where? The road? Or on the other side of the ridge?

Suddenly Jake sprang into motion, gathering her clothes and thrusting them at her. "Quick," he said. "Get dressed. We have to get out of here."

Megan didn't argue. She put on her clothes while Jake tugged on a shirt, boots, and the holster containing his pistol. Then he slid a window open wide and unlatched the screen. "This way."

On the porch, he had her wait while he entered the dark living room and returned with something in his hands.

"Follow me," he said. "The road may not be safe, but I know a place that is."

He led her around the clearing, staying in shadow, to the workshop. There he retrieved the keys and opened the door for her.

"There's a door here behind the wood storage shelves," he said, leading her across the room to show her. "It leads to an old cellar. If anyone does think to look in here, the cellar is so well hidden no one will find it short of an all-out search. Take this." He thrust something into her hands.

Megan felt the cold metal of a weapon. "Oh, no," she said. "You're not leaving me here alone, Jake Kenyon. You're not going up that hill without me."

"Megan, trust me in this. I have to know who it is. I'll be back, I promise, and then we'll get the hell out of here, safely, if we have to walk out by way of Texas. Got that?"

She reached out and grabbed his arm, pulling him close to her. "And if you get yourself shot up again, I will never forgive you. Got that?"

"Got it," he said, wrapping her in a tight hug. For a moment she stayed there, close against him, feeling the accelerated beating of his heart in cadence with hers. Then he took her mouth in a brief, almost bruising kiss. "Lock yourself in," he said. "I'll be back. That's a promise."

She followed him to the door but she didn't try to stop him. He had to do this; she had to wait. Why she knew it, Megan didn't want to explore. She watched until Jake blended in with the shadows and disappeared, and still she watched.

I remembered that the sky had been cloudless when last I looked outside, to see if the scrabbling noises in the leaves were caused by the raccoon that so often frequents our cabin looking for an easy food supply.

Megan shuddered at the memory of that entry, even though she knew the scrabbling noises outside the workshop now were caused by her imagination.

The engine noises, however, were real. With headlights dark, the shadow of a car moved into the clearing from the road and stopped just beyond the house. Two men, hidden by darkness, stepped from the car and made their way to the house silently. A moment of silence followed, and then, one by one, each light in the house came on. Megan heard the sounds of slamming doors, overturned furniture, shouted curses.

Then she saw the men come from the house, each carrying a gun, and begin a systematic search of the cars, the barn, and the shed, and finally head toward the workshop. Quickly she backed away from the door, ran into the hidden cellar, and threw the bolt she found on the inside of the door.

The room was small, dark, and damp, and Megan didn't want to think about what might live on the floor at the bottom of the steps. Was this how Lydia had felt the night she waited alone in her cabin? Megan's hand, damp and slick, slid on the grip of the gun while she listened to the outside door crash open and to the voices and footsteps come into the outside room. One voice had a decided Oklahoma twang, which she recognized: Deputy Mark Henderson. The other had a slight but unmistakable Spanish accent.

Jake was right!

But if Jake was right, there was more going on with Henderson that an unresolved political battle, more involved in his not having come to Jake's rescue months ago than incompetence.

"Don't worry," she heard Henderson say over the roaring of the blood in her temples. "She knows where it is. That's the only reason she could have for coming here. We'll get her. And Kenyon. There's no way in hell he's getting away again."

Jake silently worked his way to the top of the ridge. Two men stood outlined against the backdrop of a battered four-wheel drive pickup. He crept closer, keeping to the trees, until he could make out their features.

One was the stranger Sarah had described. The other wore jeans and a shapeless long sweatshirt with the sleeves torn out. Jake recognized him too, from a much more recent contact: Mack, lumberyard employee, Sarah North's job applicant, and what else?

"This is a hell of a place for a tea party," the man called Mack said, leaning back on one foot against the pickup. "Where are we anyway? I thought we were supposed to be damn near in the national forest. Isn't that a house down there?"

"I believe that is Mr. Jake Kenyon's residence," the other man said.

"Kenyon? Hey, he's bad news. We don't need to be anywhere near him."

A soft chuckle echoed through the night, raising the fine hairs on the back of Jake's neck. He'd heard that laugh only once before, in a little town in Central America just before five people died.

"But we do," the stranger said. "And so we wait."

For what? Jake wondered. And then noises of the search at his place carried up the hill on the night air. Megan. He'd left her there thinking it would be safer. What in the hell did they want?

They wanted Megan. He knew that. That was why he had hidden her. *He told you.* Megan's assailant had whispered those words to her. And even though Roger *hadn't* told her, no one involved in this deadly intrigue would believe it. Should he go back down the hill? Was she hidden well enough? Would he do more harm than good if he ran to her side now?

Damn! He was ruined, worthless, if he couldn't figure out how to keep one fragile woman safe in the middle of several thousand acres of trees and rocks and hiding places.

Once again he heard engine noises, and this time he knew where they came from. The truck was coming from his house, in this direction, with its lights on. Their time for stealth had passed.

As the truck pulled into the small clearing, its headlights swept the trees. Jake ducked just before the light cut across where he had been standing. He closed his eyes briefly to accustom them to the darkness and then looked toward the truck. Two men got out. He recognized the deputy, Henderson. He shouldn't be surprised, but he was. He always was when one of the guys who was supposed to be wearing a white hat turned. It was a bit of naïveté that had almost gotten him killed on assignment. Damn! It was a bit of naïveté that had almost gotten him killed three months ago.

Jake didn't recognize the second man, except by type. He was undoubtedly in charge of this operation. Short black hair, an almost military cut. An almost military posture. He looked as though he would be more at home in pressed khakis than Henderson. Megan's army officer? The suspicion grew when he spoke and Jake heard his accent.

"Gentlemen. I believe we all know each other." He nodded toward Mack. "You have the package?"

Mack shook his head. "I left it in place. It's about half a mile from here."

The leader's mouth twisted in a smile. "But you do have a sample so we know our night's work won't be wasted, I trust."

"Sure." Mack reached into his shirt pocket and pulled out a small wrapped package, which he tossed to the leader.

The man opened it, sniffed at its contents, even wet a finger and touched it to the powder and tasted it. He rewrapped it and tossed it to the man who had waited with Mack. "Thorough, very thorough. But then what else would we expect from the DEA. What a shame they're going to lose another agent to this uncivilized back woods. Henderson?"

Jake had watched Mark surreptitiously draw his gun while the package was being examined. Mack had watched too. Now Mack stood with his booted foot still propped on the side of the pickup. Mark stepped forward.

DEA. Damn! The fact that Jake didn't recognize him was no surprise. Once stated, Jake supposed Mack was probably an agent. What did surprise him was that Mack had been in place since before Patrick had made his call.

Mack nodded toward the deputy. "You want to explain what's going on?"

Henderson shook his head. "No. Any explanations would be coming from you, and we're really not interested in anything other than you're not who you say you are. Oh, yeah, and if you really found the missing package."

He glanced at the man who had examined the powder, who shook his head.

"The boss says he doesn't think you did."

"Based on what?" Mack asked softly.

Jake recognized that tactic. Delay. Think of some rational way out. Hope like hell the cavalry will arrive in time. Know that it won't.

Hell, it looked like *he* was the cavalry.

He didn't need this. He was getting too damned old to be riding to the rescue. What he needed to do was get back to Megan and get her out of here, back to someplace where she really would be safe. But would there ever be any safe place for her so long as any of this scum thought she knew anything?

Damn.

He eased around the clearing until he stood behind the leader. One step, then two, and he had his gun in the man's back.

"Probably either because your stuff's too good or because

it's been cut too much. Want to bet it isn't the latter?" he asked companionably.

"Kenyon?" Mark's startled question rent the night just before Mack uncoiled from his seemingly relaxed stance and lunged for him. At the same time the man Jake held captive rolled to one side, and the third man fired off a volley of shots that was echoed by an answering volley from across the clearing.

Jake felt the slug tear into his left side, high. "Oh, hell," he muttered, as the thrust sent him to the ground. He rolled with it and came up with his automatic in his hand and his knee in the back of the man he had dubbed the leader.

"Don't even think about moving," he growled. Two other men lay on the ground. "Mack?" he called out.

"Yeah, here. You okay?"

"What in the hell are you doing here?" Jake asked.

"That's my question, Kenyon," the man said with a shaky laugh.

"Saving your butt."

"Yeah, and winning my thanks. Look out for the weasel over there while I make contact. I'm not sure he's dead. And Henderson got away. How's your man?"

Jake pulled back on the man's collar until he could see his face and his rage-filled eyes. "Mad. Real mad."

Still holding the pistol he had produced without Jake's seeing from where, Mack reached up under the wheel well of the pickup and retrieved what Jake recognized as a signaling device. He pushed a switch and set it on the hood of the truck before walking to the man he'd called a weasel and turning him over. He then walked to Jake, tucking his gun in his belt up under his sweatshirt.

"Damn. He got you again."

Jake felt a laugh building which turned to a cough that left him weak and gasping. "Him?" he asked. "He was along on that last little hayride?"

Mack nodded while stripping the belt from the man Jake still held at gunpoint. "Him, and this creep here, and—on your belly, buddy," he said to the man, pushed him down, and began lashing his wrists together. "And—hell, you're going to find out anyway, Roger Hudson. As best we can figure it, Hudson intercepted the man who shot you, took the delivery away from him, and finished him off. What he did with the goods is anyone's guess, but the big money has been on the hope that he planted it somewhere near here."

Jake felt no surprise at what Mack said, except in the fact that Roger had actually gotten his hands dirty. "And Henderson? Was he involved?"

Mack grunted as he tugged the belt into place and began stripping laces from the man's shoes. "Up to the brim of his four-X white beaver Stetson."

And Henderson had escaped into the woods, suspecting that Megan knew where a fortune in cocaine lay waiting. "Are you about finished with this one?" Jake asked.

"Yeah. You got something better to do?"

Jake nodded and stumbled to his feet. "I've got a lady to see to, back home."

Mack whistled. "The senator's daughter. Shit. I think I got him, but I don't know how bad. Henderson's—"

Jake shifted the gun to his left hand and felt his shoulder. He could still move it, barely, but the blood was beginning to soak his shirt, front, back, and even the sleeve where he held his arm against his body. "Got a handkerchief?" he asked.

Mack yanked the last knot tight on the man on the ground and stood. "Let me see."

Jake shook his head. "There's no time for that. Put some pressure on it, something to slow down the blood. I'll be all right for a few minutes more."

"Damn, you're as hard-headed as everyone told me."

Jake smiled at him. "Just send in the troops when they get here, will you?"

Send in the troops, Jake thought, minutes later. Send them in now, because he wasn't sure he was going to make it back. Blood soaked his shirt, and he felt his breath wheezing through his lung. He stopped and ripped at his soaked sleeve in a futile effort to tear it loose, to have something to hold in place over the wound, trying for a little more pressure, a little more time.

He heard a rustling in the trees ahead of him and stopped, waiting, listening, wasting time he didn't have.

I'm coming. He sent the message silently to her. Hang on just a little longer. I'll be there. I promise.

It felt very much like a promise he had made sometime in the past, a promise he hadn't been able to keep. As he was afraid he wouldn't be able to keep this one.

Megan listened until the footsteps left the workshop. After a minute the stream of light under the door blacked out. She heard two car doors slam and the truck left the clearing and headed, she thought, toward the ridge. She emerged from her hiding place in the cellar into darkness.

Funny that they'd turn out the lights, she thought, until she looked out the open door and saw that the entire clearing lay in darkness.

She stood in the doorway watching the headlights as the truck made its way to the ridge. Stood there even after it stopped. Stood there until the sound of gunshots broke her from her paralysis.

Jake! "Damn it, Jake Kenyon, don't you dare get yourself shot," she murmured as still she stood there.

Stood there like some helpless Victorian maiden waiting for someone to rescue her. Megan felt a shudder run through her. She couldn't go after Jake—she didn't know where he'd gone—but she'd lay odds he was somewhere near the gunfire. She couldn't jeopardize his safety by putting her own at risk. But by God she could do something.

Help. She could summon help. And if Rolley P was involved, she would just bypass him. Would he be listening at the tapped phone? Did she care?

Patrick. She could call Patrick.

And he could call her father. What good did it do to have a powerful father if she couldn't call on him? Surely, with Patrick's voice added to hers, he'd believe her. He had to believe her. For Jake's sake.

She remembered the skirting path Jake had taken in bringing her to the workshop. Clutching the gun, she repeated that path, heart pounding, until once again she stood on the porch. The front door gaped open. Carefully, cautiously, she made her way inside. Just inside the door she paused and gasped. The pleasant, comfortable room had been trashed almost as badly as her bedroom. The furniture lay overturned as though some child, angry with his toys, had tossed the chairs and tables around.

She groped her way through the darkened room to where the telephone should be. She found it, the receiver in one place, the body in another. Both, she noted thankfully, were still connected to each other and to the wall. But there was no dial tone.

And then she heard the sounds from outside: an odd shuffling step on the front porch, a harsh breathing, and finally, Mark Henderson's voice.

"Oh, Megan? Ms. Hudson. I know you're in there. You might as well come out now. It's all over. It's just us, and you have something I want."

Lydia? You might as well tell me. You can't hide in there forever.

"Megan. Kenyon's dead. I saw to that. Now we can either share what Roger left you or I can take it. It's up to you."

Lydia? Oh, Lydia. Open the door, Lydia. You know there's no one to save you now.

Megan bit hard on her fist to keep from crying out. Jake was dead? No. This man lied. He had to be lying.

She crouched behind the overturned sofa as he entered the living room and walked in that strange shuffling gait toward the bedrooms. She knew she had no chance of getting out the front door, but the kitchen was close. Carefully she worked her way toward it and saw that the back door stood open, probably from their earlier search.

She heard a yelp from the back of the house and then a yowl of pain. She cringed as she recognized a kitten's cry but couldn't stop to help it now.

"Damn cat!" Henderson yelled, and the cat cried out again. Sending the kitten a silent apology and thank-you, Megan darted out the back door.

The woods? she thought. Would she be safe in the woods? No. Jake had told her to wait in the workshop. In the cellar, with the darkness, she would be as safe as anywhere else. And that's where he would look for her. Please, God, he *would* look for her.

A benevolent cloud covered the moon for the last twenty yards of her dash. She ran into the workshop. Bolt the door? Or leave it open and pray that Henderson remembered that he had left it open and think she couldn't possibly be there?

"Megan? Oh, Megan." She heard his voice from the direction of the stable. Oh, God. Somewhere he had found a flashlight. To hell with subtleties. She bolted the door, or tried to. Something jammed the lock. Almost sobbing, she prowled through the lumber until she found a board that had to be the right length. She shoved it under the knob. Yes! It fit. It would hold, at least for a while.

"Megan, it won't do you any good to hide."

She fought a whimper and backed toward her hiding place.

Who is he?
Why won't he leave me alone?
I don't know anything!
I don't want to know anything!

No, that was Lydia. Megan knew who was outside. If Jake was right, she knew what he wanted. But she didn't know where it was, any more than Lydia had known.

And she knew what he'd do if he found her: she'd be dead. As dead as that young girl at Villa Castellano, not quickly like Helen or Roger.

Jake? Oh, Jake, where are you?

Was he dead? Oh, please, no. Not Jake.

She heard the doorknob rattle, heard what she could only describe as a malignant chuckle. "So that's where you are. Stay cozy. I'll be back."

She stayed frozen in place for seconds she couldn't spare and then shook herself to awareness. She couldn't stay in the cellar; she'd given her hiding place away. The back door. She could go out the back door, around the pile of equipment that Jake was slowly amassing there, and hide in the woods. She'd be safe there. Oh, yes, please—she'd be safe.

The cloud drifted away from the face of the moon just as Megan unlocked the back door. Through the panes of glass she saw the outline of a man approaching, a man bent unnaturally. A man walking with a stumbling, shuffling gait. Her hands fumbled on the lock as she tried to relock it. Not sure that she had, only that she had to get away from the door, Megan backed away and lifted the gun in her hand. There was a shell in the chamber; Jake had seen to that. The safety was off; Megan had taken care of that herself.

It's all over. It's just us, and you have something I want.

Had those innocent people at the clinic just been in the way of something someone like Mark Henderson had wanted? The girl was screaming again. Megan put her hands to her ears, but that would never block out the sound of her screams. Or the shots. Or the noises of destruction and death. Or the screams she herself would be making very shortly, if—

She choked back a cry as she heard the knob being tried.

Not her. By God, no one would make a victim of her! Not like they had Lydia. Not like they had that poor child at the clinic. She might die, but she'd take at least one of them with her.

Kenyon is dead. I saw to that.

"You bastard," she whispered. "How dare you hurt him again?"

She lowered the gun to firing stance as the door opened and the man stumbled through.

What stayed her hand? Later Megan was never sure of anything but the memory of Jake telling her, *Lydia killed him. He went home from the explosion, and she shot him as he walked in the door.*

She hesitated only a moment, a moment in which she heard Jake's labored voice whisper "Megan?" before he collapsed in the doorway.

Her moan echoed through the room. She lowered the gun, staring at Jake, frozen in place and unable to move toward him.

And another figure filled the doorway.

"Well, well," Mark Henderson said, stepping over Jake and obviously not able to see her clearly in the dark interior of the workshop. She saw him cleanly outlined by the moonlight. She saw the deadly looking gun in his hand, which he pointed at Jake's head. "I believe we have some unfinished business to take care of. Or do you want me to make sure he's not going to inconvenience us again before you and I go for a walk? Yes. I think that's what I'll do."

She heard the words spoken calmly, rationally even, before their meaning penetrated. He was going to kill Jake. Kill him with no more passion than he would swat a fly, just because he was an inconvenience. And he was going to do it right now, unless Megan stopped him.

"You bastard," she said again, raised her gun, and fired.

He stumbled out the door just as Megan heard the

whop-whop-whop of a helicopter circling the clearing and saw powerful searchlights sweep over the workshop and house.

Voices in the clearing shouted, and one yelled, "I don't care who he is, kill those damned lights."

The cavalry, as Jake would have called it, had arrived.

Megan ran to Jake's side. She knelt by him helplessly until she saw his labored breathing. Then she lifted his head from the concrete floor and into her lap. He was alive. Thank God, he was alive. He opened his eyes and gave her what he probably intended as a smile but managed to look like a lop-sided leer.

She realized that tears were raining down her cheeks, but she didn't care. All she cared about in this world was lying in her arms, near death.

"Don't you dare die on me, Jake Kenyon," she yelled at him over the noises of the men filing into the clearing. "Don't you dare die!"

He hurt like hell. His arm and side and back. Even his leg screamed in agony. And now his head. He slitted open one eye, bit back a groan as the dim light in the room proved to be too piercing, and closed it. He was in a hospital. He recognized the tubes and monitors and the stark white sheets.

He recognized the cotton-candy state of his brain as a reaction to the painkillers they had probably given him. Painkillers that right now didn't seem to be doing a whole hell of a lot of good.

And he recognized his headache as a drug hangover, which meant he'd probably been in this bed for a while.

Megan! Was she safe? The last he remembered was her standing in front of him, holding that gun as though she were facing off an invading army. No. The last he remembered was her swearing at him, holding him and crying and saying over and over, "Don't you dare die."

"I won't, babe," he said through parched lips and a dry throat. "I won't."

He felt a soft hand on his and once again slitted open an eye.

She sat in a chair dragged to the side of his bed. Her head lay on her crossed arm on the bed by his thigh; her hand rested on his. Slowly she raised her head, as if from sleep. Her eyes searched his face, and when she saw his opened eye, her face lit in a smile.

"You won't what?" she asked softly.

"I won't die on you. There's no way on earth I'm leaving you now."

"Thank God."

She rose from her chair to lean over him, and he felt the cautious touch of her fingers on his face. "You scared me, Jake," she said, with a funny little catch to her voice. "Damn it, I told you not to get yourself shot up again."

The cotton candy was closing in on him, but not so much yet that he didn't hear the pain in her voice. He turned his hand under hers and did his best to squeeze her fingers. "Never again," he promised.

She hiccuped once. "I'll hold you to that," she said and returned the pressure of his hand. "I love you, Jake Kenyon. I don't care that I've only known you a week. I don't care that we've got all this shared history and unresolved trauma to work through. I don't care that I'm the one who's saying it first. I love you. And I was so afraid I'd never have the chance to tell you."

He was going down fast. Damn. Why did the lousy medication have to kick in now? From recent history, he knew he'd be out of it soon and unable to say anything to her for hours. "Love you too," he managed to whisper.

When he floated up to consciousness again, he found Megan asleep in the chair beside his bed. The pain was as bad, the cotton-candy fog worse. Memories of dreams of Megan and Lydia Tanner floated through that fog, dancing just beyond comprehension. But one thing was clear. He had to tell her.

"She didn't kill him."

Megan came awake instantly at his croaked words.

She leaned over him, taking his hand in one of hers, tracing her fingers across his cheek.

"Lydia," he whispered. "She didn't kill Sam."

How did he know? "It's all right," Megan murmured. "Even if she did, she redeemed herself." He felt a shudder run through her. "She saved your life. She kept me from pulling the trigger when you came through the door."

When he awoke again, he was in a different room. Bright light flooded through the windows. Patrick sat sprawled in a chair across from the bed.

"Where's Megan?" His words grated his throat and hung in the stillness of the room.

Patrick pulled himself up out of the chair. "Welcome back to the land of the living, my friend," he said easily, but he didn't answer Jake's question.

Jake looked around at the absence of monitors. He decided to try his voice again. "How long?"

Patrick flashed that maddening grin of his. "Three days. Long enough to miss all the excitement." He chuckled. "You'll be pleased to know that Deacon the Wonder Dog is once again the hero of the day, having been taken out, so to speak, so that the bad guys could get to you and the senator's beautiful daughter."

Jake groaned. "Is she all right?"

Patrick nodded. "Right as rain. Her daddy came running to her rescue in a military chopper just as law enforcement from no fewer than three federal agencies swarmed over your property. That, apparently, was his fact-finding trip. He vindicated her allegations about Villa Castellano after your guys identified the head honcho of this operation as a captain in the army of that misbegotten little country, one who was doing some moonlighting without the knowledge of his government.

"And, of course, with Henderson up to his eyeballs in this mess, she's been vindicated in her charges against Rolley P, which, by the way, she has made."

So her father had come to the rescue. Jake let that thought work its way through him. She'd needed that. Needed Jack McIntyre's support and belief. Needed it enough to go back to Washington with him?

"Where . . . is . . . Megan?" He spaced the words out, but only a deaf person or a very dense one would miss the intensity of his question. Patrick was neither. He immediately dropped all attempt at humor.

"Barbara took her out to the house for a shower and a change of clothes," Patrick told him. "She's been here for three days, Jake; she's dead on her feet."

Jake felt some of the tension drain from him. "She didn't go back with McIntyre?"

"Go back with him?" Patrick repeated incredulously. "My God, Kenyon. This is the first time we've been able to pry her away from you for more than five minutes in the entire three days you've been here. What kind of a stupid-assed question is that?"

The pain was every bit as bad as it had been before, but suddenly Jake felt younger, as years and injuries and losses seemed to fade into his past.

I love you, Jake Kenyon. And I was so afraid I'd never have the chance to tell you.

She had said that. It was a memory, not a dream, and not just wishful thinking.

Patrick leaned over the foot of the bed and peered at him. "And what kind of stupid grin is that?"

Jake laughed weakly, then caught his hand to his chest to hold the pain in place. "The kind you'd better get used to seeing, my friend."

The door opened gently, and Jake turned his head on the pillow.

Megan stood there, wearing a softly draped, flattering blue silk dress he had never seen in her closet or his. She'd taken time to have her hair cut and styled, and now it made a feathery frame for her delicate features. And she wore softly applied makeup that gently highlighted her beauty and the new maturity she seemed to have gained. Her whole image was soft. Soft for him because that was what he needed now. But strong, so strong, when that was what they both had needed.

Barbara stood behind her in the doorway, but other than noticing her, Jake had no strength left to do anything but look at Megan. She smiled hesitantly. So did he. And that was apparently all she was waiting for. She crossed to his bed, took one of his hands in hers, a nd placed her other one gently on his face.

"I love you, Megan McIntyre Hudson," he said.

Vaguely he was aware of Barbara tugging Patrick from the room. Vaguely he was aware of the door closing behind them, leaving him and Megan cocooned in privacy.

"Thank God," she said, and he heard echoes of those words from another time but couldn't remember when.

"How many kids?" he asked.

"What?" She gave a choked little laugh and ran her fingers into his hair.

"My house or yours? What will you do? Will you want to work?"

"Jake? What are you doing?"

He was doing what he thought he'd never do again. "I'm proposing, Megan. But I thought it would be nice if we knew a few things about each other before I actually asked."

"Ask," she said softly. She bent and brushed her lips across his. "As for the rest, we have all the time in the world for that."

Epilogue

Megan lay back on the blanket spread across the largest of the flat rocks surrounding Waterfall Canyon. Only a trickle of the waterfall survived in the annual droughtlike weather of late August. But there was a trickle, and a respectable pool, and a surprising light breeze tickling the leaves and grasses.

Jake lay beside her, his eyes closed, his hands crossed on his flat belly as he napped after their picnic. Deacon lay softly snoring a few feet away, with the two cats curled up against him.

Her wounded warriors.

Deacon's hair had not completely regrown to cover his wound, and the scar from his surgery constantly reminded her of how much she had almost lost. And how much she had gained.

Jake had wanted to claim a shoulder wound, but the truth was, this bullet had taken a bite out of his lung. The truth was, she'd told him, he was running out of parts to sacrifice. And he'd agreed. So when Rolley P resigned in disgrace, Jake had refused to take the office.

Mack had taken the job as sheriff of Pitchlyn County: Mack, the DEA undercover agent who'd been sent in to check on all the irregularities in the investigation of Jake's shooting and the buy gone bad. He said he found he liked small-town living, and that while he wasn't sure it would be any less eventful than his days at the agency, based on what he'd seen so far, he wanted to give it a try.

Jake had never again talked to her about what he'd said while still drugged, that Lydia had not shot Sam. She doubted if he even remembered saying it, so she knew it would do no good to question him. But he had gone with her and Mattie to visit Sam Hooker's overgrown grave in a rural cemetery a few miles north of Prescott.

How alone he had seemed in death. As alone as he must have been most of his life.

No one knew where Lydia was buried, *if* she was buried at all. A cryptic comment found in the cemetery records of the county genealogical society mentioned the grave of a woman found in a field near Wilton's sawmill, with no name, no age, no date. And though Wilton's sawmill was located miles from where Sam's had been, surely someone would have recognized Sam Hooker's wife, Daniel Tanner's daughter.

They visited that grave, but there were no answers there.

She did remind Jake of what she had told him, that she felt sure Lydia had been responsible for her not shooting him. And Jake, standing at the foot of Sam's lonely grave, had been the one to make the suggestion that now seemed so right.

"That notebook of yours," he'd said. "How did Kent describe it? A way of putting all the pieces of your life back together?"

Megan had nodded, not understanding where he was leading. A place to explore choices made and those not made as though they had been, she remembered. "A way of exploring things done and those not done. A way to make me whole again."

"And how much of it is Lydia?" he'd asked.

Except for two brief pages, which Megan removed, all of it was.

Sam Hooker had loved Lydia. Even though he'd never told her, every word written in her fine copperplate penmanship sang of that love. He'd told her he never wanted her to be frightened again, but she had been. And he hadn't been able to keep his covenant with her that no one would ever hurt her again.

Now, even in death, they were separated.

Jake understood those things as well as Megan. He also understood when she'd told him she had to go back into the notebook one last time. He'd stood silent watch over her while she did so, and although she knew he wanted to ask her what she had discovered, he did not.

That morning they had gone to the cemetery: Megan, Jake, Mattie, Patrick, and Barbara. Earlier they had spent days cleaning the gravesite, ordering the headstone, and building the black metal fence that surrounded an area large enough for the two graves the double stone suggested. Now Patrick and Jake opened a second, much smaller grave while Mattie looked on in approval. And then, with words both from Mattie's tradition and from Megan's, they had buried the notebook that contained the essence of Lydia Tanner Hooker next to her husband.

The picnic had been an afterthought. Just Jake and Megan, together in the heat of a lazy August afternoon. One of the few lazy afternoons remaining to them, because Jake's business had just received orders for millwork for five reconstructions, and Megan had dusted off her degree and the certification that neither her father nor, later, Roger had wanted her to use and signed a contract to teach history at Prescott Middle School.

She felt Jake shift and stretch by her side and smiled. Life was good.

"What would that rich white aunt of yours think if she could see you now, Liddy?"

"Perhaps she would refuse to let me live with her."

Jake jerked to awareness beside her. Quickly she put her hand on his arm. "Shh," she said. It was happening! She hadn't expected it, but she had hoped. Now this, too, she could share with Jake.

The larger black kitten looked toward the pool and arched his back, hissing. Deacon jerked awake, looked at the pool, and then nudged the cat back into place and slathered its face with a wet tongue.

Megan raised on her elbow to look at the pool. Peter and Liddy waded there as before, Liddy with her long dress tucked up between her bare legs, Liddy with a wisdom and maturity about her that had not been apparent before. Together they played out the scene that lived so vibrantly in Megan's memory.

If I had let Peter win the argument about our visiting Granny Rogers's house, if I had let him convince me that Sam was not at home, if we had gone wading as we had done so many times before, would any of the subsequent events have happened? Lydia had written in her diary.

Would they have? Or were they already set in motion by then? Megan didn't know. But she did know of this moment, a moment so strong it lingered for others to see.

"My God," Jake whispered. "It's—"

"Yes," Megan said. "Yes."

A sound from the opposite bank drew Lydia's attention. A tall travel-worn man stood there, hlding the reins of an equally travel-worn sorrel horse. His dark hair showed strands of silver, and his hair, his clothes, even the day's dark stubble on his jaw wore the dust from his ride.

"You're back!" Lydia cried. With joy lighting her face, she waded from the pool, dropped her skirts, and crossed the stone dam to stand in front of Sam. "I was afraid you wouldn't get back in time."

Sam reached a tentative hand to her cheek. "I tried to stay away. God knows I tried."

Lydia caught his hand to her face and held it there. "I knew you wouldn't let me leave you."

"You're so young, child, and so innocent. I wonder—could you survive me?"

She stood straight and tall and proud before him. "I only know that I cannot survive without you."

He shuddered as he drew her against him. "So be it," he said. He looked over her shoulder to the young boy in the pool. "Peter," he said. "We're going to have to elope, because your father will never give his permission. Will you be our witness?"

At some time Jake's hand had captured hers and now held it tightly.

It had worked. Oh, sweet heaven, it had worked.

In our language, the words for "to go" and "to have gone" are the same. . . . I felt a peace there, a continuity too often lacking in my world, a harmony with all that had been, all that was, and all that would be.

Mattie's words mingled with the half-remembered directions for her journal. They all faded as she watched Sam Hooker lift Lydia onto the sorrel horse and lead her from the clearing.

Jake let out a deep sigh and turned her in his arms. "That was why you went back into the journal, wasn't it?" he asked.

She nodded and he pulled her against him.

"Does this mean that none of it happened?"

"I don't know," she told him. "I only know I had to try to do something. And now, somewhere, they are together."

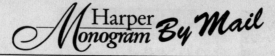

Harper Monogram By Mail

Looking For Love?
Try HarperMonogram's Bestselling Romances

TAPESTRY
by Maura Seger
An aristocratic Saxon woman loses her heart to
the Norman man who rules her conquered people.

DREAM TIME
by Parris Afton Bonds
In the distant outback of Australia, a mother
and daughter are ready to sacrifice everything
for their dreams of love.

RAIN LILY
by Candace Camp
In the aftermath of the Civil War in Arkansas, a
farmer's wife struggles between duty and passion.

COMING UP ROSES
by Catherine Anderson
Only buried secrets could stop the love
of a young widow and her new beau
from bloomimg.

ONE GOOD MAN
by Terri Herrington
When faced with a lucrative offer to seduce
a billionaire industrialist, a young woman
discovers her true desires.

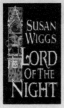